"A hot new spin on paranormal, *Descendant* is refreshingly imaginative and powerful. I can't decide which was best ~ piecing together Abby's sinister past or keeping up with her heartbreaking future. If you like your YA laced with melt-my-heart romance and a good helping of heart-pounding suspense, you'll love this book!"

~ Michelle D. Argyle,
author of *The Breakaway* series

"Nichole Giles has crafted a story that breathes from the pages. Her characters are authentic, the action intense, with powerful emotions that will keep *Descendant* on your mind long after the book ends."

~Rachelle J. Christensen, award-winning author
of *Wrong Number* and *Caller ID*

"Nichole Giles brings a fresh new voice and flawless writing technique to the world of Young Adult fiction. I was swept away to another place and never wanted to come back."

~Tristi Pinkston, author of *Turning Pages*
and the *Secret Sisters* mystery series

"This debut novel delivers in all the right ways, with heart-pounding action and a delicious romance that sweeps centuries. I loved it!"

~Elana Johnson, author of
Possession and *Surrender*

Third American Paperback Edition

Published by Jelly Bean Press
PO Box 548
Osawatomie, Kansas 66064

Copyright ©2013 by Nichole Giles
Edited by Diane Dalton
Cover design by Melissa Williams Design
Interior design by Melissa Williams Design
Cover photograph by Selins via Shutterstock
Author photo by Erin Summerill

ISBN 978-1-63034-000-1

Nichole Giles's author website is http://nicholegiles.blogspot.com

DESCENDANT

NICHOLE GILES

JBP
JELLY BEAN PRESS

For Brayden, Brittany, Madison, McKay,
and Gary

I would battle demons for all of you.

The Key to her future
lies in the past

PROLOGUE

Kye's white shirt is drenched with blood. It pools on the smooth, black floor of the cave, soaks my knees, and ruins the silk dress I bought in New York just yesterday. A river of it runs into his golden hair until it's orange and sticky. He's so still, so broken.

I've always known it's my destiny to give in to death while healing someone else. That's the one lesson Gram taught me that actually stuck. I just never imagined the day would come before my eighteenth birthday. No amount of childhood training—no crystals, herbs, or healing energy—will give back the life slowly draining away.

It's happening again. Feelings of helplessness and grief are at war as I struggle to hold on to the last shred of the person I've loved for so many lifetimes but only known a few weeks. So much has happened, and all I can think is that his car is at the airport.

Knowing that the person who did this is dead doesn't comfort me. Too little, too late. It doesn't change what's been done. To me. To him. To all of us. I've cried so much today that I'm already drained. I can't catch a breath, so I let the tears come. Emotions crash down on me; anger, sadness, frustration, love, pain. They flow into me, swirl together until flashes of memory sharpen my other senses.

His face close to mine, his thumb stroking my cheek, a heartbroken declaration of love on a pedal-cab ride through Central Park. It's not enough. Not nearly. It's not his time to go. Or mine either.

Except ...

There is a solution. Something I can do to save him. I can offer my life in place of his and hope the goddesses accept. One of us will survive. As I picture my life without him, the world without him, I know it's the only thing left for me. Because I love him that much. The world and others like us need him more than they need me, and I'm the only one who can save him.

He's already done everything in his power to protect me, to save me. I am why he's here. It's my turn now.

I bend to touch one last kiss to his swollen lips and whisper, "It'll all be over soon. I'll love you forever." Then, with all I have in me, I gather his broken energy together and call it into myself—preparing my body to die in place of his.

ONE

The Round Man

"In a time when the world is stricken, there will arise a new generation of Gifted individuals on whose shoulders shall rest the fate of the civilization."

~ *Prophecy of the Cairn Elen*

Three Months Ago

We're comfortable in Nevada. We have been for a few years. According to Gram, the problem with being comfortable is that comfortable people tend to get sloppy. Stuff happens. People get found and secrets discovered and women like us have to pack up and move on—or something like that.

One evening during winter break, my friends and I attend a show at one of the big hotels on the Strip. Halfway through, the hairs on the back of my neck stand at attention, followed by the prickling sensation I've experienced so many times before, an inexplicable knowledge that someone is watching me. I turn my head, squinting into the gray space behind us as my pulse jumps with anxiety.

The eyes that light on mine are yellow with a hint of green so they resemble burning amber. He has a round face on a round head topped with auburn hair, attached to a round body dressed in the most awful brown tweed suit I've ever seen. The man watches from the back corner of the room and nods when he sees me looking—as if I should know precisely who he is.

I feel like I *should* know, but I don't have a clue.

Then a vision hits me with a force that knocks me off my chair and sends me sprawling to the ground.

It's me, standing on a tall cliff overlooking a bubbling, steaming pool of muddyish goo and feeling more than seeing that someone important to me is in serious danger. I'm desperate to help and crazy with fear. Gram's blue and white diamond ring pulses with heat on my hand—a detail that seems odd to me, since I've never been allowed to touch Gram's most treasured possession. I'm surrounded on all sides by trees, grass, and mushy piles of snow, and wearing a beautiful silver evening gown but no shoes. The trees around me bend with the pressure of the wind, and the pool bubbles harder as I scream, and scream, and scream.

Patches of snow in the background melt and fade. The ground trembles.

Then the vision goes black.

I rasp in a mouthful of air and open my eyes. The world quivers. Several faces hover over me; my friends—and a few strangers.

My body shakes as one of the girls helps me to my feet and a security guard takes my elbow, guiding me through the doors at the back of the theater. As we pass, I scan the area where I saw the man with the amber eyes, but the table in the corner is empty.

He's gone.

The guard takes me to a desk where I call my mom, grateful she's close enough to come to my rescue.

Something's very wrong. I'm anxious, so anxious to get home, and yet as we pass through the bright lights of the Strip, nausea rolls around inside me until I nearly vomit in the car.

"Honey, are you sure you're okay?" Wrinkles tug at the corners of Mom's mouth as she pulls into our assigned parking stall.

I squeeze my lips together and close my eyes, fighting the dread, the burning in the pit of my stomach, but don't answer.

"You must be coming down with something." She opens the door and takes my elbow, and I let her help me. At the bottom of the stairs, I stop, bracing my palms on the building. A thick, black cloud of bad energy hovers in the stairwell, though I'm the only one who can see it. "Mom?"

"Breathe in through your nose and out through your mouth."

I take her advice and try again. "Mom, something's wrong."

"Do you need to see a doctor?"

I shake my head. "It's not me. Something else. I don't know—I can't see it. It's so black."

"What's black?"

"It's just outside my line of vision, but there's a black haze. Something ... something." I look up, meeting her eyes. "It's really bad."

Mom wraps her arm around my shoulders and leads me to the stairs but I turn, bolt to the patch of grass, and fall on all fours to throw up everything I've eaten today. Gram's face flashes in my mind—her gray-blue eyes surrounded by laugh-lines and the smile that says she's far younger than seventy-three. "Gram!" The hazy edges of my conscious self sharpen and fear shoots a burst of energy through me.

Abby.

She's calling my name.

"Gram!" I bolt up the stairs, taking them two at a time.

At the top, I pause, my heart racing in dread. The door to our apartment is unlocked. The sea-green sofa cushions are ripped to shreds, white stuffing strewn all over the carpet like fuzzy bits of snow. Knick-knacks Mom and Gram have collected over the years lie in pieces. Pictures have been torn from the walls, the ground littered with shards of glass from shattered mirrors, clothing scattered down the hall leading to the bedrooms. Our Christmas tree—so recently surrounded by brightly wrapped packages—is on its side, branches broken, ornaments crushed.

"Gram?" I yell. "Gram!"

"Isabelle?" Mom calls. "Isabelle, are you here?" Together, Mom and I trip over the mess to Gram's bedroom, the carpet crunching with every footfall.

"Gram!" I burst through the door, only to find the room empty. I'm vaguely aware that the bed has been stripped, the mattress pulled off, and the contents of Gram's jewelry armoire scattered on the floor. Erda barks at the sound of my voice but doesn't come running.

"Abby!" Mom calls. "She's in here. Come quick!" I tear into the kitchen where Gram lies sprawled on the tile. Her face is ashen gray and a puddle of blood has collected beneath her head, matting her silver hair with a patch of purplish-black.

"Gram! Oh no." I drop to my knees and place my rose quartz crystal over her heart. My own thumps like a drum.

"She's breathing, but only just." Mom stands, turns toward the herb cabinet, and opens it. "What do you need?"

"Um, I need ..." I run my hands over Gram's arms, down her body—making note of some broken ribs—and stop over her heart. The beat is faint and I detect a struggle. My training kicks in gear. "Hawthorne and ... um, garlic." I move my hand in a clockwise circular motion above Gram's chest, spinning the energy in her heart chakra, the way she taught me. The crystal rises into the air and turns under my hand, but the rotation is slow. "Gram, you have to help me. I don't know what to do."

Gram rasps out a breath. "Don't ..."

"Yeah, that's it, Gram. Come back to me."

Mom hands me two tiny glass bottles. I measure out a few drops of each herb and drip them into Gram's mouth. Her head moves. She catches hold of my wrist. "No."

"What, Gram? Am I doing it wrong? Help me!"

"Abby," she croaks. "Stop."

Ignoring Gram's words, I hum the heart tones, calling the afflicted energy out of her and toward my strong heart where it can be mended. Louder and louder I hum, chanting, until orange light surrounds Gram and forms a tight ball that spins over her heart. I sing louder as the light moves toward me, preparing for the pain I'm about to feel.

But then the crystal falls lifelessly on Gram's chest. The herbs I've administered dribble down the sides of her chin and the ball of light breaks into a thousand pieces that bounce around the room. "Gram!" I scream. This can't be happening.

Gram's eyes open, but the usually deep blue irises look gray. "Abby." Her voice is weak. I expect her to tell me something, anything I can do to save the life I can feel slipping out of her body.

"Yes, Gram? Tell me."

Mom kneels at my side and takes Gram's hand. A tear rolls down her cheek as she bends to hear Gram's raspy words. "Isa, it's okay. You can go. I'll take care of her."

I jump in alarm. "No. Don't say that. I'm going to Heal her. That's why I have this Gift, so I can Heal the people I love. She told me so."

Mom shakes her head as another tear falls. "Honey—"

"No!" I bend over my grandmother, wishing I could hug her. Wishing she could sit up and put her arms around me and tell me she's going to be just fine. "Gram, tell her. Tell her I can do it. You know I can, don't you? You taught me how—I just need to try it again."

"Marian. The box. Get the box," Gram wheezes. Mom nods as another breath whooshes out of Gram's mouth and I lean closer so I can hear her instructions. "Last lesson. You can't Heal ... someone—"

"Yes, I can," I interrupt. "You've seen me do it before with Erda."

"When ... it's her time ... to go."

"Right," I say. Tears burn my eyes. "But it's not your time, so I'm going to Heal you."

Gram's chin bobs. "No, baby. It is."

I look at Mom and swallow a sob. "Tell her she's wrong."

Mom shakes her head and leans toward Gram. "Isabelle, Abby and I need you here. We need your guidance. I can't teach Abby to Heal—she needs you for that."

Gram closes her eyes as she struggles for breath. "You ... already know, Abby. Dig deep ... find the light inside you. It's there."

I pick up my crystal and reposition it over Gram's heart, then spin her chakra again as the tears escape. No matter how hard I concentrate or how fast I spin, the crystal won't rise. The energy won't form. I want to scream in frustration, but I'm controlled. Instead, I hum the heart tones—direct them to Gram's chest. To her heart.

Her breathing grows rapid and shallow, and for a minute I think she's releasing her energy to me at last. Seconds later, her eyes grow wide. "Raina." She says. Slowly, very slowly, her eyes close and her lips draw into a serene smile.

She doesn't take another breath.

TWO

Grief

Gram once told me that every time the heart of a Healer bleeds, her powers become stronger. Each time we Heal another, we take on a portion of their burden, a portion of their pain, and a portion of their life energy.

But I don't feel stronger. I don't feel Gram's life energy, either. I don't feel anything.

Gripping my mother's hand, I stare at a blank wall in the busy police station. The world revolves around me. People ask questions. I try to answer through the haze, but I'm not sure my words make sense. Everything whirls and swirls around in my head while I sit, unmoving.

Then a voice breaks through. "You're free to go, ladies. Officer Stewart will drive you home." Detective Connor hands Mom a business card. "If you remember anything else, anything at all, call me. Day or night." We're like zombies, both of us still in a state of shock. The detective clears his throat as he crouches in front of Mom. "Your landlord gathered a cleaning crew and they were in the door as soon as we cleared the crime scene."

Mom squeezes my hand, hard. "Why did this happen?"

The detective shakes his head. "I don't know, Marian. I really don't. I'm sorry. We're working on some leads, so maybe I'll have a better answer soon. At this point, my best guess is that the perpetrator picked your apartment at random, not expecting Isabelle to be home. It could have been anyone."

A tear rolls down my cheek, but I hardly feel it. Gram believed that there is no such thing as random. Only now do I finally understand what she meant. I want to tell him, explain about my Gifts, but I can't. I'm not sure which secrets should be kept anymore and which truths should be told. This didn't happen to just anyone. It's my gram. And Mom. And me. My body feels numb as I stand, as if I've been asleep for days. I wish I could wake up. This nightmare has lasted far too long.

A police officer in a tan uniform leads us through the station and out to his patrol car. I climb in the back, leaving the front seat for Mom.

"Marian?" Detective Connor says something about grief counseling. I turn away, knowing it doesn't matter.

Words cannot bring my grandmother back.

Nothing will ever be the same.

After the officer drops us off, I stand on the sidewalk for a long time, staring at the top-floor windows of our building. It looks normal, like nothing bad has ever happened there. Like no one ever died within those walls.

The landlord meets us in front of the tall stucco building, offering a new key. He says he checked on my dog, and he's sorry about Gram. I don't say anything. We climb two flights of stairs and Mom clicks the lock on the new doorknob. The living room is now mostly empty. Mom drops the keys on a hall table that survived and walks to the fireplace.

Erda, who was locked in the bathroom during the break-in, growls. "It's okay, Erda," I say, weary. "It's just us." She pads up to me, tail between her legs as if she, too, is frightened to be here.

Mom stares for a long time at a picture of the three of us, Mom, Gram, and me, soaking wet, laughing, standing in the rain with our arms around each other. A tear runs down Mom's cheek as she tips the picture face down on the mantle and takes off the back.

"Mom? What are you doing?"

"I thought she'd gone loony when she showed me this."

"What are you talking about?" I put my arm around her shoulders. "I love that picture."

Mom's eyes fill with more tears. "I love it too." Taped to the back of the frame is a tiny silver key. She slides her thin hand behind a gap in the mantle and brings out a small wooden box, sighing in relief. "I've been worried they found this."

"What is it?" I rub my face with my sleeve.

"Isabelle left you some stuff." Swallowing hard, she unlocks the box. Wrapped in soft, black velvet are Gram's most prized possessions. Her antique blue and white diamond ring, a handful of Healing crystals, a pocket-sized book of herbal remedies, and a sealed envelope with my name on it.

Mom's voice breaks. "Isa made me promise to give you these things if anything ever happened to her." She picks the ring up and places it in my palm. "This is your legacy. All we have left of them. Be careful with it, Abby."

The lump in my throat threatens to choke me as my hand closes around the ring. Mom places the crystals in my free hand. "I don't remember much about our late-night conversations, but I do remember a few things Isa would want you to know. If you ever have questions ... I'll try."

The crystals feel warm in my fist. The ring fits best on my left ring finger and feels right, like it's supposed to be there, so that's where I leave it.

Mom hands me the book. I hold it between both palms and bring it to my nose to inhale the essence of lavender and rosemary I'll always associate with Gram. The pages are filled with descriptions and pictures of herbs and plants, outlining details of their uses and how to find them.

"I don't know how to Heal without her help," I say.

A flicker of pain rides across Mom's face. "That's probably why she left you this." She hands me the sealed envelope. "Don't open it until you're ready. I'm curious to know what it says, but you don't have to tell me—unless you want to. This is for you, Abby. Only you." She meets my eyes again and hands me the box.

I replace everything but the ring, then turn the key to lock it all inside. "So."

"So," she repeats.

"Will we leave tomorrow then?" I wonder how much is left to pack, what we'll even want to keep.

Mom's mind seems to turn in the same direction as she surveys our surroundings. "The next day," she says. We stand in the kitchen doorway, our eyes resting on the floor where Gram died. "We'll need time to bury Isabelle first."

I lean my head against the door jamb, squeezing my eyes shut. "Oh." I almost forgot about that little detail. We've never had to have a funeral before we moved.

Mom reads my thoughts. "Just us, Abby. Graveside. I'll call the mortuary first thing in the morning and see if someone's willing to say a few words, maybe pray."

Exhausted, I turn away from the kitchen. My bedroom door closes with a quiet click as I curl into a ball on the bed and let the wave of guilt crash down on me.

I didn't save her.

I was born a Healer—and Gram has been pushing me to study the Healing arts for years. Maybe if I had studied harder or learned faster. Maybe if I was smarter or had stronger powers—or a stronger heart—I could have saved her. Healed her. But I didn't. I couldn't. Something was missing. Something went very wrong, and it's my fault. It's my heart, my soul that lacked the ability to Heal Gram. Gram's dead because I didn't do it right. I'll be haunted with this knowledge for the rest of my life.

I hug the box and sob, letting out my grief until the pressure in my chest flows into my head and clogs my sinuses. Then I cry harder. Erda senses my despair and jumps on my bed—something she's never been allowed to do—and curls up at my back to rest her chin on my side. We stay in this position, without moving to get food or go to the bathroom or even to start packing, until the light fades into blackness. Eventually, I fall asleep and dream about Gram until I open my swollen eyes to stare out the window at the sun peeking over the horizon. However hollow I feel inside, however badly I want to lie in bed and let the dark of night consume me, a new day is dawning. It's as if Gram is urging me to get up, to find the courage I need to move on.

Erda's chin is still nestled on my side. She blinks with wide, sad-looking eyes, and whines. She is mourning Gram's loss too.

I nudge Erda's head away and crawl off the bed. My puffy eyes sting and my head throbs from crying, but neither of those things feel half as achy as the hole in my chest.

"Come on, Erda," I say, heading slowly for the bathroom. "Let's get packing."

THREE

New Beginning

I'll never get used to winter in Wyoming. Nothing could be further from the sunny weather we left behind in Nevada. My suede jacket has been replaced with a coat that makes me feel like a marshmallow. If it wasn't green, I could bury myself up to my waist in snow and pass for a snowman. Except then I would probably freeze to death.

"Watch your step." The elderly bus driver nods at the ice-coated sidewalk. "Gets slippery this time of year."

"Thanks." I use the door for support and test my footing, positive that the most graceful ballerina could easily kill herself on such a treacherous surface, even in boots with three-inch-thick rubber soles. When I'm confident I have enough traction to keep from falling—thus making a poised entrance onto the grounds of my new school—I take a long look at Jackson High.

It feels small, probably because it's contained within one building. The red roof curves into a dome on which there is no buildup of snow or ice. The large windows on the second-story level to my right reflect the jagged Teton Mountains. A positive, bluish energy surrounds the building. Seeing it calms my nerves.

Warm air streams through my lips in a puff of white as I hitch my backpack higher and take a few experimental steps toward the main entrance.

Only seconds later, a snowball whizzes past my head. Another smashes into my backpack, while a third breaks to bits at my feet. I whirl around and almost turf it right there. A group of boys barrels toward me, a volley of hard-packed snow torpedoes gunning down anyone in their path. I'm directly in the line of fire. A dark-haired boy in a blue coat grabs my shoulder and whips me around to use as a shield, and is simultaneously nailed in the forehead. He goes down, dragging me with him. "Sorry."

Icy wet cold seeps into my jeans, and I'm pretty sure my hip will be purple by tomorrow. "You sh-should be!" My teeth chatter. "Why did you do that?"

"I was under attack." His hands fly up in defense. "I grabbed the first shield I saw. Not my fault you were in the way." He gets up, brushes the snow off his pants, and smiles—showcasing a row of straight, white teeth. "Sorry. Again." More snowballs fly. He scoops up a handful of slush and takes off running.

Jerk.

Fingers of cold creep under my coat, stretching to the top of my head. I brace my bare hands on a mound of snow and push myself up. Whatever happened to the guys you read about in romance novels who offer to help a lady up from the ground when she falls, and who aren't responsible for knocking her down in the first place?

They don't live in Wyoming, I tell myself as I open the heavy wooden door, relieved by the whoosh of warm air that blows in my face. My first destination is the office. The secretary is stationed behind a long wooden counter that cuts the room in two. On one corner of the desk, a fern struggles for life, yellow and mostly leafless.

"What can I do for you?" the lady asks.

"I'm Abigail Johnson." I unzip my bag and find the registration forms Mom signed last night. "It's my first day."

The secretary's eyes soften as I hand over the papers. "Good to meet you, Abigail," she says. "I'm Mrs. Kelly. I arranged your classes the other day after your mother called, so this will only take a minute." Her fingers fly over the keyboard, and a printer hums to life. She hands me a schedule and a map. "Welcome to Jackson High."

"Thank you." I sit in a chair near the fern to go over my class list. Since I'm here, I tug the silver chain from under my shirt and spin the garnet crystal a few times, aiming my energy at the fern. For practice.

"What up, Ms. K.?"

I don't look, but for some dumb reason my heart thumps at the sound of the voice behind me. Energy spikes in the docile air. I hope no one's watching the fern. My eyes stay riveted on the paper like it holds the key to an important secret.

"Doing well, Kye," says Mrs. Kelly, her voice breathless. "How was your trip?"

"Educational," the voice responds. "Have you ever been to Ireland?"

"No, but it's on my list of places to visit when I retire." Mrs. Kelly sounds flustered. I chance a peek over the edge of my paper—she's patting her hair. *Pathetic.* I roll my eyes, refusing to turn around and look at whoever makes her act that way.

"It's amazing. You'd love it." The bell rings. "Gotta go," he says. "Have a good one."

"See you later, Kye." If voices can smile, Mrs. Kelly's does as she returns the goodbye. Fighting a giggle, I stand to leave. A sidelong glance at the now perky fern gives me a sense of satisfaction.

I make my way to English, where a stately, pear-shaped teacher named Mrs. Carlson hands me a list of suggested reading and directs me to the only empty seat in the back corner. From here I can see almost everyone without turning around. It's an advantage because I can peek into each person's energy field and find out what they're like before we even meet.

After Gram's death, I bought several books about auras, wondering how I didn't know what was coming before it happened. Turns out, I should have. Gram's aura was purple when I left that morning. Purple means serious danger.

That's a mistake I'll never make again.

"Pssst." From the next desk over, a girl with fluffy, dark-brown hair gestures at me. "What's your name?"

I tap my index finger on my lips and raise my eyebrows in the direction of Mrs. Carlson.

"Oh, don't worry." The girl waves her hand, shoving my objections aside. "She loves me. I'm her favorite."

I slide lower in my seat. "Well, I'm not. I don't want to get in trouble on my first day."

"What's your name?"

"Abby Johnson."

"I'm Rose Westover." She points to a blonde head two seats up and three seats over. "That's Jen Thomas. We've been best friends since preschool. You should eat lunch with us."

Rose shuts up when Mrs. Carlson stands to begin a discussion about the reading homework she assigned over winter break. I follow along easily and answer a few questions correctly because I've read A *Midsummer Night's Dream* before.

At the end of class, I glance up and find Rose standing next to me, smiling. Her aura is the brightest, most unusual shade of turquoise I've ever seen. She's highly energized, influential. Happy. Likeable.

"What?" I can't help but return her smile. Rose is contagious.

"For being new here, you sure know a lot about our Shakespeare assignment."

We head for the door together. "Repeated lessons are a hazard of attending many different schools."

"Oh," she says. "What class do you have next?"

My schedule is already a crinkled mess. "Drama. Why?"

"Down the stairs, right at the bottom, and then keep going straight until you run into the auditorium door. Sit near the front of the stage."

I try to memorize her directions. "Um. Thanks."

"Where are you from?"

The question forces me to push away thoughts of Gram and our experiences in Nevada. "Most recently, Las Vegas."

25

"Cool." She looks at her watch. "Gotta run, but later I'm going to track you down to find out where you live, if you have a boyfriend, and if you two ever—ya know—and when's the last time you got drunk? And I need to know *everything* about Las Vegas." She claps a hand to the top of her head. "We have to hang out. Soon."

My head is reeling as I start down the stairs. "Maybe." *Not.*

Thanks to Rose's directions, I find drama easily and am shocked and amazed when the teacher, Mr. Akers, starts class by ordering us onstage for a ten-minute Thai Chi warm up. I thought Thai Chi was one of those quirky things only practiced by fanatics and Californians.

Mr. Akers is unexpectedly good looking, in a way no teacher should be allowed. His night-black hair is the perfect frame for his pale, nearly translucent skin and striking eyes, which are a deep-aqua color too blue to be real. Those eyes watch over the class and stop momentarily on me. He towers over my five-foot-two—in the six-foot range—leaving his sculpted chest continually in my line of vision. I picture him standing shirtless on the cover of a fashion magazine. No, a billboard. In Vegas. He could totally pull it off.

His aura might be yellow, which would indicate joy and vitality, but it's hard to tell for sure since the stage is flooded with lights.

Following his directions, my classmates and I stand with our feet shoulder-width apart, eyes closed, and sweep our arms in circles, aiming first at the floor and then moving toward the ceiling.

"Push out all the dark energy, and pull in your chi," Mr. Akers says in a soothing voice. "Pull in the light, the good, and the happy. Concentrate. Breathe in the positive."

I feel calm. Balanced. Stable.

Until the door behind the stage slams open and a burst of frigid wind hits me from behind. Shivering, I turn toward the source of the distraction.

Someone forces the door closed, pushing hard until the latch clicks. He's standing in the shadows, so I can only see his outline, but my breath catches when he steps into the light and tosses his coat on a chair. His hair is short up to his ears, but from the top grows long enough to wave softly around his face. Smooth skin stretches taut over the lean muscles in his arms. This guy works out. My heart stutters when our eyes meet. His are pools of the clearest blue I've ever seen—a blue that seems to pierce straight through my soul. A spark of familiarity races down my spine. I know those eyes from somewhere.

Why won't my heart beat normally?

"Glad you could make it to class, Kye." Mr. Akers doesn't even have to look; he already knows who just came in. He continues to lead the Thai Chi movement as if there was never an interruption. "I assume you have a good reason for being tardy?"

"Yes, sir, I do." Kye's voice is musical. And familiar. He's the guy who was talking to Mrs. K. in the office, but that's not all. I could swear I've seen him before, heard his voice before. "I can get a note if you want," he says, tearing his eyes from mine. "Val sends his regards." He takes a place on the stage, far away from me, assumes a Thai Chi stance, and mimics our movement like he's been doing this his entire life. His breathing is even and slow, as if he hasn't just come bursting in from the Arctic. As if he isn't as affected by me as I am by him.

Mr. Akers opens one eye and peers at Kye. "I see." Kye nods and Mr. Akers closes his eye again and finishes the warm up session—apparently needing no further explanation. My intuition spikes and I'm curious. There was something in the look they exchanged, but as hard as I try, I can't figure out what.

I try to see into Kye's energy field, but I can't. For some reason that has nothing to do with the stage lights, I can't see Kye's aura at all.

While the rest of us pair up to work on a characterization assignment, Kye joins Mr. Akers in the small office located on one side of the stage. Through the glass door, I can tell Kye is excited.

He talks with his whole body, not just his hands. Mr. Akers looks concerned at first, but then a proud smile spreads across his face.

I wonder about their relationship. Obviously, they're more to each other than teacher and student. It wouldn't be unheard of for them to be related, especially in a town with more snowplows than people.

My partner, Crystal, looks at her watch, clearly annoyed. "You want some advice, new girl? Stay away from Kye. Guys like him think the world—and everyone in it—revolves around them. I'm out of here." She grabs her bag and walks away.

I'm left speechless in our corner of the stage—with five minutes left before the bell.

"Don't let her get to you. Crystal often has bratty tendencies."

I turn around and find myself face to face with the boy from the snowball fight. Dark brown hair falls in pieces over his forehead and cheeks and he shakes it back, revealing hazel eyes and the perfect teeth I noticed earlier. "But don't tell her I said that or she'll come after me."

My irritation from the morning's confrontation flickers and dies. I return his smile. "I'm Abby."

"Eric." He closes my hand in both of his. "Welcome to Jackson High."

"Thanks." I drop my papers in my bag as the bell rings.

Mr. Akers pokes his head out the office door. "You're free to go. See you all tomorrow."

"Where's your next class?" Eric asks.

I glance at my schedule, unsuccessfully trying to avoid a last look at Kye. He's sitting on the edge of Mr. Akers's desk, looking amused. I shake my head and look at the paper for real this time. "Um, history, room 107."

"Wicked. You're in my class." Eric picks up his binder. "I'll show you the way."

FOUR

Memories and Plans

E ven though I dread Rose's promised questions, I accept the invitation to sit with her and Jen at lunch, because not sitting alone is eighty percent of the first-day battle. The conversation centers on an upcoming trip they're planning. I only partly listen, picking the pepperoni off my pizza and stealing discreet glances around the cafeteria. I'm not really looking for Kye. Okay, I am, but I don't want to admit it—even to myself. Something about him draws me like a paperclip to a magnet, and I haven't even officially met him.

"Abby, are you in there?" Rose waves a hand in front of my face.

"Sorry."

"So, are you coming with us?" Rose struggles with the lid on her milk chug then hands the bottle to Jen, who opens it with a faint pop. When she hands Rose the plastic lid, it looks a bit warped, like it sat too close to the heat vent.

"Where?"

"On our trip to the Park."

"What, like a picnic? It's freezing out."

Rose laughs and rests a hand on my shoulder. "The Park. As in, Yellowstone National Park. Geysers and mud pots are the most fun."

"Oh." I sip my drink. "When are you going?"

"Spring break. Jen's uncle is getting us a killer deal on rooms at Old Faithful Lodge. They're not always open by then, but I talked to the owners. No one ever tells me no."

"Originally," Jen says, "we planned the trip for Rose's birthday, but it turned into such a big deal, the principal arranged for chaperones and buses. I guess he decided it's better to get involved than leave the junior and senior classes at a lodge, overnight, without adult supervision."

"You're spending the night?"

Jen leans forward. "Hence the chaperones. Isn't it wicked? Half the school will be there for Rose's eighteenth." Jen grins at Rose. "We're going to rock that park."

"Oh, yeah." Rose strums an imaginary guitar. "Hey, if your parents will let you come, you can room with Jen and me. We have a suite so there's plenty of space."

"We'll see," I say. It's hard to imagine going on an overnight trip with people I just met. Plus, my mom will never go for it. Not after what happened with Gram.

Conversation swirls around me, but my eyes are drawn to the far corner of the cafeteria where two people are arguing. Kye and that girl from drama—Crystal. The energy around them sparkles with rainbow-colored darts.

Mostly, Crystal rants while Kye stands there. Every so often, the muscle in his jaw tenses, but though I can see his mouth moving, he never yells back, even when Crystal slaps him and the sound echoes in the cafeteria.

There is a chorus of cheers and guffaws as Crystal storms out and Kye follows, ignoring the catcalls from other students and questions from a concerned cafeteria monitor.

"Here we go again," Rose mutters, shoving half a roll in her mouth.

"You'd think he'd learn by now." Jen returns to her party planning, but I'm no longer listening. I'm remembering the one and only time I ever saw Gram lose control. She slapped my father during an argument in the living room of a house we rented in

Utah. I was six-years old, crouched behind the sofa, eavesdropping, when I should have been in bed. Gram was telling my dad he shouldn't go, but he insisted that he had to, that there were evil things happening which he couldn't ignore.

Later that night, he came to my room while I pretended to sleep. He brushed the hair off my forehead and kissed my cheek. "I love you," he whispered, and I opened my eyes to watch him leave. It was the last time I ever saw him. That's when I learned to fear my Gifts, why I resisted learning to use them until it was too late, why I couldn't save Gram.

Remembering makes my stomach ache, steals my appetite.

"Hey." Eric's voice breaks into my thoughts. "You okay?"

I nod. "Just thinking."

"You're not sick or anything?" He points at the pizza on my plate. "Pepperoni poisoning?"

"No, I'm not sick. I'm fine, really." My eyes sting.

"You look sorta pale."

I gulp the rest of my drink, trying to cool the cold burn in my throat. "New school nerves catching up to me, I guess."

Eric eyes me over his burger. "You seemed fine earlier."

"Long day." My lunch tray is still full, but the need to escape is now priority. I dump my food in the nearest trash can and bolt through the outside door. Salt crunches under my boots as my feet take me around the school toward the parking lot. The weak afternoon sun has melted the ice, leaving puddles on the sidewalk.

I take a calming breath and stare at the snow-covered mountains. The frosty air fills my lungs and, bit by bit, I regain my balance.

The loss of my father is far enough in the past that a layer of scar tissue has formed over the wound. Only weeks have passed since Gram's death, and her loss is still an open sore. My heart aches, missing her.

Gram always knew my feelings before I did, and when I hurt, for whatever reason, she always knew what to say to make me feel better. I miss the comfort of having her put her arms around me and tell me everything will work out for the best, the way she did when I was twelve and first showed signs of being a Healer.

I had found the body of a newborn puppy in a Dumpster and picked her up, planning to bury her, but instead brought her back to life. Mom let me keep her, and we named her Erda, after the Norse goddess of fate.

When I was fourteen and had my first vision—about a blue-eyed boy who was always being chased by men with otherworldly abilities—Gram made me oatmeal raisin cookies and informed me that having two Gifts is exceptionally rare. She made me believe that even among Gifted people, I am unique. Special.

But Gram's gone. *And it's my fault.*

"Hey, I wondered where you went," Rose calls from down the sidewalk.

I force a smile as she approaches, but keep staring at the mountains. "I needed some air."

"Beautiful, aren't they?" She stares too.

"I've never seen anything quite like them. Mysterious. Like a fairy tale."

"I know what you mean." Rose's voice takes on a more serious edge. "If you're looking for a fairy tale, good or bad, you've come to the right place."

"What do you mean?" I'm trying to act more interested than I am, even though I just want to be left alone.

"We have a bunch of local legends," she says. "Fantastical creatures, lots of adventure ... you should read about them sometime."

My interest piques, despite my desire to be alone. "Maybe I will," I say. "Everyone loves a nice fairy tale every now and then."

"Yeah." Rose frowns, stares at the mountains again. "As long as there's a happy ending involved."

FIVE

Don't Panic

I don't see Kye much for the next few weeks. I've never even talked to the guy and my stomach ties in knots at the simple thought of his ocean-blue eyes. It makes no sense. But then, very little in my life actually makes sense these days.

I know he comes to school—just not to drama class. We pass each other in the hall occasionally, and I feel his presence like a palpable thing. He ignores me, so I return the favor, bothered by the fact that he feels so familiar and I can't figure out why.

Eating lunch with Rose and Jen becomes a daily habit. Rose's cheerful yellow aura mixes with Jen's purplish-blue to form a calming deep green. It's no wonder they're friends—they bring each other balance. Interesting things happen when they're around, and I look forward to Rose's nonstop chatter. The two of them are relentless when discussing their plans for the trip. They insist I come, and work devilishly to talk me into it.

Then there's Eric, who is relentless in a different way.

"I'll bet you a dollar I can make you fall in love with me by the end of the month." He says when he catches up with me after drama and walks with me to history.

"Is that all my love is worth?" I lick my lips, wondering what makes the air in Jackson taste metallic and why I shiver every time Eric is around.

"Fine then, twenty dollars."

I dig through my bag, looking for gum, and ignore the instinct to jump away when Eric's cool arm brushes mine. "It doesn't seem fair to take money I've done nothing to earn." I back up, putting distance between us on the premise of offering him a piece of gum. "But I've never been a girl to pass up easy money, either."

"Oh, you'll earn it. Anyway, I have no intention of letting you win. I'm going to start by escorting you to the party this weekend."

My memory flashes to an intense gaze shared across a stage. *What's wrong with me?* Why do I feel like going out with Eric is cheating? "Party?" I ask.

"Uh, yeah. Well, it isn't officially hosted by the school, technically. It's in Yellowstone."

Oh no, not him too. "Did Rose put you up to this?"

He looks confused. "What?"

"Never mind." I sigh. It's not fair for me to pretend I like him. "Look, I was joking. I can't go out with you, and I'm not letting you make all kinds of effort just to win a bet. Besides, I'm not going to Yellowstone."

His shoulders slump. "You have so little faith in my abilities. It's discouraging."

I stop in front of my locker and dial the combination. "Thanks for the offer, but I'm not into the whole teenagers falling in love thing. Even if I was, I never stay put long enough for it to happen. I'm a waste of your time."

Eric leans on the locker next to mine, his head cocked to the side. "How long have we known each other?"

"Three weeks." I retrieve my history book and slam the locker shut.

"Three weeks," he repeats, steering me in the direction of our classroom. "And I've seen you spend time with two people. Rose and Jen. Do you not know how many guys in this school are dying to ask you out?"

Obviously not Kye. I snort. *Stupid that I even care.* "You're such a liar. You're the only guy who's actually spoken more than one sentence to me since I moved here. I might as well be invisible."

Now it's his turn to snort. "Abby! You're anything but invisible."

"Whatever. It's not like I fit in." I stop to sip from the water fountain, hoping it'll ease the almost constant dry burn in my throat.

"The problem is that you're so quiet you seem almost standoffish, untouchable. I thought you were a snob at first. Do you realize I tried to talk to you three times before you actually responded?"

"You did not."

"Yeah, Abby, I did. But you were busy observing ... other people."

Have I really stared that much? Crap. Heat creeps into my cheeks as I turn to him, my heart beating a little harder. The idea of upsetting Eric makes me shiver harder. "It's not like ... I didn't mean ..."

"It's okay, Abby." He rests his hand on my arm. "I know you aren't a snob. You're a little on the shy side, a lot on the nervous side." He moves closer. "Completely defensive and absolutely as untouchable as everyone thinks."

I shrug away from him again. "I am not. Stop saying that."

"Honey, look—"

"Don't call me honey, Eric." The burn in my throat moves into my eyes and sinuses. "I'm not your honey. And I don't want to be your girlfriend, either."

"See." His body blocks my way into class. "That's exactly what I mean. You want to be left alone, and you make sure everyone within a hundred miles knows it."

"So?"

"So, nothing. I want to know why. You're not the cold person you want people to think you are. What would be so bad about going with me to a party? I'm not going to attack you or anything." I turn away, my stomach churning with an unwelcome yet familiar sensation. Before I take a step, he wraps his arms around my waist from behind, and his cool breath is in my ear. "At least, not yet."

He's joking and I know it, but my heart hammers. I don't want him to touch me. *I don't want him to touch me.* My throat burns like it's coated with hot metal and I'm overcome with an ancient, primal terror I know I've felt before, though I have no idea when. I can't see Eric's face since he's behind me, but I See him. In another place and time. A rakish grin slashes his features, and his hair is at least two inches longer.

Drawing in a deep breath, I try to shove the vision away, but only manage to trigger my more recent memory of Gram as she lay on the floor, bleeding. Dying. The blood drains from my face. Pain spasms in my chest. There isn't enough air in the building.

Memories flash like strobe lights.

My father kisses me goodbye.

A pair of amber eyes stares from the back of a dark theater.

I run up the stairs to find Gram lying on the floor, taking her last breaths.

Violet eyes, watching, waiting, ready to strike.

A circle of Healing power breaking into a million tiny pieces and scattering around the kitchen.

Eric's touch feels very, very wrong.

"Hey." Eric spins me around to face him. "Abby? Are you okay?"

I wheeze in and out. In. Out. Close my eyes. Concentrate on getting oxygen to my brain.

"Abby? Talk to me. Please. What did I say?"

I open my eyes. The room moves in circles and black spots float in the air. The breathing thing isn't going to work. I slide down the wall and sit on the floor. Eric says my name over and over again. I ignore him.

Someone else says, "Let's get her to the nurse."

I push away the hands on my shoulders. "I think ... I need—"

"What, Abby? What do you need?" Eric asks.

I want to fight him, push him away. Hurt him. I don't know why. "I need to find the boy." I mumble. Then the world goes black.

SIX

Railroaded

I wake up in the nurse's office, where she explains that I've had a panic attack and my mother is coming to take me home.

Someday I hope I'm able to laugh about the sheer mortification I'm experiencing, but that day is not today.

Eric is in the office with us, which makes me angry. I don't want him here. The nurse must sense this because she kicks him out, sending him to class. As he leaves, I can hear him telling someone, or everyone, that I fainted.

Mom takes me home, and after a minor amount of fussing and a short lecture about me and stress and what could be the cause of the problem, she leaves me alone and finally goes back to work. I change into lounge pants and a T-shirt and curl up on the sofa to watch TV with Erda.

My vision blurs beneath my heavy eyelids. In a minute, I'll go take a tincture of willow bark for the headache that's been building in my forehead all day. Right now, I can't move, can't feel my arms or legs or anything but the pounding in my head as I watch the vision unfold, like a movie on a screen.

A small woman with blue-green eyes smoothes her hair and straightens her skirt before gliding down the stairs to rejoin her son's wedding party. As she descends, she catches the eye of the captain of her Warrior Guards and murmurs his name, "Rhys." His eyebrows rise in appreciation.

The laces on her silver-trimmed gown are pulled tight, making breathing difficult. She hides her struggle by tossing loose strands of golden curls over her shoulder and patting the pile of them atop her head. The emeralds at her throat sparkle in the bright light of thousands of candles. She picks up her skirts and cuts through the dance floor. The crowd parts, and she glides to the empty throne next to the king. Rhys stands just behind and to her right, acting as bodyguard.

"Damon," she says to her husband. "Have you seen Theron and his new bride?"

The king chuckles wickedly. "Of course not, my dear Isleen. Our son is too smart to waste his wedding night socializing with commoners and snobs."

"Well, where is he then?" She perches on her throne.

"Where do you think, darling? I imagine Theron and Raina have already given great efforts toward the creation of an heir."

A blush creeps across Isleen's cheeks. "Someone should rouse them every so often. After all, this is their party."

Damon motions to Rhys. "Captain, if you had the choice between spending the evening in the privacy of your bedchamber with your new bride or rubbing elbows with a ballroom full of courtiers, which would you choose?"

Rhys smiles, avoiding the queen's gaze. "Privacy, Your Majesty. Of course."

"He could at least show his face every few hours or so." Isleen leans against the throne as far as her full dress will allow. "I grow weary of making his excuses."

"Shall we send everyone away?" Damon sips from a silver goblet to hide his smile.

"Not yet." Isleen turns to Rhys. "Captain, fetch Theron. Inform him that I shall retire soon and expect his goodnight wishes immediately."

Damon snorts. "Surely you do not mean to interrupt the boy?"

"Damon! The Prince has been raised to respect his mother."

Rhys bites back a smile.

"Shall I bring him here or have him meet you at your chambers?"

DESCENDANT

The smile Isleen turns on her bodyguard is intimate. "My chambers will be fine. Thank you, Captain."

Rhys doesn't smile, but his expression betrays a hint of adoration as he bows. "Anything for you, Majesty."

The buzzing doorbell startles me awake. Was I really asleep? It's late afternoon, nearly dinnertime. None of my visions has ever lasted so long, and they usually involve a blue-eyed boy. Maybe it was a dream.

Erda barks as I trip to the door, stub my toe on the entry table, and bang my elbow against the wall. On the stoop, Rose and Jen are bundled in heavy coats and snow boots. Jen's eyes are hidden behind a pair of wrap-around sunglasses, which she shoves in her hair as she follows Rose in from the blinding sunshine.

Rose wastes no time getting to the point. "Did you really faint in the hall?"

I pull my fingers through my tangled nest of hair with a groan. "I guess the whole school knows by now." Especially since Rose has—no doubt—spread the whole embellished story through the grapevine.

Jen says, "You're under way too much stress. You probably need a break."

"She definitely needs a break. A sleepover of epic proportions." Rose shoves past me and into the living room. She drops her coat on the floor and plops in the recliner, reaching out to scratch Erda's head. "You're coming with us on this trip. No more arguing."

"Make yourself at home." Shaking my head, I close the door. I haven't argued so much as flat-out told them no—no fewer than twelve times. And the three of us have only been hanging out for a few weeks. I like them—both of them—but I have no idea why they're trying so hard or why they care if I go to Yellowstone. It's not like they have a shortage of friends, and I haven't exactly been Miss-Abby-sunshine-full-of-cheer since my arrival. "Remind me when you're going?"

"Duh. After school tomorrow. Spring break kick-off." Jen folds her coat over her arm and sits on the end of the sofa. It has gotten a bit warm in here since they arrived. "Haven't you been listening to anything we've told you?"

"Come on, Abby. It'll be wicked fun. Epic." Rose slides off her boots and crosses her ankles on the coffee table. "If we can scrape enough money together, we might even be able to rent snowmobiles and soar through the back country or something equally entertaining."

Since they both look comfortable, I decide to make an attempt at hospitality. "Do you want hot chocolate or something?"

"Marshmallows?" Rose asks.

"Of course." I start toward the kitchen. "Cookies?"

"Sure," Jen says.

When I come back with three cups of mint-flavored hot chocolate and four cranberry oatmeal cookies, Erda is writhing in ecstasy while Rose rubs her belly. "She's going to expect that every time she sees you now," I warn.

"I don't mind." Rose keeps rubbing. "She's a sweet dog who deserves to be treated like royalty. Don't you, Erda?" Erda groans in response, and I try not to feel betrayed.

Jen accepts a mug of chocolate. I toss a cookie to Erda, who jumps up and runs for the kitchen, catching the cookie in her mouth mid-flight, and crumbles it to bits all over the tile.

"Where's your suitcase?" Rose's mouth is full of cookie. "We'll help you pack. You'll need to get plenty of rest so you feel better for tomorrow."

"I haven't even checked with my mom." It's my last line of defense.

"Oh, we did that already." Jen sets her mug on top of a new-looking burn mark on the scarred end table. "We stopped by her office on our way here. She wants you to go and even signed permission papers. Now we just need to help you pack. Where can we find a suitcase?"

"How much is it again? I don't know if I can afford it."

Rose grins. "Your mom gave me cash. No more excuses."

"I wouldn't know what to pack."

"That's why we're here." Rose pours her whole mug of chocolate down her throat, unconcerned about the temperature.

"Trust me, Abby. You won't be sorry." Rose steps around Erda—who is now flopped on her belly, asleep—to open the coat closet. "No suitcases in here. Next."

Jen follows Rose to my room. I look at Erda. "A lot of help you are, pup." She opens one eye. "You were supposed to help me out, and instead you let her pull you in." I set my empty mug on the coffee table and follow my friends upstairs.

As I lie in bed that night, excitement vibrates through me and I roll onto my side to stare out the window. The moon gleams through the glass, turning the white curtain pale pink, and ice crystals sparkle like diamonds around the edges.

Rose and Jen have railroaded me into going to Yellowstone, but part of me is glad I've been stripped of excuses. If this trip wasn't good for me, I would feel it. Know it. Instead, what I feel is anticipation for something big—much bigger than an overnight excursion with my new friends.

A movement outside the window catches my eye and I jump up to pull the curtain back. Through a cluster of trees, a creature nibbles on a shrub. Its white hide reflects the moonlight like a pearl, giving it an unearthly glow. A great rack crowns its head as if the animal is king of the forest. If not for the antlers, I might have mistaken it for a cow.

The great beast lifts its face, gazing in my direction, and a tingle makes the hairs stand up on the back of my neck. It's *watching* me. I press my hand against the cold glass. As if sensing my desire to touch it, the beast backs into the trees then turns away and bounds through the foliage up the mountain.

"Wait." I whisper. "Come back." But the creature is long gone.

My bed beckons to me, but Gram's box catches my eye from a shelf on the wall. Reverently, I take it down and switch on my bedside lamp. Except for putting the ring away before we moved, I haven't opened the box since that horrible day.

I hold the sealed letter to my nose, inhale the faint scent of lavender, and then replace it in the box, not quite ready to read Gram's last words to me. Reading the letter will only make her absence more real, and I can't bring myself to open the envelope, to probe that still-healing wound.

Instead, I slide the ring on my finger. My skin warms where it touches, and an electric spark zings up my arm. The stones glitter in the lamplight. The crystals I've neglected wink up at me, demanding to be taken out of the box and carried in my pocket. I touch each one, feeling faint pulses of energy in them.

"How can I Heal other people when my own heart is broken?" I whisper to myself.

I play with the diamonds I was never allowed to touch when Gram was alive, and sniff the letter again, wondering what Gram would think of me going to Yellowstone. When I'm finished, I close the box and place it in the back of my bottom desk drawer, still wearing the ring.

The comforter cocoons me in warmth as I snuggle in and close my heavy eyelids, letting my mind drift. A fluttering sensation tickles my forehead and the scent of lavender touches my nose, the way it did when I was little and Gram tucked me in. "You'd love my new friends, Gram."

I must be dreaming already. The voice that responds sounds distant and far away. *I already do, baby. I already do.*

SEVEN

A Chance Meeting

Rose slams the trunk, scowling at my heavy duffle when I struggle to keep up. "If you'd let us take your bag last night, it would already be loaded with the rest of the stuff."

"I told you, I'd rather load it myself." No way am I taking chances with Gram's crystals.

"Throw that thing in the luggage compartment and meet us on board. We'll save you a seat."

Jen sends me an apologetic glance and follows Rose.

"Wait!" A mass of people moves after them, shoving me aside. "Hang on, I'm coming." They don't wait. Teenagers crowd the door and I end up at the end of the line, unable to see my friends anymore.

Someone knocks me off balance and I manage to stay upright by grabbing on to a random person, dropping my duffle bag in the process. I release the person's jacket, muttering, "Sorry," without looking up, and bend to pick up my bag, but someone else already has.

"Not cool," says a familiar voice. I jerk my head up, meet the gaze of the person I've grabbed, and find myself staring into Kye's crystalline blue eyes.

I struggle to find my voice, to force words out of my mouth. "Sorry."

"Not you, the guy who plowed into you," he says, handing my duffle over to the chaperone loading the last of the bags. "He didn't even apologize."

"No manners." I force a smile, take a breath, and try to remember what I'm supposed to be doing. "Um. Thanks." *Lame. Lame. Lame. Say something. You've only practiced this conversation two thousand times.* Nothing comes. One corner of Kye's mouth quirks up in a sort of half-smile and he nods. The silence is awk-ward.

Eventually, I make it to the door and try to step aboard the bus, but the driver looks down his nose, frowning. "Sorry, kids, this one's full."

"What?" Kye puts his hand on the door before the man can close it on me. "Seriously?"

The driver starts the engine. "Another bus should be here soon." When I still don't move, he narrows his eyes. "Look, you're going to catch up with your friends in a few minutes. You and your boyfriend will still get your weekend together—along with everyone else. Step back."

Heat floods my cheeks. The driver thinks I'm going to Yellowstone *with* Kye. "He isn't my boyfriend," I manage to squeak.

"I'm closing the door."

I take a step back and look helplessly down the row of windows. Jen opens hers and sticks her face through the opening. "What happened?"

"Bus is full. I have to wait for another one."

Jen turns, says something to Rose, and then sticks her face back out again. "Meet us in the lobby. We won't do anything fun until you get there."

Rose sticks her face out next to Jen's, but only her mouth clears the glass. The bus lurches forward. "Don't bail on us, Abby. Whatever you do, get on the next bus! Remember, you promised."

"I didn't promise anything," I murmur, though minor details like that rarely matter to Rose.

A pile of suitcases and duffle bags waits on the curb. The chaperone who was loading them earlier stands guard, watching down the street as if he expects a new bus any minute. I can see my bag on top and allow myself to feel relieved. I can still back out if I want. But I don't want to anymore. *It's only one night. Not exactly life or death. Besides, my friends will be waiting for me.*

"This sucks," Kye says.

A giggle bursts out of me. "Yep. Could be worse, though."

"Too true." Kye fiddles with a string of leather tied around his wrist and glances up at the sky. "It could be snowing."

"Ugh. Don't say that. Snow is my enemy." We find a bench, and Kye leans against it as I sit and curl my knees up to my chest.

"Hate to tell you this, but if that's true, you're in a losing battle. It snows seven out of twelve months here—at least."

I push my hair out of my face. "I was afraid of that. Too bad my mom loves Jackson, or I'd talk her into moving near a beach."

Kye doesn't respond. He's staring—mouth open, a strange expression on his face—at my hands.

"What?"

He shakes his head. "Where did you get that ring?"

I hold both hands in front of me, displaying all four rings. "Which one?"

Kye grabs my left hand and touches the only one that really matters to me. Gram's ring. Two sparkling diamond hearts—one blazing blue, the other brilliant white—twined together with swirls of shining platinum, each stone set opposite the other so one heart is always upside-down, the tips touching. "I ... from my grandmother. I inherited it when she died."

Kye slides it off my finger.

"Hey. Give that back," I yelp, jumping to my feet. "It isn't a toy."

His only response is to move away and hold the ring up to the cloudy sky, turning it so both the stones catch the weak sunlight.

"Are you listening to me?" I grab his bicep, squeeze. "I said give it back." Though Kye's muscle tightens and flexes, his arm doesn't move, even when I use all my weight. Desperate, I resort to a reaction I haven't used since kindergarten and pound on his chest. "Give. It. Back." I emphasize each word with a little more power.

Finally, Kye catches my hand, returning the ring to my finger. A flash of memory startles me when he does this, a feeling of déjà vu that only lasts a second before it's gone.

I'm shaking. Probably in anger, but I'm not sure.

Kye stares at me, his eyes full of speculation. "By any chance, do you know how or where your grandmother got that ring?"

I wrap my arms around myself and hide my hands, hoping to ease the shaking. "Why?"

Kye snorts. "Why, indeed?"

I walk away to put space between us, waiting around the side of the building until I hear the roar of an engine grumbling into the parking lot. My heart sinks when I realize a line has formed in the very spot I just vacated. I'm at the end. Again. As expected, the bus is almost full by the time I climb the steps, lamenting my bad luck. A hand waves at me from the back row.

Kye saved me a seat. I ignore him and slip into an empty spot in the front. "Sorry, miss." The driver turns the key and the engine roars to life. "That one's reserved for a chaperone."

Resigned, I drag my feet down the aisle to the only seat left—the one next to Kye. He struggles to hide a smile, but his eyes dance.

"You want the window or the aisle?" he asks.

I'm already crafting a witty retort, but make the mistake of looking into his eyes. His smile fades for real. I've spent the past three weeks convincing myself that I imagined my original gut-clench reaction to him. All over again, I'm disconcerted by the way his gaze reaches deep inside me.

Kye's expression gives no indication of what's going through his mind, though mine is moving about a thousand miles a minute. The outside storage compartments bang closed, and the moment passes. The connection breaks as the final passenger stomps onto the bus.

"Sorry, gang. Running late, as always." Mr. Akers sets down an armload of stuff and strips off his oversized camouflage coat. Kye grasps my forearm and pulls me past him to sit next to the window.

"Best seat in the place." His voice sounds rough, different. "More room, more privacy."

"Oh." I gulp, and my heart races. *Privacy? With Kye?* I like the idea, as much as it terrifies me.

While we ride in silence, I focus on how the descending sun lights the sky on fire, when what I really want to do is stare at Kye. Something about him heats my blood, stirring feelings I've never experienced and wouldn't know how to describe. Even though I'm not looking at him, I feel his every movement, hear the odd rhythm of his breathing that makes me wonder if his thoughts are as focused on me as mine are on him. Part of me wants to believe he's been plunged into the same type of turmoil I'm currently experiencing.

When his knee bumps mine, a vision appears in a blinding flash

Fingers trailing over the bare skin of my arm, lips pressed against my throat, a hand caressing the small of my back.

Kye taps my shoulder, bringing me out of my daze. "Akers has a cooler up there. You want a drink?"

I realize my mouth is dry and nod.

The road is far from smooth, but he moves down the aisle easily, chatting and joking with Mr. Akers like they're best buds, and helping himself to the contents of the cooler like it belongs to him. A few minutes later, Kye returns, handing me a can. "Here you go."

"Thanks." I pop the top and sip, needing something to do with my hands, something to cool the flames I can still feel in my face.

"Will this be your first time?" He fidgets with the leather on his wrist.

I gasp, nearly choking on a mouthful. "Um, what?"

He purses his lips, doing battle with the urge to laugh. "I mean in Yellowstone."

"Yes." Relieved to realize he didn't mean *that*, I twist a lock of hair around my finger, trying not to think about what *that* would be like. "Can't wait to see what all the hype is about."

"You'll enjoy it." Something in his eyes tells me he's talking about more than geysers and mud pots, and twin feelings of anticipation and fear go to war in my stomach.

"I ... I'm hoping to see a ..."

He tips his can up and knocks back the entire thing. My eyes follow the line of his throat as he swallows, and once again, my own mouth goes dry. Needing the distraction, I take a long swig too, chugging so hard that this time I do choke, doubling over while Kye pats my back.

"Breathe." He chuckles. "You okay?"

I shake my head. "That went down wrong." My back tingles where his hand touches a strip of exposed skin, and a line of heat circles my core.

Lips, warm and soft on mine, teeth scraping against my tongue.

"Abby?" He removes his hand, bringing me back to my senses but leaving me feeling feverish.

"I'm okay." I scoot toward the window, needing to put distance between us.

His hand curls into a fist on top of the armrest, but it's his only reaction. "You were about to tell me what you're hoping to see."

I fold my coat into a pillow and try to prop it against the seat behind my head, still holding my empty can. "A buffalo."

Kye takes both cans, tossing them both at Mr. Akers, who turns and catches each one as it arcs toward his head. Now empty-handed, Kye turns sideways, his back to the aisle, and focuses on me. "You haven't seen a bison yet? What about moose? Elk?"

I shake my head, because I don't really know how to identify what I've seen. I'm not a wildlife expert. Kye seems to get that. "Wait. Just tell me what you know you've seen already."

I adjust in my seat so we're facing each other and hear myself highlighting for him all my best experiences in Jackson with one exception—I don't mention the white creature. I'm not sure why.

Talking to Kye gets easier with each mile. I don't know if it's the privacy, or the distance from real life, or something entirely different, but I feel myself opening up to him in a way I would never have thought possible. It's comfortable. Scary comfortable.

"Sounds like you're adjusting well." Kye rests his head against the seat.

"I try to make the best of wherever I am." I wind a lock of hair around my finger, peering out the window. "Might as well appreciate it for everything I can until it's time to move on."

Kye's fingers graze the back of my hand as it rests on my knee. "You sound like you don't plan to stay very long."

It's hard to ignore the goose bumps that erupt up and down my arm, but I try. "I don't plan to stay anywhere for very long. Nothing's permanent. Life's a journey that forces us all to move forward, whether we want to or not."

I half expect Kye to laugh, but he doesn't. Something catches his eye, and he leans across me to touch the window. "Look. There."

Up ahead, a family of animals with thick, curved horns climbs a steep mountain slope. The angle appears impossible, but they never stumble, and their fluffy backsides bounce up and down with each step.

"Bighorn sheep." Kye turns his head, and I realize his face is only inches from mine. He backs away slowly, the pulse pounding visibly in his neck proof that he feels unsettled. I draw air into my lungs as my heart thump-thump-thumps.

Kye faces forward again, leaning against his seat. When his eyes close, I turn back to the window and watch the snow-frosted trees fly by. After a few minutes, the steady motion of the bus has my eyes feeling heavy too, and I lean my head on the window.

Though I'm tired, I can't slow my heart enough to sleep. My thoughts stray to Las Vegas. I wonder if I can find a way to visit during spring break. Gram loved living there. Mom claims it was because Gram won every time she sat down at a blackjack table and her odds at roulette were generally three out of five. I smile, thinking Gram had better luck than anyone I ever met. Then I remember why that's not true anymore, because in the end, her luck ran out. The end of Gram and the end of Vegas. I live in Jackson now, and Gram's in the ground, and all I have left of her is my ring.

Kye's hand covers mine. "You look uncomfortable."

"I'm okay."

His eyebrows draw together and he frowns. "You're not. What's wrong?"

Tears well up and I glance away, mortified, squeaking out, "I'm fine. Just tired."

He looks distressed, unsure. "I ... I just wanted to—" He clears his throat. "You ... you're welcome to spread out if you want."

I shake my head, wiping my cheeks with my fingertips. "I'm fine, really."

He raises the armrest dividing our seats. "If you need to sleep, you can lie on my shoulder or put your feet up here or whatever. It won't bother me."

"Okay." It's a strange offer, even though I think he's made it in innocence. Or not. Maybe he's hoping he can get a good look down my shirt.

Right. My bulky sweatshirt is really sexy shirt-looking-down material. I tug at my top, sighing, because I'm paranoid. Actually, I sort of trust him, though I don't know why. He offers me his little pillow and I scrunch it, double it over, and try futilely to stuff it into the crease between the seatback and the window. It won't stay.

A gentle hand touches my knee, offering waves of warmth to calm my frustration. "You really can relax." My heart speeds up when he tugs the pillow away from me and cushions it against his shoulder, then draws me closer until my head rests there. "Try this."

I hesitate, wondering why I'm at ease with Kye—who I've really only just met—and on edge around Eric, who I eat lunch with almost every day. My eyelids droop, and my head feels heavy. I've slept very little since Gram's death, and when I do, my dreams are riddled with nightmares and visions I don't understand. When I close my eyes, something warm and soft covers me. The flannel

DESCENDANT

button-up Kye had on over his T-shirt. I give in, grab the collar, and curl against him, comfortable, safe, and more content than I've been since Gram died. He shifts, stretches his legs around me, and leans sideways on the seat with his back against the armrest. Without thought, my head moves from his shoulder to his chest like this is something we've done a hundred times before. Here, after weeks of insomnia, I finally fall asleep.

EIGHT

Revelations and Discoveries

My dreams are riddled with Kye and Eric fighting, Kye and me kissing, more kissing, and various other activities that make my heart race and my blood run hot. The strangest part is that these dreams are different from regular dreams, and also different from visions. I have mixed senses of peace and dread, happiness and deep, profound sorrow. Then an awful laugh breaks through, rough and mean. Frightening.

When I jerk awake, the full moon bounces above the mountains like a bright ball in the darkening sky, gilding the edges of the distant cliffs. Kye rubs my arm and smoothes my hair. "Nightmare?"

Heat creeps up my cheeks as I lift my head to meet his gaze. The tenderness in his expression makes me long to stay right here, wrapped in his arms and staring into the endless pools of blue for the rest of forever.

I tear my eyes away, feeling silly, and glance at his watch. After only an hour, my crush has developed into something far more dangerous. Kye traces circles up and down my arm, and my chest tightens when his hand slides under my chin and tips it up.

A spark of recognition passes between us, something undeniably strong and just as inexplicable, and I can't look away. Conversations buzz around us, but we float in our own little bubble, focused and unmoving for what feels like eons. Then his hand moves down my arm until our fingers lace together.

He shifts, pulls me closer, his heart beating a quick, irregular thrum under my free hand. In this moment, I want Kye to kiss me in the same way my lungs want oxygen. The wanting makes me tremble from an ache I swear I've felt before, but can't for the life of me remember where or why or with whom. It is that sensation—the not knowing—that pulls me back, sends me scrambling out of his arms.

He keeps a firm hold of my hand, refusing to completely break contact. His thumb caresses the inside of my wrist, sending vibrations of energy to awaken all my senses. It feels as though time is racing, dragging me along behind it, and I experience a surge of panic. What if my time with Kye is limited? What if he's only a temporary part of my life? Will I be gutted when he leaves? *I might.*

Breathe in. Breathe out. Stay calm. Don't freak out again. Not here, on the bus. Not in front of Kye. Not while he's holding my hand. The warmth from that hand spreads up my arm, keeping me grounded, and I realize that it is because I'm holding on to Kye that I'm able to find my balance.

"You okay?" His voice is unsteady.

"Okay?" I shake my head. *Of course I'm not okay. I've completely lost my mind.* "You?"

He shakes his head too.

At least I'm not the only one.

We spend the next half hour catching up on conversations we've never had—since before today we've had none. It makes no sense, the things I hear myself telling him. None at all. This behavior is so unlike me.

The weirdest part is that Kye opens up too—like he's known me for years and years rather than just minutes. Two halves of a whole coming together after a long absence, desperate to fill in all the gaps. Even so, I can't tell him about my Gifts. I won't. Not yet.

When I mention that we moved after Gram's passing, instead of saying I'm sorry, like I expect, Kye says, "It hurts you."

"Yes." I swallow a lump in my throat. "I wasn't ready to let her go."

"Of course you weren't." Kye wraps an arm around me and squeezes. I lay my head on his shoulder and soak up his warmth. The guilt and tears I expect don't come, so I relax and allow the grief to dissipate.

"So. You officially know the story of *my* life. Now it's your turn."

"My life's boring."

"Oh, come on." I pull out of his arms and lean back, pouting. Kye adjusts in his seat, looking uneasy. "All right, fine. Where should I start?"

I listen to the soothing tenor of his voice, memorize every accent and cadence, drink him in. "How about your family?"

"Now there's a story." He runs a hand through his hair and tries to smile. "Mom's in Mexico these days, and Dad's in New York."

"Wow." *What's Kye doing in Jackson?* "That's ... far. How long have they been divorced?"

He shakes his head. "They aren't."

"Oh. Then why ...?"

"They love each other, even though they live separately. Mom does geographical and historical research—which requires funding. Dad's pretty persuasive and he has connections with important people back east, so he handles the funding. They work together, a continent apart."

"So, who do you live with?" Our knees touch, sending a shiver through me as a thousand questions tumble in my head. "And why do you live in Jackson instead of with one of them?"

"Most of the time, I live with Valdemar." Kye gnaws on the inside of his cheek. "He's a ... friend of the family, I guess, and my legal guardian. Like, if I went to jail, he'd be my one phone call. But he's gone a lot, so sometimes I stay with Akers. They've been best friends for years. I could live with one of my parents if I had a fit, but they both feel that it's better for me to stay here, so I do. It's complicated."

I open my mouth to tell him what I think of the fact that both his parents pretty well dumped him on their friend, but can't find the right words to say anything. He picks up my hand and plays with my fingers, checking out my ring again. "We get together for a reunion every few months. It's great stuff."

"Don't you miss them?" I ask.

"Every day." There's a shadow in his eyes as he pulls me close. "But we live with it."

"Why, though? I don't understand what would keep you all so far apart."

A wrinkle forms between his eyebrows and he seems to be weighing his words. "Honestly, I don't understand either. Everyone keeps telling me I will someday soon, but that hasn't happened yet. I think maybe they just weren't built to be full-time parents."

I stare at him for a long minute, feeling like a complete whiner for complaining about my mom and Gram, who—for all their faults—have never once failed me, never, ever deserted me.

He stares back, his face reflecting so many emotions I can't keep up, and seems to make a decision. Untangling himself from me, he leans against the armrest so we're facing each other and picks up my hand again, twisting Gram's ring around and around on my finger. The metal is warm—hot, almost. "I want to tell you more. A lot more. But I'm not sure I should. This is ... don't you think it's bizarre how we both just spilled our guts like that?"

"I do. It feels like I've known you for years—"

Neither of us notices the bus is slowing down until we come to a full stop in the middle of the road. The Inn can't be too far away, but I know we're not there yet.

Kye opens the window, peers into the dark, and swears under his breath. The look in his eyes makes my stomach uneasy. "What?"

He shakes his head and swears again. "I don't know, but something's not right."

I feel it too. My intuition picks up danger vibes stronger than any I've ever felt—except once. "Maybe there's an animal on the road or something."

"Maybe. I'll go check it out." He meets Akers at the front of the bus, and the driver opens the door so they can step outside.

Fear makes my heart thud as I follow Kye's path to the front and observe through the windshield. An enormous animal stands in the road, illuminated by the beam of our headlights. Kye approaches the animal, petting its glossy white hide. I can't see Mr. Akers. "Is that a moose?"

The driver, somewhat stupefied, answers with a short, "I think so. Never seen a white one before."

His words trigger a memory from a conversation I once had with Gram. "Well, a white horse would be boring. A cliché," I murmur. "Only thing missing is the knight."

Outside, Kye caresses the animal's snowy pelt, soothing it as if he alone knows exactly what to do. I step off the bus, careful not to make any noise. Kye sees me and signals for me to stay back. "Is he hurt?" My voice is soft, but Kye hears and shakes his head. He nuzzles the animal's neck, then backs away and slaps its flank.

I jump, half expecting the moose to turn on Kye and lower its enormous rack. Instead, the beast takes off in the opposite direction, stopping at the tree line to look back at us, and then disappears into the thick of the forest.

Before I can move or respond, Kye has me by the elbow, guiding me onto the bus. "What was all that about?" I realize for the first time that no one else seems conscious of what just happened. I wonder if any of the students even noticed there was an animal on the road. Mr. Akers boards behind us and takes his seat. He and Kye exchange some silent communication.

My head whips back and forth between them, questions floating around my brain like letters in canned alphabet soup. What just happened?

"I'll explain later, I promise." Kye reaches up, retrieves a large black flashlight from the luggage hold, and tucks it into his waistband. This doesn't make me feel any better. "Be back in a sec."

While he and Mr. Akers have a hushed conversation, the volume of the chatter between the other passengers increases. No one even looks up. They act like we're still driving along on our way to the party.

My mind swirls with unusual and improbable possibilities and questions until one of Gram's favorite truisms pops into my brain. "Nothing is impossible for the right person." I think I might finally understand what she meant.

Standing in the aisle, I turn in a circle, unable to figure out why I'm the only one who's so confused. A hand squeezes the top of my arm, brings me back to earth, and makes me feel stable again. I don't understand how or why.

"Abby." Kye's voice sounds funny. "I have to get off the bus now." He grabs his backpack and slings it over his shoulder.

The driver's intercom sounds. "Sorry for the delay, kids. The situation with the animal is now under control. We'll be on our way again shortly." The driver knows. Why is he the only one besides me? And Kye? And Mr. Akers?

"Wait," I say to Kye. "We're in the middle of nowhere. What are you going to do, catch a ride on the moose? Climb the mountain and sleep in a volcano?" When he doesn't answer, I block the aisle. "Tell me what's going on. Right now. Explain something. Anything. I'm freaking out here." The idea of him leaving already gives me major anxiety.

He pulls me close and kisses my forehead. I can't help but cling to him. He clings back with shaking hands. "I have to go. I'll explain as soon as I can, I promise."

Someone takes my shoulders, holding me back so Kye can force open the emergency door.

"You're going to die out there." Panic rises in my chest. I glare at Mr. Akers, who is holding me in place. "How can you let him leave like this? Don't you care about what happens to him?"

"Of course I do, Abby. But Kye is ..."

"What?" My eyes narrow into slits. "What is he?"

Kye's fingers grip the edge of the door frame. "Abby, I'll see you at the Inn in a little while, I promise. I'll be fine."

"How will you get there? On foot?" Tears of frustration burn my eyes. "It's dark."

He shares another look with Mr. Akers and says, "Trust me." He grasps my hand, linking our fingers, and my ring vibrates, glowing blue, then white, as it sends comforting warmth through my blood. Kye's lips touch mine, so briefly I'm not positive they actually make contact, and then he leaps off the bus.

A piece of my heart tears as I watch him go. I swear I've watched this happen before, said goodbye to him before. More than once. I feel like I know what he will do before he does it. He touches his lips with the tips of his fingers and holds them up, and then disappears into the dark.

I can't comprehend what just happened, but standing in the emergency doorway, breathing in the frigid winter air, my thoughts churn. I remember all the times I've seen Kye since I moved to Jackson, the way I feel when I'm near him, the way my ring flashed when our fingers touched.

Kye's like a brick wall when it comes to intuition, and I've never been able to see his aura very clearly. It takes deductive reasoning to cause a sudden realization to crash down on me. There's only one possible answer to all the questions that have been forming in my head since the first time I saw him.

Kye's Gifted.

NINE

Strangers, Rangers, and Soup

The lobby at the Inn is packed. I search for Rose and Jen, hoping they've already checked in so I'll have a place to hide out while I try to sort through everything in my head. Unfortunately, an organization project of that magnitude might take me all weekend, or the rest of the year. I spent the rest of the bus ride by myself, feeling empty and alone, my brain a blended up jumble of questions. What just happened? Where did Kye go? And why was I the only person around who was so thoroughly and utterly confused?

It's not like Mr. Akers explained after the bus started moving again. He just returned to his seat and left me alone in mine.

A wave of dizziness hits me on my way to the registration desk. Not a vision, but a premonition—a hollow ache in my gut—that tells me what's happened tonight is only a taste of what's coming. *Great.* Every seventeen-year-old girl wants to know in advance that her already unusual life is about to become downright weird.

"Are you lost?"

My eyes focus on a brown-haired Ranger in a khaki uniform. He doesn't look much older than me, but he's a lot taller. His gaze seems to take in the whole room at once.

"My friends are here somewhere—I just have to find them."

"I heard they had to call a second bus. This crowd is unbelievable—especially pre-season." The Ranger's eyes twinkle as he leans against a pillar, arms folded against his chest. "I'm Gabe."

"Abby." I offer. "You haven't by chance seen a couple of girls who—"

"Abby! Over here." Across the room, Rose stands on a chair waving her arms. "Finally!"

"Looks like they found you."

"Guess so."

Gabe turns his head, and I notice an odd swirling flame tattoo behind his left ear. I don't want to think it's sexy, but it kind of is. The radio on his belt crackles and a disembodied voice rattles off numbers, using what I can only assume is a sort of Ranger code. "That's my cue. Glad you found your friends." A secretive smile plays at Gabe's lips as he turns to walk away. "Have a good visit in the Park."

Trying to forget that tattoo, I wind through the crowd. Rose jumps off the chair and wraps her arms around me in greeting. "You made it!"

"You doubted?"

"Nah, we knew you wouldn't bail on us." Jen grabs our wrists and drags us to the elevator. Her hands are overly warm, so I peek into her energy field to make sure she's not feverish.

Rose hands me a plastic key card. "Have you eaten?"

"No." I check my watch and realize it's after seven. "Have you?"

Jen grimaces. "Only if you count gummy bears and Reece's Peanut Butter Cups as dinner."

"What's wrong with that? Sounds pretty good to me."

"It's fattening, for one thing." Jen presses the elevator button, avoiding Rose's glare. "And you'll burn through the sugar high and be starving again in an hour."

The elevator dings and we enter, Rose still scowling at Jen. "I can eat candy for dinner if I want. It's my birthday."

We settle into easy banter. Jen and I take turns teasing Rose about being an old lady who throws classy birthday shindigs for the entire state of Wyoming. This results in a small, hair-damaging pillow fight in our room.

In the end, Jen lobs a pillow at Rose. "You know we're all here just to get away from the parentals, right?"

Rose tosses the pillow at me, suddenly calm but grinning. "Sugar's all gone. I'm starving. Time for real food."

They've distracted me for a while, but as soon as the stuffing stops flying, that heart-hammering anxiety is back times ten. I'm tempted to hide out in the room and worry about Kye, but instead follow the others down the hall. A tall man in an overcoat brushes by in a hurry, and I catch a view of a smoky, dark gray aura. I've never seen one like it—and don't mean to look—but the color is so alarming, I can't miss it. Evil. Bad. Scary.

My skin prickles.

The man and I both pause, turn, and our eyes meet. His are a strange violet color, and the pale brown skin surrounding them creases like a fan into his hairline. Dark hair—almost black—swings past his pointed chin as he angles his head to stare. "Raina." His voice winds around me, wraps me up in smoke, freezing the blood in my veins until I shiver. So, so cold. "You're back."

I feel like all the air has been sucked out of me. *Can't. Breathe.* Then the elevator dings, reminding me that I'm not alone. "Abby?" Jen asks. "Are you coming?"

"Yes." The word comes out as a whisper, as if my voice has been trapped in ice and needs to warm up before it can be used again. "Yes." I clear my throat. "Sorry."

"What's going on?" Rose grasps my elbow. "You okay? You're kinda pale."

I look up, expecting the strange man to still be standing in the hall, but in the seconds since I looked away, he's disappeared. "Who was that?"

A wrinkle forms between her brows. "Who was who? That's Jen, I'm Rose, you're Abby."

"But I ... there was a guy." *Could he have been a vision? Am I the only person who saw him?*

Rose urges me forward with a hand on my back. "You need food, stat. I think you're delirious with hunger."

"Ahem." Jen stands between the elevator doors, tapping her nails on the metal frame. "Are we eating or not?"

I let Rose pull me inside and watch her punch the button for the lobby. It cannot be a coincidence that so many strange things have happened in a few short hours, but my brain refuses to make a connection. Inside my sweater pocket, my hand finds my amethyst crystal and clasps it tight, my fingers rubbing the smooth surface, begging for some sort of clarity. Healing comes, but not from the crystal. I let it go and remove my hand from my pocket. My palm is moist with sweat and the platinum band of my ring feels warm.

The diamonds glow with soft blue light—the heat source—like some kind of dormant power has broken through or been reactivated. Before the other girls notice what's happening, I shove my hand back in my pocket. The heat from my ring spreads into my blood, flows up my arm and shoulder, down into my toes, and across my chest, searching for my chilled heart. It calms me, fills me up until the cold left behind by the stranger with the gray aura is a distant memory. I'm fine. Everything is going to be okay. I'll figure out what's happening. Eventually.

Should I warn someone about the stranger? No one else saw him. Would anyone believe me? I decide to wait. If I happen to see Mr. Akers, maybe I'll mention it to him. *If it feels right.*

The restaurant has a lodge-type atmosphere with hardwood floors and rough log walls, and is packed to overflowing with kids from our school. This café is the only one open, so everyone is sharing tables. We crowd around a corner table, which we share with three guys who came in behind us.

Rose and Jen manage to arrange things so they're squeezed between the guys, flirting and giggling before I've even figured out where to sit. The booth's c-shaped bench is already crowded. "Uh."

Rose sees me hesitate and comes to my rescue. "Everyone scoot in so Abby can fit."

The guys compress their shoulders and try to squish together, like that will create more room. The five of them look like sardines already. *Thanks, but no thanks.* "Maybe I'll just—you're already packed in there pretty tightly. Looks claustrophobic."

Jen snaps glittering fingers at the guy on the end. She and Rose must have done their nails while they waited for me. "Brian, don't just sit there. Go get Abby a chair."

"Why me?" he whines.

Rose glowers at him. "Because you're on the end. Man up."

As Brian stalks away, Rose pats the spot he just vacated. "Saved you a seat."

Before I can sit, Eric slides into the empty spot, grinning. "Hey. So, since you're here, I'm going to assume you'll be accompanying me to the party. And tomorrow, a bunch of us—"

"We have plans tomorrow." Rose attempts to shove him off the bench.

"I wasn't asking you, Rose." Eric ignores her attempts to dislodge him and unrolls the flatware from one of the linen napkins, fiddling with the dull butter knife like he's nervous. "I'm thinking we could—"

Brian clunks a chair down so hard it clatters, teetering precariously before settling on all four legs. He glares at Eric. "You're in my seat."

Eric's lips pucker like he's just eaten a lemon. "You going to drag me out of it?"

"If I have to."

Rose's eyes go wide with merriment, though I can't figure out what she finds amusing.

Reluctantly, Eric stands. He glares at Brian for several long seconds before sidestepping with a sweep of his hands. Brian blocks the spot but doesn't sit. Eric looks at me, his eyes imploring. "Shall we?"

He wants me to go with him now?

Jen saves me the trouble of responding. "Abby needs to eat, Eric. None of us wants a repeat of yesterday's performance."

Eric narrows his eyes, calculating, and points to the chair Brian has just delivered. "Sit. Eat. I want you to be able to dance with me later." He gives Brian a withering look. "If you're smart, you'll keep your hands to yourself."

"You wish." Very deliberately, Brian drapes one arm across Rose's shoulders then grabs the leg of my chair, pulling me right up to his side. "Now, this is cozy."

I pick up the edges of my chair and scoot back. Eric slams a hand on the table between me and Brian.

"Boys." Rose's voice is stern, like a parent, and heads turn our way.

Eric's chest heaves with anger, his breath puffing out so hard I swear it looks like he's blowing smoke, but he doesn't look at Brian again. "Have a good dinner," he grumbles. "I'll see you at the party."

He stalks off as I sink behind a menu, wishing I could curl up and die of humiliation. *Did I or did I not tell him I don't like him? And I don't even know Brian.*

A few minutes later, a forty-something waitress shows up to take our order. She pulls a pencil out of her wispy brown bun and taps the table with it as she rattles off the specials. "What can I get for you?" she asks, apparently deciding to start with me. I haven't looked at the menu so much as hide behind it.

"Uh," I say. "I haven't … maybe, um …"

"Why don't you start with someone else? Give her a minute." A familiar voice, sweet as honey to my ears and as welcome as it is unexpected, draws my gaze behind the waitress. The woman smiles at Kye before turning her attention to Brian.

"Mind if I join your group?"

There's not much room, but I scoot over and Kye slides a chair next to me. Under the table, his fingers find mine. I'm flustered and angry and so very confused, but I allow Kye to enfold my hand in his, grateful to feel my imbalance settling. *We so have to talk.*

"Ahem." The waitress taps her menu, impatient.

Kye glances up. "Thanks for making room for me, guys." He concentrates on the menu. "What's good here?"

While Kye orders, Rose catches my eye and hisses, "Seriously?"

"When did this happen?" Jen sets a misshapen fork on the table, gesturing to the waitress that she'll need a new one.

I bite my lip, shaking my head. "Later." Except I plan to omit around ninety percent of the details. How could I even try to explain what I don't understand myself?

To my relief, now that Eric's gone, Brian directs all his attention to Rose. I still don't know the names of the other boys, and except for the occasional comment and a few speculative glances, they all but ignore me now that Kye's here. He holds the menu in front of my face, indicating that it's my turn to order. "If you don't hurry and pick something, I'm ordering for you."

Rose's gaze turns into a glare, though I'm not sure if it's intended for me or Kye. I hope I haven't unknowingly stepped into her territory. That would be bad. So bad. With a sigh, I order a cup of chicken noodle soup, wondering how on earth I'll unmake my newest mess.

TEN

Confessions and Special Gifts

The restaurant fills with people, and the low din of voices turns into wild chatter until Rose talks the waitress into turning on some music. Then the volume becomes obnoxious, leaving my head throbbing. After we've paid our bills, Kye takes my hand and leads me out. The party is just getting started.

The lobby isn't any quieter. Flames crackle merrily in the enormous rock fireplace dominating the middle of the room, surrounded by a crowd of people lounging on the floor and in log chairs. Crystal is one of those people, and judging from her frosty glare, she's still angry about something. My boots squeak on the hardwood as I follow Kye outside, away from everyone. A gust of frigid winter air hits me in the face and sends a shiver all the way down to my toes.

"Sorry, I know it's cold," Kye says. "I thought we'd get away from the noise for a minute. We need to talk."

I breathe in the crisp, pine-scented air. "Rose loves the crowd."

"Yeah. Leave it to Rose." He blows into his hands for warmth. "I bet the Inn's owners are happy. It's usually closed for another month."

"I heard." I wrap my arms around myself, shivering.

Kye's teeth chatter. "Yeah, that girl has some influence over the people running this place."

"She must," I say, thinking about the waitress in the restaurant, the cooks, check-in clerks, and housekeeping. Then I remember seeing the gift shop doors open. "I wonder how she did it."

"Rose has a ... special talent when it comes to talking to people. Haven't you noticed?"

I bite back a smile. "How could I not? She and Jen practically railroaded me into coming, and I don't even know how. I'm usually not so easily swayed."

"Now, that I can believe." Kye pulls me closer, running his palms up my sleeves, inching me toward him until his arms are wound around me and we're shivering together, the white puffs of our breath mingling in a common cloud. "Is this ... are you okay with me holding you like this?"

My only response is a nod, because I am okay. I'm more than okay. I'm home. But I still need my questions answered. "Before we turn into Popsicles, are you going to explain to me about the bus thing?"

"Yes, right. I'm sorry about that. It was unexpected or I would've warned you."

"What *did* happen, exactly?"

He takes a long, deep breath and puffs it out. *He doesn't know I know.* "What would you say if I told you I have a pet moose?"

I hear my own laugh tinkle out, muffled in the blanket of snow surrounding us. "I'd ask his name and wonder what he was doing so far from home."

Kye swallows again, his smile uncertain. *He's nervous.* "His name's Finn, and he was looking for me."

Recognizing the hesitation in his voice, I send him an encouraging look. If he was raised hearing the same warnings as me all his life, this might be the hardest confession he'll ever make. *Go on. Tell me more. Tell me all.* "How did you come to have a pet moose?"

"Funny thing is, he found me. I'd been living here for about two months and I'd never been so lost in my life. Literally. Val's house is out in the sticks, and I went for a walk and couldn't find my way back. Then I looked up and there he was, all alone and scared. He let me climb on his back, even though he was just a tiny little thing, and brought me home. Val let me keep him."

"Just like that? How did you know he wouldn't, you know, gouge you with his rack or something?"

Kye grins. "He didn't have a rack then. He was just a baby. But I knew he wouldn't hurt me, because he ... told me."

I turn my head to better see his face. "What do you mean, he told you? Like, with his eyes? Because you could see he was kind?"

"No, he—I—" Kye clears his throat, staring at the trees, his chin resting on my shoulder. "We communicate. Always have. Different from talking, but kind of the same. I understand a lot of things other people don't. The rustling of the leaves in the trees, the squeaks and sounds of animals, the language of basic elementals ..."

Gifted. The word rolls around in my head until I feel it forming in my mouth, and still I have to test it before I can actually say it. The taste is strange, sweet. Forbidden. "Gifted."

"Yes. Like you." He draws away, staring into my eyes until I can see his questions mirrored there. Knowing what's coming fills me with that frightening anxiety Gram instilled in me. The idea that if I tell, bad, bad things will happen to me and everyone I love. I am momentarily speechless. "Not your average teenagers, I guess."

He smells like pine and musk and something else—something sweet, like a mixture of tree sap and flowers—as I take his face in my hands. "Average equals boring."

My feet leave the ground when he lifts me up and twirls me around, eyes closed. "You're right. Nothing boring about us." We're both grinning when he puts me down.

"How did you know? About me?" I ask.

"I don't know how. I just—I saw you and something you did triggered a picture, maybe a memory—I don't know. I just knew. That's all."

Could he have Sight too? No. Having one Gift is rare. Having two? I'm an anomaly. An original. Even Gram didn't know what to make of my Sight.

His thumb brushes the side of my neck and my stomach leaps with desire, a longing that burns in the back of my throat. That small amount of contact makes me ache for something I don't understand. Not just kissing or even sex, nothing as simple as that—but a need that is foreign and unidentifiable.

"Tell me about you. About your Gift," he murmurs in my ear. His heart ka-thunks under my hand on his chest.

"I'm a Healer." He raises one eyebrow as if waiting for me to go on. "Herbs, crystals, life energy—"

"Have you ever ...?"

A jolt of pain seizes my heart, stealing my breath until I choke on the cold, shaking my head. "No. I've never Healed anyone. Well, except my dog, Erda."

"But you've tried."

I nod.

The moon sparkles in his golden hair as he searches my face and tucks errant auburn tresses behind my ears. "It's okay. We don't have to talk about it right now."

"Thanks. I'm not sure I could if I tried."

Leaning in, he strokes my jaw, his face so close I can feel his breath on my chin. "You can trust me, Abby. Your secrets are safe here."

Something flutters in my chest, filling me with warmth. *Kiss me! Now. Just kiss me!* But if he does, I'll be too distracted to tell him the rest, and I find I want him to know, so I whisper, "I have Sight too."

Kye's eyes pop open and he leans back a little. "Sight?"

I nod, dreading the explanation. Dreading seeing the look on his face when he realizes what an awful thing this is. Anything but a Gift. "I can see auras, energy, and on rare occasions, visions."

He tilts his head, frowning as he processes this information. "What kind of visions?"

"The kind that give me nightmares." I break away from him to stand alone, shivering with the absence of his touch. "I can't believe we're having this conversation. If Gram knew, if she were alive, we'd be living in the South Pole tomorrow."

Kye doesn't move, seemingly dumbstruck by my admission. My heart sinks, but now that I've opened the secret vault, I can't stop. More explanations spew out.

"Sometimes I see things happening to people far away. Usually it's the same boy, but not always ..." I trail off as I look at him, a sudden realization making my thudding heart drop into my toes and then start thumping again, harder. Kye looks a lot like the boy in my visions. A lot.

He crosses the space I've put between us and turns me to face him. "Wait. Not to be redundant, but I need to puzzle this together. You got that ring from your grandmother. You're a Healer who sees visions—sometimes of strangers, and sometimes of a certain person. Am I correct so far?"

The word "strangers" hits a note in my brain, but I can't place it. My teeth chatter again, as much from nerves as from the cold. "Yes."

"Have you ever seen the past?" His eyes are intent, and I sense that the answer to this question is important.

"I think once. But it might have been a dream." *It wasn't.*

"It's you." Kye doesn't ask for any more explanation, but closes his eyes and turns his face to the sky. When he looks at me again, his eyes are luminous in the moonlight. "I knew there was something, that you had a Gift, but—" He breaks off to stare at me. "I can't believe I didn't recognize you before now—or maybe I did, but I ignored it all this time. It's you."

I tuck my face into his neck as a shiver rattles my teeth, and he enfolds me in his arms. I don't know what he means—not sure he does either—but this part, where we fit together in an embrace as if we were cut from the same mold, it feels right. Peaceful.

When the cold becomes too much, Kye takes my hand and leads me around the building. The light of the full moon gilds everything with a pale silver lining and a billion stars blink above, reflecting off the snow and creating radiance in places where there are no electric

70

lights. A movement at the tree line catches my eye and I stop.

"Where are we going?"

"There's something I want to show you."

"It's like zero degrees out here and neither of us is wearing a coat. Let's go back inside."

He puts a finger to his mouth and pulls me through the snow. "In a few minutes. Don't worry, I won't let you freeze. Hurry, they're waiting."

"Who?"

The night brightens farther from the building. Tiny glowing lights flicker in and out of the snow-covered branches, and a gust of warm, sweet-smelling air invites us forward. A gentle, peaceful hum tickles my ears as it's carried on the breeze like angel music. My sensitive nose detects traces of honeysuckle and lilac, fresh grass and salt water—scents I associate more with spring than winter. Especially winter in a sulfur-soaked park riddled with volcanic activity.

At the edge of the tree line, Kye encircles my waist protectively and positions me in front of him. "What are we waiting for?" I whisper.

"The sprites are inspecting your energy field. They want to know if they can trust you."

"Sprites?"

Kye lets go and steps away. "Our fields are mixed. I'm being asked to move aside."

"Sprites?" I ask again.

His mouth drops open in surprise, but then he closes it and smiles. "You've never seen an elemental."

I move forward involuntarily, longing for more of the warmth I can feel blowing from somewhere through the trees, but Kye holds me back. "Stay still."

"What's an elemental?"

He runs a hand down my hair. "Elementals are manifestations of the basic elements that support our Gifts. They give us life and protect the earth."

I wonder why Gram never mentioned sprites—or elementals. And then I wonder who explained it to Kye. A few minutes later, he nudges me forward, grinning. "You're in. We're invited to the party."

ELEVEN

Faery Parties and Magic

As Kye leads me through the thicket of trees, I find the piney scent comforting, familiar. Warm air swirls around, engulfing us in spring-like temperatures even as snow crunches under our feet and hangs in thick strands from the foliage. Farther in, the light gets brighter and the aroma of roasting herbs urges me forward.

When the trail narrows and the light dims, Kye squeezes my hand and we duck below a heavy curtain of branches. A high-pitched squeaking noise makes me scan the area, but I see nothing other than snow and the occasional patch of green. I feel like the forest is shrinking in on me and fight off a wave of claustrophobia as we're forced to duck even lower. "Almost there," Kye says. After a few more feet, we emerge in a clearing.

Thousands of tiny lights hover in the air and a cheery fire dances inches off the ground within a circle of stones. A creature is perched at the edge of a pine log. Her greenish skin is shot through with veins of darker green and a wild array of fiery red vines cascade to the jagged hem of her filmy deep-green skirt. Her bare feet tap a rhythm on one of the stones as she turns a spit of squash, wild onions, and asparagus. A basket of herbs nestles on the ground near the fire.

The creature turns, and I shiver in surprise when the flames glint off a pair of iridescent wings.

"A faery," Kye says under his breath. He bows. "We offer thanks to Nematona and the faeries for gifts to the trees and the animals, the plants, the water, and all living things. And thank you for granting my request."

"You answered your summons earlier, and now the favor has been repaid." The faery's voice is high-pitched, musical. Warm air swirls around me like a mini tornado. "Your female possesses an elemental Gift but has never called upon us for aid. Why?"

"Her understanding has been limited," Kye says.

"You speak truth." The faery turns to me and smiles, baring jagged teeth. "You may call me Alena. I sense many questions within you." She probes me with emerald green eyes, reminding me of how I feel when Kye looks at me. "The answers you seek are buried within your heart. Only you have the power to find them."

Squeaking noises ripple through the clearing again. "Watch this." Kye's arm curls around me protectively.

My pulse vibrates in a wild rhythm as the trees sway unnaturally and large things move out of the shadows. One by one, creatures crowd the clearing. The first stands easily seven feet tall, with rough tree-bark skin and grassy hair. Its long fingers are twiggy and covered with knobs. Another has brown, grainy skin—more like dirt than bark—and tiny stubbles of wheat-colored hair running from the top of its head to halfway down its back. Closer to the ground, a tree-stump-like figure, with green moss draped over gray scaly skin clomps toward us. More creatures approach and I struggle to take them all in. Some have wings, others don't. And the balls of light—which turn out to be sprites—continue to hang in the air like tiny, glowing hummingbirds.

Alena hovers close to Kye. "You received Nematona's message?"

Kye nods. "Finn indicated it was urgent."

"Indeed." Her faery wings flutter. "A great rumbling can be heard from the belly of Mother Earth. The Dark Elen seek ancient Keys to unlock the lost city and the evil trapped within."

Kye leans closer to Alena. "What happens if the Elen find the Keys?"

"All you see," Alena's arms spread wide, "the forest, the trees, the grass, the rocks, the streams, the lakes, the air ... all will be destroyed by forces of darkness."

"That can't be good," I say, for lack of a better response.

"No, not at all." Kye shakes his head. Alena's wings flutter faster and faster as she begins to spin, whirling to the other side of the clearing. A creature catches her and whisks her through the trees in a graceful dance, leaving a trail of greenish mist in their wake.

"I have a question," I say, taking a step away from Kye and holding my hands toward the fire, noticing for the first time that some of the flames are blue. "Two, actually."

He raises a brow and comes to stand next to me. "Just two? That's hard to believe, under the circumstances."

"Well, it's kind of difficult to voice them all at once, so I'm going to start with two. Nematona and the Elen. What and who? Explain."

He sighs and runs a hand through his hair so it falls around his eyes. "Nematona is queen of the Tree Spirits. I almost never hear from her, but when I do, she tends to be majorly demanding. Like now. Not very trusting of humans, either. Can't say I blame her for that, though."

"And the Elen?"

The word causes him to purse his lips, like he's chewing on an explanation he would rather not spit out. "Elen is what people once called the Gifted."

"Oh," I say, surprised. "So, she was referring to us?"

He shakes his head, his expression horrified. "No. Absolutely not. Not anymore. A long, long time ago, there was a war, and let's just say the bad guys won. They kept the name, we—meaning the good guys, or the handful of us who survived, anyway—adopted a new one."

"What made them so bad? Well, besides the war thing."

A glowing ball of light zooms closer to us, hovering above Kye's shoulder, and its lavender-pink light blinks a few times. The rest of the forest inhabitants continue to move slowly, as if each step and sway of limb is part of an ancient dance.

Kye answers, "They found a way to steal powers from others. Not just humans—animals too. And steal them they did. Often. Two things happened. First, the person from whom they took the power usually died, turning over the span of years left in their life to the thief. So, the more powers the members of the Dark Elen stole, the longer they could live. But then the powers got hard to control, making the already scary people even more dangerous. Besides being nearly immortal, they were—are—very, very difficult to defeat. Almost impossible, actually."

Alena and her partner fly past us with an unnerving speed that contrasts the slow movements of the other creatures. They stop in front of us and Kye bows again before the pair spins off, this time far enough that the mist evaporates. All at once, the rest of the creatures begin a sluggish migration toward the edges of the clearing.

Not wanting them to leave, I reach for a nearby creature. "Wait!" His deep green skin feels cool and slick, like grass on a summer evening. His eyes are the color of blueberries and unusually large. "Where are you going? Don't leave yet."

Kye smiles and takes my wrist, urging me to let go. "Don't worry, they're not leaving."

"What are they doing?

He pulls me to Alena's cooking pit. "It takes a lot of energy for a faery to stay visible to human eyes. They need to save it for the party." The sprite hovering next to Kye's shoulder bumps into him repeatedly. He turns, exasperated. "Fine, I'll take it off the fire."

Kye lifts the spit and uses a forked stick to push the roasted vegetables into Alena's basket, then picks up a piece of asparagus and holds it out to me. "Taste."

I open my mouth and take a bite when Kye holds the tender stalk against my tongue. The seedy tip explodes in my mouth and the taste of all things green—things grown wild without pesticides or chemicals—slides down my throat, warms my stomach, and clears my mind of questions. "Wow. That's really good."

Kye throws his head back, laughing. "Yeah, the faeries are excellent cooks. I'm usually not a big fan of veggies, but ..." He waves the forked stick in a circle. "There's nothing like these."

I hold my hand out for more, so Kye breaks a tiny zucchini in half and offers me a piece. Each savory bite makes my tongue tingle. Bite after bite, I chew slowly to make it last as long as possible. I become aware of a sound so sweet and soft I have to ask Kye if he hears it too.

"It's the song of the faeries," he says. "They love to sing. I'm surprised you've never heard them before."

He pulls me into his arms and we sway, stepping side to side and back and forth. I know there was something I wanted to say, questions I should ask, but I can't force my thoughts to gel together. His hand slides to my waist, my feet move with his, and before I realize what's happening, I'm dancing with Kye to the rhythm of faery song. The volume swells. "If they sing this loud every night, I'm surprised a lot of people haven't heard them," I say.

"I bet lots of people have heard faery music in their lifetime. They just don't know what it is."

"Good point. If I hadn't seen them with my own eyes, I wouldn't, either." I lean my head against his chest, about to close my eyes, when he tips my chin up. "Look at that." All around us, tiny glimmering lights flicker like fireworks that don't die. I lean my head on Kye's chest again, inhaling the scent of woodsy cologne and faery forest that clings to his clothes, but this time I keep my eyes open.

Time slips away as Kye holds me. "Whatever happens in my life, I'll never, ever forget this night."

He shakes his head. "Neither will I. Not in this life or the next." He slides his finger under my chin and brings his lips to mine, soft, experimental at first, but more demanding as I lean into him. Our racing hearts stutter, merging like we've been waiting to find each other our whole lives. Kye smiles against my lips, and I know he feels it too. He takes a shaky breath and leans in again, this time harder, more demanding as we melt together. I match his fervor until my ring glows with power, bright as the summer sun. "Wow," Kye says, rubbing his chest with his hand and staring at my ring. "I wonder what that means."

I shake my head, breathless. "No idea."

The faery lights fade and the black sky lightens to navy. Kye looks at his watch and cringes. "We should get going. It's after four in the morning."

"Four? Are you sure?" Heat floods my face, but I turn to look one last time at what I'll always think of as the faery clearing. "We're in so much trouble." And I'm not just talking about staying out all night.

Kye grins. "Are you embarrassed that you spent the night here with me?"

I look away. "You know what everyone will think."

"So what? Who cares what everyone thinks? And we won't be in trouble, because—" He stops walking and turns to look behind us.

Something clicks in my brain and realization dawns. "He knows, doesn't he? About you, I mean. Akers knows about your Gift."

Kye nods, waving farewell to the faeries and sprites. "Thank you for a memorable party."

"Yes, thank you," I repeat. "I'll never forget it."

A sprite flutters to us, its greenish glow pulses, and I hear Alena's words again. "Don't forget Nematona's warning. The Elen must not find the Keys."

The early morning cold seeps through my clothes, touching my skin and stealing my breath. Kye wraps his arm around me and we walk huddled together back toward the Inn. With every step, the fuzziness in my brain fades, leaving a puddle of confusion. I wonder if Kye did this on purpose. He must have at least known it would happen, but I'm not as angry as I should be. I feel like I'm coming down off a sugar high, and I yawn as exhaustion settles into my muscles.

"I think I had more questions," I tell him.

"I know." He squeezes my waist as I lean my head heavily on his shoulder. "When your brain clears, you can ask them all. I promise."

TWELVE

Busted

W e're standing at the elevator ready to push the button when it dings and Mr. Akers steps out, fury dancing in his eyes. "Do you know what time it is?"

My feet feel like they're glued to the floor.

Mr. Akers takes both our wrists and pulls us in. "Did you have a good time playing with the faeries?" His words are sharp enough to cut. This isn't the man who laughed with Kye in his office. He rounds on me. "What am I supposed to tell your mother when she hears the two of you snuck off and stayed out all night?"

My eyes go wide with realization. It's a small town. Gossip travels fast.

Kye calmly punches the second floor button. "Lan, don't get mad at her. You know how easy it is to lose track of time when you're under a faery enchantment."

"So do you, Kye." Akers jabs his finger in Kye's chest. "Which is why I'm disappointed you let it to happen to Abby."

Kye straightens his back. "She needed to see. You know she needed to see what can happen. She was the only student on the bus whose vision you couldn't alter when Finn showed up. The only one who heard and saw everything. Like it or not, this thing with the Elen involves her somehow."

Akers's face pales, but the spark in his eyes doesn't die. "Nevertheless, you should know better than to let her eat faery food. Why would you put Abby in that kind of danger?"

"What danger? You once told me there's no safer place than a faery party." Kye throws his arms up. "How is giving her knowledge of things that could help her putting her in danger? She has Sight already—the faery food only helped clarify her vision. Now she'll be able to see all the creatures, including the Elen." My confusion compounds when he meets my eyes and his are soft with regret. "Besides, she needed a break. Why do you think she collapsed at school? The faeries cleared her mind—both of our minds—for a while."

"Well, hope you got good and focused at the party." Akers backs Kye against the wall with a hand on his chest—not hard, like a shove, but it concerns me just the same. "Did you have a good time? Get your hormones settled well enough to think with your head?"

Kye looks down at the hand on his chest, confused. "What's wrong with you? You had to know this was coming."

Mr. Akers lets his hand drop with a heavy sigh. "Boone was here."

"What?" The color drains out of Kye's face and his eyes grow wide. "Are you sure? You saw him?"

Akers laughs, but it's dry and mirthless. "Yes." He points at me. "And so did she."

Any hope I had of sleeping is now gone. Mr. Akers takes Kye and me to his suite where I explain to them about the guy with the scary aura.

Kye tries for a smile but fails. "Why didn't you say something before?"

I consider telling the truth—that memory, logic, and rational thought simply flies out of my brain the minute Kye walks into view—but that sounds sort of pathetic, even to me.

"Why didn't you call security?" Akers asks, exasperated. "What if he did something to one of your friends? What if he kidnapped one of them? Or attacked them?"

I can't look at either of them, so I stare at the floor, feeling guilty. Why does he have to put it that way? "How was I supposed to know the guy was dangerous? He could work here or be a chaperone from the other bus. I'd never heard of the Elen before tonight. Why would I call security?"

Mr. Akers shakes his head in disgust. "Well, it's too late to worry now. We should've warned you sooner."

"You should have said a lot of things sooner." I sigh and fall back onto the bed.

"I wish that had occurred to me before I caught him trying to break into your room." Upon seeing the panic on my face, he presses his palms together and pulls out his soothing voice. "Don't worry, he didn't succeed, and I've banished him from the building. He won't be back tonight."

While his words are something of a relief, I'm still shaken by the very idea. "So, now what? Do we pack up and go home? I'd hate to cancel the party. Rose would be devastated."

"No, let's not raise an alarm yet." Kye runs his fingers through his hair, thinking. "We should stay near the forest. There's something big happening and we need to know what we're up against."

Mr. Akers rubs his chin. "You're right. At this point, it's best if we stay as close as possible to the earth's power sources—and this place oozes with them." His eyes bore into me. "Maybe if we stick around, Abby will be able to See something that can help us."

A trickle of fear runs through me at his words. *How much does he know about me?* Kye flops next to me on the bed, his arm around my waist pulling me close so he can whisper in my ear. "It's okay, Abby. Landon—Mr. Akers—knew before I did."

I can't move for the shock I'm feeling, but as I lay next to Kye, it occurs to me that a lot of people in Jackson have special Gifts. Including my drama teacher.

Later, I sneak in my room, exhausted, and feel my way to the empty bed, grateful to know the strange man didn't actually get inside. In the dark, I strip off my boots and jeans and slide between the crisp, cool sheets. A snore reverberates against the wall. "Shut up!" someone mumbles, and after a muffled thud, the snoring stops. I grin into my pillow, wondering who hit whom.

Considering I've been up all night, I should be able to get right to sleep, but I can't shut down my brain. After lying awake for half an hour, frustration takes over and I rub the crystal hanging from a chain around my neck, quietly humming the sleep tones. Muscle by muscle, inch by inch, my body goes into hibernation mode, letting go of questions, tension, and thoughts. I feel my energy wane and am finally able to drift off, wondering if Kye is struggling to fall asleep too.

My friends are gone by the time I wake up, and I feel guilty for ditching them last night. After washing my face and applying some makeup to cover my dark under-eye circles, I braid my hair, pull on jeans and a heavy sweater, and head downstairs to the café, where I find Jen pouring syrup on a stack of pancakes at the same table from last night.

"Where's Rose?"

Jen gestures with her fork to the other side of the room where Rose is sitting on some guy's lap, feeding him bites of waffle.

"What is she doing?" I reach across the table and snatch a bite of the omelet sitting in front of the empty chair. "Oh, that's good."

"Rose wants to take you to see the Fountain Paint Pots, so she's trying to procure us a form of four-wheel-drive transportation."

"What does she want him to do, ride us there piggyback?" I commandeer Rose's water and catch the eye of the waitress from last night, pointing at the menu. She nods.

Jen shoves another bite in her mouth, talking around her food. "He came in a Jeep."

Realization dawns and I cover my mouth with both hands to keep from busting out laughing. When I'm confident I can hold it in, I ask, "Is she planning to invite him and his friends?"

"I kind of doubt it." Jen swirls her fork in the air. "There are three of us, and a Jeep only seats four people."

The waitress sets another glass of water on the table. "Know what you want this time?"

I haven't even looked at the menu, but breakfast is easy. "Can I please have some pancakes and sausage? Oh, and orange juice."

She writes my order on her pad. "Anything else?"

"Nope, that'll—"

Jen interrupts, "Can we get some ketchup?"

The waitress glances at Jen's pancakes with a grimace. "Sure."

I scrunch up my face. "Ketchup?"

"Rose will want some for her hash browns in about three minutes."

Across the room, Rose is pouting. She bats her eyes and whispers in the guy's ear. A minute later, she drops a set of keys on our table, takes her seat next to Jen, picks up a fork, and proceeds to shovel food into her mouth at warp speed.

"I hope you already ordered," she says without looking at me, "because we need to get out of here before Jared figures out what just happened."

As if on cue, the waitress bustles out of the kitchen with my plate and Rose's ketchup. I down two pancakes in five minutes, and the three of us throw some bills on the table and run.

Rose curses under her breath. "Why didn't we bring our coats with us?"

"Well," I answer, stepping into the empty elevator. "I don't know about you two, but I didn't know I'd be in a hurry to go anywhere."

Rose snorts. "Jeez. You might have had an idea if you came back last night. Where were you, anyway?"

"Um." The elevator dings. I dig the room key out of my pocket and hurry down the hall. "It's sort of a long story."

"Yes, well, we figured that." Jen sticks her card in the lock before I get there, cursing about it being warped, then takes mine and throws open the door. I snatch my coat off the rack, remembering how Kye had tried to keep me warm last night. I haven't seen him since a few hours ago when he kissed my forehead and told me to get some sleep, but I'm pretty sure he'll be looking for me when he wakes up.

Jen zips her coat and pulls on gloves and a hat. "Abby, hurry. Rose is persuasive, but sooner or later Jared's going to realize he just handed over the keys to his brand new Jeep and come after us."

I bite my lip.

Rose stops mid-zip. "Oh no. Don't tell me you're worried about lover-boy already."

My eyes fall on a pad of hotel stationery, which I use to jot down a note to Kye.

Went to Fountain Paint Pots with Rose and Jen.
Be back in a few hours.
Hope you got some sleep.

Abby

Then I fold the note in half and write his name on the front.

Rose taps her foot. "Ahem."

"I'm done." Flustered, I skip down the hall and slide my note under Kye's door. We hustle to the elevator and then make a beeline outside.

Rose hits a button on the key ring, and a black Jeep—one of only four cars in the lot—roars to life. "Gotta love remote starters." She turns to me. "You can start talking any time now, Abby. We're, like, waiting."

I climb in the back and fasten my seatbelt. *What can I tell them?* "Okay, let's start with a question. How in the hills did you talk a stranger into loaning us his new car?"

Jen's been holding in her laugh since the restaurant, and now it explodes out of her. She claps both hands to her mouth, shaking with laugher until tears stream from her eyes. "You ... should ... have ... seen yourself."

Rose only laughs a little as she shifts into reverse, even though Jen's laugh is of the contagious variety. She sounds sober when she says, "It's just something I do. I've always been able to talk people into things. My mom says it's a special talent." She smiles, but I detect a hint of sadness. I wonder about it but don't ask. I know all too well how that feels. We pull out of the parking lot and proceed along the icy road, following the arrows that indicate the direction to the Paint Pots.

When Jen calms again, she turns in her seat. "Enough stalling. Spill."

"I met Kye for the first time yesterday. I mean, I've seen him before, but we never had an actual conversation until we were waiting for the bus."

"Oh, no," Rose says, her voice full of disgust. "Let me guess. You sat in the back."

I shrug in response.

"Ew. Abby, you made out with him, didn't you?"

"Not on the bus," I protest.

"But you kissed him," Rose insists, seeming disgusted. "A guy you just met."

"Rose, let her talk." Jen sounds intrigued. "First things first. On the kissing scale of ice to fire, where did it fall?"

My face burns, but I know I have to give Jen something. My fingertips trace my tingling lips as I remember. "Fire. Definitely fire."

Rose catches my eye in the rearview mirror. She doesn't look mad, but neither does she seem very happy. "Do you even know his last name?"

I return her glare, sensing I need to tread softly. "Yes, it's Murphy. I know him better than you think."

"And did you learn this before or after you stayed out all night with him?"

I blow out a breath. *What's her problem?* "Why do you want to know?"

"Rose," Jen says.

"What, Jen? What?" The Jeep accelerates. "Give me a break, okay? I'm trying to decide if I judged her wrong or if there's something bigger going on."

Jen folds her arms and sits back in her seat. "Who gave you the right to judge anyone?"

Rose bites her lip.

Oh no. What if Rose and Kye have a thing? Or had a thing? Or she *wants* to have a thing? I swallow. "Rose, please, please tell me you were never ... hooked up with Kye."

"No. Oh, ew." Her expression reflects pure horror. "He's my cousin."

"Really?" Surprise and then relief surge through me. "So you have a legitimate emotional attachment to him. Will it make you feel better if I promise not to hurt him?"

She chuckles, but there's no smile involved. "Abby, it isn't him I'm worried about."

THIRTEEN

Boone and Finn

Rose pulls into what looks like a driveway and parks the Jeep. The snow's a foot deep in some places, while in others, bare ground is exposed. They lead me to a wooden walkway, all of us stepping cautiously to avoid ice. Falling into boiling acid would not be fun right now—or ever. Nearby, a fountain of water sprays ten feet into the air, spewing and bubbling for several minutes before it abates.

Breath catches in my throat. "Is that a geyser?"

"A real live geyser." Jen links elbows with me, her body radiating comforting heat.

Rose saunters a few feet ahead and points to one side of the walk. "Paint pot."

A gooey, gray substance bubbles and spits on the ground. We wander the length of the walkway and I reluctantly feed the girls a modified version of what happened on the bus, careful to leave out anything referring to Kye's Gift. Also how I feel like I've known him forever. Some things are too strange, too private, to put into words.

"That's sweet." Jen sighs, a dreamy look on her face. "But I just know you're leaving pieces out. Like, where were you all night?"

I stop to stare at a sputtering geyser. "With Kye."

"Obviously," Rose says. "But what were you doing while the rest of us were sleeping?" Her insinuation is clear.

"Talking."

"Talking?" Jen kicks a piece of ice into a bubbling paint pot. It immediately melts into the mud. "All night? Where?"

"We looked all over for you," Rose says. "Tell me you weren't in his room."

I scoop up a handful of snow and pack it into a ball, then throw it at a geyser. It disintegrates in mid-air. "We were freezing our tails off—outside." I catch myself glancing in the direction of the Inn. Kye is probably awake by now. Everything inside me pulls toward him. There's no explanation for this intense desire to be near him, no reason to explain why his absence feels like a hollow, aching loss.

"Look at her." Jen pushes me along the path. "She's lovesick." We've come full-circle back to the parking lot and I notice a trail of melted ice leading from the place where we started.

Scowling at Jen, I storm to the car. The ache has grown into a shooting, physical pain in my abdomen, and by the time I get to the Jeep, I'm doubled over, breathing heavily. Something isn't right. After checking my energy field and finding my chakras in fair alignment, I wander to an aspen tree and pull a twig from a low branch. "What are you doing?" Rose calls.

"Just checking out this tree," I say. "It's amazing how plants can grow here, only yards away from all that icky mud and acid and stuff." I keep my back to them and rub the twig on my sleeve, then break off a piece and suck on it. The anxiety slowly ebbs away—or most of it.

I chew the aspen bark for a while, then spit it out, staring into the forest until I'm grabbed from behind, arms pinned to my sides with powerful muscles.

"Where's your boyfriend?" The stranger's voice is low, rough.

Jen screams. Rose's voice shakes as she asks, "What do you want?"

"I don't have a boyfriend," I squeak as panic races through me.

"Could've fooled me," says the man. In our struggle, I catch a glimpse of his face and recognize him from the hallway yesterday.

The guy Mr. Akers called Boone. "You two looked awfully cozy last night."

His arms squeeze my chest, leaving me gasping, choking. "I don't know what you're talking about."

"Let go of her." Rose offers him the keys. "You can take the Jeep if you want. Just let her go."

Boone ignores both Jen's screaming and Rose's bargaining. "It was a mistake for you to come here without him."

"Why?" My voice is shaky. "What do you want?"

"Doesn't matter. You don't have to know or do anything to be bait."

Rose drapes a calm demeanor around her like an invisible veil. "You don't want to take Abby." Her voice flows across the tension like a soothing balm and Boone's arms relax around me. "She's not who you think she is. You have the wrong girl." *He does have the wrong girl. Rose is right. She's always right.*

Boone pulls back, and though he still has a tight grip on me, I feel his eyes raking me up and down. "Yeah, I'm pretty sure she's the one I want." His voice sounds sure, but his confidence cracks enough to allow doubt to flow in.

"You're wrong. Just like you've always been wrong." Rose steps closer. "Wouldn't you like to get something right for a change? Just once?"

Yes, I'm tired of always messing things up. I want to do exactly what she says.

Boone shakes his head. He seems to be waging an internal battle. "Not me. I never screw up. I always do it right. It's other people who mess up."

Rose dangles the keys on the end of her finger. "You want to get in that Jeep and drive. Run away and no one will catch you. All you have to do is let go of my friend and take these keys."

I could take the keys and drive away. Far away. Start over.

Boone tightens his grip again, and this time, I don't have a chance to take a breath. Black spots swim in front of my eyes as I struggle for air, and what I do manage to pull in tastes like smoke.

Rose moves closer. If my arms were free I could reach out and touch her. "Stay back!" Boone shouts. "I know your trick, little girl, and it won't work on me."

Everything goes gray around the edges. Rose no longer appears the confident young woman offering keys to a stranger, but rather one immobile with fear. Then an orange flame erupts between the girls, distracting them, while Boone drags me backward through the snow. He stumbles on something, his boot uncovering a fist-sized rock that my ankle then brushes against. The contact sends a tiny burst of energy up my leg. Boone moves faster and faster until we're yards away from my friends.

At the edge of the parking lot, he picks me up and I kick him, fighting with all my strength. A few times my feet connect with body parts, and each time I hear a muffled grunt, I fight harder. I've been taught it's never a mistake for a girl who's being taken somewhere against her will to fight, but when Boone tosses me on the ground and subdues me with his body—I begin to wish I hadn't.

His arm is around my chest and his other hand is over my mouth, grinding my cheek against my teeth until I taste blood. His legs clamp around mine so I can't move. I can't even scream.

Then the energy around us changes and I hear feet crashing through snow and underbrush. Something solid whooshes over us, propelling Boone away from me in a blur of movement. I sit up, preparing to jump and run, but hot air blows on my neck and something wet tickles my ear. Shrieking, I spring about three feet in the air and land on my rear with a thud.

From the corner of my eye, I catch a glimpse of Kye and Boone, wrestling on the ground in a tangle of shrubs and tree limbs, but when I look straight, I find myself staring into the bright brown eyes of the white moose.

His antlers spread at least five feet across, and his square head is lowered, prepared for battle. Never in my life have I been so close to a creature of this size. I should be frightened, but I'm not. I know he won't hurt me. Instinct tells me to run—run, you idiot!—but I can't make my feet move. Finn holds me trapped in his gaze, and I get the feeling he's trying to communicate something I don't understand.

When the wrestling comes nearer, he backs into the trees. I leap into action, searching for a weapon I can use to help Kye, and settle on a large, broken tree branch. My intentions are good, but I hesitate too long and before I have a good grip, Boone tackles me. I'm under him again and he's holding a knife to my throat.

"Let her go, Boone." Kye wheezes.

A wolfish smile spreads across Boone's face. "You see, honey, I didn't even have to take you anywhere before lover-boy came running to save you."

"I said let her go." Kye growls.

Boone's grip loosens, but he keeps his weapon in position. "You have something I want." He pulls me off the ground and drags me backward—again. "And now I have something you want. I thought we'd work out a trade."

Kye's eyes flash. "What? What could I have that you want badly enough to kidnap someone?"

"Where is it?" Boone hisses.

"Where is what?"

"The Key! Where's the Key?"

Kye looks truly baffled. "I really don't know what you're talking about. A key? What kind of key?" Something rustles behind us.

Rose's voice chimes in, "I have the keys! Right here. I already said you could have them. Just take the Jeep, already!" From the corner of my eye, I see a flash of color—Jen's lavender coat, the sleeves now scorched.

While Boone's distracted, Kye grabs the hand holding the knife, directing it at Boone's torso while I roll away. More wrestling ensues, but as soon as I make it to the others, Kye lets go and hurries to put himself between Boone and me.

Boone howls with rage and his eyes flash violet again. A blackish aura loaded with red darts settles around him. His fury is about to spill over and he's still clutching the knife.

"Kye," I whisper. "We need to go. Please." I grab a fistful of his coat and urge him to the parking lot.

Boone points at me. "Who is she?"

"Just a girl." For the first time, I sense real fear in Kye. "No one who matters."

His words pierce deep, making me stumble. A memory—or vision—jumps into sharp relief.

Fingers I can't see press Gram's ring—my ring—into a stone door, and as they do, it opens. The walls tremble and the floor cracks open.

I shake off the vision and clutch Kye's coat, trying to re-orient myself.

"Oh, she's someone," Boone says. "And you can bet I'll find out who by the end of the day. This is not over."

Something large crashes through the trees with such power and speed that I scream involuntarily, like a wimpy girl. Which I'm not. Usually. Finn charges at Boone, hurtling past us so close that his snowy pelt brushes the sleeve of my coat.

Boone plows into the forest, screaming like a girl himself. His screams make me feel better about my own.

Kye is shaking when he pulls me into his arms. "You okay?"

I nod, unable to speak.

"You're not okay. Of course you're not." He presses a kiss to my head. "I'm sorry."

"Why?"

"Because it was stupid of me to let you out of my sight long enough for him to get to you."

"Abby." Rose's voice is hoarse. "We need to talk."

"Ya think?" I lead the way to the Jeep. "What was that fire all about?"

Rose hits the remote start button again. "What was any of it about?"

"Haven't I told you never to talk to strangers?" Kye drapes his arm across Rose's shoulders. "You know how trouble always finds you."

She grins. How could she not? Cousin or not, Kye's smile is warm enough to melt the coldest heart. "And, yet," she says, "I'm still alive and thriving."

Kye's face sobers. "Well, today you're lucky. Really, Rose, you have to be more careful."

Jen sputters. It's the first sound she's made in fifteen minutes. "We're in the middle of a national park. We came in a group of three. What else should we have done?"

He cocks his head. "Duh. You should have brought me."

We all burst out laughing and book it across the parking lot to the Jeep as the snow starts coming down hard. Kye holds the seat forward while I climb in the back. When he's seated next to me, I glance out the window, noticing there are still no other cars.

"How did you get here, anyway?"

He bites his lip, leaning closer. "Didn't you meet Finn? He's my moose."

I nod. Of course. It would have to be a white moose.

FOURTEEN

Healing the Injured

By the time we park at the Inn, snow is falling in sheets of white, making me glad we returned when we did. As we run for the building, I'm hit by the weight of something else in the air. Worry. Panic. Fear.

A fire burns in the fireplace, but there are no other lights on in the building. The power must be out. Kids crowd in a half-circle near the bottom of the stairs, and the collective mood isn't good.

One of the teachers holds a cell phone to his ear, mumbling under his breath, "Please connect. Please connect." My stomach clenches at the sight of a student lying on the floor, immobile. His breathing is shallow, strained. Mr. Akers leans over him, murmuring.

I try to inch forward, but a chaperone holds me back. "You need to stay out of the way until we can get an ambulance here." As he says this, Mr. Akers moves and I get a better look at the injured person. "Eric!" I push past the restraining arm and drop to my knees beside Mr. Akers, a sick feeling welling inside me. "What happened to him?"

"He fell over the railing from the third floor." Mr. Akers looks anxious. "The phone lines aren't working and no one has been able to get cell service this morning. At this point, we don't even know how seriously he's hurt, but he definitely needs help." Mr. Akers holds my gaze, sending me a silent question.

He wants my help. My Healing help. I glance down at Eric and know I should, I could help him. Isn't this what I've always wanted? To be allowed to help my friends? To not keep my Gifts a secret anymore?

I nod my acquiescence, though I'm nervous. *What if I can't do it?* Akers instructs the chaperones to escort the rest of the kids to their rooms, "so they'll be out of the way when medical assistance arrives." But really, he's just getting rid of them. Once they're gone, I run my hands through Eric's energy field. My palms hover above his clothes while I ask his energy to tell me what's wrong.

Energy ripples as I pass over an injured rib on one side, then again over another. Pressure in a lung, bruises on a kidney. My hand trembles as I pass it over Eric's face, distracted by a memory of Gram lying on the floor dying. I pause to swallow a lump in my throat and am grateful when Kye squeezes my arm and whispers, "Don't give up, Abby. Eric needs you."

With a steadying breath, I check Eric's head again and sigh in relief when I discover his concussion is mild, something I might be able to handle. "I'm going to try to help you," I say. "In a few minutes, you'll feel much better." *I hope.*

Eric's eyelids flutter and he lets out a moan.

"Shh. Eric, it's me, Abby. Try not to move too much."

"Abby?" He tries to smile, but it turns into a grimace. "I knew you'd come for the party. You love me already."

I wish I could laugh, but I'm concentrating. "Don't count your money yet."

When I glance up, Kye is scowling at Eric. Shaking my head, I give him a list of kitchen herbs to look for and tell him where to find my Healing crystals, then turn to Mr. Akers. "Can we move him somewhere more ... private?"

Akers hesitates. "Are you sure that's wise? I wouldn't want to hurt him more—"

"His back and neck are fine. We need to be careful of the ribs on his right side—at least two of them are cracked and maybe putting pressure on his lung. He has a concussion, but it isn't too bad, considering the distance he fell." I brace my hands on the floor. "I prefer not to do this in the lobby."

"If his ribs are broken, moving him could be painful. What if I can promise no one will see?"

I open my mouth to object and decide it doesn't matter. "Fine. I'll treat him on the floor."

Akers rests a steady hand on my shoulder and lowers his voice. "Are you sure you can handle this?"

Doubt dances in my stomach, but I brush it away. "I think so." Then with more confidence, "I have to try."

I kneel, stroking Eric's cool cheek with my fingertips. His eyes flutter again. "Abby?"

"Yeah?" I unclasp the chain around my neck and set the crystal between his broken ribs.

"I think ..." he coughs, wincing in pain. "I might not be able to dance tonight."

"Probably not." His raspy breathing concerns me, so I focus on his ribs first. "Shh. Don't talk." I spin his chakra, calling the broken energy away from him. Kye approaches and sits next to me on the wooden floor, holding an ice bucket full of dried kitchen herbs and teas.

I hold out my hand, trying to stay focused on Eric. Kye drops the crystals in my palm.

"Thanks."

"Anytime." He slides a possessive hand across the small of my back and my heart soars.

Realizing I'm distracted, I swallow the metallic taste in my throat, focus again, and place another crystal over Eric's ribs, two more over his lungs, and one on his forehead. The thyme and comfrey Kye has brought me are dried, which means they have to be steeped into teas or packed as a poultice, but there is a fresh sprig of wormwood leaves.

I crush a leaf between my fingertips, roll it into a ball, and place it under Eric's tongue to help with pain. "Can you get me some hot water, and either cheesecloth or gauze?" Kye jogs back to the kitchen.

Eric opens his eyes and moves his limbs like he wants to get up. "What are you doing?"

"Hold still. You can't move yet." I replace the crystals where I want them. "Close your eyes."

"Why?"

"Because I said so," I snap. Then more gently, "I'm trying to help you. Please, just stay still and close your eyes."

I move my hands over him again, this time attempting to spin two chakras—one with each hand, both clockwise to speed the energy—and sing the Healing tones. The crystals lift above his chest and start to turn faster and faster, until Eric's energy forms a ball of bright, greenish light. I raise my hands to the sky and call the energy into myself. The crystals continue to hover over Eric, but the light moves into me, hovers above the top of my head, and sends an uncanny chill down my back. I sing louder and my heart pounds in anticipation of the pain I'm about to feel.

The energy trickles into me like a thin column of ice and brings with it Eric's agony. My head throbs, and breathing gets difficult as the pain travels to my lungs and ribs. I keep singing and continue moving my hands in the clockwise motion that keeps the energy flowing, and all the while I'm shaking with unexpected cold. Something doesn't feel right.

Focus. Focus. Focus. I try so hard to focus, but the room swirls with milky fog that feels like frost. When the throb in my head becomes unbearable and my muscles can't handle any more, my arms drop. I barely catch myself from tipping sideways onto the floor. Someone speaks, but I can't hear what is said over the wind in my ears. I'm still trying to sing, but my voice cracks and then stops working, my throat frozen. I rasp in a mouthful of frigid air, but it doesn't move into my lungs. Again and again I try, until I can no longer stay upright.

Warm, strong arms cradle me and I'm floating off the floor in a cloud of pain. My head lolls to the side and rests on something

97

solid. I hear a steady rhythm—a heartbeat. Breathing takes so much effort. I force my eyes open but can only see Kye's outline. The lights are too bright. "Did it work?" I rasp. "Did I do it?"

"I don't know." He squeezes me gently. "Are you okay?"

I close my eyes and try to relax against him. "My head hurts. And I'm so tired. I just need to sleep for a while."

"Okay." His voice is strained. "Okay."

I float in and out of consciousness, aware only that I'm buried in blankets and my whole body aches. Every so often a voice breaks through the nothingness, but comprehending words requires too much energy.

My dreams are filled with bits and pieces of things and non-things. Scary, gray-coated men trashing my bedroom at home. Faeries fluttering in the forest, cooking wild vegetables on fire that hovers above the ground. A white moose that speaks English and charges bad guys. Little round men with yellow eyes rolling down Las Vegas Boulevard ... and Kye. Dancing with Kye at a faery party. Kissing Kye. Kye's smile. Only, in my dreams, Kye has a different name and I can't remember it, even though I think I should.

Light flickers on the other side of my closed eyelids and I hear a voice. I roll over and pain shoots through my side. Someone screams, loud. Doesn't she know how bad my head hurts? I mumble for someone to tell her to shut up, and sink into oblivion once more.

Rhys, the queen's bodyguard, brings a young man dressed in royal clothing to meet Isleen outside her chambers. "There you are, my darling." Isleen takes Theron's chin in her hand and draws him down to her level so she can kiss his cheek.

Theron returns the kiss. "Good evening, Mother. I trust you're enjoying my party."

"As is the entire kingdom, dear boy. And each one asks after the newlywed couple."

A pink tinge colors Theron's cheeks. "I am sorry, Mother. We do not mean to be rude. Raina and I simply wish for time alone."

Rhys chuckles.

Isleen sends Rhys a demure look. "Honestly, son, I do understand. It was not so long ago that I–"

A shrill scream erupts from the ballroom, soon joined by a cacophony of other screams and the clashing and clanging of swords.

Rhys grabs the queen around the waist and holds her tightly to him. "Theron!"

Theron sprints to the great hall, with Rhys and Isleen close behind. The scene that unfolds before them nearly brings Theron to his knees in anguish. A group of men dressed in dark hoods has attacked the party and a large number of Dryden's subjects lie sprawled across the ballroom floor, injured– and worse.

Isleen gapes in horror. Damon's throne is empty, the king nowhere in sight. The powers of protection, bestowed upon Theron by the goddesses Morrigana, glow in his eyes as he clasps hands with Rhys. "By the power of Macha, goddess of war, you will protect my mother and keep her safe above all other things. Swear it."

Rhys nods, grasping Theron's hand tightly. "I swear protection to the queen until peace and order is restored. My life and hers are joined from this moment." Their clasped hands glow.

"The goddesses will hold you to this bond." Theron releases his friend's hand. "If Tynan is behind this, my mother's life is in danger. You must flee."

Isleen grips her son's arm before he can rush into the melee. "What of you and Raina? What of Damon? Our people are injured. I must help Heal them!"

Theron shakes his head. "It is too risky, Mother. Go! For the sake of our people, you must live." He shakes out of her grasp and rushes forward.

"Theron." Rhys meets him at the door. "Find Sergeant Liam. Swear him into the protection of Raina. When Tynan doesn't find Isleen in the castle, he will attempt to take Raina in her stead. He is looking for a Healer."

Theron nods, wrapping an arm around the man who has been as a father to him. *"Live well, until we meet again."*

Rhys returns the embrace. *"And you."*

The bright winter sunshine soaks through my eyelids. I turn my head slowly, testing the ache. Finding the pain bearable, I open my eyes. The curtain over the sliding glass door is pulled back, revealing a foot of fresh snow on my tiny wooden deck. Crystals of all colors and shapes hang from the doorframe and rest on the windowsill.

Erda dozes on the hardwood floor in a pool of sunshine, her favorite tennis ball between her front paws.

I take a deep breath. It doesn't hurt too badly, so I try again and smile when my lungs fill with herb-scented air. Several potted plants adorn my desk, along with another handful of multi-colored crystals. My heart warms at Mom's attempt at Healing. I shift and try to sit up.

"You're awake." The voice is familiar. And male.

I pull the blankets up higher and roll to my other side. "Guess so."

Kye leans forward in my rocking chair, holding a hand out as if he wants to touch me but is afraid I'll break. Dark circles shadow his eyes and his hair looks like he's run his hands through it at least a thousand times. A shadow of brown stubble makes his chin look dirty. "How do you feel?"

With one arm braced on the bed, I ease myself up. My head spins a little, but since my stomach is growling, I decide the dizziness has as much to do with hunger as pain or injury. "I'm starving."

Kye looks relieved. "That's a good sign. Do you hurt anywhere?"

I wiggle my toes, circle my ankles, and repeat the action with my fingers and wrists. "I don't know yet." It occurs to me that we're in my bedroom—at my house—instead of at the Inn. "How did I get home?"

He rubs the smooth arm of the chair, standing to stretch. "I brought you."

I laugh, and then wince when a pain shoots up my side. "Not on Finn?"

Concern and worry flicker across Kye's face as he perches on the edge of my bed. "No, in that guy's Jeep. Are you sure you're okay?"

I nod and throw off the covers, realizing for the first time that I'm wearing my flannel pajamas. Heat floods my cheeks. *Who changed my clothes?* "How long have I been asleep?"

Kye checks his watch. "Forty-five hours and thirty-nine minutes."

I rub my eyes, squeeze them tight. That can't be right. "Really, Kye. How long?"

"I'm not joking, Abby. It's 10:52, Monday morning." His hand kneads my foot while he talks.

"Seriously?"

"Yes."

"Oh, crap." I jump up, ignoring the stabbing pain in my side, and move the plants around on my desk so I can see the clock. "I missed Rose's party. I missed the bus. I missed breakfast." In shock, I plunk down on the bed. "I'm late for school."

With his hands on my shoulders, Kye turns me to face him. "It's spring break. And I hate to tell you this, but even if it wasn't, being late for school is the least of our problems right now."

FIFTEEN

Déjà Vu

Kye tucks a lock of hair behind my ear, extra gentle. Too gentle. The look in his eyes makes my stomach clench in fear.

"No. Oh no." My eyes burn and my voice cracks with emotion. "He's dead. Eric's dead. I killed him, the same way I killed my gram."

"What are you talking about?" With gentle fingers, Kye brushes wisps of hair off my forehead. "Eric's fine. Well. He has two broken ribs, a concussion, and a whole lot of bruises, but he'll be fine. You, on the other hand, have hardly stirred since you passed out in my arms Saturday afternoon. I've never been so freaked out. What happened? What went wrong?"

Frustrated, I free my feet from the covers and curl my knees up to my chest. "I screwed up somehow. Gram tried to teach me Healing, but obviously I never caught on." I squeeze my eyes shut. "I really wanted to help Eric. He's been nice to me since my first day here. Even if I don't like him the way he hopes, I would like to be his friend. He deserves that much."

"But?" Kye's eyebrows wrinkle together like he's trying to figure me out.

"But something about him feels off. He makes me uncomfortable. There's no real reason. He's never been anything but nice. Except ... I don't know. There's just *something*."

Kye pats my knee and stands. "Listen to your instincts. You never know who people are under the masks they wear."

I ease myself off the bed and take the brush from my dresser. "I'm trying, but ever since we moved here, my intuitive senses are hazy. They're all smooshed together like meatloaf."

"What do you mean? Are you talking about your Sight?"

I set the brush down and try to demonstrate with my hands. "Say you're driving through really thick fog. You can't see the road, but you smell something unusual, something out of the ordinary. You know it doesn't belong, but have no idea what it is. And while you're trying to figure that out, you hear muted sounds. You should know what's causing them, but you can't match it to anything in your head. You reach out, try to feel your way, but everything you touch slips out of your grasp. There are a zillion tastes in your mouth, but no way to know which ones are important. I'm completely handicapped."

Kye scrubs the back of his neck with his hand. "That must be scary."

"It is." I pick up my brush again and attempt to pull it through my hair, but pain shoots across my torso. My ribs are sore. Very sore. "I've always had such clarity. Well, almost always. Everything was fuzzy when Gram died, but that was just one incident. This feeling I have right now has been almost constant since we moved here. Like a radio with jammed frequencies."

Kye stares out the window, lost in contemplation while I dig through my drawers, looking for clothes.

A wave of nausea hits, disorienting me, and I grab the edge of the dresser. "I'll hurry. I bet we can make it to class by fourth period."

He catches my arm as I move into my closet to find jeans. "Abby, didn't you hear me? It's spring break. No school."

"Oh. Yeah." I back into the door and hit my side on the knob, gasping when pain slices my midsection and black spots dance in front of my eyes.

Wincing, he wraps his arm around my waist, holding me upright and ignoring my muttered curses. "Your mom said you're going to experience aches and pains similar to Eric's for a while. Somehow, you took his injury into yourself but didn't Heal him."

"She's right." My head throbs. "I'm going back to bed."

His eyes are a mixture of sympathy and anxiety when they search my face. "I hate to bring it up, but we told Alena we'd help look for those Keys. Boone thinks we already have one, which means we need to move soon."

"Soon. As in now?"

He cringes, looking torn. "When you're up to it. But today, if possible."

"Why me?" I ask, feeling weary and confused and a whole lot of other conflicting emotions. "What do I have to do with this?"

"I'm not sure. First your ring and your Gifts, and then Boone tries to kidnap you to get to me. And he was right. It did get to me. I've never been so scared—and I've been in some pretty precarious situations. We've known each other for, like, three days, and the thought of leaving your side makes me want to throw up. No joke. I haven't even been home since Yellowstone. You're involved. I don't know how, I just know it's true." He touches his forehead to mine. "So do you."

"Great." I lean against the doorframe, feeling shaky. "So, assuming you're right, what comes next?"

"I don't know."

"You don't know?"

"Look, I don't have all the answers. I don't think anyone does, but my dad might have some."

"Okay." Holding my things to my chest, I back into the hall. "Why don't you give him a call while I get cleaned up?"

"It's not that simple." He follows me into the bathroom where I set my clothes on the counter.

"What do you mean, not that simple?"

"We have to talk to him in person."

I lean against the cabinet for support and grimace at my reflection in the mirror. I'm not exactly looking my best. "Fine.

We'll go see him after I get dressed." I can probably handle it. I think.

"Uh. About that ..." He looks away, his eyes focus on the counter top, and he rubs a scratch with his thumb. "Remember how I told you my dad lives in New York?"

It takes a second for his words to sink in. "Oh. Yeah."

"Listen, it's all arranged. I've already talked to your mom, and she agreed to let you come with me for a few days. I promised—"

"Wait, what? You talked to my mom? What exactly did you tell her?"

His Adam's apple bobs. "Um, all of it."

"All of what? Like, about the bus? The Mud Pots? The faeries?"

He gulps, nodding. "I brought you home unconscious. What else was I supposed to tell her?"

Groaning, I bury my face in my hands. "You could have told her I got drunk, partied all night, and passed out."

"Why?"

"It would probably be easier to have her worried about underage drinking than that I went to a faery party and nearly got kidnapped and then tried to Heal someone I hardly know. Do you realize that in the world of Abby and Marian, this could mean I'm moving to Alaska tomorrow?" I grab his shoulders to shake some sense into him, but only manage to hold myself upright. "And how is she supposed to react when her seventeen-year-old daughter runs off to New York with a guy she just met? Let's not even mention that I'm about to be caught up in a battle between good and evil that ninety-nine-point-nine percent of the human population will never freaking know about."

Kye laughs out loud and rubs his thumb across my bottom lip. "Your mother will be fine, I promise. And as far as Alaska goes—well, that can't very well happen while you're gone, can it?" He turns away and backs into the hall. "Get ready. We'll talk more over breakfast."

"Thanks for letting me clean up first. I feel like I haven't showered in days—oh, wait, I haven't."

Kye starts down the stairs, ignoring my sarcasm. "I hope you like eggs, because it's about all I know how to cook."

It's easier to breathe in the steam from the shower, with hot water soaking my hair and running down my back. Every time I lift my right arm, pain shoots through my side and down my leg. It makes shampooing tricky. *How did this happen? What went wrong?*

After I dry my hair and apply enough makeup to make me look less haggard, I rub one of Gram's homemade herbal lotions into my skin, knowing the concoction will help the pain fade faster. Though I have no visible bruises, a deep ache resonates in my ribs and throbs in my head—leaving me weak, despite my lack of success in Healing Eric. *It doesn't add up.* I must have started right, because his pain became mine. But at some point I screwed up, because I lapsed into a Healer's coma without finishing the process. *That's not supposed to happen.*

Kye seems at home with a plate of scrambled eggs near his elbow, the newspaper spread in front of him, and Erda at his feet. I'm flooded with the strongest sense of déjà vu that Kye's been here before, that we've had breakfast together dozens of times—maybe hundreds. Except the picture that comes to mind is not of Kye sitting at a polished oak table wearing a sweatshirt and jeans and eating eggs. Instead, I see him wearing a long cloak and traveling boots, sitting at a crude pine table, eating mush out of a clay bowl. The pictures superimpose themselves on each other until the vision disappears, leaving only Kye. I can't place the memory.

Or is it a vision?

As I sit, Kye folds the paper on the table and pushes a plate toward me. "If you hurry, we can catch the 4:30 flight."

"That's fast." I push the eggs around my plate, wondering why I haven't seen my mother yet. "Where's my mom? Does she know what's going on?"

"She went to work to handle a couple appointments that couldn't be cancelled. I called her while you were showering and told her you're awake. She wants to see you before we go."

I manage to swallow the bite of egg I was chewing. Barely. "You called her for me?"

"No, I called because I promised I would let her know when you woke up. While I had her on the phone, I filled her in on our possible flight plan."

It takes some effort to find my voice again, but find it I do. "And she's okay with this ... plan?"

He taps the table with his fingertips, his mouth moving like he isn't quite sure what to say next. "Yes, I—"

"What if I refuse to go?"

The kitchen falls silent. Kye doesn't move.

"It's a valid question. I have every reason to believe that going with you could be hazardous to my personal health and safety. Give me a good, solid reason why I should agree to this. And don't say because my mom already paid for a ticket, because I know she doesn't have the money for that."

Very slowly, Kye braces both hands on the table and leans in until we're nose to nose. Logically, I know I should back away, probably run screaming from the house, but that's not what I want. Being this close to him makes the pulse pound in my ears and heats my blood to boiling. What I want is to jump into his arms and hold on forever. Who cares where he takes me? What he expects from me? All these things race through my head, but I don't actually *do* anything except blink, waiting for Kye's answer.

"Here's one," he murmurs, his breath tickling my chin. "Because you want to go with me as badly as I want you to come."

The tips of our noses are the only parts of us touching, but that contact alone makes my insides feel like I'm being electrically charged. *If I die on this trip, at least I'll go having felt what it's like to be on fire.* I try to form the word no, but my lips refuse to do it.

"And two," he continues, his lips so close to mine I can feel them moving as he speaks. "I need to be close to you. If you don't go—I won't either."

I'm afraid to move, afraid to break the contact that has brought my senses alive. The thing is I know he's not trying to guilt me into going. He's stating facts. He won't go without me, and I doubt I could let him. But I have to think, need to keep my head before I lose myself, so I lean back in my chair to put distance between us. "Where in New York does your dad live?"

"Manhattan." He sits back, blinking like he's trying to form a coherent thought. "Also, we'll make a pit-stop in Las Vegas on the way."

Once again, I can find no words.

He looks pointedly at my plate, then his watch. "Something wrong with your eggs? I swear I didn't drug them."

"You promise?" I clear my throat and take a bite, realizing Kye's a decent cook. Although, I haven't eaten for days, so it's possible dirt would be delicious at this point. "Thanks. I didn't realize I was so hungry."

He watches silently while I shovel in every last bite. "Do you want more?"

I shake my head and lean on the table, gathering my thoughts. "Las Vegas?"

He stands to clear our plates. "Akers knows a guy there who might have the location of one of the missing Keys."

Erda licks the crumbs off my chair when I follow Kye to the sink. "Does my mom know about this detour?"

"Um." He shuffles his feet and looks at the ground. "What's the right answer to that question? Can I please have a hint?"

I groan, staring at the ceiling. "Let me guess. You told her and her response was, 'Sure, boy-I-don't-know, go ahead and drag my daughter all over the country unsupervised. Don't worry about a thing. Oh, but if it's not too much trouble, try to use condoms when it's convenient. I'm too young and hot to be a grandma.'"

Kye blushes. Even through my anger, his pink cheeks give me a warm buzz of affection. "I promised her we'd sleep in separate beds," he says, "and swore on my life that I wouldn't try anything like that. I'm supposed to protect you."

"But she didn't object to me going?" I scrub the dishes clean working through the ache in hopes that a little pain will help me find some clarity.

"Hey." Kye turns me around, offering the comfort of his arms. "What's all this about?"

"I don't know, I just ..." I lean into him, drawing strength from his solid chest. "Is she trying to get rid of me? She certainly deserves to have her own life, and now with Gram gone ..."

"Shh." Kye strokes the top of my head and runs his hand down my back. Jealous, Erda rubs against our legs, whimpering. "She's not trying to get rid of you. You should have seen her these past few days. She's been in a tailspin."

"Then why isn't she here?"

"It costs money to buy herbs and groceries, and she had to work. Besides, she was making me crazy. Honestly, I think she needed some space. I wasn't exactly willing to leave." He pulls back to look in my eyes. "Abby, she doesn't know how to help you, what to do for you. Without Isabelle's guidance—she was terrified about what came next. Then I brought you home unconscious and compounded her stress by, like, a thousand percent. Akers came too, and we explained about your Gifts and my Gifts, and how there are more of us, and that we all need to work together to help each other. Even though she didn't understand everything we were telling her, she realized I can help you, and you can help me, and together we can find these Keys and stop the Dark Elen from whatever they're planning. So, she agreed to let you go with me on the condition that I—ahem—keep it in my pants or risk losing it forever."

The breath catches in my throat. "That's all?"

"Her open threat—which was actually rather graphic—was the only birth control mentioned, I promise."

Relieved, I let out the breath I don't remember holding. *I can do this. I should do it.* "What now?"

"Pack whatever you need in a travel bag." He gives me a gentle shove toward the stairs. "We have an hour."

"We need to stop and say goodbye to my mom on the way."

He grins, patting Erda's head. "I'd be a dead dog if you didn't."

Halfway up the stairs, I pause. "The airport. We're flying."

"Yes, we've established this." With a hand at the small of my back, Kye propels me to my room.

"How much ...?" I'm trying to recall my account balance. It doesn't matter—it's unlikely I can afford it.

Kye hands me the duffle I took to Yellowstone. "Don't worry about the tickets. Just pack the essentials."

"How long will we be gone?" I pause at my underwear drawer and motion for Kye to turn around.

"I don't know. Two days? Four? Maybe a week. Pack light, though. We might have to carry everything at some point."

Shaking with the enormity of what I'm about to do, I zip my bag and clasp a square-shaped pendant around my neck, glancing back at my room. "I guess I'm ready."

He takes my things and leads me down the stairs, and as I do a quick doors-locked-stove-off check, I find myself anxious to be on our way. When I meet Kye at the front door, he fingers my necklace. "That's pretty. What is it?"

"Alexandrite. Maybe it'll help clear up some of the fog for me."

"How does it change colors like that? One second it's purple, the next it's green."

"Depends. Mood. What my body needs. Sometimes it's lighting." I fill Erda's bowls with food and water. "Watch over Mom for me."

Kye pats her furry head. "Is she a good watchdog?"

I squat down to hug her and scratch behind her ears. "Only if licking a robber to death makes a good defense."

Erda only whines a little when I leave her inside and lock the door, but it gives me a sad pang just the same. Kye stows my duffle bag in the back of a black SUV and opens the door for me. "What does it mean when your necklace turns that purple-blue color it is now?"

DESCENDANT

I slide into the seat, my ribs throbbing again. "It's giving me strength to take a risk."

"Well, now, that's handy, isn't it?" Kye closes the door and walks around the car, as steady on the icy road as he was in the moving bus. *Oh, yeah. A big-enormous-giant-crazy-stupid risk.*

SIXTEEN

The Journey Begins

"Are you okay?" Kye asks as he buckles his seatbelt.

Our plane—small as it is—has two seats on one side of the narrow aisle and one on the other. The airline staff includes two flight attendants and two pilots, because—I assume—it's some kind of law that every airplane has to have at least two people on board who know how to fly the thing, and two to keep everyone calm if we go down.

I clear my throat and try to shake away my nerves. "Yeah. Why?"

"You seem a little ... off."

"Really? A little off?" I snap. "Huh. And here I thought I was doing so well, all things considered."

He freezes, glancing sidelong at me. "What's wrong?"

I stare out the window as the attendant seals the door and the engines roar to life. *Don't take it out on him.* "Sorry. I don't mean to be a brat. I have a massive headache." *Might as well admit it.* "And I'm sad. I feel like this is it, you know? Like I'm growing up and leaving home and nothing will ever be the same again. Ever. I didn't expect it to come so soon." My voice cracks on the last word and I turn my face away to hide the sheen of tears in my eyes. *This is not the time to turn into a crybaby.*

"I'd love to lie and say you're wrong, but I can't." His hand caresses my cheek. "It's okay to be sad, though. Some parts of growing up really suck."

"Yes. They really do." As the plane moves onto the tarmac, I do my best to get comfortable and close my eyes. I'm still so tired.

"Do you want some aspirin? I'll ask the flight attendant for something."

"It won't help. The broken energy has to funnel out while the good energy stitches back together. This really isn't the best day for me to travel."

His fingers graze my cheekbone again and my heart stutters like it did on the bus. Then his lips touch mine—soft as the brush of a feather. "I'm sorry," he breathes. "Go ahead and sleep."

And I do.

The next thing I know, Kye's shaking me awake. "Come on, Abby, time to change planes."

My eyes pop open. "Where are we?"

"Salt Lake City. One more flight and we'll be in Las Vegas."

He looks so cheerful, so encouraging, I don't have the heart to tell him that all Eric's bad energy is about to find a way out of my body via my mouth. It's a good thing we're taxiing to the gate. As we disembark, the coolness of the breezeway soothes my nausea a bit. I breathe deep—taking in the winter air perfumed with airplane fuel—and will myself to hold in the contents of my stomach until we find a restroom.

Upon seeing the sign with the gray triangle lady, I bolt, leaving Kye calling after me. When I emerge several minutes later, I feel like a new woman. Not only have I expelled the majority of the bad energy that was causing me pain, I've washed my face and gargled an entire fifty-cent bottle of mouthwash from the dispenser.

"Feeling better?" Kye looks me up and down, as if inspecting me for defects.

I nod. "Lots. Do we have time to eat? I'm starving."

His eyebrows crinkle together. "But you just ... I thought you were sick?"

"I was." I dig into my purse, looking for my wallet. "Most of the bad energy's gone now, but I need some protein to help finish the

113

job. Another couple hours of sleep, a few more trips to restrooms, and I should be good as new."

With an arm around me, he steers us to the nearest food vendor. "You bet. How do you feel about cheese?"

The lights from the Strip cast a festive glow in the dusky sky as the plane circles to land. We catch a taxi and head for the Luxor, where the guy we're looking for supposedly works. Thousands of blinking lights wiz by, making me feel as if I've stepped into a time vortex. *Too bad I can't go back to the night Gram died and undo everything.* "If this guy is Akers's friend, why couldn't we just call him? Why come all the way here for our answers?"

"Lan doesn't think it's safe to talk about this stuff over the phone. He's probably right."

The pyramid is built from blocks of black glass rather than Egyptian clay, and a bright light pierces the sky in a straight line from the top. Our driver stops at the curb in front of the entrance.

"Why didn't he come himself?"

"Landon and this guy, Juri, had some kind of falling out," Kye says. "He wasn't sure the guy would talk to him."

The line for the check-in desk winds around the lobby only feet away from tables where women in flashy mini-dresses sit next to men in T-shirts with poker chips stacked at their elbows. Egyptian symbols have been etched into walls, and another pyramid—a smaller version of the building in which we're now standing—advertises an IMAX theater. We move with a strong sense of purpose, up an escalator, past the theater, and stop near a shop boasting a King Tut display to look closer at a board etched with fake hieroglyphs.

I touch the symbols for peace and happiness, hoping this journey will end with both.

Kye's looking at a marking without a caption. It isn't in line with the rest and it's not made from the same characters. The shape looks like an upside-down Y with a line through it and two small marks in the upper corners.

"Whaddayaknow. This place is marked." Kye removes a piece of paper from his pocket, unfolds it, and holds it up to the symbol. His paper is stamped with an identical symbol.

"What is it?"

"The mark of the ancient Elen. Not to be confused with the Dark Elen."

"Does that mean we're in the right place?"

He studies his paper again. "Hope so."

From the corner of my eye, I catch movement in a nearby shadow—a short man in a brown trench coat, watching us. My stomach clenches. The man is shaped like an orange, and something about him feels both familiar and wrong. "Kye."

Kye grabs my hand, dragging me down the escalator into the casino. The man doesn't follow, but I can't shake the feeling that he's watching us.

"Creepy." I murmur.

"Yes," Kye agrees.

We enter a door marked employees only and walk down a wide hallway into a utility room filled with computers. A tiny imprint of the symbol on Kye's paper is etched on the side of an enormous metal box.

On a large door, almost as big as my bedroom wall, the symbol is stamped into the frame about halfway up. Kye tries the knob but it's locked, and when he knocks no one replies.

I follow him back into the casino. "Maybe we should just ask for him at the front desk."

"We will." He runs his fingers through his hair as we drop onto a bench. "I wanted to get a feel for the place, scope out escape routes. I hope this will be easy, but with our luck, it won't. We have to prepare for the worst, you know?"

No, I don't know. I wonder again what I'm doing here.

Kye pulls out his phone and hits a button. "We're here. This place is marked and I don't know what it's supposed to mean. We haven't talked to that Juri guy yet, but I'm not getting a good feeling. Call me when you get this. It's ten hours till we're in the air again." He glances at me and frowns as he deposits the phone in his pocket. "I wonder why Lan didn't answer. He always answers."

"Maybe he's in the shower. Or didn't hear his phone ring."

A savory aroma tickles my nose and my stomach growls. Kye sends me an apprehensive glance. "Are you going to be sick again?"

"Not yet." I lean against the wall, probe my ribs with my fingers, and realize that the pain has diminished to a dull throb. This is good, since I expected them to be sore for another day or two. "But I'm getting hungry."

"Me too. Let's find this guy so we can get out of here." He pulls me up and keeps my hand in his as we head back through the casino to the front lobby. The lady at the information desk frowns when Kye asks for Juri but doesn't know if it's his first name or his last. She picks up her phone receiver and turns her back on us, speaking in a hushed voice. Facing us again, she gestures at a security guard. "Walt will take you to Mr. Juri's office."

Walt, a big guy in a scary-looking uniform, eyes us up and down, causing my heart to pound in apprehension. *No turning back now.* We follow him down the same hall we explored a few minutes ago, but this time a cloud of dark energy looms, threatening to overwhelm me. The lights flicker and dim.

I squeeze Kye's hand until my fingers ache, trying to tell him something's not right. He squeezes back. He feels it too.

Walt opens the enormous door, and terror slams into me as I'm met with a pair of familiar cat-like yellow eyes. I know this man. I remember seeing him the night Gram died. His eyes bore into me and I feel an evil kind of heat in him. The blood drains from my face and the air backs up in my lungs. Kye squeezes my hand. "Abby?"

"It's him," I whisper. "I know him."

The man shakes his head. "Can I help you?"

Kye's muscles go rigid and he pulls me close with a protective arm. "Mr. Juri? Landon Akers sent us."

SEVENTEEN

Landon and Juri

The round man swivels back and forth, resting his elbows on the surface of an expensive desk with his fingers locked together. Shelves line the walls, crammed with books and Egyptian-style artifacts that may or may not be authentic. Walt directs us to two metal folding chairs, then steps out and drags the heavy door closed as Mr. Juri starts to speak. "How is Landon these days?"

"He's doing well." Kye leans back in his chair, faking a calm I know he doesn't feel, exchanging pleasantries with Juri. My attention falls on a dusty, framed picture propped on a shelf near my head. I pick it up and rub the dust off. A much younger Mr. Akers has his arm draped around a younger Juri. I notice Juri's eyes seem greener rather than dull yellow, and he wasn't nearly so round. The men are standing next to a wooden sign that reads Welcome to Mount St. Helens. A tall, cone-shaped mountain forms a distant background. The picture is date-stamped March 14, 1980.

"We were best friends," Juri says, indicating the picture. "A very long time ago."

I hand the picture to Kye. "Is it rude to ask what happened?"

Juri sighs. "Take it out of the frame."

Kye does as he says. There's a note on the back:

To Juri—my best friend and fellow adventure seeker. May you someday find the freedom you're looking for and the life you deserve. If you change your mind, you know where to find us.

Landon

I glance at Kye, wondering what he's thinking. He takes a deep breath as if unsure how to proceed, then says, "What can you tell us about the Elen?"

Juri sits back and taps his lips with his index fingers." Why?"

"The Dark Ones are looking for some Keys. It's important that we find them first."

Juri cocks his head to one side. "So, what do you want from me?"

"Landon suggested you might have information that could help us," Kye says.

I squeeze my fingers together and lean my elbows on my knees to help me keep calm. My gut clenches again, hard.

"Why should I help you?" Juri says, his eyes flicking to a shelf behind us. *He's considering it.*

"Because," Kye says, "something really, really bad will happen if we don't track down these Keys."

"Like, maybe end-of-the-world bad," I add.

Juri throws up his hands like he doesn't care about the world potentially ending.

"What about friendship? You and ... Landon were friends. I can tell you loved him." I hold out the picture. "Look how happy you were here." Juri stares at the picture but doesn't take it. "He sent us to you because he trusted that you would help us. Please."

Juri stands, leaning against the desk. "Was," he grunts. "He was my friend. Past-tense."

"We're in trouble," Kye murmurs, looking stricken—hurt. "Landon's in trouble."

Juri picks up the photo and tosses it in a drawer. "The day after that picture was taken, everything fell apart. The world exploded around us, and when the dust cleared, we stood on opposite sides. I got no loyalty left for Landon. Haven't seen or talked to him since."

"But you care about him. I can tell." I inch my way around the desk so I'm facing Juri. "Whatever happened between you back then is history. Or it can be. If you help us, maybe you and Landon can make amends."

A look of despair flickers on Juri's face. "That's not going to happen. But ..." He stands, drags a heavy book off a shelf, and sets it on the desk. Then, reaching up the sleeve of his jacket, he produces a tiny silver key. "He saved my life once. I'll share what I know, but then you're on your own. My debt to Landon will be repaid in full." When he turns the book around, I realize it's actually a lock-box.

Juri inserts the key and opens the top. Nestled in a bed of black velvet, a large, flat slab of clear quartz carved with a series of odd shapes around its edges gleams in the dim overhead lights, casting an eerie, greenish glow.

"What is it?" Kye asks.

"A Cairn Elen." When we both give him a blank look, Juri explains, "An ancient slab stone that marks a spiritual pathway. They're usually embedded in the ground at a sacred crossroads. This one holds a great deal of history and future prophesies of Dryden and the royal family."

On the opposite side of the room, Juri pushes aside more books to reveal a wall safe, from which he removes an object wrapped in gray linen.

"What does it do?" I ask, glancing back at the enormous stone.

"I'm getting to that part." He unwinds the cloth and draws out a crystal blade with a jeweled silver handle. "It's a dagger," he says in response to our questioning looks. "Made of crystal quartz. Very, very old." As he speaks, he slides the sharp point into one of the triangular shapes in the top of the Cairn Elen.

A rainbow of colors spins around the room like a whirlwind, settling above the stone and melding into random shapes and forms. Kye and I lean forward, awestruck, as the hovering colors take shape and turn into a moving picture, not unlike a digital movie. An auburn-haired lady smiles, clapping a hand to her mouth as a handsome young man kneels, holding up a sparkling ring. She nods, and the man jumps up, hauls the woman off her feet, and swings her around in a circle. The picture fades and another one forms. Another woman—tall and statuesque—looks over her shoulder and crooks her finger.

I recognize her from my dreams. My visions.

Behind the woman, the colors form a middle-aged man in chainmail armor. He bows with a playful smile as he runs toward her and scoops her into his arms. Her emerald pendant catches the light and flashes as she takes his face in her hands. The embrace is intimate—and inappropriate between a queen and her bodyguard— yet I'm positive the man resembles the guard more than the burly king.

Again, I keep my thoughts to myself.

Next, a fatigued, war-worn man stumbles across a castle courtyard and falls on his knees in front of an enormous door. The door opens, and the man holds his hands out, begging, but the king's servant glares at him, eyes full of scorn, and turns him away. With a look of desperation, the man reaches into his cloak, producing a jewel-encrusted crystal dagger, and offers it to the king. The servant shakes his head and closes the door as the man crumples to the ground, weeping.

The colors swirl together and become the hands of a child, lifting a glowing stone off a crude rock pedestal. A young face is illuminated in the stone's glow as the boy kisses it and drops it in a brown leather pouch tied around his wrist. He crows in triumph, only to have the world around him quake and rumble. The picture pans out, becoming a forest of trembling trees. The mossy dirt on the ground breaks in half and the fissure spreads rapidly between the child's feet. Smoke erupts from the new crevice and billows after the boy as he runs and runs and runs, screaming in terror.

When the lights fade, Juri whispers, "One more. There should be another." Smoke pours from the place where the dagger meets the Cairn Elen and the picture blazes brighter as the colors swirl like a whirlwind, not taking a solid shape for several seconds.

When it does, newborn twin boys lie naked on a cloth. One has his mouth open in a wail and his eyes glow amber, nearly red. His skin is deep purple, wrinkled and puckered from birth. The other baby appears to be the polar opposite of his brother. He smiles, his bright blue eyes curious and wise. A healthy blush tints his perfect, smooth skin, offset by downy-white, angel-soft hair.

Rough hands reach out from under a dark cloak and take the darker baby away without ever being held to his mother's breast to nurse. The lighter brother cries, but the scene leaves him behind to follow the cloaked figure, whose face remains concealed. He carries the other infant through a forest to a door in the side of a mountain. Holding the child above his head, the figure falls to one knee and calls out as if offering a sacrifice. The door opens.

The breath backs up in my lungs.

Sinister-looking creatures with large, red eyes float out in massive numbers. Their physical bodies look human, but not. Some have claws or talons in place of their hands, others are covered in fur, and still more have wings protruding from their shoulder blades. Yet, when their feet touch the ground and they surround the child, every one of them appears human.

Well, their bodies do. Their energy is markedly different. It flickers and rises like black fire, and I wonder how something that vile isn't visible to the naked, untrained, and un-Gifted eye.

"Demons," I breathe, backing away. Kye squeezes my hand.

The cloaked figure rises, thrusts the infant higher above his head, and yells something we can't hear. He repeats the motion again and again, rhythmically, chanting a mantra, and the evil-looking creatures fall on their knees and bow.

My heart hammers as the lights fade and the picture falls apart. Juri removes the dagger and rewraps it, then closes the box and turns the key on the Cairn Elen.

When he looks up, his eyes are sad. "When I was young, I went on a quest for the Arawn Keys." The corners of his lips turn up as he replaces the wrapped bundle in the wall safe. "Did Landon tell you about that? He came with me."

"No," Kye says, surprised. "He didn't mention it."

"Oh yes. All those years ago, Landon, Valdemar, and I set out to conquer the forces of evil all by ourselves." Juri frowns. "Turned out we all wanted different things. Too bad. We never completed the journey."

Feeling nervous, I brush the hair out of my eyes and manage to get my ring tangled in it. "Did the three of you keep in touch at all?"

Juri doesn't answer. He's staring at me. The back of my neck prickles with a sense of danger and a tingle of alarm races along my spine. My ring is still glowing, as it has been since we walked in—just enough to be conspicuous. I shove my hand in my pocket, trying to appear casual, but I'm ready to run.

"Where did you get that ring?" Juri asks.

Fear dries out my mouth and my mind blanks. Kye stands, taking my hand. He's getting ready to run too.

"Where?" Juri's voice changes and the lights flicker under his power.

Kye drags me behind him and backs us slowly to the door. "I bought it for her. Cheesy airport gift shop."

"You're a terrible liar, boy. There are probably fewer than ten people in the modern world who'd recognize the Ring of the Princess. I happen to be one of them." He inches toward us. "Tell me, little girl. Do you understand what happened to that ring's original owner?"

"Yes," I squeak. "I was there when she died." *What if he killed Gram?*

"Oh, to be so innocent. So clueless." He shakes his head. "I assure you, Isabelle Johnson was *not* the original owner." At my shocked expression, he explains, "Yes, I knew her. Quite well, actually. I followed her for years—never quite positive she actually had it."

"My Gram. You killed her, didn't you?"

He strokes his jawbone with short, stubby fingers. "Not personally. Another story for another day."

If only I wasn't frozen with fear, if I wasn't absolutely certain that we needed to leave right now, *right now*, I would find a way to make him tell me about what happened that night. I would find a way to punish Juri for hurting my Gram. Except I can't speak. Without Kye backing into me, I'm not sure I could think to move.

Juri's thick legs swish together as he gets closer to us. His arms swing and I picture his knuckles dragging on the floor. "Seeing as how you're Landon's kids, I'm willing to offer you some extra assistance. It would be handy to know how to save yourself when the Dark Ones come after you."

"No thanks," Kye's hand on my arm trembles.

"Perhaps it would be prudent for you to stay here. I can protect you." Juri is only a few feet away, looking directly at me. "The ring makes Key number three. Only one more left to find. I save you from imminent death, and you help me with a special project of my own. It won't take long. I'll even make sure you have a nice room to share—and I won't tell Landon." He offers a nasty insinuating smile. "You know what they say—it all stays in Vegas."

Kye's body quivers like a spring at its limit. "I said no. But thanks for the offer."

Juri pushes a button on his desk and Walt enters, followed by another security guard. Juri continues to advance, and now his guards are coming at us from behind.

My ring pulses again. Through the roaring in my ears, I hear Kye mumbling. Following an inhuman screech, five or six rats scurry in from the hall. One brushes my pants and I scream, but it ignores me and lunges for Juri—a mad look in its eyes. The rats sink their teeth into Juri's shoes and proceed to climb his clothes, biting along his legs and arms, until one jumps for his face.

We lunge for the door, but there is no way we can get through the guards until a gust of wind fills the hallway with a rank smell, accompanied by the screeching of bats and a reverberating buzz not unlike a swarm of bees. The disoriented guards fall to their knees, stunned, while bats pelt their heads and backs.

Miraculously, the creatures leave me and Kye alone and we run. Clasping hands, we manage a speed made possible only through sheer adrenaline, down the hall, into the casino, out the door. Everything we pass is a blur as we run for what feels like miles through parking lots and around buildings and tourists. I want to turn around to see if we're being followed, but Kye drags me with him until my breathing is ragged and the pain in my side forces me to slow down.

"Come on, Abby, we have to keep going."

"I can't," I wheeze. "I'm too tired. I hurt."

"Just a little farther." Kye breathes more evenly than I, but slows so I can keep up. When we first arrived, there were taxis all over the place, but now that we really need one, I can't see a single car.

We're several miles from the hotel by the time we finally stop in an outdoor mall that's closed for the night. I collapse on a bench and wrap both arms around my stomach, breathing hard. Kye sits next to me, stroking my hair. "Are you okay?"

"No." I double over as pain shoots through my ribs. "You?"

He stretches his legs out, leaning back to stare at the stars. "I'll be fine. I'm more worried about you."

I try to straighten, then change my mind. "Oh man, I hurt."

He pulls me into his lap, and I let him, because being held will help keep my mind off the ache. Once my breathing evens out and I can talk, I ask, "What happened back there?"

Kye picks up my hand and plays with my fingers the way he did on the bus. "Juri wanted your ring."

"Yeah, I got that part." I relax into him, leaning my cheek on his shoulder. "But why? And what did you do in that room?"

"The rats came from the crawl spaces and the bats and hornets were hanging out in the parking garage." He shrugs. "Calling them was all I could think to do."

"We're lucky. It worked." The rhythm of his heartbeat calms me, allowing me to release some of the pain with each ka-thump.

"Yes, it did." Kye pinches the bridge of his nose like he has a headache. "I've been thinking about what we saw in the Cairn Elen, putting it together with some research I did while I was waiting for you to wake up. I have a theory." He runs his hands through his artfully messy hair. "The Arawn Keys are powerful objects rumored to unlock an ancient prison that houses a demon army, but they have to be used all together. Over the years, hundreds of Gifted have attempted to find the Keys. I'm pretty sure that dagger in Juri's office is one of them. That's the only way it could've activated the Cairn Elen. So. There's one Key located."

Not that we'll get our hands on it anytime soon. "If that's true," I ask, "why didn't Mr. Akers tell us Juri has one of the Keys? Do you think he knows?"

Kye looks away, but I can see the tension in his jaw. "He must. They must've found it together. Why else would he insist we come here?"

"No. He couldn't. He wouldn't keep it from us."

"If he did, there's a lot more to it."

"Like how their friendship ended and how many Keys they found."

"And where they ended up, and which ones were left to locate." Kye shifts me off his lap so he can stretch out to lie lengthwise on the bench with me snuggled close.

A shooting star stripes the sky and I close my eyes, wishing I could talk to Gram. She would know what we're missing. "What did he mean by the Ring of the Princess?"

"From what I gather, the original Elen lived in a place called Dryden, around four hundred years ago or something." He pulls me closer when I shiver, wrapping me inside his jacket. I breathe deep, relaxing even more and ignoring my rumbling stomach.

Kye's voice sounds sleepy. "Guess the king was a pretty popular guy, known for being fair. Diplomatic. People liked him, but they absolutely adored the queen. She was this raving beauty who loved the people, especially children. She had a strong Gift for premonition, which gave her visions of things to come." He pauses, and I feel the weight of Kye's words settle over me. "But more importantly, she had the Gift of Light. I don't know much about Light, but it sounds like she could persuade enemies to become good and change loyalties and stuff. She could cheer people up and maybe even mend—though not Heal—broken hearts. Val says her Gifts were heart-based. Pretty rockin' Gifts.

"But when she had Prince Theron, something happened to deplete her powers. She almost died. King Damon had an emerald pendant made to give her strength, and she always wore it, but she never completely recovered."

I stifle a yawn and fight off a sudden heaviness in my eyes. "What happened to them?"

Kye runs his fingers up and down my arm on his chest. "The Prince spent a lot of time with Dryden's Warrior Guards. Rhys, the Captain, treated him like a son. In fact, Rhys spent more time with Prince Theron than King Damon ever could. The king was a busy guy." Kye leans his head on my hair. "Are you comfortable enough?"

"I'm fine." I yawn. "Was Rhys married? Did he have his own children?"

"No. Rumor was he had his heart broken not long after being assigned to the Guard. His true love was promised to someone else, and Rhys couldn't do anything about it. I guess he never recovered.

"Anyway, Rhys and Theron became inseparable. Then, during a hunt, Theron ended up lost. Three days later, they found him in the forest, and he had a maiden with him."

Goosebumps rise on my arms. Something about the story strikes me. "Who was she?"

"No one knew. She came out of nowhere. But Theron fell in love with her, and they were soon engaged. Theron designed a diamond ring for the maiden—Raina—as a betrothal gift. She never took it off, even to sleep. It was said to have the power of true love."

"You think my ring is four hundred years old?"

"I'm just saying it would make sense if Juri thinks it is."

"I know it's an antique, but it's not *that* old. It can't be the same ring." It's becoming difficult to keep my heavy eyes open. "I'm falling asleep. When do we have to be back to the airport?"

"We have a few hours. Go ahead and rest." He strokes my hair and traces his fingers up and down my spine. "I'm sorry. I never intended for this to happen."

I yawn. "It's okay. Just make sure I'm awake when it's time to go." The world fades around the edges and my eyelids fall closed. "Tell me more about Theron and Raina."

"Too tired. I'll finish later." He yawns. "We're safe for now. Sleep."

"I think I have to."

Kye replies, but I'm already falling under the cloud of slumber and can't comprehend his words. Sometime during the night, I dream he takes my hand in his and calls me his love—and I really, really like the sound of it.

EIGHTEEN

The Key

"Abby." Kye jerks awake. "We should get to the airport."

I sit up, blinking away the fog in my eyes, and try to rub out the throbbing bench slat indentations in my shoulder and back. The sky is turning a lighter shade of navy—sunrise isn't far off. "What time is it?"

"Quarter to five." Kye stands, stretches his arms over his head, and then offers to pull me to my feet. His eyes go soft as he brings my hand to his mouth, kissing my fingers above the ring. It warms to a soft glow.

My stomach rumbles as we walk toward the street. We still haven't eaten. "So, bus or cab to the airport?" I ask.

"Cab."

This trip has to be expensive. After considering my budget, I have to ask. "How much do I owe you for the plane tickets?"

"Don't worry about it."

"I am worried. How much?"

"It's taken care of."

"How? By whom?" *Does he have a job?*

"I have enough money. We'll be fine." He laces his fingers through mine and we head down the boulevard.

"You have money." I turn to glance in the direction of the bench where we slept. "You couldn't have mentioned that earlier?"

"Yeah, not so well-planned, was it?" His cheeks puff out as he exhales through his teeth. "In my defense, I'd hoped Juri would comp us rooms, or at least let us hang at the Luxor for the evening."

"Good thing we didn't."

"Yeah. But I promise we won't spend another night on a bench. As much as I enjoyed holding you, that thing sucked as a mattress."

"Even though I enjoyed being held, I agree."

He signals an approaching cab and then opens the door for me. "Come on. Let's get outta here."

The airport is crowded with early morning passengers as we check in and go through security. Once we've found our gate, I decide a trip to the ladies room is my top priority. No matter how hungry I am, hygiene is more important. After braiding my hair, brushing my teeth, and changing from my grimy T-shirt into a cable-knit sweater (purchased on clearance at the gift shop), I emerge feeling awake, alert, and infinitely more human.

Kye has cleaned up too, and has in his hand a pastry sack and two bottles of juice. "Breakfast is served."

I sit next to him and choose a blueberry muffin from the bag. My mouth is full when I remember to thank him. "You're my hero."

"Remind me to bring you muffins every day."

"You have no idea how badly I needed that."

"Hard to miss." He grins around a bite of his own muffin. "Luckily, it didn't take much to vanquish the growling monster in your stomach."

I glare playfully at Kye. "Yeah. I'd apologize, except I blame you."

He scrunches his face into a frown—and I'm utterly charmed. "If you're keeping a list, it'll be holy-crap-long when we get home."

"I'll just keep track of the big stuff, then."

The last drops of juice slide down my throat with a satisfying tang, and I toss the bottle in the trash as we line up to board, still flirting. Our plane lifts off the ground as the first rays of sun crest over the tops of the buildings, tinting the pale sky with shades of purple, pink, and gold.

Kye peers out the window with me. "Beautiful, isn't it?"

"Um-hm." We're cheek to cheek, and my heart races in anticipation, but his attention is focused out the window. Saliva pools beneath my tongue. Kye runs his hand up and down my arm as he leans back, his eyes dropping to my mouth as if he's trying to make a decision.

I inch closer, licking my lips in anticipation.

Then he sits back.

He hasn't kissed me—really kissed me—since the faery party. I'm starting to wonder if his earlier clinging was brought on by remnants of the faery enchantment. Stung by his rejection, I swallow and sit back, wincing when my ears pop and a tiny hammer drums inside my head.

The airplane seats are of the extreme straight-backed variety, but I lean mine back the full three inches and close my eyes. Between the cold air, noise, and the crappy airline pillow, I can't get comfortable. When frustration wins the battle with pride, I rest my head on Kye's shoulder. As he did on the bus, he encircles me in his arms and covers us with a blanket. Sticking with what feels like a new habit, I drift off listening to the sound of his steady heartbeat.

A dark-haired woman stands in a stone doorway, a look of horror pasted on her face. Her hands fly to her mouth and she stifles a scream as a group of angry men drags a headless body—dressed in royal finery—through the corridor. Her skirt skims the floor as she backs into her room and slams the heavy wooden door, dry heaving.

Silent tears trickle down her cheeks as she searches for a place to hide, knowing there will be no escape. Something crashes in a room nearby and she knows the army will soon make a thorough search of her chamber as well. Her ring glows, and she rests a hand on her heart, relieved to know her true love still lives. For now.

With a new resolve, she dumps out the contents of a drawer, glancing behind her every few seconds. The soldiers are coming.

She removes strands of golden hair from a brush and rolls them into a ball in her palm, then retrieves vials from a drawer, opening some, tossing others aside. From each opened jar, a drop or two of liquid or a pinch of powder falls into her hand where she massages it into the hair. Satisfied, she rips a gem off her jeweled dress, dumps everything into a pestle bowl, and crushes it all together with a mortar.

The noises become louder and panic makes her throat feel thick. She opens her mouth, chanting—no words, just notes and sounds—tones of protection. The gems in her ring glow more brilliantly each time she passes her hand over the mixture. A smile lights her eyes. She will succeed.

The wooden door splinters into pieces, but the woman still sings. The room fills with men. One snatches the bowl and dumps the contents into the chamber pot, a sneer turning his eyes coal black. The glowing stops and the woman cries, anguished. The spell is broken.

The sneering man grabs her around the waist and she shrieks, lashing out with all her strength. She's no match for him, and he carries her away.

As the plane touches down, I jerk awake and wipe a bead of cold sweat off my forehead. My fingers brush Kye's cheek. The blanket is on the ground and we've curled into each other to compensate.

He smiles, his face unguarded, intimate. "Good morning. How'd you sleep?"

"All right, I guess. Better than the bench." I stretch my back, peering out the window at the jumble of towering buildings. "So that's New York."

"Yep." he says. "Been a while since I was here."

"Never for me." My excitement builds. "Will we have time for sightseeing?"

Kye runs both hands through his hair. "Maybe."

After we have our luggage and are standing in line for a cab, Kye makes a call on his cell phone. "It's me," he says. "Did you talk to him? Well, it's kind of late to warn him now. We're just leaving the airport. Listen, we need to talk about Juri—"

I deduce he's probably talking to Mr. Akers. A skycap holds the door as we climb in a cab. Kye shakes the man's hand, still on the phone, but I don't miss the subtle transfer of money.

"How long before he recovers? I'm afraid he'll follow us here. He thinks Abby has—yeah. We need to talk about what we saw in his office, too. Listen, we're in a cab. I'll check back later tonight. See what else you can find." He hangs up and scrolls through his contact list to give the driver an address. "I love technology."

A thick layer of brownish-yellow smog hovers over the buildings, darkening the sky as we drive into the city. When I can't stand the silence anymore, I ask Kye to tell me more about Theron and Raina.

Kye clears his throat. "Where did I leave off?"

"The prince was in love."

"Right." He takes my hand and traces along each finger and into my palm. "So, they planned a royal wedding. The biggest celebration Dryden ever had. The whole kingdom was invited to a three-day party."

"Sounds amazing." I have a momentary flash of guilt over missing Rose's birthday bash.

"Theron and Raina hid in their room after the ceremony. Isleen made them come out and mingle every once in a while, but they really wanted to be alone.

"On the third day, there was a fight in the ballroom. Theron went to check things out and discovered that the castle was under attack. Everyone at the party was either dead or injured or gone. Theron ran around calling for Healers and searching for his parents.

"He found his father's body in the courtyard. The head was about fifty feet from the rest of him."

"Ew." I shudder. "TMI."

"Sorry. So, Theron searched the castle for his mother and Rhys, but there was no trace of them anywhere."

My brow furrows as the somewhat familiar story takes an unexpected turn. "Are you sure that's how it happened?"

"This is the story as I read it. Well, okay, not in those exact words, but yeah. Why?"

I bite my thumbnail. "I dreamed this—or at least I think I did. But it was different."

"Shall I tell you the rest? Or do you already know how it ends?"

"No, that's as far as I got." I sigh. "Please finish."

"The guards cleaned up the mess and buried the dead, and Theron sent groups of knights to search for any trace of Isleen or Rhys."

"What about Raina?" I can't forget how she screamed as the man carried her off. "What happened to her?"

"Well," Kye says, his voice measured. "When Theron went to tell Raina what was happening, she was gone. The only signs of struggle were a bowl of herbs spilled on the floor and a double-heart-shaped burn in the wood. Theron found her ring under the bed.

"The thing is Theron and Raina never told anyone about their time in the forest. No one knew how they fell in love, but when Theron ordered Raina's ring, he asked for two heart-cut diamonds, one blue and one white. Individually, each stone was highly powerful, but together, they held the unbreakable power of true love."

Kye rubs my ring with his thumb. "If these are real diamonds, there's a really good chance this is it. We both know it has power."

"Yes." My eyes widen as realization sinks in. I knew the story would end this way. The movie of it has been playing in my head in bits and pieces for weeks. "Raina disappeared."

"Theron searched for a long time but never found a trace of her. A few years later, Theron returned to Dryden, heartbroken, and swore he'd never love again."

"So, so sad." A hard ball of grief forms in the pit of my stomach. "What did he do with the ring?"

"That's where the legend gets hazy. No one knows for sure because it was never seen again. Or so we all thought." He flashes a grin at me. "I bet your gram knew something about that."

I return his smile, let my eyelids flutter flirtatiously, and sit up as the cab pulls to a stop. "Probably."

The streets here are much less crowded than those in the heart of the city, and though there's still a hungry quality to the air, this neighborhood feels more peaceful. Kye pays with cash and grasps my hand, striding to a tall red door to ring the bell.

A voice, deep and male, crackles in a tiny speaker, "Yes? Can I help you?"

Kye grins, looking younger than I've ever seen him look. "I sure hope so, Dad. If not we're in a mess of trouble."

NINETEEN

Raina and Abby

E oin Murphy's home isn't what I expected. When Kye first told me his father lives in New York City, I envisioned a man who wears designer suits and rides around in a limousine. I imagined him living in a sprawling penthouse apartment in a fancy high-rise building. A tall, blond demi-god who is classy and loaded—because who else could have fathered Kye, and what else would explain his lack of worry over the cost of this trip?

Given my background, and considering my current circumstances, I thought at this point that nothing could surprise me. Of course, I thought wrong.

We climb three flights of stairs because the elevator is broken, and knock on the door. The man who answers has an over-large nose and straight, sandy hair that sticks up in the back. He is slightly shorter than Kye and wearing a rumpled T-shirt and crooked basketball shorts. "My boy!" He throws his arms around Kye. "What are you doing here? You're supposed to be going to school in Jackson. Or has that changed since last month?"

"No, I'm still there. It's spring break." Kye pounds his father on the back, affectionately returning his father's embrace before pulling back to make introductions. "Dad, this is Abby."

"Good to meet you, Abby. Welcome." Eoin grasps my offered hand.

"Thank you. You're not what I expected."

He chuckles. "Well, I didn't expect either of you. But come in, come in."

He moves some things off the sofa, making a place for us to sit, and offers us herbal tea. Kye and I are situated so close together our elbows touch every time we move. The space Eoin has cleared is the only available seating I can see. We're surrounded by stacks of books and papers, odds and ends, and interesting-looking trinkets that cover all available surfaces, including the bookshelves lining the walls. Most of the books appear old, possibly even antique.

This may be a home, but it feels more like a box to me. The kitchen and living area are basically the same room, with a short counter running between carpet and tile. I haven't seen the bedroom, but I imagine it's the size of my closet at home.

Kye gestures to the books lying open on the table. "It's research. Dad works best in an environment of controlled chaos. The funny thing is he knows exactly where to find everything he needs whenever he needs it."

Eoin clears a space on the counter and sets down three mugs of steaming tea, a package of bagels and a tub of cream cheese. "Sorry, it's the best I can offer on such short notice." He glances around with a shrug. "If I'd known you were coming, I'd have cleaned up a bit."

My stomach rumbles as I help myself to a bagel. "This is perfect. Thanks."

"We haven't eaten since the airport in Las Vegas, and that was hours ago." Kye opens the cream cheese tub and hands me a butter knife. "Sorry about the communication breakdown, Dad. Lan was supposed to call you."

Mumbling about needing to find his smart phone, Eoin takes his mug to the table. He stacks the books and papers together and sets them on the floor to make a place for us. I sit at the table across from Eoin. Kye sits next to me, chewing vigorously and gulping his tea.

Kye's dad watches us down our snacks, patiently keeping his questions to himself until we're finished. "If you're still hungry, we can order pizza. Or go out to a restaurant, if you prefer."

Kye leans back in his chair, glancing at me. "Maybe in a bit."

Eoin clears his throat. "So ... don't take this the wrong way, because, I love you, son. But what are you doing here?"

"You really need to find your phone, Dad," Kye says. "A lot has happened in the last few days. The Elen are looking for the Arawn Keys."

Eoin frowns at the mention of the Keys. "That's nothing new. They've always been looking."

"Yeah, well, they must be getting closer, because now the Fae are involved, which drags Abby and me into the search." At his father's look of confusion, Kye shakes his head and continues, "Long story. Lan sent us to see Juri in Las Vegas—not a friendly guy, by the way—and he showed us that Cairn Elen thing."

I draw in a deep breath as Kye tells him the full story, shivering at the memory of what has transpired in the last forty-eight hours. Kye notices and takes my hand, lacing our fingers together and absently stroking my thumb with his. Considering that Eoin and I have only just met, Kye's off-handed yet blatant gesture of possession makes me self-conscious. I have to remind myself we have much bigger worries than whether or not our parents approve of our relationship. *If that's what this is.*

"Anyway," Kye continues, "we could really use your help, Dad." He holds my hand up so Eoin can see my ring. "What do you think of this?"

Eoin's mouth falls open. Here's an expression I recognize. He lets out a slow breath. "Where did you get that, Abby?"

I swallow, fighting the urge to hide. "It was my grandmother's. I inherited it when she ... died."

"Do you know where she got it?"

I shake my head because I really don't have a clue.

Eoin studies me. "Are you sure?"

"Yes, I'm sure." I untangle my hand from Kye's and fold my arms to hide my hands.

Eoin rubs his knuckles over his lips and exchanges a glance with Kye. "Okay. Am I correct in assuming your gram was Gifted with a special ability?"

"She was a Healer."

"And you?"

I hesitate. After a lifetime of keeping my Gifts a secret, I'm suddenly telling a whole lot of people.

"Abby has two Gifts," Kye says. "She's a Healer like her gram, and she has Sight as well."

Heat creeps up my cheeks as I stare at the scarred wooden surface of the table, thinking of Gram and Eric and how miserably I've failed to ever Heal anyone. Maybe I don't have two Gifts. Maybe I only have Sight and we just thought I was a Healer because I picked up a natural instinct from living with Gram. Maybe if I stop telling myself I can Heal people, I won't feel that sick dread that comes whenever I think of my future. Maybe if I accept it now, I'll be able to focus on the things I can do instead of the one thing I can't. "We might be wrong about my Healing ability," I mumble. "Gram wanted it to be true. She said it was true, but it's never actually worked. I've never been able to Heal anyone. Maybe Gram was wrong."

Kye rubs my shoulder. "Don't say that, Abby. I've seen you. I saw you work on Eric."

"Who consequently could have died, and me along with him." I let out a shaky breath, leaning away from Kye. "I've patched cuts and scrapes, and once saved a dog—probably a total fluke. It's possible that anyone with the right herbs and healing crystals could've done all that."

While Kye stares at me in stunned silence, Eoin clears his throat. "Tell me about your Sight."

I comply, and as I talk, I mentally draw a line between my visions from the past and my life in the present. What if Kye is that boy? Maybe he's the one I've been searching for all this time. It would explain our connection, that instant recognition. It would explain why touching him feels so right, so familiar. It would explain everything. When I'm finished, Eoin runs a hand through his hair, the same way Kye sometimes does. "How old are you?"

"Seventeen." I lean my elbows on the table, reeling with my newest realization. *Soul mates?*

Kye and Eoin exchange another surreptitious look.

"What?" I snap. "What are you not telling me?"

"Nothing." Kye sounds exasperated. "I already told you I think your ring might be the one Theron gave Raina. I just—what if it was more than a wedding ring? What if it's one of the Arawn Keys?" He looks again at his father. "Is that possible?"

"Entirely." Eoin picks up a book, opens it on the table, and flips through the pages until settling on a specific one. He turns the book around, pushes it toward me, and taps the faded script. "Take a look at that."

The sketch is faded and the artwork questionable, but the design is eerily similar. I hold out my hand to compare. "It could be, I guess."

Eoin's fingers graze the page. "There's no proof, but if what Kye says is true—if what I see in you with my own eyes is accurate—then yes, I'm guessing that is the same ring."

"What does that mean? What you see in me?"

"I see that your soul is older than your body. You have an unusual depth of compassion, and trust, and ... something else, but I can't find the words to describe it." Eoin takes the book back and turns the page. "How much Gifted history do you know?"

"Kye told me about the King and Queen of Dryden, and the story of Theron and Raina."

Eoin nods in approval. "Good place to start."

"He said Raina's ring has the power of true love." I lift my hand so the stones catch the sunlight and reflect sparkles of color all over the walls.

"May I?" Eoin asks. Nodding, I drop it in his outstretched palm.

"Wow, that was easy." Kye jokes. "As I recall, you pounded on me when I first looked at it."

I glare at Kye, annoyed. "He asked nicely. You just took it. I hardly knew you at the time. How was I supposed to know you'd give it back without throwing it across the parking lot?"

"Well. I have been known to throw things from time to time." Kye's grin infuriates me, so I shove him away and accept my ring back from Eoin, who returns to the pages in his book.

"When the Ring of the Princess was lost is unclear," he says. "After Raina disappeared, rumor circulated that Theron kept it on a chain around his neck, holding on to the hope that he would someday find his princess and return it to her. But after Theron died, the ring was never recorded as having been seen again in all the history of Dryden."

He taps another section of text and reads aloud. "Theron, heir to Dryden's throne, was many years in his searching. Neither Queen Isleen nor Captain Rhys ever returned. The kingdom fell into disarray. Crime became rampant, and the peaceful lives in which the community had lived crumbled without a leader to enforce the laws. Rumors spread, suggesting that Rhys and the queen had run off together. Theron's parentage was called into question. The name of the beloved Isleen was defiled and defamed.

"While Theron was abroad searching for his family, his cousin, the Duke of Nairn, came to visit and, finding the palace devoid of the royal family, immediately laid claim to the throne.

"He took control, cleaned up the city, and restored order within the realm. But Nairn was not meant to be King of Dryden. He ruled it with an iron hand, ruthless in punishment, raw in temper, and hateful in vengeance."

I shudder, strangely reminded of Hitler.

Eoin continues reading. "Nairn fell in love with power and prepared to do battle with Theron for the throne. But when Theron returned, weakened by his shattered heart, he was in no condition to reclaim the throne. For forty days, he locked himself in the room he had shared with Raina, refusing even an audience with the cousin who had ruled in his absence. When he emerged, it was with plans to build a memorial fountain in honor of his missing family, after which he would reclaim the throne and resume his duties as King of Dryden."

"That poor guy," I murmur. Suffocating sorrow hangs in the room. "First he loses his parents, then his true love, and then he has to fight for his kingdom."

"Theron never actually fought, though," Kye says. "Didn't he disappear after the memorial was dedicated?"

"Yes. He was presumed dead. Then the Duke ran the kingdom into the ground." Eoin turns the page, pauses in unmasked surprise, but then shakes his head and picks up the book to pace with it. "Prince Theron's disappearance was the catalyst for the people of Dryden. They had lived in fear of Duke Nairn, waiting and hoping for the return of the royal family, but Nairn reclaimed the throne the day after Theron's memorial service. His first order of business—after crowning himself king—was to destroy the fountain and call in an army of demon guards to enforce his new laws. Eventually, the people rose up against Nairn and the demons, and the kingdom went to war ..." Eoin's voice trails off, and he stares out the window.

"Dad?" Kye takes the book from his father. "Are you okay?"

Eoin shakes himself. "Yes, sorry. Just imagining what a horrible battle it must've been. A lot of innocent people died. When the war was over, the destruction was so complete that the city had literally disappeared. It sank into the ground, and was never seen again."

I draw a pattern on the table with my fingernail. "It doesn't seem possible an entire city could sink like that."

"Well." Eoin picks up another book. Toward the end, he stops turning pages. "Listen to this:

'By magic did the kingdom fall.
Below the earth its demons sleep.
The Morrigana did forestall
The fate that makes all mortals weep.

141

The Arawn Keys have sealed the door
The keepers spreading far and wide
Until the day the Keys restore
The powers that are locked inside.'"

The book thuds onto the table as Eoin sets it down. The room is silent as we all work out the poem in our heads. I break the silence. "The city sank by magic, then?"

"You could call it that." Eoin runs his fingers through his hair again. Kye does it too, and I hide my smile. "The magic—or powers—of three goddesses. Badb, Macha, and Morrigan, otherwise known as the Morrigana or the Great Queens. The ladies had a special attachment to Dryden, and I think that was their way of preserving what little was left of it."

"They sank an entire city?" My head throbs with incredulity. "Why?"

"It wouldn't have been the first time in history, would it?" Eoin clears his throat. "From my studies, I gather that the city and all beings living there—mostly demons at that point—were sealed behind a door. Val and I figure it's a sort of tomb."

"A tomb containing an enormous cache of power." Kye lays the book on the floor at his feet. "Evil power."

"Don't worry." Eoin pats my hand. "They can't get out by themselves. The tomb is made of poisonous stone, so their Gifts are rendered useless. For now."

"And my—Raina's ring is one of the Keys." I'm starting to believe Eoin's theory about my ring might be right. "But why would Juri want to open the door?"

Kye's face lights up. "I bet he's after treasure."

Eoin shakes his head in disgust. "That's probably not far from the mark. Dryden was a wealthy kingdom. A handful of Gifted people escaped before the city sank, and they helped seal the tomb by combining their powers with the magic of the jewels that would become known as the Arawn Keys. By doing so, the people bound their powers, unknowingly giving up the bulk of their special abilities.

"Theron was not one of the sealers—we know this for certain. But that ring of yours must have been one of the sealing Keys. Or that's my theory."

A sliver of sunshine creeps through the closed curtain and I follow it to the window to look out at the street. "But there's no real proof. No one knows for sure if this was really Raina's ring."

With his hands on my waist, Kye draws me backward into his arms. "I know it," he whispers, holding me tight. "Whoever carried that ring out of the city helped close the demons behind the door. Whoever it was must be related to you."

Eoin joins us at the window, staring at something in the distance. "Everything I've read indicates that the only people powerful enough to seal an entire city underground were members of the royal family, yet they were all missing at the time. There's a big piece of this puzzle still absent and I'm running out of places to look."

I lean the back of my head against Kye's chest, still surprised at how comfortable we are together. "Could one of my ancestors have stolen it?"

Eoin shakes his head. "It's not likely."

"Why not?"

Eoin turns to stare at me—hard. "Your eyes. And your abilities. It's entirely possible you could be a blood relation to the royal family—a direct descendant, even. It would explain where your grandmother got the ring." He picks up a book and hands it to me, pointing out a full-page portrait of a young woman. She has high cheekbones, a slightly crooked chin, and waves of auburn hair that frame her porcelain skin and bring out the roses in her lips. There are more similarities, but none so striking as her eyes, which are round and full, a mix of blue, green, and gray.

They're my eyes. My face, my crooked chin. If I didn't know better, I would swear the portrait in Eoin's antique book is a picture of me.

A *small figure creeps through the forest, pulling her cloak more tightly around her shoulders to keep out the chilly winter air. In the shadow cast by a grove of trees, she waits, knowing he will come. Sooner or later, they'll bring him here, and then she'll save him. A cough shakes her body—the cough of the dying—and the hood of the cloak slides down to reveal her face.*

She is me.

TWENTY

Run

The flash of vision leaves me trembling. I droop to the floor, holding the book to my chest. "Princess Raina?"

Kye searches my face apprehensively as if trying to decide what to do and ends up in the kitchen searching through cupboards.

Eoin sits across from me on the floor. "Yes."

My fingertips trace Raina's face over and over again until the look on Eoin's face makes me stop. These pages are hundreds of years old. Gently, I set the open book on the table. "Sorry, I can't help but touch. It's eerie."

He pats my knee. "Quite all right, honey. They're copies. Very old copies, but not originals. And, if my theory is correct, they belong as much to you as to me. I may be the historian, but the story belongs to your family."

"Dad, you're the historian because you're good at finding information." Kye returns from the kitchen and hands me a glass of water. "Here you go."

I drink deeply, soothing my dry throat. "Thanks."

"You're pale. Doing okay?" He sits next to me, frowning at his father.

I nod at Kye then turn back to Eoin. "Why would these books belong to me?"

"Still going in the vein of you being a direct descendant of the princess—and honestly, given that you look so much like her, I'm left with little doubt about the truth of it—that would technically make you heir to the throne of Dryden. It's not much of a throne anymore, but if it were ever restored, we could refer to you as Princess Abby, making these books—and a number of other things—officially yours to inherit."

Eoin's words stun me into silence for about ten seconds. He's so serious. So sure. I'm gluing thoughts together, trying to make them stick, and then laughing because it's the funniest thing I've ever heard. I can't help it. Me? A princess? Kye's befuddled expression makes me laugh harder. Eoin's joking. He must be joking.

"Of course you think it's funny," he says. "But, Abby, this is a serious situation. You could be in a lot of danger."

Part of me, somewhere deep down, knows he's right, and I make an attempt to stop. But the idea sounds so absurd, so irrelevant to my current life, that I can't help it. Eoin's stern look gets me going again until I'm laughing so hard I can barely breathe, bending over, kneeling, then lying on the floor. Kye watches me for a while, trying to keep a straight face—for his father's sake, I think—but after a few seconds, he's rolling on the floor too, one arm around me while the other holds his stomach.

By the time I regain my composure enough to sit up, Eoin has left the room.

Kye leans against the couch, his breath still hitching every time our eyes meet. "I'm sorry. I don't mean to laugh. You'd make an awesome princess. I don't know why it feels so funny right now."

"Are you kidding?" I drag myself to the table where the book lays open. "What girl doesn't dream of being someone's long-lost princess? That's what makes fairy tales so popular. The thing no one expects is discovering that their so-called kingdom has been overrun by demons and buried underground." Another giggle bubbles up in my chest.

Kye stares at the picture, grinning. "Yeah, that sounds about right, doesn't it? Just our luck."

"Ahem." Eoin returns with a piece of paper in his hand, looking resigned. "Are you finished? Because we really should talk about the Keys."

I bite my lip, feeling better than I have in days, and spread my arms wide. "Lay it on me, Dad."

Finally, Eoin smiles. "That's a pleasure I don't have very often, being called Dad. If you kids can stay for a day or two, I'd love to play the role. I could show you around the city, buy you dinner, take you to a show ..."

There's a new light in his eyes, and I want to feed it. I want to get to know him better because I love the idea of sharing Kye's dad for a few days. It's been so long since I had my own. "I vote we go to the top of the Empire State building."

Kye swipes his hand over a dust-covered end table, glancing around. "Where will you put us?"

"Good question." Eoin scratches his head, surveying his tiny apartment. "We'll figure it out. I suppose Abby can have my bed, while we men camp out in here on the floor." He waves the paper and hands it to me. "You've distracted me again."

"What is this?" On one side it looks like a blueprint, but the other side is filled with symbols and writing in another language.

"Something I would never, ever be showing you under other circumstances." He resumes his pacing. "If Abby's ring is in fact one of the Arawn Keys, it's the only Key for which I haven't found much data in all my years of research.

"I've uncovered the locations of two, and have actually held one—besides Abby's—in my hands. Years back, some friends of mine went looking for the Keys. In hindsight, I'm not sure why—because using them could only cause destruction. But they were young and stupid and ..." his voice trails off as he stares out the window. "That was a long time ago. It turned out badly."

"Juri's dagger?" Kye asks.

"Yes. It wasn't a good idea to begin with." Eoin rubs his chin. "Anyway, to my knowledge, there are a total of four Keys. About a month ago, while combing through some texts, I came across newer information that makes me believe the Pendant of Sadira is here in the city ..."

Eoin is still talking, but his words become a distant buzz as a vision slams into me like a tornado-force wind.

Pale violet eyes are reflected in the window of a cab, driving past rows of tall buildings. A hacking cough drowns out the heavy metal song playing in the background. A cell phone rings.

"Did you find the address?" asks a raspy voice. "Good. I'm nearly there." Another cough. "Don't worry, I'll bring the ring. Remember our deal. You get the ring, and I get Raina."

"Abby!" Kye shakes me. "What? What's wrong?" He has me cradled in his lap on the sofa, though I have no memory of moving there.

I sit up, shaky, my eyes darting to Eoin. "He's here. He's coming for me. For my ring. They know where we are."

Kye tenses, his voice alarmed. "Who? Who's coming?"

I shake my head as I push myself up to stand, looking around for my duffle bag. "I don't know. Someone." Another flash—eyes reflected in glass. "The guy from Yellowstone."

"Boone?"

"Yes."

"Are you sure?" Eoin hurries to the window and looks down at the street.

"I'm sure." I shove my arms into my coat sleeves and strap on my duffle bag. Kye frowns and trades me for his backpack, claiming it's lighter and we'll be faster this way. I shrug and sling his pack over my shoulders.

Kye zips his coat and turns to Eoin with a look of regret. "Sorry, Dad. Wish we could stay."

Eoin slips the paper inside Kye's backpack. "Maybe you should wait to retrieve the Key. Come back in a month or so?"

Kye shakes his head. "We don't have a month. Besides, if we leave New York without that Key now, we risk losing it to the Dark

Ones. They must know that's why we're here. We can't take the risk."

Eoin taps his head with his fingertips. "You're right. Be careful."

"You aren't coming with us?" A knot sinks into the pit of my stomach. I had so hoped to have a parent around to be responsible.

"No. I need to preserve the records. I'll catch up with you in a few days." Eoin wraps his arms around me. "Be safe."

I hug him back. "We will. Thanks for everything."

"My pleasure, Princess Abby." He lets go of me and says goodbye to Kye. After a few murmured words and manly pats on backs, they pull apart, and Kye and I race down the stairs and burst onto the street. On the run for the second time in two days.

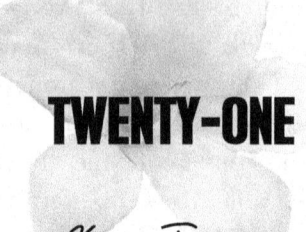

TWENTY-ONE

King Tynan

As the door closes behind us, a cab stops at the curb and Boone gets out, a frighteningly large smile spreading when he sees me. My heart thuds in fear. There's someone else with him, but I can't tear my gaze away from those violet eyes. Kye drags me around the corner and we take off down the alley.

"Don't let them get away!" Boone yells. Shouts trail after us, combined with footsteps pounding on the pavement, but I don't look back. Kye's forward momentum won't let me. He has my hand, and his legs are longer than mine. Adrenaline is the only way I can keep up with his speed.

The cold air stings my throat and burns in my chest, but I don't dare slow down. We leave the alley and blow through an intersection where—luckily—the light is green. We run down another alley, onto another street, around corners, past buildings and cars. My feet move methodically, heavier and heavier with each step as I burn through the bagel I ate earlier. My heart thumps so hard I wonder how it doesn't break through my skin. The footsteps trailing us have faded significantly.

"Kye," I wheeze. "Are they still behind us?"

His breathing is as labored as mine. "I think so."

"I can't ... go anymore." Afraid to stop completely, I slow my pace because I can't keep up any longer. Every part of me hurts.

"Come on, princess," he urges, turning down another alley. "Just a little farther."

I remember him saying something like that in Vegas, too. "Where are we going?"

"To get—" He takes a breath as we dodge a stream of people flowing out of the subway exit. "To get the other Key."

"Where?"

"Liberty Island." Kye slows down too, his eyes wild and urgent. "Come on, princess, we have to keep moving."

"Don't call me princess." I take a detour down the stairs to the subway. "I'm sick of running. Let's ride."

Kye closes his mouth on what appears to be a protest and smiles instead. "Good idea." He follows me through the station and stands guard as I buy two tickets to wherever, and then we board the train.

As the doors close and we pick up speed, I notice him looking over his shoulder. "Do you think they saw us?" I ask.

"If they did, they won't know what train we're on or where we're headed." We squeeze together in the crowded car, holding on to a rail in the middle for balance. It's hot in here, muggy. Claustrophobic.

"Boone wasn't alone," Kye murmurs. "Did you get a look at the other guys?"

I shake my head. "I was too scared. Did you?"

"Not a good one. Too busy running."

"Do you meet guys like Boone often?" We're inches apart.

"Here and there," he murmurs. His eyes drift to my lips and he leans forward. *Finally.* I sigh against his lips and move into him as his hand covers mine on the pole. Then someone behind us loses his balance and tumbles onto the floor, nearly pulling me down with him. "Watch it!" Kye catches me, keeps me on my feet and holds me close.

I want him to kiss me like I want air to breathe.

His lips find mine, an explosion of heat and light that sends ripples of sensation across my skin and leaves my insides burning. His tongue glides over my teeth, dips in to find its mate as his smooth lips keep mine busy, their taste evocatively familiar. *This.* This is that thing I've searched for. Kye is that person who has haunted me for so long. Whatever lingering doubts I had disappear one by one as we lose ourselves in each other, knowing there's nowhere we can run right now.

We've only been riding for a few minutes when a bright flash startles us apart and a lilting voice says, "Don't you two make the prettiest picture? All hearts and love and big hopes for happily ever after."

Kye's body goes rigid. He pulls me into his chest and answers over the top of my head. "Mind your business."

"Now, now. That's no way to talk to your brother." The voice has a hard edge to it. "Theron."

"What did you call me?" Tension radiates off Kye as he maneuvers me behind him. "Should I know you?"

I shiver, feeling the beginnings of something—a vision that wants in. I shake it off, determined to stay in the present. Now is not the time to black out.

"You did. Once upon a time." Dark, piercing eyes sparkle under a fringe of jet-black hair. His skin is pale, his face all angles and lines to go with his accent. He stands around six feet tall and isn't much older than me and Kye.

Kye looks confused. "I did?"

The stranger smiles and my breath catches. Everything in me feels drawn—urges me to go to him. And I thought Kye was good-looking. "You really don't remember, do you?" he says.

Kye shakes his head and reaches back to grab my wrist.

"Another life. Another time. Another world." He focuses on me. "Come, Raina. Come to me now." That voice is compelling, hypnotic. Every muscle in my body strains toward him and my thoughts center only on that beautiful sound. I want to push Kye aside and run to the mysterious stranger—but Kye won't let go. He rubs my arm with his free hand. "Stay with me, Abby. Don't let him trick you."

This guy is good. I shake my head to clear it. "Who are you?"

He folds his arms. "Come now, little princess. Don't tell me you've forgotten me too." He looks meaningfully at Kye's hands, holding me in place. "I can see you've missed me."

The vision swims again, stronger this time, and I can't force it away. I tighten my hand on the pole and feel my eyes roll up.

The woman's knees are pulled up to her chest as she alternates between sobbing and screaming. Shaking in fear, she raises her eyes at the sound of footsteps. Glowing veins of red mineral streak the black stone walls, the only light by which to see. A heavy metal door clangs open.

The wrinkled man who enters has only wisps of gray hair hanging to the nape of his neck. A bronze cloak wraps around and billows behind him, shimmering in the unnatural light. A jeweled crystal dagger rests in a sheath at his waist, and around his neck is a white stone shot through with the same red mineral that shimmers in the walls.

The woman huddles on the dirt floor, careful to stay clear of the glowing walls as tears wear rivulets through the dust on her cheeks. "Please," she begs. "Please. She's dying. I'm dying. Let me go. I can't do what you want. I can't."

With great effort, she lifts her head to meet the eyes of her captor. "Have mercy."

"Mercy? You mean the same mercy Damon showed me?"

"No!" she cries, her voice feeble. "The kind of mercy I know you have in you. Or at least you did once. Be a man, Tynan. Keeping me captive is not the answer. Killing me and my child won't solve anything."

His chuckle sounds morbid. "No. No, you're right about that. I have other plans for you and your ..." he grimaces as she sits straighter, her abdomen bulging, "offspring."

More shaking, more tears. "Please let me out of here. This room is killing us. Both of us."

"Soon," he says. "Once my curse has fully developed, you will all be free. Free from my prison, free to kill each other with your very presence. Free to die. Over and over and over again."

The train jerks me out of the vision. "Come on, Abby, don't do this to me now." Kye's arm around my waist keeps me upright, though my head lolls on his shoulder. The stranger advances on us. "Babe, snap out of it."

My feet find solid ground and I lift my head. My eyes struggle to focus on our pursuer. A crystal dangles from his neck—white with red streaks through it. "Who are you?" I demand, my voice weak.

"That's it. Come back to me."

Come back to me ... come back to me ... come back to me.

A knight on a black stallion gallops across a field, his face handsome and strong yet twisted with tormented grief. The stallion grinds to a halt and the knight falls to his knees to pray. "Come back to me, Raina. Please. Oh please, goddesses Morrigana, I beg of you, bring her back to me."

"Abby!" Kye's voice is now rife with panic. "Help me out here."

I'm falling, pushed into the arms of another passenger as Kye readies himself to fight. The passenger looks at me in disgust and shoves me to my feet. "What's your problem, lady?" He doesn't seem to notice the evil presence advancing on Kye.

"Sorry." My hand feels warm, and a surge of power ripples down my spine. I clutch Kye's shoulder and the diamonds in my ring radiate with a soft, powerful glow. The bad guy flickers like a TV when the cable is about to go out. He roars a string of curses.

"This isn't over, Theron. I will have those Keys! After four centuries, my power will be restored." His image fades and then, with a flash of light, he's gone.

The other passengers seem oblivious to the spectacle, and I wonder how that's possible. Having others not notice what's going on isn't a first for me, but Akers isn't here this time.

Kye picks up our baggage, his eyes mirroring first fury, then despair. "You okay?"

"Yes." I hesitate. "Are you?"

He shakes his head as the train slows to a stop and the doors open. "I can't do this. I don't know how to do this." We move with the flow of passengers onto the platform and up the stairs.

"What can't you do?"

"I can't save the world from them, Abby. And neither can you. We're doomed to fail."

"Wait." I catch his arm, stopping him halfway up. "What are you talking about?"

"Tynan!"

"Who's Tynan?"

"The guy on the train."

A lady bumps into me and we start walking again. "You mean the ghost-guy?"

"That was no ghost. I don't know what it was, but you have to be dead to become a ghost, and I'm pretty sure Tynan is very much alive."

"So how did he get in the train with us? And then out again?" I shade my eyes as we step into the too-bright sunlight. "It doesn't make any sense. If he wasn't really there, how bad could he hurt us?"

"He can always hurt us, and I don't want you to think otherwise." Kye shades his eyes too and peers around at the classic-style buildings with the beautiful large windows and artful spires. We're on the east side of the city, near the park. "The fact that he's able to appear like that a thousand miles away from where he's trapped—that's a bad sign. His powers are stronger than ever, which means someone's helping him from the outside, feeding him or sacrificing for him—I don't know. Something. There's no telling what he can do."

"Oh."

"Also," Kye continues, starting down the street, "never underestimate the power of the Dark Prince of the Elen. He has more Gifts than we'll ever know."

"But he left us alone just now. Why?"

"I don't know. It bothers me. It shouldn't have been so easy. Something's up."

I stop to wave my arms at a cab. It doesn't stop. Neither does the next one.

Kye keeps walking, but when he realizes I'm not with him, he turns around. "What are you doing?"

I roll my eyes. Isn't it obvious? "Hailing a cab."

"You're doing it wrong."

Aiming a scowl at him, I drop my hands to my hips. "Then you do it!"

He holds out an arm, whistles, and a car stops against the curb. "Where to?" the driver asks.

"Battery Park," Kye says. Looks like I'll get some sightseeing in after all.

In a low voice I ask, "Why are you suddenly so sure we're going to fail?"

Kye leans against the seat and closes his eyes in exhaustion. "Didn't you hear what he said?"

"About him getting the Keys and having his powers restored? Yes, I did."

He opens his eyes. "No, not that."

I start to brush the hair off his forehead, but he captures my hand and presses it to his cheek. "What are you talking about?"

"We're cursed, Abby. You and me. I didn't put it together until he said it, but I should have. It only makes sense. The missing piece of our puzzle. You'll be the great love of my life, and I'll be the great love of yours—and in a few months, we'll be forced to separate forever."

He's talking gibberish. With a touch as soft as a breeze, I trace the lines of his face. "You're exhausted and you're hungry and you're hearing things. Tynan didn't say anything about a curse."

"No, he didn't." He sighs, closing his eyes again as my finger traces his features. "It's part of the story you haven't heard yet, and one I would never, ever guess applies to me." He opens his eyes again, an ancient agony in their depths. "I can't save you from this, and I'm sorry. I'm so, so sorry."

His throat is working, and I watch—baffled. "Kye, what are you talking about? I didn't hear your dad or Tynan say anything about a curse."

"No. But, Abby, Tynan called me Theron."

TWENTY-TWO

Mermaids and Symbols

"Yes, and he called me Raina," I say. "He's obviously confused."

Kye squeezes his eyes closed and takes a deep breath. "You know what? We have enough to worry about. Right now, we should concentrate on tracking down that Key."

Part of me wants to pursue his thoughts, find out why he looks so devastated, but instinct tells me to let it drop for now. He's right about needing to focus on the task at hand. Finding the remaining Keys is starting to feel like a race.

The cab drops us at Battery Park, where Kye gets us tickets for the next ferry. We have thirty minutes to wander the park, hunched against a chilly breeze that's blowing off the river. We have our picture taken with a person dressed as the Statue of Liberty, and I buy two "I ♥ NY" T-shirts. It would be a crime to leave here without one for each of us, and I want tangible proof of where we've been, what we've done. Something to prove that this experience was real. We run onto the ferry, laughing, and elbow our way to the front, dropping our bags at our feet.

Kye stands behind me, arms braced on either side of my waist, hands on the rails. The wind sends my hair flying, so he catches it and tucks it in the neck of my coat, leaning his chin on my shoulder while we watch the great American icon growing larger. My eyes drift closed as I breathe in the salty air. Kye breathes too, but his nose is in my neck. I cringe, realizing I haven't showered since yesterday. He doesn't seem to mind, though, and replaces his nose with his lips for a too-short second.

Before long, I'm aware of an eerie ringing that sounds almost melodic. At first I think it's a police siren, but then the pitch changes. It reminds me of the faerie song we heard in the forest.

"What is that?"

"There must be mermaids in the river."

We're surrounded by people, but none of them act like they hear anything unusual. On our right, something resembling a fin catches my eye. "Look."

Kye grins. "Shall we see if they'll wave?"

"Is that a good idea?"

His breath is warm on my neck. "Why wouldn't it be?"

"All these people. Don't you think it would be kind of a big deal if the general public were to see a mermaid? The story would be headlined for weeks."

He presses closer, wrapping his arms around my middle. "Unless they've eaten faery food or have a specialized Gift, they can't see her. Only those who possess certain magics can see magical creatures—well, most of them. Our eyes have an extra sensitivity that others don't." He pauses, and I think about Finn stopping the bus in Yellowstone. How no one noticed him. I thought that was Mr. Akers's doing, but maybe not.

Kye cups his hands around his mouth and makes a strange, deep-throated noise to answer the mermaid's song. Something blue bobs in the water. I don't realize it's a head until a long, thin arm sticks up and waves with webbed fingers. Bright blue hair flies wildly around a pointy, angular face. Her skin is a shade lighter than her hair and blotchy with what looks like scales. Sharp, white teeth gleam as the sun breaks through the clouds and a beam illuminates her. If Kye hadn't told me what I was looking at, I would chalk it up to being a trick of the light.

Kye waves back and calls out again. The head bobs, then the mermaid slips under. With a puff of steam in the cold air, she pops back up, jumps like a dolphin, and dives head-first into the river with a splash. Drops rain down on us.

Farther out, another arm waves, another fin dips. "It's a pod."

"Where do they live?" I ask.

"Way, way, way below the surface. So deep even submarines can't go there."

I fill my lungs with the briny air, my ears straining for the mermaid song as it grows more distant. They're swimming away. "I'd love to see an underwater city. Have you seen one?"

He snorts. "I've never been to a mermaid colony. Humans can't survive at that depth. But if I could, I would totally go there. Probably the coolest thing I'd ever see. Dangerous, though."

"And what we're doing now isn't?" I lower my gaze as realization opens a hollow ache in my chest.

"Scariest thing I've ever done." He quirks an eyebrow as he closes the distance between us, making it clear that he's not talking about looking for the Keys or facing down people like Juri.

Heart racing, I let go of the railing and turn into him, winding my arms around his neck as his lips crush mine. His hands thread into my hair, gripping, while he presses me against the railing. When his teeth graze my bottom lip, I taste desperation, an unquenchable thirst. It no longer matters that there are mermaids in the river, or that we're searching for an object that could help us save the world from a demon army. It doesn't matter that mythical creatures really exist. The only thing that matters is that I'm here with Kye and my world feels complete because of it.

We jerk apart when the ferry docks and I'm finally able to catch my breath.

A crease forms between his brows as a mix of emotions tangle in his eyes. "Sorry. I'm not helping us focus, am I?"

Feeling bold, I wind my arms around his neck again and drop a kiss on his chin. "I don't mind. In fact, feel free to distract me anytime." He grabs me, pulls me up until only my toes touch the ground, and leans his forehead against mine, closing his eyes as he breathes me in.

The ferry is mostly empty when we disembark, following the flow of traffic.

"Now what?" I ask, still a little punch-drunk from his kisses.

"My dad thinks it's hidden in or around the statue." He digs in his backpack for the paper Eoin gave him and studies it, turning it front to back and back to front as I crane my neck and stare at the towering structure.

"That's what we're looking for, I think." He traces a circle around a symbol that resembles a flaming cinnamon roll.

"Where should we start?"

He eyes the blueprint side of the page and retraces the symbol again. "Well, this is just a theory, but if I were going to hide something that important in a public place, I'd make sure to put it wherever it's least likely to be accidentally found."

I stare up at the towering copper giant. "Okay. Translation?"

His eyes follow mine. "Inside, at the top."

I don't believe we'll be allowed to go up there—there are signs indicating that it's highly unlikely—but strange things happen when Kye's around, so I follow him in the museum entrance and up some stairs. The guards stop us, informing us that the statue is closed to tourists for the day. We thank them, then wander to a display and pretend to be interested in the architecture. We wait. Five minutes. Ten. Fifteen. At last, the guard closest to us is distracted. An elderly man doubles over coughing and needs assistance. While the guard's back is turned, we slip past him and sneak up the stairs, holding our baggage to our chests to minimize sound.

As soon as we can no longer see the ground level behind us, we run. This is our only chance, and if we're caught, things will become extremely complicated. As it is, I'm afraid they'll figure out someone's up here before we find the Key. We keep going until intense pain in my ribs forces me to pause for a breath. I sit to rest on one of the steps and Kye sits next to me, not nearly as winded. "Why aren't you tired?" I ask, forcing musty air into my lungs.

"I run a lot."

"You suck. I run a lot too. But not stairs."

"I could piggyback you."

"Shut it. I don't need you to piggyback me."

He stands and pulls me up. "We're halfway there."

After what feels like miles and miles straight up, we make it to the crown. Kye half-drags me up the last step into the small space. I lean against a window, panting, and stare out. The sun tints the clouds pink, highlighting the New Jersey skyline. "That's something you don't see every day."

Kye grins, wiping beads of sweat off his forehead. "Look fast. We should get to work before we lose the light."

We search the crown—the ground, the windowsills, the walls. It doesn't take long, but it feels like hours because I'm so worried about security catching us.

When we're sure it's not here, Kye starts up a ladder affixed to the wall. "It must be in the torch." We climb the narrow passage to the torch and emerge in a room only big enough for a few people. He slides his hands along the walls in the poorly lit room, and I mirror his actions on the opposite side, working toward him. "What if it's not here?"

"It has to be," he says. "My dad seemed positive the Key was re-hidden in the statue. Downstairs I read that the torch was closed in 1916. It makes complete sense that the keeper would hide it in the one place no Elen can look."

"Why can't they look here?"

"Why would they? She's only been around since 1886—about three hundred years too late to have been an original vault for one of the Arawn Keys. But more importantly, this beautiful lady is copper, and copper is poisonous to Dark Elen."

This surprises me. "If it's poisonous to them, how is it not poisonous to us? What about cooking pots and pennies and all the other things made of copper?" I remember the ugly copper clock Gram hauled from house to house with every move. Every time, she insisted on hanging the hideous thing next to the front door.

"It has something to do with the metal content in their systems. Every time they steal someone else's power, their blood metals rise.

They can handle being around some metals, but not copper. It does something to their brains. Scrambles them, shuts them down. Like turning off a power switch."

The idea makes me shudder. "How exactly do they to steal powers?"

"Something to do with the Arawnian Dagger and cutting out people's hearts—"

"Ew. Okay, that's enough." The room is too dim. I pat the top of Kye's backpack. "You wouldn't happen to have a flashlight in here, would you?"

"Wouldn't that be nice." He's still running his hands over the walls. "I had one, but lost it in Yellowstone."

"Yeah. If searching for stuff in dark places is going to be a regular thing, it might be good to pick up another." I lean against the wall, close my eyes, and beg my mind to guide me to the symbol. Focus.

"How did you do that?" Kye breathes, sounding amazed.

"What?"

"Your ring. It's glowing." I open my eyes. A bright beam reflects off the windows and casts rainbows on the walls, like color showing through a raindrop. My whole body vibrates with warmth. Power. Love.

"Huh. No idea." I grin. "But we should take advantage."

We get back to work, running our hands along the walls, the floor, around the windows. Dust tickles my nose and I sneeze. When the light dances on something above my head, I direct it at the ceiling, heart pounding in excitement. "Kye! There it is. I think I found it."

TWENTY-THREE

Scaling the Beast

Kye's head jerks up. "Brilliant." He stretches to his toes but isn't quite tall enough to touch the symbol etched on the low ceiling.

"Give me a boost," I demand.

Kye looks incredulous, but steps into a manageable squat. After kicking off my shoes, I wedge my foot on his thigh and swing up onto his shoulders. From here I'm able to scrape the ceiling with my fingernails. Dust and crumbling mortar rains on my face and stings my eyes until I'm sneezing like crazy.

Kye's hands tighten on my ankles to keep me steady. "You okay up there?"

"Just a hundred years of dust build-up falling in my face." I've rubbed off enough grime so the symbol is visible.

"What are you doing?" Kye leans his head to look up and whacks my hipbone with his skull.

"Ow. Careful."

"Sorry."

I probe the ceiling with my fingers again, my stomach sinking in defeat. "There's nothing." He crouches enough so I can drop onto the ground, and then straightens. He wipes sweat off his forehead. "It's here. It has to be."

The final rays of sunlight cast long shadows on the floor. I wander to the window, raking my fingers through my tangled hair.

"Abby ..." Kye trails off.

"What?"

"Look at your ring. It's fading."

The radiance that shone so brightly only a minute ago has dimmed, though the diamonds still glitter. "Why would it do that? How?"

"There has to be something here. A clue at least." He circles the room and looks up one last time. "I think we need to try again. Wish we had a ladder."

"We can add it to the list of travel must-haves," I mutter, "along with my flashlight."

He crouches again, motioning for me to climb up. "One more time?"

All I can think to do is to rub the dust off the symbol and the area around it. As I do, my ring starts to glow again, the platinum heating my skin. Simultaneously, the lines in the symbol sparkle to life, outlining cracks around the edges. I open my hand and brush the dust with my palm and a burst of color shoots a circle around the symbol, bright enough to hurt my eyes. I yank my hand away in fear of the heat, the light, but the symbol keeps glowing. Pieces of ceiling crumble and rain down on us, leaving a hole the size of a fist. I blink the grit out of my eyes. "Kye, you have to see this."

A plume of dust falls on his head and he's coughing as he leans back. "What did you do?"

"I don't know."

The opening is small, so I have to squeeze my hand through the hole to feel around inside. The texture is smooth like metal, probably copper, the same as the rest of the statue. My fingernail snags on a piece of cloth. I catch it between my fingers and tug until a small bundle is in my hand.

"I've got something," I say, coughing away more dust.

"Good." Kye squeezes my ankles. "Are you ready for me to put you down?"

"Not unless you want me to lose my hand. I'll have to work it through the opening." The fabric is wadded and tangled, and it takes several minutes for me to wrestle free. Something hard and heavy tumbles out and lands with a tinkling clatter on the floor.

"Are you out now?" Kye's shoulder muscles quiver beneath me.

"Yes. You can put me down." He sets me on my feet and I run over to pick up the pendant. A large, brilliant-green emerald set in an intricate platinum scroll dangles from a shiny platinum chain. The clear green stone flickers with power and feels warm to the touch.

My eyes go misty. "I dreamed about this necklace."

He stares at the pendant, speechless. The chain drips fluidly through my fingers and I close my hand around it.

"It's the Key," Kye says. "I can't believe we actually found it."

"If my ring is one Key, and this pendant is another, that's two of the four." I drop the pendant in his open palm so he can take a closer look. "And if Juri's dagger is also one of the Keys, then we still have one more left to find." I beat the dirty cloth against my jeans to get the dust out.

Kye shakes his head, twisting the pendant so it catches a ray from the rapidly fading twilight and washes the room in flashing green sparkles. "Juri has the fourth, remember? He said he has two."

After a thorough search of my memory, I realize Kye is right. Juri did say that, though we have no idea what the Key is, or if he was actually telling the truth. "What do we do now?"

"We take the Keys we have to Valdemar and hope he knows what to do with them."

"Can't we just ask your dad?"

"No, it has to be Val." He crosses to where we've left our bags. "Dad has a lot of information because he's studied it, but Val was there. He experienced the fall first-hand."

Two loud bangs echo in the lower stairwell and we both freeze. Another bang, then footsteps coming our way. My heart thuds as I look around, futilely wishing for somewhere to hide.

Muffled voices and clanging announce someone—or several someones—climbing the ladder.

"Someone's coming," I whisper.

"Time to go." Kye wraps the pendant in the cloth and shoves it in his pocket. He tosses me the backpack and straps my heavier bag across his chest, his eyes darting around the room. "Guess we're not going down the way we came." His gaze lands on a door. I assume it leads onto the observation deck. Kye tries the knob.

It's locked.

He pulls, twists, and bangs, but it doesn't budge.

Overwhelming fear threatens to consume all logical sense when I imagine spending the night in a New York City jail cell. "Kye! They'll arrest us. We shouldn't be up here."

Our eyes meet, and my terror is mirrored in his. He kicks the door. It doesn't open. He kicks it again. On the third try I grab his hand and kick with him, and finally the door flies open. We climb onto the observation deck and push the door closed.

The cool evening wind buffets my ears and whips my hair. The sun has set, leaving only a rim of golden orange on the horizon. Kye unzips his backpack—still on my back—and digs in it, producing a lumpy black bag. He dumps the contents on the ground, mumbling, and sifts through, finding some black straps and threading them between his legs. After hooking the straps to his belt, he connects them with a metal ring and attaches a smaller bag to his buckle. All this is managed in a matter of seconds, as if he's done it hundreds of times before.

From the bag attached to his waist, he loops the end of a thin, high-tech cable through another metal ring and attaches it to the bottom portion of the iron railing. Once he's satisfied the cable will hold, he pulls on a pair of fingerless gloves. "Do you trust me?"

"Uh." I stare at the ground hundreds of feet below. "Do I have a choice?"

He tests the cable again and swings his leg over the railing, letting out more slack from the bag at his waist and wrapping it under his backside, holding with his right hand.

"What are you doing?"

He swings his other leg over and braces against the rail, waiting. "Not getting arrested." He holds an arm out, looking expectant. "Come on. Climb over and hold on to me."

Nichole Giles

I shudder. Being arrested doesn't sound quite as scary as dying. "Kye ..."

He glances away from his white knuckles, searching my face. "You trust me, right?"

Angry voices bark in the torch room. "They were here. I knew they snuck up here the moment I took my eyes off them. Look at this mess!"

"Well, there's only one way down, and we would have run into them. They're up here somewhere."

"Where?"

"Abby!" Kye hisses. "Come on."

With a jolt, I scramble over the rail and wrap my arms around Kye's neck and my legs around his waist. His biceps shake as he lowers us from the edge. I fight the instinct to look down as we slide farther, stopping when Kye's feet hit something. I open my eyes long enough to see that it's one of Lady Liberty's giant fingers. Tangled together, we lean against the base of the torch to catch our breath, listening to the door as it scrapes across the observation deck and feet shuffle out.

"They aren't out here."

"Where'd they go?"

"How am I supposed to know?"

"They didn't disappear into thin air!"

"Well, they didn't come down. We would have seen them."

"They didn't jump, did they?"

"Man, I hope not. Who do you think would get stuck cleaning up that mess?"

I tighten my grip on Kye and close my eyes—praying I won't throw up on him—and fight the urge to scream when I open them again and accidentally look down. I cling to Kye, huddled against the torch handle. His steadiness renews my confidence, and I loosen my stranglehold on his neck. "They almost caught us."

"You did well." Kye drops a kiss on my lips.

My body quakes. "I didn't do anything but hang on to you." I gulp, still trying to avoid looking at the ground. "What do we do now? We can't get back up there."

Kye squeezes my waist as if bracing me for bad news. "Nope, we aren't going back up."

My arms tighten involuntarily around his neck. "Um, I hate to tell you this, but I'm *not* scaling down the rest of this beast." I pat the statue's finger. "No offense, Ms. Liberty."

"Just keep your arms around me and hold on tight," he says. "You won't have to scale anything, we're rappelling down."

"What if someone sees us?" I fight for control of my growing panic. This day just keeps getting better. "How do you know your little contraption-thingy will hold us?"

"This *contraption* was designed for military special forces and can hold as many as four full-grown men. I promise it'll hold us just fine." He rubs my back, comforting. "Let's just hope it's too dark for anyone to see." He retightens his grip on my waist. "Hold on."

I do as he asks—what other choice do I have?—and close my eyes as he kicks off the statue.

When I open them again, we're dangling three hundred feet in the air with nothing below but the star-shaped building and the rough ground. An involuntary scream escapes my throat.

"Shhh," Kye soothes. "Don't panic, I've got you. I promise I won't drop you." I wrap my legs around him tighter, and then we're moving, dipping lower and lower with nothing but a thin cable and a little piece of metal to keep us from falling to our deaths. I keep my eyes closed and try not to wonder if anyone sees us or is staring at our backsides this very moment.

We make it to the observation deck on top of the pedestal at Lady Liberty's feet and Kye releases the clip connecting the cable to the harness so we can drop the last few yards. He sets me down, and then catches me when I sway. "You okay?"

"Uh-huh." Bracing my hand on the building, I peer up one last time as the contents of my stomach prepare to make a reappearance. "Yeah, that was awesome." Then I run to a garbage can a few feet away and throw up.

TWENTY-FOUR

Narrow Escape

As I wipe my mouth, Kye removes the harness straps and clips and crams them back in his pack, leaving the cable dangling.

"Over there, officer. Someone was trying to climb the statue." The agitated voice is followed by footsteps pounding up the concrete stairs.

"I saw him too. But he was coming down, not going up."

We've been seen.

Kye grabs my hand. "Now would be a really good time to disappear."

We slide through an open door, trying to look casual as we wind around tourists and personnel, doing our best to blend in. Not long after we've "joined" a tour group, a security officer jogs past, radio in hand. As he heads for the door, not even glancing in our direction, his radio crackles. "Suspects appear to have climbed down the statue. Be on the alert for two teens, one male, one female, unknown descriptions, possibly armed."

I shake my head. *Armed?* "That was close."

"Too close." Kye pulls off a glove and gingerly touches his palm. His hands are red and irritated, starting to swell with blisters. I want to Heal them, to take those hands in mine and kiss them better, but now is not the time.

We stay with the group, trying to look casual and blend in, while security guards swarm the island. Twenty minutes later, I'm starting to worry that they're going to question every teenager here, so we slip outside and head for the ferry.

"What if they're looking for us at the dock?" I choke. "What if they won't let the boats leave until they find us?" It's what I would do if I were them.

"Don't even think that," Kye says. "We're not getting trapped here."

Near the concession stand, I see a restroom. We burst through the door and lock it behind us, panting with nerves. I turn on the tap and wash my hands, then lean over the basin and rinse my mouth. "What do we do now?"

Kye's brows furrow as I move aside. He lets the water run over his hands, grimacing when it stings. The water washing down the drain is pink. "Do you think they're still looking for us?"

"Yes." Shaking my head at his injury, I dig in my bag for a specific jar and rub Healing silver cream over Kye's already festering blisters, massaging his palms until his fingers wrap around mine.

"They'll stop running the ferries soon," he murmurs. "We can't hide forever."

I look up, meet his worried eyes, and—thinking of Raina—come up with a sort-of plan. "Take off your coat." I remove mine as well, dump my peach-colored airport sweater in the trash, and pull a bulky gray one over my head. Kye catches on and changes into a khaki-green hoodie, then stows our coats. While I shove my hair into a knit beanie, Kye dons a baseball cap. As a final touch, I slip Kye's backpack under my sweater—in the front—and evaluate myself in the mirror. It's not exactly a natural looking pregnant belly, but it might pass if no one looks too closely.

"You're kidding, right?" A look of almost-panic flits across Kye's face, but is quickly replaced by a forced smile. He picks up my duffle and peers outside. "Guess we'll leave our coats?"

Not knowing what else to do, I shrug. "Guess so."

He goes first to make sure the way is clear, and I follow. We walk slowly toward the dock, trying not to bring attention to ourselves, and are beyond relieved when the ferry captain calls all aboard. We fall in with the shuffling crowd and no one even gives us a second glance as we find seats near the front railing.

A security guard boards behind us, and it takes all my willpower not to break down and have another panic attack and confess every misdeed I've ever committed. Kye sees him too, but rather than freak out, he pulls me close, wordlessly encouraging me to lean my head on his shoulder while he rests his hand on my fake-pregnant belly, then he tips his head so the visor of his hat conceals his face.

There's no mermaid song coming from the river as the ferry casts off. I glance at Kye, my eyes asking the silent question. "Probably long gone," he says. "It's pretty unusual for them to be here in the first place."

"Nothing about this week has been usual." I close my eyes with a sigh, exhausted, and try to ignore my rumbling stomach, which seems to get louder by the minute. Kye sends me a sympathetic look and offers me a piece of mint gum.

The security guard walks by. It appears as though he's checking out the passengers, watching for something. *Probably us.* He pauses a few feet away, his gaze skimming over us at first, but then he turns and looks again.

"What do you think of the name Isabelle?" I say, rather louder than necessary. "I mean, if it's a girl."

Kye frowns for a second before catching on. "Hm. Bella for short?"

"No, Izzy. Cute, don't you think?"

He nods. "I like Jack for a boy. Or Jake."

"What about Collin?"

He makes a face, shaking his head. We continue this conversation, throwing out baby names and discussing possible nicknames and the bullying ramifications until the security guard frowns and walks on. Kye's fingers loosen on mine, and I realize he's been squeezing my hand until it's numb. I want to sigh in relief but don't dare. We haven't escaped yet.

I'm afraid to ask what's next. The thought of going anywhere besides home—even if it isn't mine—is enough to bring tears to my eyes. Right now, I need sleep—in a bed—and a solid meal to fill my empty stomach and calm my shaky hands, but I have no idea when I'll get either. The water is choppy, so I spend the duration of the ride with my eyes closed, drifting along with the toss and roll of the boat, grateful that mint helps fight nausea.

The sky is completely dark by the time the ferry docks. I shiver, wishing I had my coat. The guard disembarks behind us, so I take care to walk slowly, painfully even (not hard to do, since my muscles ache anyway) and we talk about how much we have to do before the baby comes.

I'm starting to worry we'll never get rid of this guard when the ferry boat captain yells to him and waves him over, and we beeline down the street.

That was way too close for comfort.

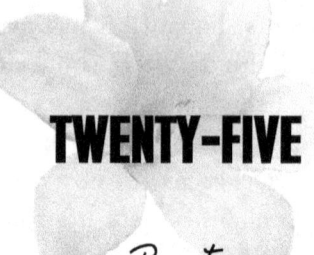

TWENTY-FIVE

Beat

"You can probably take my backpack out of your sweater now." Kye drops my duffle on a bus stop bench. "Have I ever told you you're brilliant?"

I slump down on the bench. "Not since we left the statue."

"Abigail Johnson, you are the most brilliant woman I've ever met." A piece of hair has escaped my hat, and he tucks it behind my ear. "We make a good team."

"Thanks." I pull off my beanie and finger comb the tangled locks, my stomach rumbling again.

"You need food." Kye pats his backpack in my middle.

"Yes. And sleep. Don't you?" I maneuver my arms in the sweater sleeves and let the backpack fall on my knees.

"Yes." He flexes his fingers, shaking his head at the burns. "What's worse? Hunger or exhaustion?"

I yawn, the effort of covering my mouth almost requiring too much energy. "It's a toss-up."

"If you had to choose one or the other, sleep or food, which would be most important right now? Your answer decides where we go from here."

It's childish, I know, but I can't stop my whimper. "Both. I need both."

"Okay."

We take the subway to Times Square and wind through the crowds for a couple blocks before choosing a building. The adrenaline that has kept me going is long gone now, and my eyes blur. Kye leads me—walking in a zombie-like trance—to a desk, where he talks to someone, but my brain is too fuzzy to understand his words. We're ushered into an elevator and up one floor to emerge in a lavish lobby filled with floral-scented candles and a water scene projected on a blank wall. It doesn't hit me that we're in a hotel until Kye asks the receptionist if they have any rooms available.

There are a lot of things I don't know about Kye, but I learn something at the Marriott.

He has a fake ID.

I never realized hotels have a minimum check-in age requirement, but he must have done this before. Kye claims he's twenty-three and hands the woman his license and a credit card.

I stare at the ground, nervous. Kye squeezes my hand and accepts two plastic key cards. Another elevator takes us up seven more floors, my heart pounding the whole way.

When Kye opens the door and I realize our room has two queen beds, I breathe an audible sigh of relief. Still, my hands tremble— and not because of hunger. *Is this going to be the night that changes everything?* The beds are piled high with soft pillows and puffy white down comforters. "It's nice."

"Should be. It's a four-star." He fidgets with the zipper on his backpack, not looking up.

"Why are we nervous?" I ask.

"I have no idea." He shakes his head and looks around the room, but not at me. "Why are we?"

A giggle escapes my lips.

Kye finally looks at me and laughs. The tension breaks, and I remember that I trust him. Care about him. *Maybe even love him.* "How does pizza sound?" he asks. "We can have it delivered."

"Perfect." While he orders, I close myself in the bathroom and run a bath to soak away two days' worth of grime. Washing my hair almost feels like a luxury, and though I rarely wear much makeup, I'm glad to wash what's left of it away. The hotel has provided us with lavender sage lotion, and I use it liberally, then pull on cotton shorts and a faded T-shirt.

"It's all yours." I drop my bag in the closet. The slice of pizza Kye is eating is almost as big as his head.

"Okay. Food's here."

"I see that." I shake back my damp hair, noticing the pizza already has three pieces missing. "Glad you left me some," I tease.

He grins, handing me a yellow flower from a vase on the desk. "For you," he says, heading to the bathroom and pausing outside the door. "I got us on a red-eye back to Jackson tomorrow night. It doesn't leave until one AM, but it's the best I could get on short notice."

"Oh." *I should be relieved. Why am I disappointed?* "We're going home?"

"We're taking the Keys to Val." He smiles half-heartedly. "You can finally see where I live."

While Kye is in the shower, I relax against the pillows and gobble a slice of pizza, flipping through the TV channels. *What would Mom think about where I am and what I'm doing?* I haven't even tried to call her yet.

If Gram knew I was staying in a hotel with a guy, I would be grounded until I was ninety. Self-conscious, I pick up Kye's cell and dial. When I get home, I'm getting a cell phone of my own, whether Mom likes it or not. I'll figure out how to pay for it myself. I've never needed one before, but now—this can go on the list of things that are changing.

She answers on the second ring.

"Hi, Mom." Something in me sighs at the sound of her voice. *Everything will be okay.*

"Abby." She sounds relieved. "Why didn't you call yesterday? I've been worried sick. You were supposed to let me know when you got to Vegas."

"I know. I'm sorry."

"What's wrong, honey? You sound exhausted."

Everything. "Nothing. I *am* exhausted. We've been on the go since we left."

"Doing what? Honey, you've got to rest. It's not healthy to travel like that. You need to stop and sleep if you want to accomplish anything productive. Where are you?"

I stare out the window, holding the flower to my nose. "New York."

She blows out an audible breath. "Already? I thought you were going to Vegas first?" I can hear murmuring in the background. *Is she with someone? A man?* I'm not sure I want to know, so I don't ask.

"We did, but it was quick," I answer. "I'll tell you about it when we get back."

"When you get back, we will also be discussing the hole in my sofa cushion. It looks like a burn mark, and if I find out someone was smoking in my house, heads will roll."

Even though I have zero idea what happened to the cushion, I burst out laughing.

"It's not funny, Abby. You know I can't afford to buy new furniture."

"I know, Mom. Turn the cushion over. We can talk about everything the day after tomorrow. I should be home sometime in the morning."

"Where are you staying?" she asks, her voice low.

I hesitate, knowing it doesn't help my case, but unsure how to put it any way other than straight. "The Marriot."

There is an audible intake of breath. "Are you and Kye—" I hear another murmur and Mom mumbles something in response. She sounds distracted when she says, "Abby, whatever you do, please be ... careful."

I shudder, because I think she's talking about sex as much as personal safety. "Gotta go, Mom. Love you."

When Kye comes out, I'm standing at the window, staring down at all the people on the street. The lights of Times Square blink, reflecting off of everything they touch. Billboard images bigger than my house cover the front of every building as far as I can see. "Amazing, huh?" he says.

"I've never seen anything like it. Well, Las Vegas, but that's different. More sparkle and glitz, less glamour."

His hair is damp and the dark circles under his eyes make him look vulnerable. I stroke his cheeks with my fingertips. "You're beat."

"I was going to say the same about you." He inspects my face and pushes a strand of hair off my forehead. His plaid flannel pants brush my leg, and my eyes wander down to the T-shirt stretching across his chest, hinting at the muscles beneath. "You should get some sleep," he says.

I stroke the hair above his ears then let my hands drop to my sides. "We both should." His hands slide down my arms until our fingers lace together. He draws me toward one of the beds, and I feel a shiver of nerves before he kisses my forehead and takes a step back. I sit, testing the firmness of the mattress. "Why didn't we go back to your dad's apartment?"

"It isn't safe anymore. They know where he lives, and that we were there. If I were them, I'd keep someone watching for us to go back. Thanks to Juri, they probably know you have Raina's ring, and they'll eventually figure out we have the pendant too. So my dad's apartment is probably the most dangerous place we could go right now. To be honest, it's only a matter of time before they find us again."

"How?"

"I don't know. Tynan projected today." Kye crosses the space between us and sits next to me. "He must be more powerful than anyone thought. He found us on the subway. We have to assume he can find us again. Only next time, he'll probably send someone who won't fade away."

"Someone else? How many of these thugs actually work for him?"

"A lot. The worst ones were locked away, but some Dark Elen are still out there, and they get more powerful every day. There are tons of Gifted people in the world, but very few recognize their power. Those who do carry the burden for the rest." I stare at the floor. With a finger under my chin, he tips my head to look at him. "Your grandmother was right, Abby. No matter what you do, you'll never be completely safe. Not while the Dark Elen are after the Keys."

I shiver with the knowledge that I might never be free, and twist my ring around my finger. "What would happen if I gave this to them? Would they leave me alone? Or maybe we could hide it, bury it somewhere in a remote desert or something." The idea gives me a pang of intense sadness.

"No." Kye clasps my shoulders. "You don't understand. They'll find it. You can't ever let them get their hands on that ring. Ever. Giving it to them would only make you weaker. Hiding it might slow them down, but eventually, they'd find it, the same way Juri found the dagger. And that would be really bad. They might not be able to use the ring without you, but they could use it through you. And if they did …" he shudders. "Do you remember those things we saw in Juri's office in Vegas? The demons?"

I nod.

"That's what's locked in that tomb. An entire army of demons. If the Elen get their hands on all four Keys, that's what will be unleashed."

I curl up on my side and pull the comforter tight around my shoulders to stop a sudden chill. "Why me, Kye? What does this have to do with me?"

He leans over, one hand on each side of me. "Because in another life you were Princess Raina. And even in this life her blood runs in your veins."

The thought swirls around in circles and I try to catch up with it. Me. A princess in another life. I know, of course. I've always known on some level. It does sort of make sense, in a weird, convoluted way. But what does that make Kye? Could he really be Theron?

He interrupts my thoughts. "I'll keep watch tonight."

"No," I protest, fighting to open my heavy eyelids. "You have to sleep sometime. We're safe here, I can feel it."

Kye finds my hand sticking out of the covers and entwines our fingers. "Abby, you aren't safe anywhere right now." His thumb plays with my ring. "I want you to promise me you won't let your guard down. Not ever. Not even in your sleep."

"I promise." I murmur.

Kye blows a kiss across the space between us, and reaches to turn off the light. "Sweet dreams."

"Kye?"

"Yes?" he whispers, his comforter rustling.

"Can they find us here?"

"Don't worry," he assures me. "This is a big city. They'll have to sift through a lot of people before they do. Go to sleep."

TWENTY-SIX

Found

*I*sleen's skirts brush the tall blades of grass and her boot heels sink into the soil with every step. The pendant sparkles against her throat. Droplets of ice cling to trees and shrubs on one side of the path, but as the queen comes closer, the ice melts, leaving behind fresh, new-flowering buds.

She continues down the path, waving her hand over struggling plants and dormant trees, which perk up and bloom as she passes. A group of sprites flutter around her head, buzzing like bees. Isleen holds out her hand, and one—whose glow has grown dim—lands in her palm and brightens immediately. He says something in another language, and Isleen laughs as he bobs in front of her before speeding away through the forest.

"Thank you, Murtagh!" she calls after him.

In the courtyard, Isleen stops near a barren rosebush. Pinching a thorny branch between her fingers, she breathes warm air all the way to the roots until it's covered with peach-white blooms.

"'Tis nearly as beautiful as you, my lady." Rhys leans against an archway, shadowed by the walls and the position of the setting sun.

Isleen doesn't smile. Her eyes simply drink him in as she forces a second rosebush to bloom. Rhys's hard expression softens as he watches her give life to the dormant plants. "Do you like what you see?" Isleen's stare doesn't leave her captain.

"Far more lovely than the sunset. More beautiful than the flowers. The strength within your heart could hold my gaze for hours." Rhys bows. "My lady."

Isleen laughs, lifting the hem of her dress to curtsy. "My captain, Rhys the poet."

Rhys smiles ruefully. "My queen, Isleen the ... noble."

Anguish is reflected in Isleen's eyes. "I do what I must for the survival of the kingdom. As do you."

Rhys takes a hesitant step forward. "Would that my heart could stop beating for the one I cannot have. Every day I swear I shall leave, and every night I find ten reasons to stay."

Another step. "I would not survive if you did leave," Isleen murmurs. "Nor would Theron. You are needed here."

"My heart breaks here, every minute of every hour."

Tears sparkle in the queen's eyes. "Do you think you are the only one who hurts? Who lies awake in bed night after night, longing for the tender touch of a forbidden love?" She steps closer. "I taste you on my lips when I sleep, and wake with an aching heart. It aches still."

Rhys closes the distance between them in one bound, sweeps the queen off her feet and into the shadow of the doorway, wrapping his arms around her as the tears course down her cheeks. "Shh. My love. I cannot bear to see you cry." He dries her tears with his lips and claims her mouth briefly before setting her on her feet and stepping away. "The king has not yet returned from his hunting expedition?"

Isleen shakes her head. "Come to me, Rhys. I cannot bear to be apart from you one more day."

A tortured expression flits across his face. "I'll be hanged for treason."

"I would never let him do that to you."

"You would not be able to stop him if he hanged you, too."

Isleen grabs hold of Rhys's sleeve before he can turn away. "If my choice is to live in agony or die with you, I choose the latter." She swallows. "A life without true love is no life at all. If I am to die tomorrow, let it be with the satisfaction of knowing that I spent one more night with you."

Rhys hesitates. "If only one night could last a lifetime."

I wake to a loud bang and something rattling. Kye untangles from his covers and vaults to the door. "Yes?"

"Housekeeping," says a gravelly voice.

Kye turns on the light and checks the chain. "We're sleeping."

I scramble out of bed and to his side. "Bring me the desk chair," he murmurs.

"Orders are for now, sir."

"We're sleeping." Kye shoves the chair under the doorknob. "It's six o'clock in the morning. What kind of hotel wakes their guests at sunrise?"

"Very sorry, sir," the voice says. "We'll come back later."

Kye's frantic movements shoot my blood pressure into overdrive. He thrusts his backpack in my arms and seizes my duffle bag. This whole carry-your-junk-all-over-the-country thing is getting old. I stare at the door with wide eyes, my sleepy mind scrambling for a plan. A way out. Somewhere to hide. A weapon to protect us from the bad guys who might be on the other side of the door.

He urges me to the window. It opens out from the bottom—toward the street—just enough for a really thin person to slide through and splat all over the road. "No way. There's no fire escape. We'll die."

"Abby." Kye's voice is strained as he unzips his backpack. "There's no other way out and I think they've found us." He digs in his stuff and dumps half of it on the floor, grasping his rappelling harness and looking lost.

"Uh." I hate to point out the obvious, but since he's looking for it ... "You left the rest of it attached to the Statue of Liberty."

"Dammit." His fingers dig into his hair again. "I can't believe I forgot about that."

I push the window open farther, and can't resist teasing. "You want to try flying?"

"Come on, Abby. This is serious." He shakes his head. "I guess down the outside of the building isn't an option this time."

He grinds his teeth as I zip his pack and grab our shoes. A snicker dies in my throat when the door handle jiggles and something buzzes. Something like a drill. Or a saw.

Kye's lips move in silent horror as his gaze swings back and forth between the window and the door. I frown, my eyes landing on another door. An adjoining door. "What about that way?"

He shakes his head. "Locked from both sides. Someone in the next room would have to open it, and even then, it only puts us one room away."

"One room away is better than nothing." I throw his shoes to him as something slams into the door.

"Yeah," he agrees. "Probably our best option. Try knocking."

Clutching the handles of my bag, I open our door and pound on the other while Kye sifts through more stuff and comes up with a handful of thin metal rods. "What are those?"

A third slam, and something sharp and white pokes through the wood, then disappears.

"Lock picks." He crouches in front of the smooth metal plate and pries it off with a screwdriver, revealing a regular deadbolt, and then chooses two picks and gets to work.

I don't even know how to respond to Kye owning a set of lock picks, let alone the fact that he knows how to use them. Another hit against the door sends the chair skidding across the carpet. The white object slices through again, leaving a second hole.

Hysteria threatens to take over, so I squeak, "Not to sound pushy, but any chance you can hurry up?"

Something clicks and Kye grins. Cautiously pushing the door open, he peeks through to the other side and then sighs in relief. He swings it wide and ushers me into the empty room, scooting the dumped contents of his backpack with his foot.

Another bang rattles the lampshades as he closes both adjoining doors, locking our side again. Even so, it's hard not to hear the next blow, and the rattle that sounds like the whole doorknob has flown across the room.

Frantic with fear, I pull on shoes and a sweatshirt and attempt to repack everything we've dumped out. "We can't keep carrying all this stuff around with us."

He eyes me warily, tying his shoe. "Are you suggesting we leave it here?"

"Not everything. We'll condense." A change of clothes, my cosmetic bag, and a brush go in his backpack, along with everything of his that fits. Kye pulls on his hoodie and takes the pack as we hear a loud splintering of wood, followed by shouting in the next room.

"Time to go," I squeak.

Silently, Kye pulls open the outer door and we run. Down the hall, around the corner, and into the elevator. As the doors close, I catch a glimpse of Juri storming toward us, his eyes darting from room to room. Boone isn't far behind him. I'm not sure if they've seen us, but the elevator engine whines as it moves. That's probably all they need at this time of morning.

My chest constricts, feeling heavy, and my eyes blur. I squeeze Kye's hand. "Oh no. *Not now.*" The elevator walls close in on me.

Kye crouches in a corner as the demons advance on him. The creatures are at least eight feet tall with smoky black skin and eyes filled with heat. Fire shoots from their fingertips as they close in on Kye, but he never backs down, never lets on that he's afraid. "Run, Abby!" he yells, searing me with a piercing look. But I don't run. I stand frozen and watch the demons consume him in a funnel of flames.

I come to, doubled over, my heart beating so fast I can't catch my breath. "Kye ..."

He grabs me around the waist and holds me up. "Big breath. Come on now, we have to run."

I'm swaying. "Can't."

"Yes you can. Come on, babe, let's go." The elevator dings and the doors open to the empty lobby. Kye tows me behind him, his head swinging back and forth as he looks everywhere at once. We sprint down the stairs to the ground level and burst outside into the chilly air. I'm suddenly very aware that I'm wearing shorts.

Footsteps echo behind us and we take off down the street, running. Several blocks later, we slow. I'm panting, out of breath. "Kye, I can't keep going like this. Can't we take a cab?"

"To where?"

"Away," I say. "To wherever we're going." His eyes travel my length—my shorts, shoes with no socks, goose bumps up and down my legs, and me bent over holding my ribs—and he tries to hail a cab. Footsteps pound the ground behind us. I turn to look behind us and almost trip over my own feet. Juri's running fast, despite his stubby legs. Boone's in front of him. They're closing the distance rapidly.

Someone has propped open the entrance to a coffee shop and we dash through, dodging early morning customers, then out a door on the other side. Finally, a cab at the curb. Kye throws open the door and we dive in, shouting, "Go!"

The car moves at the pace of a snail. "Um, excuse me," I say. "We're kind of in a hurry here." Juri and Boone are now standing on the corner, looking for us.

We both slide down in the seat as the driver merges into traffic and we're swallowed in the sea of vehicles. We've lost them.

For now.

TWENTY-SEVEN

Strawberry Pancakes

Since our flight doesn't board until after midnight, we have the driver drop us off in front of a museum on the east side of town. There's a statue of a man riding a horse, and large stone pillars that look like they're holding up the arched roof. The building looks familiar.

"Isn't this the museum from that movie?" I ask. "The one about the displays that come alive at night?"

Kye laughs. "Yeah, I think it is. Shall we go in?"

"It's closed."

He shrugs. "Can't hurt to try."

The morning chill raises goose bumps on my bare legs and has me shivering. "We should find somewhere to change."

"If we can get in, the museum will have restrooms." Kye wraps his arms around me to keep me warm.

"The question is how long we'll have to wait to go inside." I don't relish the idea of hanging out in this cold for hours. Especially in my pajamas.

We find an unlocked service door and sneak into the lobby where dinosaur bones tower over us. Four arched hallways branch off the main room, each labeled with a different section heading.

A janitor sweeps by on an electric buffer. When he sees us, he frowns and shuts off the motor. "How'd you get in here? Museum doesn't open until ten." He points to a clock on the wall. It's 7:23. I swallow, shivering again.

"We know," Kye says. "Could we please use the restroom? We'll hurry." The man hesitates, but doesn't immediately say no, so Kye continues, "Come on, man. It's freezing outside. Ten minutes and we'll be out of your way. You won't even know we were here."

The janitor's gaze sweeps us up and down, taking in our rumpled appearance. "You two homeless? Runaways?"

I shake my head. "No."

With a roll of his eyes, the janitor points. "Down those stairs and follow the signs. Hurry up. If my boss sees people in this building who aren't supposed to be here, I'll lose my job. Nothing wrong with helping people every so often, but we're not a shelter. Understand?"

"Yes," we agree together.

Adrenaline keeps me moving, despite the fact that I can't stop shivering. Kye takes a few things out of his backpack before handing it to me. "Use whatever you need. I'm sorry we had to leave so much behind."

"My fault. It's fine." I change into the only clothes I have—a pair of jeans and my new "I ♥ NY" T-shirt—then brush my tangled hair and wash my face. As I fold my sleepwear into the pack, my fingers brush the cosmetic bag and I decide to take two more minutes to be a girl, knowing it'll make me feel infinitely better. Lip gloss, concealer, mascara, and the tiniest bit of eyeliner, and I feel more awake and refreshed than I have in days.

Even after the makeup, I've been in the restroom for less than ten minutes. "Wow," Kye remarks. "That was fast. I've never met a girl who could put herself together in such a short amount of time." He looks like he just stepped out of the shower, all fresh and pressed. His hair is combed, waving slightly on the sides, and he's changed into slim-fit jeans and the T-shirt I bought him. He turns in a slow circle. "What do you think of my new shirt?"

I laugh. Other than the fact that my shirt is pink and his is black, we match. "It suits you."

He brushes a kiss on my forehead and takes me in his arms. "Thanks. I love it."

We stop for breakfast at a deli a few blocks away. The waitress brings me pancakes with strawberries, and Kye an omelet with wheat toast.

"You know, considering how people have been chasing us pretty much since the bus, I'm starting to wonder if you're bad luck," he says. His eyes sparkle with mirth as he laughs over a frosty glass of orange juice, and my heart swells in a way it never has before. I can deny all I want, be afraid and apprehensive and adolescent, but my heart screams.

I've fallen completely, absolutely, and unchangeably in love with Kye.

My throat clogs because I understand that this is it for me. The thing people spend their whole lives searching for. Maybe several lifetimes. The feeling poets write sonnets about. All the sappy love songs on the radio finally make sense. This is more than TV sitcom love, this is movie love. Storybook and fairy tale love. Except we're writing our own story. Whatever hesitation I felt getting on the plane, whatever unease trembled up my spine when I left my mother behind, I would follow Kye anywhere. Whatever the sacrifice, I'll make it willingly to be with him. To protect him. Us.

In this moment, he's become my whole world. Everything that came before him pales in importance to the boy who is really a man. Warmth spreads from my heart and heats my cheeks to a bright blush as I smile into his eyes.

"What? Do I have something in my teeth?" He runs his tongue over them.

"No."

"Then why are you smiling?"

"I'm smiling at you," I tell him. "Because you're just so pretty."

"Right back at ya." His hand trails down my back until his arm is around my waist and he pulls me closer, chair and all, and leans his cheek against my head with a sigh.

My ring hums to life, drawing my attention to the softly glowing stones. Kye notices too, but his expression is hard to read. He seems bothered by it.

"Are you okay?" I press my lips to his chin.

Nichole Giles

He kisses the tip of my nose. "You know, this isn't the first trip I've taken trying to protect the world from the Dark Elen."

I scoop a forkful of his omelet and taste it. "Mm. I figured."

"But you're the first person to come with me. Well, besides Val. But he doesn't really count." He samples my pancakes before paying the bill—refusing the money I offer—and follows me outside. "Did I tell you Val taught me how to use my Gift?"

"Val? Not your parents?"

"Are you kidding? For the first half of my life, they thought the genes skipped a generation. Their abilities are so obvious." We start down a quiet side street that is mostly devoid of foot traffic. "They sent me to live with Val, hoping he could teach me to have one of *their* Gifts, but it didn't happen.

"Val had a cat. The thing started talking to me as soon as I walked through the door. A few weeks later, Val realized I was communicating with his pet and started teaching me about the Earth Guardians—you know, faeries, merpeople, animals and plant life—and that's been my calling ever since."

Near the entrance to Central Park, a bicyclist towing a carriage slows to a stop. "Get you a ride, kids?"

"Yes," Kye says, drawing me aboard the carriage.

"Where do you want to go?"

"Surprise us." Kye puts his arm around me and I lean my head on his shoulder. "Just make sure we end up in a completely different place from where we started."

The guy grins. "Mind if I put in my earbuds? I gotta have music to keep going in the morning."

Kye shrugs. "Sure."

All around us, tall buildings skewer the sky above the trees like spires on a castle, enclosing the park and making it feel smaller than it really is.

When I shiver, Kye tucks me under his arm. "You cold?"

"Not like I was earlier." I turn my face to the gray sky. "This whole thing seems so unreal, so dream-like. Do you ever get used to it?"

190

He kisses the top of my head. "Not really. For a long time I tried to keep my worlds separate. I had a life at school, where I was a normal guy with homework and friends. And then I'd leave campus and go to Val's—where my other life took over. The one where I could communicate with plants and animals, and fairies and sprites sent me messages. And on top of my school work, Val had me studying a whole other curriculum. Ancient texts about communication, how to rappel, climb, scuba dive, survive in the wild ... all kinds of fun stuff."

"Like picking locks?"

"Yep." He grins. "Like that. About the time I turned sixteen, I realized I was attempting the impossible. I couldn't keep up."

"No one can live a double life forever," I murmur.

"I came to understand that my Gifts have a purpose—that I can actually make a difference as a bridge between the natural and supernatural worlds. So, I decided to embrace my abilities and my heritage—which meant accepting that I would never be able to have certain things most people take for granted. Only now ..."

His breath is shaky. "I realize that even embracing everything else, I'll still to have to give up the thing that has become most important to me."

A knot of dread curls in my stomach. "What's that?"

His Adam's apple bobs as he swallows hard. He leans his head back and squeezes his eyes shut. "You don't want to know."

The misery in his expression makes it impossible not to believe him. "Tell me anyway."

His eyes are tortured when he opens them. "You, Abby. Heaven save me, I'll have to give up you."

191

TWENTY-EIGHT

Debt

"What are you talking about?" I untangle myself from his arms and lean back, confused. "We hadn't met when you were sixteen."

He swallows again, grinding his jaw, his eyes glassy. "I know. But I've been dreaming about you my whole life. I didn't know who you were or how I'd ever find you, or if you were even real. Part of me thought you were just a girl in my dreams, sometimes my nightmares. I didn't put it all together until yesterday—in the subway." He takes my hands and I can't tell who's shaking more. The look in his eyes burns a hole in my heart.

"What are you saying? I don't understand."

"If you're really Raina, and I'm really Theron, then we're cursed. Something happened during the war. One of Raina's protective spells backfired. It was meant to protect them, to save them, keep them together, but instead, it killed them. No one knows how or why, but in all the years since, none of the scholars or historians has found a way to fix it. We have about two months—three at most—as long as Raina and Theron were together before the war."

Kye presses his fingers to his eyes. "They warned me not to get attached. They said I can't keep you anyway, but at the time it didn't make any sense. We hadn't even met yet, so I had no idea how it would feel—that it would be so hard." He scrubs his hands over his face. "Abby, I swear, I had no idea that day on the bus. I wouldn't have put you through this on purpose. You have to believe me. Please believe me."

His voice cracks on the last words, and my heart cracks with it. I pull his hands away from pressing against his eyes. "Kye, you're babbling, and I still don't understand."

"Okay. Okay." He threads his fingers through his hair and presses down like he's trying to hold his head on his shoulders. Like it's going to explode. "Theron and Raina can't stay together. We can't stay together."

"Why?"

"We'll die."

My stomach pitches. He said this once before, and I think ... I know he's right, feel the truth in his words. Sick dread bubbles in my gut and I experience an entirely new form of nausea. "Who tried to warn you?"

"The faeries. The sprites. The animals. Even ... even the mermaids in the river." He looks stricken. "I was so caught up in you that I didn't even listen to their song."

"What were they warning you against?" I'm trying to stay calm for him, so I turn his face toward me with my palm on his neck. "Being with me? Or fighting this supposed curse?" This feels like an important detail. Something I should know.

He closes his eyes and shakes his head, his throat working.

"Has anyone ever asked the faeries—or animals or plants—for help in reversing it? Do they know what went wrong?"

He opens his eyes again. "Val wanted me to build a relationship with the elementals because he hopes Dryden will someday be restored. But before that can happen, both worlds have to be balanced. That's what I've been working on for the past two years. Trying to help find balance. They know what has to be done. But, Abby, we've been through this—or Theron and Raina have, anyway—five or six times. It's all documented. If the elementals could have helped with the curse before, they didn't, so why would they now? I doubt there's anything they can do."

He shifts in his seat, pulling me into his lap, seeming to calm a little with the contact. "The thing is, despite all the warnings, even if I'd known, I wouldn't have stopped myself from falling in love with you."

My heart skips and my blood warms. "You love me?"

The sound he makes falls somewhere between a whimper and a choke. "Abby, I love you so much my heart wants to explode with it. I want to touch you all the time, and hold you, and ... just ... be with you. I want—"

My arms wind around him and my lips cut off his words. I kiss him until my heart feels like it could beat out of my chest and into his. Until we melt together like we're one person, until the energy surrounding us turns a perfect pale lavender that glows through my closed eyelids. Our lips and tongues tangle together, creating a taste sweeter than anything I've experienced and completely, uniquely ours. His arms slide up my back until his fingers tangle in my hair and send shockwaves of happiness down to my toes. My fingers stroke the short hair at the nape of his neck while I kiss him like we're the only two people in the universe who have ever truly loved—because in that moment, we are.

My heart is his. Irrevocably.

By the time we break apart, my face is flushed and my skin tingles, and I don't care about curses and demons and death. Right now, what matters most to me is that I've found the boy in my dreams, and I finally understand why I've always needed him. Holding his face between my hands, I tell him, "I love you too. Whatever happens, I'll love you until the day I die."

He swears, his arms tightening around me. "This is impossible. I can't love you the way I do, but I can't help it. You can't be with me here, but you are."

"I wouldn't want to be anywhere else." I lean my head on his shoulder and nuzzle his neck.

"Even if it kills you?"

My eyelids flutter closed, tickling his skin with my lashes. "It won't. We won't let that happen. There has to be a way. There just does."

"No." He gently nudges me onto the seat. "No, no, no. This is like déjà vu. I told you, we've been through this before. A lot. It doesn't work. And there's something else."

I lean back, stare at the tops of the buildings towering above the trees, then glance at the back of the guy who is pedaling so hard. A spot of sweat has soaked through the back of his shirt, even though his breath comes out in puffs of white.

"Raina died because of me." His eyes change, filling with pent-up emotions that seem hundreds of years old. An image superimposes over his face and his voice takes on a thick Irish brogue. "I won't let that happen this time. The world—I couldn't survive it again."

My heart races as I reach out tentatively to touch Theron's face, needing to assure myself that Theron and Kye are one and the same. But the image is gone. Now it's just Kye and me again. Kye drops his head in his hands, the muscle in his jaw ticking. "I dreamed about you last night—only not you, Raina."

"Kye." My voice is soft. "Just because Raina died doesn't mean I will."

"History repeats itself, Abby, and we've never beat this before. It's like a fast-spreading cancer."

"But I'm fine right now—and I think you are, too." I stroke his hair.

"We have weeks. Maybe a couple months." He gulps. "When it's over ..."

"Oh."

The bike stops on the opposite side of the park from where we started. Street vendors have set up tables along the sidewalks, selling souvenirs and paintings, works of art a person can only find in New York City.

Our conversation swirls in my head until I'm dizzy, so I block it out, searching for a distraction. We both need it. I look at every charcoal sketch and every picture on display. We stop to watch an artist dip her brush in paint and create shadows and light on a canvas. It's an amazing likeness of the city. I dig out my camera and snap pictures.

We're walking in Central Park when a knot forms in the pit of my stomach and overpowers everything, all my conflicting emotions and thoughts. *Something isn't right.* The energy surrounding us turns dull gray as Kye slaps a hand over my mouth—which is a good thing, given my startled cry—and drags me with him behind the cover of an eight-foot shrub.

Two businessmen pass by. One—wearing a charcoal suit and black tie—has immaculately styled, unnatural fire-red hair. The other man—much more casual in a pair of tan pants and a flowered tie—is also perfectly coifed, though his hair is boring brown.

As the men continue down the street without so much as looking in our direction, Kye breathes a sigh of relief and hails a cab, directing the driver to take us to Chinatown.

"What was that about?" I ask.

Kye keeps looking behind us, anxious. "Juri's henchmen. Didn't you recognize them? They were at the hotel in Vegas."

My forehead scrunches as I try to remember. "Are you sure?"

"I'm positive."

The cab lets us out at a market in a shabbier part of town. Little open-air shops, practically bursting at the seams, squeeze together like bodies on a packed subway train. I ogle the variety of goods with a sense of wonder. "What is this place?"

"Canal Street. Good shopping, easy to blend with the crowd." Kye turns me toward the shops. "We need a break. There's nothing more we can do to stop the Dark Elen from here, and it's hours until our flight. Let's have some fun."

When I'm not looking, Kye buys me a pair of dirt-cheap emerald earrings that must be stolen. I try to argue, but he's already forked over the cash, so it's not like he can take them back. It occurs to me that I probably owe Kye money. A lot of money.

"This trip must be costing a small fortune." I shake my head, clueless, wondering how much I owe him. I don't even know where to start adding. "I'm going to pay you back for my half of all this. As soon as we get home, I'll get a job. I'll—"

Kye tips my chin up, forcing me to look him in the eyes. "Abby, stop."

"But—"

"Stop," he says, firmly. "If I was worried about money, we wouldn't be here."

"How can you not worry? You don't even have a job." *Does he?*

Kye shakes his head and steers me past a pushy vendor selling designer knock-offs. "Are you getting hungry?"

"Yes." We decide on Chinese, because it's like a law when you're visiting a place called Chinatown. We choose an authentic restaurant where bright dragons painted rust red, shiny purple, and bright green float across tapestries on the walls, each decorated with a different symbol. The chipped tabletops are scrubbed clean, edged with aluminum, and topped with fake white lilies. A waitress brings us water and takes our order.

Finally, I ask, "Are you ever going to tell me?"

"What?"

"The money, remember? Our bill must be ginormous. I need to know how much we've spent so I can figure out how to pay you back."

The waitress sets our drinks on the table, and I sip mine, waiting for her to leave so he can answer.

Kye takes my hand on the table, looking suddenly apprehensive. "Abby, you won't be paying anything back. It isn't my money we're spending. It's yours."

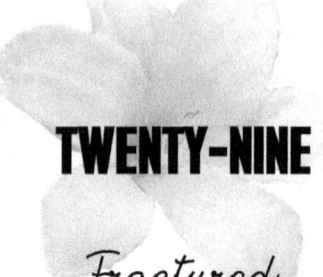

TWENTY-NINE

Fractured

It's my turn to laugh. "Oh, right. The two hundred dollars I brought got us plane tickets and a hotel room, ferry tickets, cab rides, food. And let's not forget our recent shopping spree." I jiggle the handbag I bought for my mother.

His head bobs, conceding. "All right, not exactly yours. It's Raina's."

"I thought Raina didn't have any money."

"She didn't have anything but the clothes on her back, but when they got engaged, Theron set her up to buy whatever she wanted. Like a dowry or bride-price. And because he wanted her to know it was really her money—regardless of her new title—Theron had it stored in a church outside of Dryden, where the priests could guard it, sort of like a bank."

"Right." I pinch the bridge of my nose to ward off a headache. "Next you're going to tell me you're carrying gold pieces in your pocket like Pippi Longstocking."

"Does a platinum card count?"

"Oh, brother."

"Val handles the money, investments and stuff." He rests his hand on my arm. "Raina's money has become a central source of funding for all research and projects aimed at restoring Dryden to the Gifted."

I wonder if I can buy a remedy to break the curse. *Do fairies take bribes?* "Even if I was Raina once, I'm not her now. I wouldn't feel right claiming her money."

He stirs the ice in his glass, unsmiling. "Maybe you should. Consider it a consolation prize for the life you'll never have." He meets my eyes and I feel the familiar burning sensation of threatening tears.

Does he mean a life of normalcy or a life with him? "How did Val end up with Raina's money?"

Kye taps his fingertips on the table. "After the demons were locked away, the goddess Macha made Valdemar—the last surviving priest—guardian of the money. He was the only person who knew where the treasure was hidden. In fact, he's still the only one who can access it. All I know is that when stuff comes up, he makes sure money gets deposited in the right places. In cautious, non-concerning amounts, of course."

"Well, that's handy, isn't it?" I stare, one eyebrow raised, not sure how to feel about this new revelation. "And strange, in a money-laundering-drug-dealer-ish way."

"Hey, I'll pay you back," Kye says, only half joking.

"It's not *my* money." I lean closer, searching his face. "I'm not her, Kye. Not anymore."

He wraps his hand around mine on the table. "I know."

The waitress brings steaming plates of cashew pork, orange-pineapple chicken, brown rice, and egg rolls. I scoop a portion of each onto my plate and take a bite, licking the sauce that drips on my finger. It has just the right combination of crunch and tang, the sweet chicken so tender I barely have to chew it. Flavor explodes on my tongue and my eyes roll back in my head. It's so, so good. I devour everything on my plate, barely pausing between bites.

"Wow, you were hungry," Kye says through his own mouthful. "I've never seen you eat so much."

I wave my fork and swallow. "I don't always remember to eat, so when I do, I make sure to do it well." Kye watches me scoop another portion, looking fascinated. He's barely touched his own food. "Aren't you hungry?"

He gazes at his plate as if belatedly realizing it's there. "I'm just enjoying the show."

I look up long enough to grab an egg roll and dip it in the sweet and sour sauce. "You mean the one called Abby the Pig?"

"You can call it whatever you want as long as I get to watch."

I throw my napkin at him and pick up our conversation. "Tell me about the laws."

Kye pauses, his loaded chopsticks poised in the air. "Laws? For what?"

"You know, for Gifted people." I dip the last of my eggroll in sauce while Kye purses his lips. "Don't you watch TV? Every society has rules. What happens if you break them? Are there Gifted police people who keep us in line?" These are things I need to know if I'm going to figure a way around the curse.

"We have Dragons—but not of the legendary variety. More like a council of really powerful Gifted. As for rules, no harming, stealing from or conning regular people, and if we want to keep our powers, they have to stay under wraps.

"If we screw up big enough, the Dragons will know and they'll be by to visit. They're good guys, but still scary. Also, we follow laws of the land—otherwise we'd never blend into society."

"Not to mention going to jail." I lean against the seat, rubbing my full stomach. "You know, if we like, robbed a bank or something."

He grins. "There is that."

"What happens if someone finds out?"

"Power can't be hidden from another Gifted. That's why so many Gifted end up in places like Jackson—near natural sources of Earth Power. All that volcanic activity is just bubbling with power-boosting energy. Plus, as more of us gather together, our Gifts feed each other and we get stronger, our abilities more pronounced. But if someone else discovers what we can do … well, let's just say steps would be taken to relieve that person of the knowledge." He shudders. "Safety precautions. And the person who revealed the Gift would be punished.

"In the case of someone like your mom, who isn't Gifted but has a blood tie to you, it's a little different. There's no way to keep it from her. Mothers know all, right? Only problem is now that the Elen know who you are, they'll find her eventually. But Val thinks she'll be protected as long as you're in her care."

He smiled at my look of surprise. "Didn't know that, did you? Your Gifts protect your mother just because you live in her house. Like a magical shield. One of Raina's spells that didn't backfire. Anyway, I don't know enough to tell you more than that. Val can fill you in on the rest."

I swirl the ice around in my glass as I contemplate the new information. "Do you really believe he doesn't know how to break this curse?"

Kye scoots closer. "If he did, it wouldn't be an issue anymore. And yes, he would tell me. He has no reason to lie." His arms slide around my waist. "If the Elen get their hands on all the Keys, none of it will matter anyway. We'll all end up dead. Or wishing we could die."

"The weight of the world is a heavy load." I brush a lock of hair out of his eyes, swallowing a lump in my throat.

Pain flickers across his face. "Yes," he says, squeezing my hand.

"Will my mother be in danger when I move out?"

Kye nods, slowly. "Probably. Unless she ... uh, moves in with another one of us. If she were to move in with Akers or Valdemar, even if the family bond wasn't active, they'd at least be able to protect her. To sense danger before it got to her. Or she could get remarried."

I try not to choke on that idea. "Okay. So, there are some options then."

Kye picks up his chopsticks and stirs them around in the leftover sauce on his plate. "Look, I know what you're planning. Or trying to plan. It's written all over your face."

I look away, guilty.

"We could try it. I don't know if it would work, but we could try running. Don't think I haven't been searching for a way around this thing. You can't make a decision like this without knowing all the facts."

I smile, more confident. "Then tell me the facts. I already know what I want."

He buries his face in his hands, blowing out a long breath. "Babe, I wish it was only about what you want. Or what I want. Because we both want the same thing, trust me." He presses his palms against his forehead like he has a headache, so I rub my Alexandrite necklace, humming, and gently massage his forehead with my fingertips.

"If we ran away, we'd have to keep moving to stay out of Tynan's reach. They'll look for us forever. You couldn't go home to visit your mom—not even for the holidays. No Rose or Jen or Erda. Ever. If we actually succeeded in getting away and staying alive and hidden—which would be a miracle, considering the strength of your energy field—we'd probably both lose our Gifts because we'd have to stay away from the power sources that feed them."

I bite my lip and stop humming. "I can't just never see my mom again."

"That's what I'm trying to tell you." He pulls my hand away from his head and laces our fingers so we're palm to palm, then leans his forehead against mine. "If we run away, the Elementals will see my departure as a betrayal and leave the other Gifted to fight the Dark Ones alone. The people we love will be even more handicapped in fighting against evil. And if the demons are set free, the entire planet could be in jeopardy."

"Right." *How can I live with that? How can I ask him to?* I feel selfish for wanting to run, but the idea of walking away from Kye gives me stomach cramps that threaten to tear up my insides.

"And the curse will make us terribly, horribly sick. We'd both be dead within a few months. Our life together would end in pure and utter misery."

Now *my* head hurts. I push my plate aside and press my cheek to the tabletop. "How do you do it? How does a person live with all this responsibility? With the threats?"

He slides his hand under my cheek and lifts my face to look at him. "I take it one day at a time. Do you see why it's so important to have all the facts? Because what you see as options really aren't options at all."

"I don't know how to do this," I choke. Tears well in my eyes, burn there, and I blink them away. "I can't be responsible for so many people."

He strokes my hair when I bury my face in his neck. "Shh. Don't think about it now. You don't have to decide right this minute."

"Decide what? Either I embrace my Gifts and commit to using them to help save other people—maybe even the world—without you, or we run away together and probably die."

Kye's eyes glisten and he swallows. "We're both going to die someday anyway. Maybe whatever time we can steal will be worth it. If that's really what you want, I'm willing. I'd do anything for you."

"Stop it!" A tear escapes and runs down my cheek. "Don't talk like that. Do you really think I'm that selfish? That I'd knowingly sentence the people we love to death just so we can try to live a dream?"

"No, I don't think that." He wipes the tear away with his thumb, his hand shaking. "It's what I want, too. I just don't know how to make it work." His next breath is uneven, and so is his voice. "It's killing me to see you cry this way."

"I can't handle all this," I whisper, wiping my eyes. "I'm just a kid."

"Abby, you're strong. You can handle anything." The waitress approaches, and Kye pays our bill with the infamous credit card, then takes my hand and leads me outside.

Since we still have a few hours before our flight, we decide to get tickets to a play. I've always wanted to see one, and we need a distraction. We snag two prime seats to *Phantom of the Opera*, and Kye says, "We have a little over two hours, a platinum card, and about a million places to shop. How about we make tonight extra special? I think it's the least Raina owes us, under the circumstances." His lips curl into my favorite uneven smile and the light from the setting sun turns his eyes into sparkling blue sapphires. He is everything that matters in my world.

I choose a simple silver dress with a wide scoop neck and long, fitted sleeves. The silk hugs my curves past my waist and flares at the bottom, pooling around my new silver spike-heeled sandals. As a concession to Kye's insistence that I get a coat, I top off the outfit with a long, white velvet wrap. A coat would be more practical, but the wrap reminds me of a distant memory I'm determined to cling to. It'll be warm enough.

Kye pays while I change in the fitting room, taking an extra minute to twist my hair into a knot at the crown of my head and secure it with bobby pins from my makeup bag. A few stray tendrils escape the knot, refusing to be tamed into the bun, so I let them be.

When I meet up with Kye again, he's wearing a charcoal suit and tie. His hair is wet and combed, though the naughty waves fight away from his scalp where it's dried. I can't breathe for looking at him. *Theron.* I don't know how I didn't see it before today.

His wide-eyed appraisal makes me squirm. "You don't like."

He blinks. "I like. I like a lot."

"But ..." I say, prodding.

"But something's not quite right."

I run my hands down the front of my dress. "What? Is it lumpy somewhere?"

He reaches into his pocket and pulls out the pendant.

It's so pretty. It would look great with this dress, but too much could go wrong if I wear it in public. "I can't wear that. It's really valuable and it doesn't belong to me."

"It belongs to you right now." He clasps the pendant around my throat, his fingers lingering on the bare skin behind my neck, sending goose bumps down my spine. "See? Perfect."

I've never seen a more stunning stone in my life. Kye reminds me about the earrings he bought me, and I put them on. The pendant warms my skin and energy surges through me in a way I've never felt before. The lights flicker and the tips of my fingers tingle, then my toes, and then the rest of my body. My head spins. I sway.

The music swells and he takes my hand. Cheering and clapping erupts in the background. I don't look away and neither does he. It's as though the world melts around us as we dance our wedding dance. All is well, and we're safe inside our little bubble. Theron and me.

Kye braces me with a hand on my back. I turn into him, wind my arms around his waist, tuck my face into his neck. We stay like this, our bodies fitted together like puzzle pieces, unmoving and unbreakable, until a salesperson shoos us away.

Shaking his head about my choice of outerwear, Kye drapes the wrap over my shoulders. "Tell her to buy a coat and she picks out a blanket with holes for arms."

"It's called style." I drop my wallet and camera in his jacket pocket.

He offers his elbow and escorts me outside, saying, "You better not end up with pneumonia."

The show is amazing; Christine's terror, the hypnotic Phantom, Raoul's haunting voice. My chest aches with emotion and tears pool in my eyes as I clutch Kye's hand, watching the story unfold. We stand for the curtain call, clapping until my palms are sore, then Kye slides his arm around my waist. "We should get going."

We stop in front of the theater to pose for a few snapshots, and then Kye puts the camera away and brushes a soft kiss across my lips. I grab his lapel and pull him closer, kiss him harder, afraid to let go. *What will happen when we get home?* He pulls away with a shaky breath. "We should find a cab."

I nod, shivering with nerves.

"You're cold." Kye shrugs out of his jacket and drapes it around my shoulders over the top of my wrap.

"Not really." But I put my arms through the sleeves and hold the jacket close, breathing in his scent. I'll never forget this day—this entire trip–with Kye. Glowing energy spreads from the top of my head, pouring like soft, warm liquid to the tips of my toes.

My heart will shatter if I have to let him go, but nothing in the past or future can change what's between us right now. I'll never forget what he is to me, always. And what he can't be.

Unless we fracture the curse. Reverse the spell.

The line for cabs is long, so we cross the street and walk another block. Not far from the theater, an eerie feeling of danger ripples in the air. I open my mouth to warn Kye, but before I can make a sound, someone grabs me from behind, wrenching me out of Kye's grasp.

Then all I can do is scream.

THIRTY

Self-Defense

"**K**ye!"

"Abby!" he screams.

With my arms pinned to my sides, I'm dragged backwards into an alley, losing sight of him.

"Didn't think you could hide forever, did you?" The gravelly voice belongs to Juri.

I kick him, struggling to free myself while he hauls me into the shadows. "Let me go."

His breath is hot in my ear as he cuffs my wrists together behind me. "I don't think so, princess." Juri runs his hand down the side of my jaw—a mocking caress—and I shudder. "You've given me more trouble than expected."

"Back atcha." I try not to swallow, letting the saliva pool in my mouth so I can spit in his face when the angle is right.

"Landon always had too much faith in people. Some things never change."

Wishing I could turn around and see his face, I say nothing.

"You know, you interest me. Raina always interested me. Pretty enough to start the whole bloody Elen war. Pretty. Not beautiful, not breathtaking or stunning. Just pretty. A woman who can cause a cataclysm of that proportion is a curious thing. Makes a man wonder about her other attributes."

I shudder again. Disgusted. Terrified. *Where is Kye?*

Juri's fingers trace my collarbone and caress the necklace at my throat. "This is an added bonus," he says, wrapping his fingers around the center stone. "Two prized items in one. Saves me some work." I think he's going to yank it off, but he lets it drop as his hand moves lower to cup my breast.

My mouth goes dry. *Run away. Get away, run away, get away.* Shaking, I hit, scream, kick, gouge. But Juri has a firm grip on my wrists. I'm trapped.

"I love a girl who fights." He heaves me off my feet and dumps me on the ground, my hip thudding on the cold concrete. The rough surface scrapes the skin off my elbows and shoots pain up my arms. Desperate, I continue screaming, struggling.

"If you stop fighting, I'll make it less painful. You'll never escape on your own." Breath wheezes in and out of his mouth. He drops to his knees, his hands fumbling with his belt buckle. *No.* My sandal heel scrapes across the ground as I pick up my foot and kick, connect with his groin. Juri falls on his side, howling. My hip throbs as I drag myself up to stand, to run. My entire body feels bruised.

Without Kye, I'm not fast. Juri tackles me again a few feet away. His amber eyes glint and an angry sound rumbles in his chest. "You don't know when to stop, do you? Tell you what. I'll be gentle with you if you give me the ring first."

"I'd rather die than have your hands on me," I say through ragged breaths.

"I can arrange that." He yanks me up by the front of my dress and pins me against the brick wall, breath streaming out like a mouthful of smoke. His right arm pulses with a greenish glow and the skin—starting from the tips of his fingers—rolls back over his elbow, the bone mutating into a gleaming white sword.

Before I can process what's happened, the sharp edge of his blade is pressed against my throat.

My insides clench and I'm frozen in terror when he fumbles with his belt, the button on his pants. The blade bites into my skin, deeper with his every move, and a trickle of blood rolls down my neck. Juri's teeth graze my ear with a feral hunger as he nudges aside Kye's jacket and bites my shoulder until he draws blood.

As pain blossoms across my entire shoulder, a void breaks open inside me, a wide chasm of distance that tells me Kye will not come charging to my rescue this time, because he's gone. Taken far away. My ring, powerful in his presence, is now still, dormant.

Gram's voice echoes in my head. *Concentrate, Abby. Find the light inside you. Knowledge is power.*

Still struggling against my captor, I close my eyes, digging deeper than I ever have, searching for anything that will help me.

I will not give up. I will not give in.

Juri lowers his sword to slice open a slit in my dress, and finally my self-defense instinct kicks in. I wrench my arm free and aim for his face with the heel of my hand. The impact sends a shockwave up my arm. He screams, blood spurting from his nose.

While he's disoriented, I whirl around and plunge my spiked heel into his upper thigh. He shrieks, and I yank my shoe out with a sickening pop, watching as a river of blood oozes down his leg.

He thrusts the sword under my chin, cutting a thin line of skin all the way across. The back of my head hits the wall and pain explodes in my skull.

"Kick me again, and you'll lose that pretty head of yours. We only need your heart and a few vials of blood to take your powers."

Bile rises in my mouth, but I swallow it, allowing anger to override fear. Balling my hand into a fist, I swing hard and low, catching him in the gut.

As he doubles over, stubby spikes force through his scalp and a sharp, hot pain rips into my thigh where Juri's sword stabs, just below the slit in my dress. Blood spills from the wound, surging down my leg.

Black spots swim in front of my eyes and I force them away, knowing I won't survive if I pass out. "Kye!" I cry feebly, picturing his face.

"He won't be saving you today, princess. I'm afraid he's busy—if Tynan hasn't killed him already." Juri twists the sword in my leg, sending searing fire through my body, and I scream in agony.

I hear Gram's voice, louder this time, and stronger. *Find the light.*

A warm breeze catches my hair. I reach deep, gather all my courage, all my strength, and bring it up until my body shakes with unused power. The gemstones against my throat, in my ears, and on my finger heat and glow until I'm surrounded by a pocket of light. Juri's sword is forced out of my thigh and he falls back, looking afraid.

I've never experienced power like this, but I somehow know how to use it. In a flash of brilliant light, I cross my arms over my chest and fling energy at Juri. He flies backward with the force of a speeding car and hits the brick so hard that pieces of it crumble, raining on his head while he lies face-down on the pavement, unconscious.

There is nothing left for me to do now except run.

THIRTY-ONE

Desperate

Adrenaline propels me to the street where I last saw Kye. Blood pours down my leg at an alarming rate. All pain and feeling is now centered in my throbbing wound, while the rest of me feels numb.

Tears streak my cheeks as I wrap Kye's jacket around me, stumbling down the street with no idea where I'm going or what I should do next. "Kye!" I sob, knowing he can't hear me. "Kye. I need you." A cold breeze blows past, wraps around me like a glacial funnel, sparkling with crystals of black ice, and I feel a frighteningly familiar tingling sensation.

Less than a block away, a group of people huddle together, laughing and carrying on a conversation, but none of them notices me, or the man who materializes out of thin air, here to terrorize me further. "Hello, Raina."

The first time we met, I didn't pay close enough attention to see that Tynan and Kye have the same facial structure. They're the same height, the same build, and have similar voices. They have different hair colors, skin tone, and eyes, but otherwise, they could be twins.

Polar opposites, like the babies we saw in the Cairn Elen.

"Where's Kye?" I choke, fighting the black spots again. "What have you done with him?"

"He's gone to where it started."

A vision—short but strong.

Kye hangs by his arms from a ceiling in a dim room. Blood trickles down his face, past his swollen, bruised eyes, and soaks into the dirt beneath his feet where a large, reddish stain spreads into a puddle.

I stagger. "What do you want? You've already cursed us to death. Why can't you just leave us alone?"

"Happy to—as soon as you set me free. Unseal the door you closed, undo the curse binding me here." He blinks out of focus, like an image projected from a camera. "You must deliver the remaining Keys into the jaws of the beast. Free the lost civilization and restore the true order of Dryden."

"What does that mean?" Tynan's image blinks again, fades away. "And where do I go?" It does me no good. Tynan's gone.

Black spots pop and float in my eyes, and the toes on my right foot feel numb from lack of blood. One step at a time, I move forward. I brace against a building so I can assess the damage. The cut on my neck is shallow but should still be treated, and blood gushes from the wound in my leg. This one needs to be cleaned and bound to protect against germs and the cold, dirty air, and to prevent me from losing too much blood. I'm grateful Juri didn't hit an artery—I'd be dead already.

Kye is too far away to help me now. I have ten dollars in my wallet, which is still in the pocket of Kye's jacket. If I go to a hospital, no one will believe the truth and I'll miss my plane. It shouldn't matter, but going back to Jackson is the only thing I can think to do. Kye's dad was going to meet us there, so he's probably already on his way. It's the only place where I can get help. If I can find a way to get to the airport on time, and not bleed to death.

I rub my neck where Juri's knife sliced, swearing when my fingers come away red.

Tears of anger and frustration burn my eyes, and I let them fall. Healing is about taking broken energy into a whole vessel and sending it back repaired. Gram never taught me how to Heal myself. Drops of cold water drip into my hair from somewhere high above, and I bury my face in my hands, sobbing as the cold seeps all the way to my bones.

Use pressure to stop the bleeding.

Gram's voice.

Swallowing another sob, I rip a strip off the bottom of my new dress and tie it around my leg, pull tight until the circulation slows. Pain burns all the way down—I won't be able to walk far—but I brace my hands against the wall and limp stiffly forward.

Once again, I clutch Kye's jacket closed at the neck, taking strength from his unique woodsy scent while hiding my injury. Feeling a smidgen of energy Kye left behind, I wrap my arms around myself to absorb whatever I can. A stiff crackle from inside the breast pocket leads me to one of the crisp fifty-dollar bills Kye withdrew from an ATM while we were shopping. *Maybe it's enough.* I hail a cab.

"Newark airport, please. And hurry, I'm going to miss my plane."

The dark-haired man turns, and I cower, half expecting violet eyes and a wicked sneer. "You sure you don't want a hospital?" he asks. "Looks like you need stitches."

I shake my head. "I don't have time. It may already be too late."

"Suit yourself." As we shoot into traffic, I dig through my cosmetic bag until I find my homemade Healing ointment and smear a liberal amount on my neck, hoping it works fast. Then I lean back and stare out the window, watching the crowds, lights, and neon signs fade into the distance. When I'm sure we're out of the danger zone, I focus my third eye on Kye, trying to see where he's been taken or what's being done to him.

Clouds of steam pour out of a cave protected by a boiling pool of gray liquid. Bits of greenery fight through the dirt in patches. Farther away, several feet of snow are piled high, but there's none near the mouth of the cave. More steam puffs out and a roar, like that of a dragon or a waterfall, fills my ears.

"You're bleeding through." The driver's voice breaks my concentration. I glance down, and see that he's right. A bright red circle is forming on the outside of my makeshift bandage.

"You know," he continues, casually. "Security probably won't let you board, bad as you're bleeding. Having passengers die in the air don't make for good press."

My heart sinks. *Of course not.* "What should I do? I have to make that plane." I'm not exactly asking him—a complete stranger—so much as I'm asking the universe, which seems to be out to get me lately.

"I don't know, lady. I'm not a doctor or an airline official. I just call it like I see it."

Swallowing another lump, I unwrap the bandage. Though the flow of blood has slowed significantly, I'm still losing too much. My driver's right. If I leave the wound open, they won't let me on the plane. In fact, I need to clean up a lot if I want to make it through security.

My eyes fill with tears as I press down on the fabric, try to force the blood to clot, desperately humming Healing tones I only vaguely remember from Gram's lessons and leaning over so the pendant can swing in a clockwise circle above my leg wound. As the pain eases, I focus my concentration harder. *Maybe it will work. Maybe.*

Clots of blood coagulate inside the cut as the Healing process cleans, and then begins to mend. I watch in fascination as the muscles and tissues shrink and then slowly knit back together, bit by bit like a vacuum. The action sucks the oxygen out of the car until I can't catch a breath. "Hey, can we roll down a window?"

Outside, horns are honking wildly, people shouting.

When the driver doesn't respond, I look up and realize he's slumped in his seat, breathing shallow. We're stopped in the middle of the road.

I lean over the seat, shove the driver back, and hit the automatic window button, worried he's passed out from lack of oxygen. "I'll take over from here."

DESCENDANT

My wound isn't completely closed, but the bleeding has slowed enough that a good strong bandage will hold it for a while.

Careful of speeding traffic, I swing the door open and shimmy into the driver's seat—shoving the man out of the way. "I'm really sorry, mister. I don't think I could lift you." With my uninjured left leg, I press gently on the gas—worried, because I've never in my life used my left foot to drive. The car jerks forward, and I let up a bit. The driver's body slumps against me and I push him away again.

Then I notice the blood.

THIRTY-TWO

Murtagh

The driver's pant leg is stained dark red from blood oozing out of his thigh. A heavy ball of guilt settles in my stomach as my mind reels. "I ... what the ... this is ..." I can't form coherent sentences, but as my brain swirls, I must have unintentionally used the driver—the nearest whole vessel—to Heal myself. "I'm sorry, I'm sorry, I'm sorry." I pat the man's arm, as if that makes it better. "Please, please wake up."

He stirs, moans, but doesn't open his eyes. Cold air, perfumed with asphalt and car emissions, streams through the open window, and I let it slap me in the face, praying for a miracle.

Unless I figure out how to get to the airport on my own, I'll never make the plane. Tears slide down my cheeks and I swipe at them with the sleeve of Kye's jacket Just outside the tunnel, a buzzing dragonfly zooms through the open window and lands on the dash. I'm too busy scanning the sky for signs of landing planes to worry about it—until it starts talking.

"Why you cry, *mo chara?*"

My foot slides off the pedal and the cab slows. I stare at the dragonfly, squinting through my tears. "What?"

"You need help, no? Pray the goddess, not?" The little bug flits around, hovering near the cabbie's bleeding wound. I pull to a stop on side of the road. The lump in my throat grows from golf ball to baseball size and I swallow around it. "It was an accident."

When I look again, I realize he isn't a dragonfly, but a sprite with a set of rapidly fluttering iridescent wings. His blue skin and yellow hair—along with his size—work together to give him the appearance of an insect, but now that I've experienced a faery party, I know better.

He clucks his tongue at my cab driver, who's slumped against the passenger window, and flits between my Healing leg and the driver's wounded one. "Transference, yes?"

I shake my head. "I don't know what that means."

After a long string of untranslatable phrases, the sprite finally seems to realize I don't understand him. Switching to broken English, he strokes his chin and points at the unconscious man. "You heal self. Use him."

I shrug. "Sorry, I don't—"

"Man un-powerful. No Gift."

"Yes—I mean, no. He—I'm the one who—I didn't mean to hurt him, but I ..." I pause to swallow another lump. "I have to get to the airport, fast, and I need his help."

The sprite nods as if he has the answers to all my problems, but says nothing.

I blink, wait a few heartbeats, then say, "Can you wake him up?"

With a slow shake of his head, the sprite clucks his tongue again. "Not a Healer."

"Oh." Of course not. I put the car in gear and merge into traffic, watching the sky again.

He taps his chest with his thumbs. "Murtagh. Friend."

"Abby." I offer my pinkie to shake. My head pounds and my neck itches like it's on fire—a sign of healing—so I grind my teeth against the pain. The wound in my leg aches like nothing I've ever felt before, even though the bleeding has stopped. "You don't happen to know how to get to the airport?"

"Know to flying place. That way. That way." A light blinks from his middle when he gets excited. "Turn there."

By the time the airport lights glow through the windshield, the driver's eyelids are fluttering. He moans, coming to, and finally opens his eyes.

"How are you feeling?"

He squints, focusing first on me—driving his cab—then Murtagh. "What the ..." He sits up straighter as I park behind a white limousine. "A witch!" he yells. "You're a witch!" He glances at his leg and points a shaky finger at me. "Get out! Get out of my cab. I don't care what happened to you, I just want you gone. And take your freaky bug with you. Out!"

His accusation stings. Now I understand why Gram warned against calling myself a witch. It's become a label, a bad word, a curse. I can't really blame the guy, though. Look what I did to him. I wonder fleetingly if this is how Gifted people started being labeled in the first place.

The driver shoves me out the open door and chucks Kye's jacket at my face. I hug it to my chest, my only possession, and offer money through the open window. My voice shakes. "Thanks for the ride."

He snatches the bill, throws the car in gear, and guns the gas, tires barely missing my toes. Murtagh urges me on. "Hasten, *cailín* girl! Must go."

"Right." A swell of anxiety threatens to drown me when I think about getting on the plane without Kye. I feel like I'm leaving him behind, even though I know I'm not. I know. *He isn't here anymore.* And I have to hurry. Find him. Save him.

I stop outside the automatic doors. "Thanks for your help, Murtagh. I can take it from here."

He shakes his head. "No, *mo chara.* Take you to sacred place. Fly. With you go."

For some reason, Murtagh's words comfort me. It makes me feel better to know I won't be traveling all alone, even if my companion is a sprite. I slide on Kye's jacket and hold open a pocket. "All right, then. In you go."

Pain surges up my leg into my spine, sending shockwaves through my head with every step as I limp to the restroom to clean myself up. I'm relieved that the cut on my neck now resembles a long scratch, and once I clean off the blood, my leg doesn't look nearly so scary, either. After smearing some Healing balm on my leg wound, I rinse the bandage and retie it, adjusting my skirt to cover as much as possible. Then I pull on Kye's jacket and button the front to cover the stains on my dress. It's not perfect by any means, but I look a lot better than I did when I came in.

With Murtagh still urging me to hurry, I limp to the check-in counter. The lady looks concerned when she types in my name and gets my flight information. "Honey, you're one lucky woman. Plane's already boarding. Luggage?"

I shake my head, wondering what happened to Kye's backpack.

"Speeds things up some." The woman hands me a boarding pass. "What about your traveling companion? Mr. Kye Murphy?"

A few tears escape and I wipe them off my cheeks with my fingertips. "He's not coming."

Her fingers pause on the keyboard and her eyes fill with sympathy. "I'll call the flight attendants, have them hold the plane— but you'll have to run."

I let another tear escape. She calls a skycap to drive me in a cart, and I slide through the security line at warp speed, finally having found a moment of luck. To my relief, they don't question my injuries, even when I take off Kye's jacket, so I must have hidden the worst of it well enough. It still takes all my strength to not limp to where the skycap is waiting.

I'm ushered aboard and settled into first class, glad for once that Kye splurged. The crew seals the door and reads the emergency instructions as we roll onto the tarmac. Then the engines rumble, the pilot makes an announcement, and we hurl into the sky with a jolt.

The city lights fade as I huddle under a blanket, shaking, chilled all the way through as the adrenaline that has kept me going abates. With the blanket drawn up to my chin, I open my pocket to check on Murtagh. He's curled into a ball with his wings wrapped around him so he looks like a shiny pebble.

His inner light pulses and fades, the rhythm of his breathing the only indication he isn't actually a rock. "Are you okay in there?" I whisper. "Murtagh?"

He doesn't answer, but his wings ripple. He's asleep.

I prop my head on a pillow and bury my nose in Kye's jacket, once again searching for his scent. My mind's too troubled for sleep, but I close my eyes anyway. The way things are going, this will probably be my only chance to rest.

THIRTY-THREE

Explanations

It's a rough flight. Rather than sleep, I chastise myself for all the should-haves. Should have tried harder to find Kye. Should have called Eoin. Shouldn't have gone to the play. Should have walked the other direction. What else should I have done?

Is Kye suffering?

Am I selfish for getting on the plane?

Murtagh is still rolled up in my pocket. Maybe I should be suspicious of him, all things considered, but instinct tells me to trust him, and I'm learning to trust my instincts.

Once we reach cruising altitude, I ask the flight attendant for a first aid kit. She obliges with a frown, and I take it into the restroom and bandage my leg with actual gauze and medical tape. It isn't a pretty sight by any means, but heaps better than the strip of satin I've been using.

At the airport in Denver, I veer into the restroom and change my dressings again, grateful that this one lesson from Gram—how to make Healing balm—has proven its worth. Then I search for something that would've helped me in New York even more than the money in Kye's jacket. A phone.

I dial my home number, hoping Mom hears it and answers. She doesn't.

My flight boards in ten minutes and I don't have anyone else's number, so I dial Rose's cell. She answers on the first ring with a husky, "Hello?"

"I'm so glad you answered." The sound of her familiar, friendly voice fills me with relief.

"Abby?"

"Yes." My voice breaks, so I clear my throat. "Sorry to call so early, but I don't know what else to do."

"What's wrong? What happened?"

I sniffle. "I need a favor."

"What's up?" She sounds alert now, more awake.

"Can you get a hold of Mr. Akers? Tell him I'm coming home—alone—and ask him to meet me at the Jackson airport in an hour. I need to find a guy named Valdemar."

She hesitates. "Where are you? I thought you were sick."

"I was. I'm in Denver."

"What are you doing in Denver?"

"Changing planes to get my stupid-self home. I'll explain later."

Rose pauses. "You really are in trouble, aren't you?"

My fingers twist in my hair, pulling, as I try to keep my emotions in check. "You have no idea." A few early-morning passengers wander around the terminal and I turn my back to the wall, suspicious of every unfamiliar face.

"Are you okay?"

I can't hide the tremor in my voice as I answer. "No, Rose, I'm not."

"What kind of trouble? What else can I do?"

I stare down at my strappy heels and hold Kye's jacket closed at the neck. "Could you have Akers bring me a coat and some shoes? You wouldn't believe what I'm wearing."

Rose groans. "This has something to do with Kye, doesn't it?"

I hear the announcement that my flight is boarding.

"Yes. Listen, I have to go. Thanks for your help."

She yawns. "You better be prepared to share the deets first thing."

"I will. And Rose? One more thing."

"Hat? Gloves? Socks? Underwear? You name it. I am your friend-in-waiting."

"Sorry I missed your party. I really wanted to be there."

She tries to laugh, but it sounds brittle. "Don't worry, you didn't miss much."

Murtagh makes an appearance during takeoff. He moves around in my pocket, so I look inside and find him cradled in the seam, kicking to get my attention. "So tired." He yawns, stretches up to his full three-inch height.

"Then go back to sleep. We're almost there."

"No, *cailín* girl. Sacred place, very far. Must walk." Murtagh sits up. "Find warrior-prince."

I wonder how he found me, why he's still here. "Who are you, Murtagh? Where did you come from?"

With a proud smile, he pats his chest. "Murtagh water sprite. Called by warrior." He points at me. "Help young woman. You, *mo chara*."

Murtagh's English is so broken, he's hard to understand. "*Mo chara*. What does that mean?"

He taps the top of his head with a tiny finger, then, seeming to have translated my question, says, "*Mo chara*. My friend."

"And *cailín*? What is that?"

Again, the pause for translation, then, "Girl."

It dawns on me that Murtagh has probably been providing me with the translations to his words all along and I've just been to overwhelmed to hear them. Promising myself that I'll listen closer, I decide against asking him to translate more. "Okay, back to how you got here. What did you say about a warrior?"

"White animal. Moose. Friend warrior-prince."

I lean against the window. "Finn?" It makes no sense to me, but that's nothing new.

"Go to sacred place, fight battle. Murtagh hero!"

My confusion is only getting worse, but the corners of my lips turn up at his determined posture. "Is that what this is about? You want to be a hero?"

Murtagh spreads his arms wide. "Murtagh brave."

I shake my head, smiling wider. I believe him, though I shouldn't. "Yes, Murtagh the water sprite. You are brave."

And despite his size and broken English, Murtagh is already, in a way, my hero.

As the plane descends, the sky turns from ink black to navy, royal blue, purple, and finally the smallest hint of pink creeps up over the mountains in the east.

The freezing Jackson air seeps into my skin as I disembark bundled in Kye's jacket, watching for a familiar face. I'm shocked to find several. Rose is here, with Jen and Eric, Akers, and a white-haired man I've never met. Something about his eyes—steady and so dark they're nearly black—seems familiar to me.

Rose dashes to my side, horrified, as she takes in my appearance. Dress ripped and stained, hair hanging in strings around my shoulders, and cheeks probably streaked with mascara. Not to mention my wounds that are healing but still appear red and angry.

"Abby! What's going on? What happened to you?"

I open my mouth, ready to spill everything, but my throat is clogged and my eyes burn. A heavy weight settles on my chest as the enormity of everything that's transpired over the last three days hits me. Swallowing, I try again.

My pocket vibrates and Murtagh flies out, fluttering around and speaking his strange language with almost no English mixed in. I do manage to catch a few words, though. "No fail. Cannot fail. Must find sacred place."

"What is that?"

"Is he talking?"

"What's he saying?"

I hear all the questions, but still can't find my voice. Luckily, Akers answers for me. "That, kids, is a water sprite. Abby's picked up a friend. Water sprites don't attach themselves to just anyone, and they especially don't often travel long distances from home."

Murtagh buzzes around my head, repeating the same jumbled words over and over again. Jen looks enchanted. "What's he saying?"

The white-haired man answers, his voice grave. "He says, 'Death, pain, misery. Must not fail. Powerful magic. Must find sacred place.'" He turns to me. "Young lady, you have some explaining to do. What exactly is going on? And where is my boy, Kye?"

My gaze darts from person to person, finally settling on the familiar eyes belonging to the only person I don't know. "Kye's gone. They took him. He's gone."

THIRTY-FOUR

Rally the Troops

At my own words, my knees buckle. Rose wraps her arm around me and helps me to my feet.

"Who took him, Abby?" Mr. Akers asks.

"I think it was Boone." Jen hands me a tissue and I wipe my eyes. "Juri grabbed me. They separated us, so I didn't see what happened to Kye, and by the time I got away, Kye had disappeared. Then Tynan showed up, only he wasn't really there, he was projecting, and he told me Kye was gone, and I knew it was true because I felt it first, then saw it in a vision, and then Tynan said if I wanted to find Kye I would have to deliver the Keys into the jaws of the beast and unseal the tomb. Whatever that means." I stop to take a breath. "I had a vision of Kye hanging from a ceiling by his wrists, and they're hurting him. He can't escape by himself, so we have to help him." Hysteria bubbles in my throat; my breathing is quick and shallow.

"Calm down, Abby." Akers squeezes my hand. "We're going to help him."

Again, I realize how many people have come to pick me up. "What are you all doing here?"

Rose clears her throat. "You said you needed help. So, I rounded up the troops—so to speak."

Eric coughs. He's standing apart from the rest of the group, nursing his arm in a way that reminds me he's still injured. "How are you doing?"

He shrugs. "Could be worse. It's my own fault. Well, and Johnny's. I never could resist a dare."

When he coughs again, I wince, feeling a touch of sympathy until I realize he's laughing.

"What's so funny?"

"You should see yourself." His shoulders are shaking. "You took off with that guy and came back looking like you did battle with a small army. You're a wreck, and now you've come back needing us all to rescue you? I'd say I told you so, but I never got the chance to warn you before you left."

I cross to him in two strides and haul my fist back, but Jen catches my elbow, shaking her head. "Not now. We have more important things to deal with." She scowls at Rose. "I can't believe you got me into this."

Rose flips back her rumpled hair, smoothing it behind her collar. "You were born into it. No amount of denial's gonna take it away. Besides, Abby's our friend and Kye's my cousin. They need our help."

Jen won't meet anyone's eye. "My assistance might burn the place down. How is that helpful?"

Everyone objects to Jen's comment at once—except me. I'm curious what she means. The white-haired man shushes them and herds us out the door. "Are you sure it was Tynan? What did he look like?"

I hang back from the group. "Not to be rude, but who are you?"

He stalks over and shakes my hand. "I'm Valdemar. Nice to meet you."

Valdemar. The man who raised Kye. Suddenly, I'm flustered, but I manage a smile. "I've heard so much about you, Valdemar."

"Yes. I'm sure you have. Call me Val." He drags me to the parking lot and hits the remote start on a waiting Suburban. "Can you describe Tynan for me?"

I tell him everything I remember while we all pile into the car. Murtagh buzzes around but doesn't get in. "Aren't you coming?" I ask.

He flutters near me, looking torn. "No, *cailín* girl. Murtagh find sacred place. We separate."

Murtagh's leaving now? The thought makes me feel like I've been stabbed in the chest. I'm surrounded by people who care, so why do I feel like I'm losing my only friend? My voice catches. "Where will you go?"

"No worry, *mo chara*." He points at the carload. "Friends, not?"

A tiny smile plays at my cold lips. "Yes."

"Murtagh fly to sacred place. *cailín* girl go with friends. Yes?"

"Okay." I nod and swallow some threatening tears. "Will I see you again?"

"Soon, yes." Murtagh bobs up and down, and in a flurry of light and shiny wings, he's gone.

At Mr. Akers's insistence, I sit in the front passenger side, where he covers me with a heavy blanket. My teeth are chattering when he closes the door.

Valdemar hardly glances in the mirror as he pulls out of the parking lot. "How much has Kye told you about Dryden's royal family?"

I recount a shortened version of what Kye and Eoin told me.

"It's good you know all that." Val rubs a hand over his stubbly cheek. "You should also know that Tynan is Theron's biological brother."

"Kye has a brother?" As I say the words, I realize my mistake.

"No, Kye doesn't." Val shoots me a startled look as he turns north toward the parks—instead of south to Jackson. "Theron does. They were twins. Theron was to rule as King of the mortal Elen, while Tynan's destiny lay in the Otherworld with the immortal ones. The boys were like the sun and moon, opposites in every way. They were evenly matched in power and ability, and were forever in competition."

"Bet the king loved that." Snow flurries land on the windshield, so cold they flutter around like leaves on the wind rather than melting where they land.

"Isleen saw to it that he didn't know. But the lie cost her. My theory is that, in the process of giving birth, each child took approximately one fourth of Isleen's powers—which she should have recovered under normal circumstances but never did. I suspect it's part of the deal she made with the Morrigana. I'm not sure. Regardless, the deception cost Isleen a full half of her powers."

"That's why they made this pendant." My fingers stroke the warm stones.

"Presumably. Isleen knew what Tynan was before he was born, and also that she couldn't keep both children. When she gave birth, she turned Tynan over to the Dark Ones, having never laid eyes on him."

"How could she do that?" The horror of it shocks me. How did I not know this of the woman I've seen in so many visions?

Valdemar sighs. "She didn't have a choice. If she wanted to keep Theron, she had to give up Tynan. He was a preconceived sacrifice."

"Why would the queen have to sacrifice a prince?"

Val bites his lip as if trying to decide the best way to explain. "Because of the way the boys were conceived. See, King Damon wasn't the father of Isleen's babies. Rhys was. Those boys were created in a mix of love and betrayal, splitting the queen's heart—and her embryo—in two. The goddesses Morrigana gave Isleen a choice. She could abort the fetuses and remain childless forever, or she could carry them to term and give one away. The child born as the manifestation of Isleen's betrayal would be taken and raised as Prince of the Otherworld Elen. He'd live on one of the Phantom Islands as a royal child, raised with every privilege until he could be crowned at eighteen. She felt it a better alternative than abortion."

"That doesn't sound so terrible," Rose says from the back.

"Raised as a prince and crowned at eighteen?" Jen says. "Sounds good to me."

He was raised by demons. I glance up at Val, sick to my stomach. "He didn't have a chance."

"No, he didn't." Val tips the rearview mirror so he can glance at Rose and Jen. "I'm certain Tynan didn't live the life you're picturing." He returns his eyes to the road. "Anyway, fast-forward a few years. Tynan wasn't happy living in the Otherworld—"

"What's the Otherworld?" I interrupt.

"The Otherworld is where the opposites live," Val says.

"Opposites?" Eric says. "I wouldn't call them that."

Eric's statement gives me a nervous tingle, and I wonder how he knows about the Otherworld. I feel like I'm missing something.

"I believe that's exactly what they are." Val turns his head, his expression calculating. "History tells us that every positive energy is counter-balanced by a negative one. Like when cold water is mixed with hot water and becomes warm. The same is true for human souls. We're born with both positive and negative energies. Most of us use parts of both, finding a neutral balance that allows us to experience the highs and lows of life. Every once in a while, the energies split, leaving a positive embodiment or a negative one. When this happens, the positive energy is absorbed into the universe, taking on another form—for instance, a special ability, or Gift, as you all have."

"All of us?" I turn around to smile at my friends.

"Yes." Val nods. "All of you. And many more."

"What happens to the negative?" Jen's voice is barely above a murmur, but we all hear her.

"Negative energy can be absorbed into a balanced person. It might be manifested in the form of a cancer or severe bitterness or hatred, which is often fed by more negative energy until it becomes destructive. Or it might take a form of its own. Shadows. Demons. Banshees.

"Those negative beings eventually become immortal Elen, and they live in the Otherworld, which is located among the Phantom Islands. Most of these islands are said to be lands of eternal youth and beauty—eternal bliss, if you will. But once you cross under the crystal bridge to get there, you can never come back. Tynan's Otherworld—the one he created in rebellion—is not the same. His kingdom is the place where shadows or demons might go to retire, if they were able to get through the portal."

"They can't get in." It's more statement than question. Piece by piece, my mind connects the dots. *Raina locked the door. And I have two of the Keys.*

"No," Val says slowly. "Tynan and his army have been attempting to escape for almost five hundred years."

Eric pipes up again. "If someone locked me in a poisonous cave, I'd try to break out, too."

Val's head turns with a jerk, his eyes narrow at Eric. "How do you know the prison is poisonous?"

Eric looks away, muttering, "Just something I heard."

Outside the windows, the Teton Mountains spear the skyline. Dark gray peaks tipped with snow rise sharp and angry through the pale blue backdrop. Deep green and brown foliage is buried in a blanket of white. Miles fall away as we climb in elevation.

"When Dryden fell, the Morrigana stepped in." Val slows our ascent when patches of ice make the road slippery. "They couldn't allow Tynan's demons to completely take over, so they created a prison out of poisonous stone and directed the Otherworld portal into it. To ensure no one person could open the door, they forged four Keys, which had to be inserted simultaneously to open the lock. Tynan and his army were lured there and locked inside. When the war ended, there were seven mortal Elen survivors, besides myself."

"Seven?" A violent shiver rattles my teeth and I crank the heater up to full blast. "Of how many?"

"Thousands," he says. "Three couples and one other person. These people became guardians of the Keys and dispersed into different parts of the world to live until the Morrigana saw fit to rise up a new generation of Gifted." He glances at me, then in the rearview mirror at each of my friends. "You four and Kye are only a part of this reemergence."

I slip off my shoes and hold my feet under the dash where the heat is blasting. I can't seem to get warm.

Val clears his throat. "You need to understand why Tynan's army was locked up in the first place. This wasn't simply a matter of competition between brothers. It was a struggle for power. Tynan had powerful Gifts–lots of them–and he used them to obtain things he wanted, things he coveted, and things he never should have had. Greed became his best friend, his lover, and his constant companion. The things he acquired were never enough. Not even when he started stealing Gifts.

"Unfortunately, greed has a twin sibling in fear. Tynan feared his brother more than all else. When Theron married Raina, Tynan was furious. We thought he had finally come after Isleen, angry with her for giving him up. We thought he intended to take her Healing powers."

"You were there?"

Val taps the steering wheel with his thumbs. "Yes, as much as I'd like to claim otherwise."

Tynan's face swims in my mind, glittering and fading into smoke that drifts away on the wind, and it hits me that Tynan wasn't so much angry as afraid. "He really came for Raina. Raina had the power to bear Theron a son who could possibly be twice as powerful as either of the brothers. A descendant who could balance both worlds."

"Probably." Val punches the gas and changes gears as we travel up an icy incline. "No one realized Raina was already stronger than both brothers until it was too late."

"What about the pendant?" Eric cuts in. In the rearview mirror, I catch his eyes boring into my neck, where the emerald still hangs. "Didn't Tynan want Isleen's pendant? Wouldn't it have given him dominion over both mortal and immortal worlds?"

Val hesitates. "We can speculate, but no one really knows. All we know is that he gathered an army of demons and used them to destroy the royal family."

I study Val's profile, wondering about his age. "Have you ever taken someone's power?"

He looks at me, startled. "Absolutely not. No."

"How are you still alive if you were there?"

"Old magic." He sighs as if reluctant to tell the story. "Before the fall of Dryden, the three sister goddesses—Badb, Macha, and Morrigan—paid a yearly visit to the kingdom, during which the highly Gifted people demonstrated their Gifts. Those with exceptional power were monitored for a period of ten years. If the Morrigana determined the chosen one used his Gifts for the good of others, that person was given an opportunity to become immortal by plucking a white blossom from a silver bough and eating it. Then, after serving the mortals for a period of time—usually a few hundred years—they were given passage to the Phantom Islands—the good ones, not the Otherworld—to live for eternity. I accepted a blossom."

I tuck the blankets more tightly around me as goose bumps erupt across my shoulders and down my arms. "How much longer will you serve?"

"Until balance is restored."

"That could be a really long sentence," Eric mumbles. After what I've seen, I have to agree. The conversation falls to a lull as we cover more distance, but after a while, I grow restless. I wonder if Kye is still alive, how badly he's hurt. "What do we do now? Where are we going?"

Val rubs his chin. "We need help. It's time to introduce you kids to the Dragons. Only they have the ability to locate the portal." He frowns as his eyes travel to the torn hem of my dress and my bare feet. "I wish you were better dressed for the occasion."

I've always pictured Dragons as enormous creatures with long tails, scales, and jaws that spewed fire. Even though Kye told me about the Elen Dragons, I can't get the old picture out of my head.

Rose tosses me a pair of hiking boots that are two sizes too big but remarkably better than wobbling around in high-heeled sandals.

I lace them on and accept a coat from Jen, leaving my wrap and Kye's jacket behind.

We hike for almost a mile, using mostly pre-cut trails and the boardwalks that float over the unstable volcanic crust covering the ground. After a while, Valdemar leads us away from the path and up a hill through a section of fire-burned forest. My breath catches as we crest the top and catch a view of a volcanic pond. Natural greens and blues circle the middle, surrounded by yellows that turn into oranges, reds, and then browns. The spring is more like a lake than a pool, and by my guess, somewhere close to the size of three football fields.

"There's no one here." I'm worried, tired, cold, and beyond hungry.

Eric's arm drops around my shoulder and he rubs the sleeve of my borrowed coat. The hike has my blood moving steadily enough that for the first time all morning, I'm not shivering—until he touches me. I shrug away, attempting a friendly smile and failing.

"First lesson," Akers says. "Just because you don't see a single Dragon doesn't mean there aren't a hundred nearby." He steps to the edge of the cliff overlooking the spring, waves at us, and leaps.

THIRTY-FIVE

Dragons

"**A**kers!" Instinct has me lurching forward. "What are you doing?" Val stops me with a hand on my arm.

Time seems to slow as Akers plummets toward the boiling acid. I don't want to watch, but I can't drag my eyes away. Part of me half expects someone to fly out and catch him, save him, Superman style. No one does, and in the time it takes a heart to beat once, my favorite teacher slides beneath the surface. Oddly, the water doesn't change and his body doesn't float to the top or cause the acid to sizzle.

Eric lets loose a string of curses that would embarrass a trucker. A guttural sound comes out of Rose, completely unintelligible, and Jen screams like a banshee. We are all shocked, panicked, sickened.

Val shouts over the din. "It's okay, kids. Calm down. Let me explain."

After all I've seen this week, my brain is overloaded. No words come to mind, just pure and utter shock as I stare into the water, the acrid scent of sulfur stinging my nose.

"Never try that alone," Val says louder. "It's difficult to tell a portal from an actual acid spring."

As if on cue, the water ripples and a froth of air bubbles to the surface, bringing with it a strange buzzing that touches our ears with an electric hum.

A murky shadow moves at the bottom, grows larger, and takes on the shapes of bodies that rise gracefully to the surface. Figures emerge from the pool—completely dry—and float to us on clear, reflective spheres of light that glimmer with the same colors as the spring.

They hover in a triangular formation and lower the hoods of their midnight blue cloaks in perfect sync. Powerful red energy encompasses them, so bright it hurts my eyes. Mr. Akers smiles at me from his position just behind and to the right of the leader. When he turns his head, I notice a small tattoo behind his left ear. It looks like the same symbol that marked the spot where Kye and I found the pendant in the Statue of Liberty. I think back, wondering why I've never noticed Akers has a tattoo before.

The Dragon leader appears to be about eighteen, but his deep emerald eyes tell me that looks are deceptive. His golden skin picks up highlights in the dark brown mane of hair that is combed away from his crown and secured at his nape with a strap of leather. "Valdemar," he says. "It's good to see you. I understand your protégé has run into some trouble?"

"Apparently." Val's expression is carefully neutral. "Kye Murphy recently became acquainted with the newly appointed guardian of the Ring of the Princess, and soon after, Nematona, goddess to the Elemental Fae, invoked an oath that he would find the rest of the Arawn Keys to prevent them from falling into the wrong hands and aiding in opening the Tomb of Demons."

The Dragon clicks his tongue. "The Arawn Keys were hidden to prevent such an occurrence."

"Yes." Val's eyes narrow and his voice takes on an edge. "However, it's come to my attention that an old friend and former Dragon is currently in possession of the Arawnian Dagger. A dangerous weapon, even without the other Keys."

Murmurs spread through the ranks. The Dragon's face remains stoic. "That can't be. The Dagger was protected by powerful spells. A disturbance in the magic would have caused enough destruction to alert the entire planet."

Akers whispers something in the Dragon leader's ear. A look of horror passes over the leader's face, and he mumbles something angry and unintelligible to Akers before saying, "Forgive me. I was unaware that the Dagger's movement was the apparent cause of a volcanic eruption in Washington some years back. Unbeknownst to us, the Dagger has been traveling around for some time."

Val and Akers exchange a guilty look. Val says, "Long enough for the followers of the Dark Prince to gain uncountable powers. Whether or not their sacrifices are being kept alive, clearly many Gifted have been cut, their powers drained."

More murmuring among the Dragons. The wind shifts, momentarily clearing away the acrid air and replacing it with tiny snow flurries that sparkle in the weak sunlight. A finger of air blows up my dress, raising goose bumps along my back.

"It has begun," the Dragon leader murmurs. And then, "Introduce your students."

Val presents each of us. "This is Eric Fisher, Gifted with Ice Conversion."

"Rose Westover, Gifted with Tongues of Persuasion."

Okay, I really should've figured that one out on my own.

"Jennifer Thomas, Fire Summoner."

"Ah, yeah. About that." Jen shakes her head. "Not exactly something I can control. I'm not sure I'll be of any help to anyone. Just so you know. In fact, if you feel the need to take it from me, I'm cool with that. I wouldn't mind not having to worry about burning holes in everything I touch." Val shushes her.

The Dragon leader bows, offering Jen a brittle smile. "A Gift cannot be removed except by use of the Arawnian Dagger. The means are painful, dangerous, and potentially deadly. Think very hard before thoughtlessly offering to toss away a Gift from the goddesses. There are those who seek to take that ability, and in doing so, will not hesitate to forfeit your life. And that, I'm afraid, would be a lucky thing indeed." Jen gulps but remains silent as the Dragon leader moves to face me.

Nerves make my mouth feel dry and sticky. With a hand on my shoulder, Val introduces me. "This is Abigail Johnson, Gifted with both Healing and Sight, current guardian of the Ring of the Princess."

"This is our new guardian?" The Dragon rubs his forehead, looking bewildered for the first time since he appeared. The wide sleeve of his cloak falls around his elbow, exposing the pale, pale skin on his forearm and a snakelike tattoo. "And two Gifts? Very unusual." His deep green eyes bore into mine, like he's trying to see inside me, through me. Then he murmurs, "Can it be?"

"Can, and is." Val smiles, looking like a proud father. He makes me feel bold, important.

I straighten my back, annoyed by their secret communication. Mr. Akers notices and grins at me. The head Dragon bows, ever the gentleman. "You may call me Sir Zane, Dragon Master."

Dumb title. Sounds like a video game login. "How about just Zane?"

He looks taken aback, but shrugs. "Whatever suits you."

To Zane's left, a fair-haired man with perfect white teeth and deep blue eyes bows as Zane introduces him. "Captain Tobias, my second-in-command."

"Call me Toby, Mistress." The tattoo on Toby's neck peeks out from beneath his hair as it falls forward. He winks and straightens, then moves aside to make way for another cloaked figure, this one with hair like muddy water and eyes gray as the pre-dawn sky.

"Captain Gabriel," Zane continues, "who usually stands at my right, except when Captain Akers decides to grace us."

Gabriel playfully slaps Akers on the shoulder, dancing aside to avoid a return slap, and I gasp, worried he'll fall off his floating sphere. "Gabe, at your service, Miss Abigail, Guardian of the Ring of the Princess. And serving your boisterous friends as well." His cheeks are tinged pink when he stands upright, biting his lip, clearly trying to hold in a fit of laughter. The expression hits a memory. I've seen Gabe before.

"Have we met?"

Gabe lets his laughter free. He's much more informal, more comfortable than the rest of the Dragons. I like him. "Yes."

Of course. The lodge. "I thought you were a Ranger?"

Gabe's lips twitch as he sinks into a bow. "My day job."

"Well, it's nice to see you again, Gabe." To Val, I whisper, "Why are they all bowing?"

Val folds his arms. "Protocol, I suppose. The Ring of the Princess was lost to us when Theron died, and the royal bloodline lost with it. Or so we thought. If your ring is the one Theron gave to Raina, the fact that you've shown up wearing it and haven't been burned to ashes by its powers indicates you carry the bloodline of Theron and Raina. Theoretically. Didn't Kye or Eoin explain all this?"

"Not about burning to ashes. Or the bloodline either, come to think of it."

"Well, let's call the bowing thing a show of respect. The Dragons were fiercely loyal to Raina. If that loyalty has been carried forth, it is only to our advantage right now. Why don't you tell them what you know and see if they can help us find Kye?" The wrinkles at the corners of his dark eyes deepen. For the first time since I met him, Valdemar appears vulnerable.

On a moss-covered forest floor, a crumpled form struggles for life-sustaining breath. Blood flows from the tips of his reddened hair and runs down the sides of swollen, purple cheeks. A sticky, red trail spreads away, as if someone dragged him to this place and flung him carelessly in a corner like garbage. I run to him, screaming his name, but can't reach him before the monster that guards him stops me cold. "Only one of you can live." His fetid breath blows in my face, the smell only explainable by centuries of decay. "Which one will it be?"

Cradling my rounded belly, I coax movement from the life inside me, wondering how I can ever choose between the two, the death of my love or the life of his child.

"Abby." Valdemar murmurs. "Focus. Draw away and focus."

The bitter taste of bile has risen in my mouth. I swallow it, concentrate, twisting my ring around and around. I won't let it come to anyone's death. Not this time. Power zings up my spine. I draw myself up to full height, shaking off the effects of the vision, and meet Zane's eyes. "Sir Zane, we need your help."

THIRTY-SIX

The Council

Geothermal heat radiates from the walls in the underground Dragon Council chambers. The temperature stifles my breath and causes a sheen of sweat to coat the back of my neck as I explain what happened in Las Vegas and New York—minus some personal details.

Eric stares at the table, gripping the edge with white knuckles, and when I get to the part about sharing a hotel room with Kye, beads of sweat roll down his forehead. *Guilt, guilt, guilt.*

Zane hunches over a notebook, scribbling fast. When I tell him what Tynan said, he looks up, frowning. "Into the jaws of the beast?" I nod, and he taps the tablet with his pen, staring at the smooth wall. "To restore the true order of Dryden?"

Val asks, "What are you thinking, Zane?"

Zane leans back, rubbing a hand over the tattoo on his neck. "They must have taken Kye to the chambers where the sealed tomb is located. It's not far from here."

Kye is close. I can go to him. My heart flutters. *I can save him.*

"The question is, why?" Zane continues. "Why him? Why there?"

"Because of me," I say, my eyes refusing to focus. "They want my ring. I have to go to him."

Whispers echo across the room as the Dragons speculate on the possibilities. Valdemar, Zane, and Akers lean together for a hushed conversation. When the buzz finally dies, Zane looks at me again.

DESCENDANT

"The Dragons can't go into the chambers with you. Only guardians in possession of one of the Arawn Keys can pass through the portal that will take you to the tomb."

A knot forms in my stomach. "I have two Keys."

Val nods. "Yes. Which means two people can pass through."

I glance around, wondering who I should take with me. *Whose life am I willing to risk?* Zane grips the back of my chair. "Who will you send?"

I shake my head, unable to make such a choice. "I'll go by myself."

A chorus of disagreements rumbles around the table.

"No!"

"Abby, you can't."

"That isn't a good idea."

I ignore them and ask Zane, "Will you show me the way?"

Chair legs scrape against the floor as Zane stands, weary. "I can take you there, Abby, but you need to think this through. It's a trap. They *want* you to come, and they expect you to bring both Keys. By taking Kye, they've set you up to lose one way or another. Either you surrender yourself—in which case they'll take the Keys, your Gifts, and probably your life—or they kill Kye. If you are the one to go, the chances of you both surviving are slim to none. I understand you care about him—"

"Let me tell you something," I say, and the room goes silent. "I've spent my whole life running from things I didn't understand. I'm tired. Kye is the first—the only—person who truly understands me. He taught me to face my problems and find a way to solve them rather than run. I have to go after him."

"Listen." Zane and the other Dragons stand on one side of the table, facing off with me and my friends. "However much you care about him—and I promise I understand—going through that portal means risking the Keys. Do you know what will happen if Tynan's people get their hands on all four? This isn't just about you and Kye."

Furious, I lean toward him, bracing my hands on the table. "No, it isn't just about me and Kye. It's about Theron and Raina. How will Dryden ever be restored if Theron is killed again?"

Zane takes a calming breath. "Theron isn't here."

"You're right, Zane. He isn't. Wanna know why? Because Boone took him. Kye is Theron. Tynan called that one, not me or Kye." Zane drops into his chair, suddenly looking old. "Now tell me what's at stake, Zane. Tell me I'm being selfish, that I haven't considered the consequences."

No one answers for a long moment, and then Val rests a hand on my arm. Strands of white hair fall into his eyes and stick to beads of sweat on his forehead, and for a second I can See him wearing a priest's robe, offering fatherly advice and congratulations to the newlywed royal couple. "It's your choice, honey."

"All right, then." I straighten, resolved. "Let's go."

Gabe holds me securely in front of him as we glide over the snow on his opalescent disk, my eyes closed against the wind as we swish past pine trees and around rocky outcroppings. Rose and Jen cling to Zane on his disc, Eric rides with Toby, and behind us are Valdemar and Akers.

"Sorry to hear about your friend," Gabe says. "I wish there was more we could do to help."

"You and me both."

We fly past geysers, hot springs, and a wandering bison, and I do my best to push away the terror brought on by my most recent vision of Kye. The sun is falling toward the western horizon by the time we stop near the side of a mountain. Not far away, clouds of sulfuric steam twine a white trail around the tree trunks, winding about until the wisps evaporate somewhere near the top of the tallest ones. Gabe hops nimbly to the ground, his boots passing through a layer of snow, and offers me a hand. Behind us, Jen and Akers are arguing.

"Jennifer," Akers says, "your skills will save Abby a lot of valuable time. It's not going to get out of hand, I promise."

"You can't make that promise." Jen stomps snow off her feet, only to have more build up.

"Come on, Jen. Look around." Rose's consoling hand is shaken off Jen's arm. "Everything's soaked. There's nothing here to burn."

"Except people," Jen says. "I could burn people."

Val folds his arms. "Young lady, you underestimate my ability if you think I would allow you to burn your friends. Now, are we going to stand in the snow, or are you going to clear a path?"

Jen's shoulders tremble and her eyes shoot killing looks alternately between Akers and Valdemar. Feeling like they've unfairly put her on the spot, I pull her aside, turning our backs to everyone else. "You don't have to do this," I tell her. "Really. I can dig my way through. I'm getting good at that."

With a half laugh that turns into a deep sigh, she hugs me, holds on tight. "Thanks. I'm just—I'm so afraid. When I was twelve, I caught my mother's kitchen on fire and my baby brother ended up with third-degree burns down his back. He's scarred forever. I don't ever want to be responsible for hurting someone again."

Understanding completely, I squeeze her back. There are certain things that are too much to ask—too much to expect. "Don't do it. I'll find another way to get to Kye." Releasing Jen, I turn to eye the several feet of snow that currently stand between me and the portal. I can't walk through it, and shoveling will take hours, but I won't ask for something Jen can't give. I glance at Gabe, whose muscles bulge beneath his cloak. "What are we all doing standing around when we could be digging? Let's go, people."

Fifteen minutes later, we're kneeling on the snow and have managed to scoop out a path almost two feet by two feet when Jen grabs my arm. "Stop. This is crazy. It's going to take hours. Kye doesn't have that long."

I want to scream at her how much I know that. It's all I can think about as I dig handfuls of snow while the boy I love suffers, but everything I want to say is lodged in my throat and all that comes out is a wail.

Jen pulls me up and hugs me again. "Stop, okay? I'm going to do it. It's too selfish of me not to try. Just—" She glances at each of us. "Just stand back." Her hands shake as she aims her palms at the ground. Her energy changes as red heat flows from her core and into her arms, then slowly down to the tips of her fingers until flames shoot out in short bursts, melting random patches of snow and coming precariously close to melting Toby's boots.

The flames stop and Jen takes a breath.

"Focus," Val murmurs. "Concentrate on a small area at a time. See the snow melt in your mind's eye. See the fire bow to your command. See the wind be still. Force it to obey your thoughts. You control the fire—it does not control you."

Jen tries again. Moving her palms in slow circles, she closes her eyes and listens to Val. As she does, a funnel blazes forth, melting a path that looks half a mile long, setting a number of trees and shrubs in its path aflame. Unfortunately, the path is going in the opposite direction from where Val wanted it, and Toby and another Dragon—whose pant leg looks suspiciously blackened—rush to put out the residual fires before anything else catches.

It takes more encouragement, and a reminder from desperate, frustrated me, but Jen agrees to try once more. Again, the fire pulses from her core, but this time the flames lick to life more slowly, wavering but steady as Jen commands the heat. Like ice cream in the summer, the snow shrinks into the sodden earth, evaporating under Jen's power. After several minutes, she has melted enough to allow us through, only four small shrubs are left burning, and no one has been terribly injured aside from Gabe's eyebrows getting singed. It's good enough.

Jen's arms—shaking with the exertion—drop to her side and her eyes roll back in her head as she lets out a relieved breath.

"Could've been worse, I guess." She turns to Val. "How did you know what to do? How to help me?"

"Decades of training."

Drooping from the energy drain, she clasps the arm of the nearest Dragon for support, still talking to Val. "Will you teach me more?"

"One thing at a time." Val turns his attention to me. "Let's get Abby through this first."

Zane and Akers lead me to a muddy gray pool, boiling beneath the entrance to a tall cavern. The mud pulls and spits in and out of the cave like the breath of an enormous beast, and smelling just as bad. We step over a short fence and climb the hill to stand above the sloshing, belching water. "That's not a portal," I say.

"I know." Zane frowns, an I-warned-you look in his eyes. "The portal's inside the cave."

THIRTY-SEVEN

The Prison

Zane's brow creases as I gape at the gurgling mud. "Is that water or acid?"

"A mixture of both, and it's around two hundred degrees, so you won't be swimming."

"How, then?" I bite my thumbnail. "How do I get inside?"

Val and Zane exchange a look. "Any ideas?"

"Probably something to do with the Keys." Val blinks, glancing at my ring.

I point at Gabe's hovering contraption, now green in the weak sunlight. "What if I borrow one of those disk thingies?"

Zane shakes his head. "Solar-powered. They've run all day already, and I'm afraid you'll lose the charge in the dark. Also, you don't have the clearance you'd need. Even crouching low you'd still have to skim the water—and the acid content will dissolve the disk."

A breeze winds around my legs, raising goose bumps on my skin. I zip the coat up to my chin. "There has to be a way."

Jen throws up her hands. "I know. Rose can just talk it into submission."

Rose snorts. "Yeah, like that would work."

The Dragons do their murmur-whispering thing again, and I decide I'm really sick of people having muted discussions right in front of me. Finally, Eric hops over the railing and climbs the hill. "What if I freeze the surface of the water? At that temperature I could only ice over a small area at a time, so I'd have to go with her." I blink and he shrugs. "It might work."

Val rubs his whiskery chin, looking skeptical. "Are you sure you can handle it? It's a lot to ask—even for someone with experience using his power, which isn't necessarily you."

Eric shrugs. "You have a better idea?"

"What about the acid?" I ask, wondering if Eric's ability is as sporadic and unpredictable as Jen's. "Wouldn't the acid burn your skin?"

"Not if I don't touch it. I'll have to really focus, the way Jen did."

I catch up to Eric and turn him to face me. "Are you sure you have to go with me? That you can't freeze the surface enough from the edge? All I need is a path."

"I'm sure," he says, annoyed.

I really, really need him to understand what he's getting into. "They could kill us both." *Probably will.*

His head droops and he lets out a weary sigh. "You really have no faith in me."

"I'm sorry, but I don't have a lot of faith in anyone right now. This whole thing is just ... a lot."

He raises an eyebrow. "Ya think?"

After another short conference in which it is decided this is an option worth exploring, Zane and Val lead Eric and me to the edge nearest the cave, warning us to be careful. Eric grasps my wrist, a strange light in his eyes. "Ready?"

I blink and nod, but say, "No."

He holds the palm of his free hand over the water, cold seeping into my arm where he touches me. A patch of thick ice forms and Eric guides me onto it, leaning over to repeat the action so we can take another step. For every foot we move forward, one behind us melts, and the faster we go, the thinner the ice. There is no turning back.

We slide across the smooth surface, Eric gripping my wrist and me shivering, trying really hard to concentrate on keeping my balance and not falling into the boiling acid.

When we're halfway across, Rose yells, "Um, Abby? Turn around." I glance behind us and see that the single square foot I've considered our safety zone has completely melted, leaving us standing on a ribbon that feels awfully thin. Thin enough that I can feel the heat through the soles of my boots as the last of the ice disappears. We probably don't even have a minute before we're dumped in the acid.

The mouth of the cave is still several feet away, but hot clouds of steam billow in our faces. "Can we hurry this up?" I choke.

"Doing my best here," Eric snaps. He does manage to freeze a larger section this time, which—hopefully—buys us a few more seconds. Still, it's not enough. I'm having visions of what it will feel like to be boiled alive when we finally duck under the top edge of the cave and Eric stops.

"What?" The energy inside the cave is anything but calm, and that scares me as much as being boiled alive.

"We can't go any farther. This must be the portal, because I feel like an invisible wall is blocking me."

From the outside Zane yells, "Are you in?"

"Not yet!" Eric answers. "Give me the ring."

My stomach clenches at the thought. "No."

"I have to get in somehow. The necklace, then."

I lower the zipper of my coat enough to touch the warm stones. Powerful, yes, but I'm far less connected to the pendant than to Gram's ring. As long as I have my ring, Gram will be with me. I unclasp the chain and drop the pendant in Eric's hand. With a triumphant smile, he shoves it in his pocket, but nothing happens. We still can't move forward.

Val calls, "Abby, are you in yet?"

"I don't know what to do," I shout. "We're both holding a Key and nothing's happening."

The section of ice on which we're standing shifts, cracks, and Eric refreezes it, but I can feel how his terror mirrors my own. Voices blend together, trying to send words of advice or encouragement, but I can't make sense of them. Then, as if I've called her to me, Gram's voice is here, whispering in my ear like the wind in the trees. Like a song driven into the cave from the awful steam that blocks the entrance.

Concentrate. Work from the heart. Pull the broken energy inside you and send it back whole.

Closing my eyes, I think of Kye and take a breath of rotten, stinky air, pull it inside me, and let it swirl into my core until it's fresh and clean. My ring hums, emitting a sound I've never heard or maybe never recognized—birdsong and harps, the fluttering of down in a comforter, the pop and sizzle of water hitting an open flame. Soft music and loving voices and the sunrise breaking through the clouds at the end of a storm. The sound of a rainbow.

With the help of the power swirling around us, I release the energy, and in a blinding flash of light, Eric and I are shoved forward, tossed to our hands and knees on solid ground. Rock, not ice. The noise from outside is now behind us, muted and distant as the portal shimmers, shrinks, and then disappears altogether. The acrid smoke that blew in my face moments ago is now gone.

"Wow." Eric pushes himself to his feet, wiping his hands on his jeans. "That was ... interesting. How'd you know what to do?"

I brace my palms on the cave wall to pull myself up. "I don't know. It was just ... there." Once again, geothermal activity heats the place like an oven. After I wipe my hands on my coat, I tug it off and tie it around my waist.

We're on a ledge made of slippery black rock. Steam and water surge in and out from the mouth of the cave. We can see it, but not hear it. When I swipe the air near the portal, my hand meets resistance.

The cavern opens into a corridor, which branches off farther in. Sunlight filters down the hall from behind us and is the only light by which to see. "Do you think they know we're here?" Eric sounds nervous.

"I don't know," I murmur. "But let's not alert them, just in case. We should try to be quiet."

His breath tickles my ear. "What are we looking for, exactly?"

"Kye. We're looking for Kye."

A hint of something—anger? jealousy?—flashes in his eyes, but he banks it. "And then what?"

"Then we'll see, I guess." My sweaty feet slip around in the borrowed boots, which sometimes catch on the hem of my dress and threaten to trip me. Landing face-first on rock isn't a pleasant thought, so I hike my dress higher with one hand and support myself on the wall with the other.

When we reach the split, we have two choices. To our left, the opening leads down another long corridor, which is black as space without any stars. From somewhere far away, we can hear water dripping, and a strange, unnatural-sounding hum. On the right, smoky black mist swirls around and around.

Though sweat beads on my forehead and at the nape of my neck, the mist sends a chill into me. An awful moaning wail hangs in the air, not really continuing from one ear to another or rippling up and away from the source, but rather circling as if caught inside a cold, wet whirlwind. A strong metallic tang coats my tongue and I swallow, shivering.

Instinct—or maybe fear—tells me to go left, so we head into the blackness of space. Eric digs in his pocket and produces a cell phone, but when he tries to turn it on, nothing happens. He presses button after button, but his phone appears to be dead. He swears under his breath. "What I wouldn't give for a flashlight right now."

"A flashlight would be rather handy." I remember saying something similar to Kye in New York, and what happened not long after that. "Oh," I twist my ring. Nothing happens, so I close my eyes and concentrate really hard on sending energy into it, sighing in frustration when that doesn't work either. With no other choice, we continue down the tunnel, feeling our way and learning the real meaning of true dark. Eventually, a speck of gold glimmers in the distance. Eric grabs my shoulder and covers my mouth. "Shh. Someone's coming."

The beam of light grows bigger and is accompanied by the unmistakable sounds of footsteps and murmuring voices. We flatten ourselves against the wall, holding our breath. The voices become more distinct as the light draws nearer. "Don't know why we can't just kill him."

A lower, gravelly voice responds. "How many times do I have to tell you, the kid's leverage. He's our bait."

"I know, I know," whines the other. "I don't understand why we didn't just take the girl to begin with."

A loud harrumph. "Told you, the Keys can't be teleported like furniture or people. We tried it with the other two. Doesn't work."

I suck in my stomach, trying to blend into the wall as the men come closer. About fifteen feet away, the light arcs around, glinting off something on the floor, and then fades, and so do the sounds.

Eric leans into me, bumping his nose on my ear. "Did they go down a hall?"

"I think so."

"Should we follow?"

I run my tongue around my teeth, swallowing salty fear. "Yes. I'll lead. Hold on to me." I feel the air with my hands, waiting to meet the wall, and slide my foot toward the direction in which the lantern disappeared. Eric holds on to my shoulders, his footfalls matching mine. Slide, stop. Slide, stop. Slide, stop, until my fingers brush smooth stone, and then we move sideways, using the wall as our guide. At last, more light flickers in the distance and I follow it.

The temperature drops steadily, but I don't want to stop and put on my coat for fear I'll lose sight of the target. After a while, the light stops moving. I focus on it and keep going.

A cough echoes nearby and I turn to Eric, confused. "Did you just cough?"

"No. I assumed it was you."

Miraculously, my ring comes to life, giving off a soft glow, and then I know.

"What did you do?" Eric grabs my wrist and stares.

I snatch my hand away but can't help smiling. Can it really be the power of true love? "It's Kye. He's close."

Another cough. I try to pinpoint the source, but the echo makes it hard to tell where the sound is coming from. "There must be a door somewhere. Help me look." With the aid of my ring, Eric and I search for an opening in the wall. At one point, I trip over what feels like a large root sticking out of the floor, and look down to find that a number of cords and wires have been run along the ground. *What the what?* There was a dim light in my vision of Kye. It could have been artificial. I follow the wires to see where they lead, what they do, until the glowing fades. "Too far."

We start on the other side, and the ring throws a bright flash in my eyes as I pass a thin crevice. It's only a crack, barely large enough for a slim person to squeeze through. "Kye?" I shove my arm in ahead of me. No response, so I shimmy forward, only to be stopped by my boots, which are too wide for the opening. "Kye?"

Still no response, but my ring is getting warmer. I kick the boots off and hand my coat to Eric. "I'm going in."

Eric grips my shoulders. "Are you sure that's a good idea? What if it's a trap?"

I remove his hands, one at a time. "Of course it's a trap. This whole thing is a trap. But I have to try."

Eric's arms drop, his bleak expression hard to read in the dark. "Your suicide."

My feet are now agile enough to slide through the narrow bottom. Claustrophobia closes in on me and my heart gallops with panic. But then Kye coughs again, and I scoot farther until my hand reaches empty air. Every inch of exposed skin scrapes against the rough stone as I drag myself through, and the hem of my dress catches on something sharp, ripping a gash across the bottom.

The ring shines bright now, illuminating a dark lump in the corner. I fall on my knees. "Kye."

DESCENDANT

The lump doesn't move, so I shake him gently. "Kye? Wake up." Tears burn my eyes and dread curls in my stomach as I lift a corner of the fabric. He coughs again and relief trickles in, but is short-lived.

He's in bad shape. His shirt is stained red in numerous places, though I can't tell where he's bleeding. His face is bruised, swollen, sticky with dried blood, and he's cradling his arm. It's hard to tell where else he's hurt, since he's curled his legs toward his stomach. "What have they done to you?" I swallow a sob. Crying won't help him. With no other option, I run my hands over his body, trying to focus enough to assess his injuries.

My fingers ripple in the energy near his head and face. He's suffered several blows. His shoulder is dislocated, possibly broken. Two—no, three—injured ribs on the right, four on the left. His left ankle or foot is damaged. Possibly a torn ligament or a bad sprain. There's something else, something big I can't identify, though I know it's important.

I run my fingers over him again, this time spinning his core chakra, asking it to tell me what's wrong. A strong metallic taste burns in my throat when I close my eyes and listen to Kye's energy. Chemical. Something chemical. No, not chemical, mineral. Wrong. Very wrong. Poisonous and wrong. Nickel. Nickel arsenide.

My eyes fly open and I jerk my hand away from Kye's limp form and aim the light at the wall. Shimmering silver reflects back at me and I turn to another wall, and then the next in the oddly shaped room. All the same metallic hue. The mineral's gritty taste trickles down my throat, gagging me with its strength. "Oh no," I groan. "No, no, no. Nickeline." A poisonous room. A prison that will slowly kill the occupants.

THIRTY-EIGHT

Heartache

Another turn around the room reveals a chain attached to a low-wattage light, which I switch on, realizing as I do that there really is no way out besides the fissure through which I came. I know there has to be another exit. Though I hate to touch the nickeline, I squeeze between the rocks again. "Eric. I need your help." He doesn't answer.

"Eric." I wrench free. "Eric?" Eric isn't there. He's gone, along with my boots and coat. He must have wandered away.

Or.

Or he's been caught and is now being held hostage and tortured—or worse—by Juri's henchmen. The sob I swallowed a minute ago climbs back up my throat, but I pull myself together. *I'll get Kye to safety, and then find Eric.*

I remove the blanket covering Kye and realize it's actually an old fashioned cloak. He jerks, moaning in pain when I move his injured shoulder, and a tear slides down my cheek. "I'm sorry. I'm so sorry." Another tear falls as I caress his bruises and kiss his forehead. "Kye, I'm here. I don't think I can Heal you now—not with the amount of poison in this room—but I'll try to help you wake up." My heart aches because I know this will be painful for him. For both of us.

Since the poison has likely spread throughout his body, I start with his blood. By placing my ring on his stomach between the second and third chakras, it becomes my Healing crystal, and I spin both areas, one with each hand. My throat is scratchy as I hum the tones of blood Healing, but my voice grows stronger until the energy lifts from Kye and funnels into me. I only let it linger briefly before coaxing it around and sending it back, only partially mended. I can't pass out. Not this time.

Kye's eyelids flutter and he groans. My vision blurs, but I manage to fight through it, pushing hard against the metallic taste in my saliva. "Hey, you," I say into his ear. "Wake up now. Time to go."

"Abby." His eyes pop open and swollen lips make his smile crooked. "Am I dead then?"

I shake my head and another tear drips on his filthy shirt as I return the ring to my finger. "I hope not, because we're a long way from heaven."

He tries to move and whimpers. "I must be alive because I hurt everywhere."

"I know." I cover my face, try to regain some composure. "You're injured pretty badly, Kye." My fingers stray to his face, trace invisible lines from his forehead to his cheeks. "But it's important that we get out of here. Do you remember how you got in?"

He lifts his head, squinting. "There was a door."

"A door?"

"Yeah, a sliding door."

Sliding? "Electric or manual?"

Kye's head drops again, like he doesn't have the strength to hold it up. "'Lectric, I think." His speech slurs.

I touch his face again. "Stay with me. We need to move. You have to try walking."

"'Kay." His head lolls to one side. "You gonna help me?"

"Yep." I stand, inspecting the walls for the hidden door. "As soon as I find the door."

"Can't," he says. "Locked."

I inspect every dent and crevice. "Then we'll find a way to unlock it." There are wires on the ceiling, but I couldn't even hope to reach them, and there are so many there is no way to tell where they go or what they do. It seems like hours pass. I'm about to make Kye try to squeeze through the gap when one of the walls slides open.

My stomach squeezes so tightly with fear that if I had eaten in the last twenty-four hours, it would all be coming up about now. Shaking, I cower closer to Kye.

"So, the lovers are reunited." Juri looms in the open door. Behind him, I can see a brightly lit, fully furnished office. There's even a plush rug on the ground. *Why would anyone bother bringing office furniture into a cave?*

Kye levels himself against the wall, clasping my hand.

There are a lot of things running through my mind, but one look at Juri's ugly brown suit and all I can think is that it's the one he wore the first day I ever saw him, before I moved to Jackson or met Kye or inherited Gram's ring. Before I knew anything about Theron or Raina or the Arawn Keys or curses or wicked traitors. Before he dragged me down the alley in New York and stabbed me with a knife carved from his own bones. The brown man. Everything about him round.

Waves of boiling anger burn until I finally understand the meaning of true hatred.

"Aw, the princess is angry." He clucks his tongue, seeming to read my thoughts. "Even after I allowed you a moment of private time together before you both die."

"Leave her alone," Kye croaks.

Juri's smile is nearly as wide as his entire round face. "Oh no. No, no, no. See, Boone and I were just discussing how excited we were for her arrival. And look! Here she is. No, this calls for a celebration. Let's party, shall we?"

"I said leave her alone." Kye trembles, but his voice is stronger and he pushes himself up the wall until he's on his feet.

"No thanks," I tell Juri. The metal in my throat makes my voice sound hollow, rough.

"What was that?" Another shadow looms in the doorway. It's Boone. "No? Did I just hear you tell him no?"

I reach down inside, to my very core, and try to bring up all usable energy, preparing to fling it at the both of them, but something heavy weighs it down.

Juri scowls. "You're going to wish you hadn't said that. I'll leave you with some beautiful scars before this is over." His teeth gleam in the light as he draws the jeweled dagger from his belt.

"We could take her powers now," Boone says. "A few slices, transfer of blood, cut off her finger to take the ring—done."

I tuck my fingers into fists and hide my hands by folding my arms.

Juri licks his lips. "Tynan needs her alive. Do whatever you want to her, as long as her heart keeps beating."

Boone grins. "Whatever I want?"

A feral gleam lights Juri's eyes. "Whatever we want."

Kye looks ill as he slides his arm around my waist, whispering, "I hope you have a plan."

"Nope. Totally winging it."

The men advance on us, their expressions reminding me of cavemen who want to throw me over their shoulders and haul me into their respective caves for ravishing. Except we're already in a cave, so they're ahead on that count.

"Don't let them cut you with that dagger," Kye murmurs, still unsteady on his feet. Boone moves out of the doorway, letting the light flood the small cell, bathing us in a warm yellow glow. The path to our salvation.

A flash of metal catches my eye as Boone draws a gun out of his waistband—black and sleek with a large barrel and big, deadly bullets.

"Leave her alone. Please." Kye's hand trembles on my waist. "She shouldn't be here. This is my fault."

"Oh, I'm sorry. My mistake. Of course. We'll just send her home to Mommy." Juri clucks. "After that stunt in New York, I think Tynan will want to see what she can do under pressure."

"I'd rather die than help the Dark Prince," I say.

Juri nods at Boone.

Boone aims the gun at Kye's chest, his finger caressing the trigger. "Bye bye, animal boy. You know, I've enjoyed chasing you around the country for the last few years. I can honestly say I'm going to miss you."

"Wait!" I shout. "Don't. Please don't. What do you want me to do?"

"Abby, no." Kye leans against me. "You can't."

I wrap my arms around him. We're both trembling with fear. "I have to."

"Ah, isn't that sweet." Juri grabs my wrist and yanks me away from Kye. "Let's go." Then he says to Boone, "Shoot him."

"No!" I scream. Juri flings me onto the plush office carpet and the door slides closed behind us. I fight, kicking and screaming and hitting with my free hand until he pins me on a decorative metal chair. He wrenches off his tie and uses it to bind me, then forces the ring off my finger. His eyes rake over me, stopping to linger in certain places long enough to make my stomach churn. Finally he says, "Too bad Tynan's in a hurry. It's really too bad." He inspects the ring then pounds on the wall. "I got it!" Then he disappears into the black corridor, leaving me alone.

I try to stand, but my arms are bent at an awkward angle, and maneuvering my body away from the chair feels literally impossible. My fingers pick and work the knot, pull and tug the silk, but it doesn't loosen. I scoot the chair toward the large mahogany desk hoping to find something with which to cut my bindings and have managed to make it halfway when a gunshot echoes through the caves.

THIRTY-NINE

Betrayed

"Kye!" Terror slows my world. Grief runs rivers down my cheeks while my chest heaves with the pressure of sobs being ripped from my stomach.

At some point, I find myself wondering if we've messed up the cosmic balance by not conceiving a child like Theron and Raina did. What will happen if the bloodline ends with me? This time a baby doesn't exist between us. Because I wasn't ready to take that step. Because we haven't had any time.

Just when I think I'm empty of tears, a fresh wave hits me.

What happened to Eric?

After the longest half hour of my life, the door scrapes open. Panicking, I knock a stapler off the desk with my toes, wondering how I can use it as a weapon while my hands are still tied.

A hoarse voice says, "What were you going to do, staple me to death?"

Shock steals my breath when I look up and meet the clear blue of the most perfect eyes I've ever seen. The eyes I love. "You're alive."

Kye leans on the wall for support, clearly still weak. "For now, anyway."

"Can you untie me?" As he limps over, I'm able to see his energy, and it's grayish. Not a good sign. The hand he drops on my shoulder is heavy, like he isn't doing well holding the weight of his limbs.

"I thought Boone shot you." I whisper through more tears. "I thought—"

"But he didn't." He crouches, takes me awkwardly in his good arm, and lets me cry. "Shh, babe, I'm here. That guy had terrible aim. Missed by inches. The bullet ricocheted—caught him square on the forehead." He shudders. "Never saw it coming." He pauses, glances around the room. "Where's Juri?"

I shake my head, on the verge of falling apart. "I don't know, but he has my ring. He took it, Kye. He took my ring."

Kye kneels behind me, working on the knot with his good hand. "Don't worry, he can't open the door with only three Keys. As long as he doesn't have the pendant ..."

"He might."

"What?" His hand stills.

"Juri might have the pendant. Eric and I had to use them to get through the portal, so Eric had the pendant in his pocket. He disappeared when I found you. We have to find him." *I hope he's still alive.*

"Juri has all four Keys?"

"No." I shake my head, trying to convince myself. "No, he only has three. We're not positive about the fourth one, remember? No one even knows what it really is. Right?"

Kye works more vigorously at the tie until it's loose enough for me to pull my arms free. "It's a rock. A glowing stone that gives off enough power to supply lights to Las Vegas for the rest of eternity."

"But how?" I open a drawer, search for a flashlight, a weapon, anything we can use.

Kye dumps the contents of another one on the desk and sifts through it. "That's why he was working at the Luxor. Juri's the guardian of the Arawn Sunstone."

The bottom drawer's locked, so I kick the handle with my bare heel until it comes off and the front slides open. Kye sways again, then seems to reach into a reserve of energy, because he catches himself and continues to help look.

"He used to be a good guy," Kye says. "Anyway, I saw the Sunstone right after Boone brought me here. If they have the pendant, that's all the Keys. We need to hurry."

"There's nothing here." He stands upright, and I notice a gun sticking out of his waistband.

"Why do you have Boone's gun?"

"Better to take it with us than leave it here." Kye leans on me as we hobble down the tunnel, the lights from the office illuminating our path enough so we're not completely in the dark. After the light and warmth of the office, my eyes struggle to adjust, but now that I've seen the office, I notice little things. Like lamps mounted intermittently along the walls, and the smell of some kind of fuel.

After leaving the poisonous room behind, some of Kye's strength trickles back until he's holding himself upright without support but still limping. We hear voices echoing off the stone before we see the faint light shining ominously from an inner chamber.

"Why won't it work? We have the Keys, what are we doing wrong?" Juri bellows.

"You're an incompetent, bumbling idiot. Tynan gives you way too much credit. I would have had her voluntarily if not for your interference. I swear, the two of you screw up more than you ever help." The voice is familiar, and as I comprehend his words, my heart breaks all over again for things I don't understand but know I have to do.

Kye's lips touch my ear as he whispers, "Is that ...?"

I nod against his cheek. "Yes. It's Eric."

FORTY

The Tomb

Wow. *How stupid am I?* "I thought they were torturing him." My throat burns with anger. "He came with Akers to meet me at the airport. He helped me through the portal. I trusted him."

Kye's whispered curses echo in the hollowness. *If they didn't know we were here, they do now.*

We turn around and come face to face with Juri, bone sword exposed, eyes wide and shocked. I can feel Kye's pulse raging where our skin touches.

"Glad you're here," Juri says. "We're having a terrible time figuring out how to make that ring work. Your assistance may be required." He presses the tip of his sword to Kye's side, seizing the gun and tucking it in his own waistband. Then he shoves Kye toward Eric, who appears slightly less surprised. There is no missing the guilt written on the face of the betrayer I considered a friend.

"Go to hell." I tell him. "I will never help you again. Ever."

"I told you she was feisty." Eric's voice is raspy, different, and he avoids my accusing gaze. "You'll help us, Abigail. It's the only reason I let you get this far." To prove his point, he removes the crystal dagger from a sheath strapped to his thigh, jabbing Kye in the back until the sharp point pokes through his shirt.

"How could you do this to me?" I croak. "We were friends. I wanted to help you. I even tried to Heal you."

Eric's smile is cruel. "But you didn't. If I'd let you in that far, you'd have figured me out, and Tynan's work over the past thirty years would have been wasted." He shrugs off the suffering I endured all because of him. "Good call on my part, especially now that I know you're not merely a Healer."

My head fills with indignant confusion. "What do you mean? I am a Healer."

"You haven't figured it out yet?" Eric nudges Kye with the dagger, urging us into the cavern. "You don't have two Gifts, you have one. Witch light."

My mind whirls as I try to piece everything together. *Witch light?*

Kye's face contorts with pain when Eric shoves him. Dark mist hovers a foot above the ground, filling the air with a soupy texture and stifling, cold humidity that steals my breath, like walking through fever chills.

"Light." Kye's posture sags and he leans on me again, murmuring. "Heart Light. Witch Light. Like Isleen. I should have seen it. Val would've seen it for me if we'd gone to him in the first place."

I clutch his side, alarmed at the rapid decline in his energy field as his face goes deathly pale. "What are you talking about?"

"He's talking about you." Eric's tone changes—almost as if his determination is wavering. Like he's hesitant to push forward with whatever he has planned. "It's a rare Gift, even in the ancient world of Elen. It was originally known as Heart Light, but most called it Witch Light because only women could possess it, and those who did were all encompassing energy manipulators. Isleen had it, and according to rumor, Raina had it as well."

Juri claps—hand against sword—and the sound echoes, repeating a hundred more times like applause before the sound waves disappear into the black abyss. "Enough history." He pins Eric with a look. "Master grows tired of waiting."

For the first time, I notice a faint red glow outlining gaps in the walls. The lines create a perfect square on which is carved a number of glowing red symbols. The door to the tomb.

As Eric spins away, a crystal around his neck catches my eye. White with streaks of black. Juri has one too, on a brown leather strap. How did I miss those before? Kye droops, fighting a losing battle with consciousness, and I tighten my hold around his waist. My eyes are drawn to the walls, then to the floor and ceiling. Glowing veins of red shoot through the black, like blood veins in tired eyes. "Is that ...?" I lean closer, not daring to touch.

Juri's grin is wicked, gleeful. "Cinnabar. Highly poisonous and terribly potent in such a small space. You know, because of all the mercury. Worse for you than copper is for us." He pinches the leather strap off his collarbone and taunts me with the stone. "Howlite, for detoxification. Want one?" He lets it drop against his chest. "Oops, that was rude. I'm afraid I don't have a spare."

Eric smacks the back of Juri's head. "Let's get to it." His eyes narrow at my arm around Kye's waist, then, finally, he looks at me. Something flickers between us, though I'm not sure what it is. "Let go of him, Abby. That ring is no good to us without your power. You're going to have to help us."

"No."

Juri's sword pokes the small of my back, stinging as it threatens to break the skin. "You'll help us or I'll run you through."

Kye's head lolls, but he whispers, "Don't do it, Abby."

Eric shakes his head, disgusted at Juri. "I have to do everything around here. You were instructed not to hurt her. Let me show you how she works." He digs the point of the crystal dagger into Kye's chest, over his heart, until the tip pierces his skin and a line of blood runs down the front of his shirt. "Open the door, Abby."

Another drop of deep red rolls onto the blade, and the jeweled handle lights up. Kye jerks and fights to stay standing, but I let go of him. "What do you want me to do?"

"Good girl. You see, Juri? You just have to give her the right motivation." Eric twists a handful of Kye's shirt in his fist to keep him standing, and the blade digs deeper. "Your ring is in place, there, in the center position. Go make it glow. Make it do whatever it does so I can let my master out of prison."

The pendant is pressed into a cutout near the top, and an iridescent stone near the bottom. There's no place for the dagger, and I wonder why. I'm halfway across the room when Eric's words sink in, stopping me midstride. "Your master? You've been working for Tynan all along?"

"What else was I to do when you turned me away?"

I pull my ring out of the door and put it on, watch the diamonds light up. "What are you talking about?"

Eric's knife digs deeper and Kye's face contorts. "You broke my heart into a million pieces, Raina. Tynan was the only person who cared. He helped me see light again and gave me new, stronger powers until I stopped needing you. Stopped missing you. He treated me as if I was his flesh and blood son, and I'll repay the debt by setting him free. Now, open the door!" He shrieks his last words, sounding desperate.

Kye gasps, trying not to scream as Eric plunges the dagger deeper and his blood flows more freely. Desperate, I turn back to the door and pray for forgiveness. How will I ever fix this mess? My fist shakes when I take off the ring and press it into the poisonous stone, fitting the diamonds into the center.

Thunder rumbles from the earth's core, shaking the walls until dust and chunks of poisonous mineral rain on our heads. The cinnabar glows brighter as the lines around the door explode in a flash of red light. The ground quakes, tossing me around until I end up on the floor next to Kye and Eric. Blood pours from Kye's wound, but Eric has dropped the dagger.

I crawl to the passage and press my back against the stone, trying to hold it closed. Black shadows seep around the edges, accompanied by a horrid screech. Large chunks of cinnabar roll away, leaving a hole in the center. I duck to avoid a falling rock and close my eyes against the dust. The door inches forward, my body weight doing nothing to hold it. A sulfuric odor burns the inside of my nose and stings my throat until I cough and cough and cough.

A few feet away, Eric sits up, his face a mask of both rage and panic. "What is that?"

I turn and brace my palms against the stone. "Your *master's* demon army. What did you expect? A rosy homecoming parade?" The door keeps moving, so I yank my ring out. Nothing happens. On the far side of the cavern, Juri cowers in a corner, his arms over his head as a waterfall of debris rains on him until a blow from an exceptionally large chunk renders him unconscious. Eric gapes in horror as shadow demons slip one by one through the cracks.

My eyes find Kye. He's lost his battle against the cinnabar and is lying unconscious where Eric dropped him.

I'm it.

The temperature skyrockets and the ground shakes harder as a voice thunders through the cavern. "King Tynan lives!"

A shadowy form quivers to life in front of Eric, the same person I saw in New York, twice. "Son of my heart," he says. "You've almost completed the task. One more step and we're free."

"Father of my soul." Eric steps forward to embrace Tynan, but his arms glide through the thick, flickering air.

Tynan laughs, almost mocking. "Not yet. I'm not free yet."

Eric nearly falls forward but rights himself. "How are you here if you aren't free?"

"Sacrifice, my son. We must all make sacrifices if we hope to ever be free of our bondage."

I move away from the door, hoping—needing—to see Eric's face when Tynan tells him that the next thing he has to do is kill Kye and me. "What kind of sacrifice?"

Tynan whirls around, narrowing his eyes into slits. "We meet again, Raina. Ironic and, I suppose, fitting that the woman who sealed the tomb should also be the one who re-opens it."

The floor is still tossing and I brace my hand on the wall for balance. "I'm *not* here to free you."

His brittle laugh tinkles around the room like bits of broken glass. Thousands of echoes escalate into a chorus of laughter. "Aren't you?" He turns back to Eric. "In answer to your question—and for your future knowledge—my powers have increased by three parts out of four. That is, three of the four original guardians have been sacrificed to strengthen my power. Their Gifts now belong to me for as long as I possess their hearts." He rips open his shirt and reveals a chest that crawls like something living is trapped inside it. Bright red scars crisscross his skin, radiating a purple glow. Power flows in his voice when he says, "Finish this, my servant, my son. Raina is here now. The time is right. Spill her blood and permit her heart to become the final Key."

Eric's breath hitches and his eyes flick toward me. "Kill her?"

"Take the dagger," Tynan says. "Cut out her heart and place it in the opening. When her powerful blood has pooled at the base and her heart beats in my chest, the seal will be forever broken."

Hearing Tynan's words, my muscles contract and I shrink back, my fingers flexing against the hard rock. Eric staggers toward me, clutching the dagger in one hand and holding his stomach with the other. It might be the lighting, but his skin has a greenish hue. "Father, Tynan, I—"

"DON'T!" Tynan roars. "Don't tell me you can't do it. Do not tell me you love her, or that you did love her, or that you wished to love her. She doesn't love you. She never did. Raina married Theron. She bore Theron's child, not yours. Remember how she broke your heart into pieces? For that alone she deserves to die. Kill her, my son. Mete out your justice now, even as you did then. Use your anger to free the only person who ever truly loved you—I, who have become your soul father."

Expressions race over Eric's face as he crosses the room and grabs my arm. Rage, hate, love, heartbreak, and then terrible, aching sorrow. His chest heaves and his Adam's apple bobs as he clears his throat and attempts to speak. When he finally does, it isn't the youthful voice I know as Eric's, but instead a weary, aged one.

"I never understood why you sealed them in, Raina, any more than I understood how you turned away from me, your childhood love, to marry Theron. I loved you outrageously, obsessively. And you knew. We could've been happy together. So happy." His voice breaks. "Why couldn't you love me back? What does he have that I don't?"

Centuries of memories flood my mind, and suddenly I understand. Eric—whose name in that time was Erim, servant of Tynan—loved me. In that time when I was Raina, an orphan who worked at the palace of a tyrant. As Erim and Raina, we shared a special friendship, and I did love him in the way a sister loves a brother. I did. But he loved me so much deeper, and I knew. Erim was there, hiding in the bushes near the pathway between worlds the day of the hunt. The day I—Raina—met Theron and the whole world changed.

I swallow fresh tears, pouring emotion into my voice, into my eyes for him to see. "I'm sorry, so sorry I hurt you, Eric. I did love you, just not the way you wanted."

With a sound I can't identify, he grabs a handful of my hair and pulls my head back, the dagger poised against my throat. I won't close my eyes. I intend to make him look at me, to see what he's doing when he slices the knife through my neck. So I stare at him, into him, and wait for him to kill me and be done.

Instead, his eyes fill with longing as his face hovers inches from mine. The dagger slips lower, and before I know it, we're so close I can feel his breath on my cheek. His free arm slips around my waist. "Just once," he whispers, pulling me close. "I've loved you for an eternity. I can't ... I need ... just one taste." He crushes his lips against mine. I don't return the kiss, won't return it while he's holding a knife to my throat, so I stay still, wide-eyed, and stare at Kye—still unconscious—praying for strength and shaking as Eric's lips assault mine. A tear rolls down my cheek, threading to my lips where Eric laps it up and jerks away like I've slapped him.

His fingers clench more tightly in my hair and he stares, horrified. My eyes fill with more tears. The look on his face is the most frightening thing I've seen all day. "Please," I plead. "Eric, please don't. Don't do this. I did love you. I still do."

He blinks away the shock of my rejection, weary all over again. "Not enough. Not the way you love him."

"I'm sorry," I breathe. My voice shakes when I tell him, "My gram used to say 'the head cannot choose what the heart will feel.' I loved you in that life. You were my best friend. My heart bled for the pain I caused you."

"And now, it will bleed for the pain you've caused me." Tynan moves closer. Bits of onyx and cinnabar rain on our heads and in my eyes as the walls tremble. "It's time, Erim. I've allowed you to have your goodbye moment. Now, set me free and you'll have your choice of women to love."

Eric draws my head back again, and once more I wait for him to slit my throat. Something out of my line of vision crashes and I close my eyes, no longer able to watch. He draws the dagger down to my chest where it hovers for what feels like several long minutes until his grip on my hair loosens and he brushes his hand through it, caressing.

My eyes open, watching his gaze as he follows the curve of my throat, lower, then returns to my face. A sad smile plays on the corners of his lips. "I killed you before, but it wasn't on purpose." He lets go of my hair, his hand drifting to the small of my back, and he pulls me into a hug. "It was supposed to be Theron. I meant to kill Theron, but you wouldn't let him die. Why wouldn't you just let him die?" His voice breaks. "You sacrificed yourself to save him, and I never understood. Until now." Eric slips the detoxifying crystal from his neck and loops the strap over my head, bending his face to mine. I think he's going to kiss me again, but instead he whispers in my ear, "In ten seconds, duck."

"Enough!" Tynan bellows. "It's time."

We break apart, and Eric grips the dagger with both hands and raises it high above his head. "I'm sorry," he shouts above the din. His voice echoes with force I've never heard. "I'm so sorry."

I duck, and he brings the dagger down with all his strength, stabbing it into the stone where my ring opened the gateway to hell. The ground heaves once more, opening a three-inch crack that runs across the cave and under the rock walls. An icy wind blows around the cavern, circling until it turns into a furious cyclone, pulling in the mist, the loose minerals, and everything around it. Tynan screams. "You are not my servant or my son! You are a coward. I knew you would fail me, and still I put my faith in you, loved you as my own flesh and blood. How could you do this?"

Eric grabs my hand as a mournful wail blows through the image of Tynan, who then flickers and vanishes. The cyclone circles, swirls, gathers into itself, and then disappears.

When the frenzy dies, the silence is eerie. No more demons come through the cracks, but the boulder doesn't move back into place. My breath feels stuck in my chest and my heart beats so hard I wonder if everyone in the room can hear it. Eric drops the dagger and sinks to his knees, head bowed. His pale face reflects the horror I feel.

A low moan breaks the awful silence, filtering through the partially opened magical door. Eric raises his head. "We should close that." We work together, pushing and shoving at the heavy boulder.

Juri coughs as he's coming back around. "Am I alive?"

Eric snarls at him. "Yes, you idiot. Now get over here and help us reseal this door."

Juri sits up. "Reseal it? No! Tynan's coming through with a royal procession. That's the plan. It's been the plan for five hundred years. You can't change your father's plan."

Eric leaps at Juri, draws back a fist, and punches him in the face. "Shut up. You just shut up about Tynan being my father. I'm not his flesh and blood. After being locked up for four hundred and fifty years, he still knows nothing about loyalty. Or love." He gazes at me. "But I do. That's why he's in there, and I'm not. And that's how it has to be." He sighs again. "It's just how everything has to be."

He drags Juri to the door by his collar and shoves him against the wall. "Stay."

Juri doubles over, clutching his face and wailing about his nose being broken.

The two of us heave the boulder into place, then Eric backs up so I can turn all the Keys counterclockwise until a green glow snakes around the opening once, twice, three times. The cracks around the door fill with mortar, and then all goes still. I clasp the pendant around my neck and close the glowing stone in my fist.

Eric wrenches the dagger from the center just as the door becomes a solid wall and disappears altogether. "Well, that was fun. Let's not do it again for at least another five hundred years, huh?"

I pat his arm. "Deal."

On the far side of the cavern, Kye stirs. "Abby."

My breath hitches. I rush over and fall on my knees next to him with Eric right behind me. "I'm here, Kye. Right here. Are you okay?"

"I've seen better days," he rasps. His eyes flutter open, the deep blue irises cloudy as his pupils struggle to focus.

Eric strides over, yanks the white stone off Juri's neck, and hands it to me to tie around Kye's. "Do you think you can walk?"

"Traitor." Kye growls, a wolfish sound. "I'll kill you if you hurt her. Abby, whatever you do, don't open that door."

The sound that ripples from my throat is too brittle to be a laugh. "Okay."

As I help Kye sit up, he takes in the chasm in the floor and the broken bits of onyx and cinnabar scattered everywhere. "What happened?"

I scoot closer to him and lean against the wall. "Long story."

Eric walks back to the door and runs his hand down its length. "I've failed you again." His voice is weighted with emotion. "I couldn't go through with it. I just couldn't kill her, Tynan. Not this time. I'd rather see her live, loving another man, than go through the agony of watching her die again." He touches a small crack—the only indication that the door ever existed—then slides down to the floor, sobbing.

Kye and I avert our eyes to give him privacy. For now.

Blood pulses in my throat, and that odd sensation of danger prickles along the back of my neck. I think Kye feels it too, because his body tenses as I help him stand.

Juri, still leaning against the far wall, glares at us. "Thirty years I've devoted to tracking down those Keys," he says. "Thirty years. I even brought Tynan the hearts of the guardians and passed them through the seal. I gave him vials of my own blood to help strengthen his powers." He's yelling now. "What have you done? What the hell have all of you done? You've destroyed everything! Everything I've worked for is ruined. Ruined!"

In a blur of movement, the skin peels back from his arm, becomes the sword again, and he lunges at me, screeching. Kye dives between me and the blade, and time slows as I watch the gleaming sword pierce the front of his chest until the tip comes through his back.

Kye's face goes paper white and he gasps. "Abby." Juri pulls the sword out, grinning, while Kye falls to the ground, bleeding and bleeding and bleeding from his enormous, gaping chest wound.

FORTY-ONE

Another Attempt

Juri's sword drips Kye's blood in two thin lines along the floor as he paces back to the tomb, wearing a vicious grin. "I wonder if *his* blood would be enough to reverse the seal? There's certainly going to be enough of it."

Eric's eyes are wide, his expression one of stunned panic. "Not again. It's happening again." He turns to me. "No."

Juri taunts him. "You've always been a coward. Why do you think I'm here? Master knew you wouldn't go through with killing her. You never do. But this time, I will."

Eric hangs his head, looking defeated.

"You can't change fate, boy. No matter how many times you try."

Juri dives for me and Eric lunges, dodging the sword as it slices the air, and manages to wrap his hands around Juri's throat. "Run, Abby. Go now and don't look back."

I'm frozen in place, my legs shaking because I know I'm not leaving. "I can't. Kye's dying." My voice catches, breaks. "I have to help him. I have to try to Heal him."

Eric closes his eyes, his jaw tightens, and his throat works with emotion. "Okay." His energy field glows blue and his fingers squeeze, flexing when Juri slices a gash in his leg, and then in one of his arms.

The cavern crackles with cold as a gust of frigid air swirls around them. Ice forms on the tips of their hair and in their eyelashes and a thick block of it wraps around Juri's sword. He opens his mouth to scream, but Eric has him frozen from the inside out before he can make a sound.

Kye's blood pools at my feet and I drop to my knees, trying to staunch the flow with my hands. His hand brushes my arm and I fall apart, sobbing until I can't breathe, and lay my head on his chest near his wound. Memories of the past few days streak through my mind like a distant movie I once watched. His heart heaves, stutters, and his energy hiccups, blinks, starts to fade very quickly.

"Eric, help me." I push myself up. "I ... I have to ... do something. I have to fix him."

Eric kneels next to me, his hand covering mine on Kye's chest. "What can I do?"

I'm reminded of the day in Yellowstone when their roles were reversed, and hate the grim reminder of my past failure. "Make sure I stay conscious. If I look like I'm going to pass out ... just don't let me. Slap me if you have to. Whatever happens, keep me upright. Watch my hands and make sure they don't stop moving until the light around us turns clear, okay?"

"Raina." Eric's voice is thick with emotion. "Abby, you could die. Healing something this serious could kill you. I'm not going to help you die. I won't watch that again. I can't live with it."

I ignore his hand on my shoulder and unclasp the pendant to place over Kye's wound, along with the Sunstone. "Yes, you can. It's not like you haven't done it before." My voice has an edge of cruelty. "You lured me here, betrayed me, and then almost murdered me. Again. You *should* have to watch me die if that's what it comes to. And then you can live knowing that it didn't have to be this way. Again."

"All right." His hand falls away from my shoulder and he gives a curt nod. "I deserve that. And worse. But please ... Abby, please don't die. I'm begging you. I didn't mean for this to happen. I just wanted to free the man I consider my father."

My hands start the familiar spinning motions of chakra balancing. "Well, it did. It happened. *You* screwed everything up and now I have to fix it. I have to make it right, just like I did the last time." The pendant glows green, the energy so bright it hurts my eyes. "Just promise me you'll get him out of here, get him help. And if I ... if something happens to me, bring my body to my mother so she knows I died doing what I couldn't do for my gram."

He sits next to me, stiff and formal, but nods.

Kye's eyelids flutter. He reaches for me and croaks, "Abby, don't."

"Shh." I put my fingers to his lips. "We aren't going to argue over this, okay? I have to try. I'll never be able to live with myself if I don't."

"Come here," he says.

I stop spinning long enough to lean in and steal one last moment with him. "I love you," I whisper. "Through space and time and however many lives we live. Forever and ever."

He strokes my cheek with his thumb. "I love you too. Don't worry, I'll find you again. And again and again and again. I'll keep finding you until this curse is broken. I promise. I'll never stop looking. Never."

I swallow, closing my eyes while a tear slips off my face and onto his. "Forever."

Kye's hand slides to the ground and his eyes glaze over when his heart stutters again. My hands—covered in his blood—shake as I spin Kye's chakras in a rhythm as sure as my own heartbeat. The Healing tones flow strong and true from somewhere inside me and the stones glow stronger, brighter. Light floods into the tunnels. Kye's energy streams out of his body, broken in millions of jagged pieces, and funnels toward me, spinning and spinning in a tornado of colors. The broken pieces rise and fall, rise and fall, and then surge into me with a blinding flash. I taste nickeline in Kye's blood, then iron and cinnabar. A flood of poison burns down my throat. Spots blink in my eyes—white, red, blue, black, yellow, orange—but I keep my arms moving, don't let myself pause, even when my muscles get tired, and a hot ache like nothing I've ever felt before spreads through me. I spin and spin, swallow more energy, more poison,

275

more and more and more. Everything, every virus, every illness, every scar Kye has accumulated in his life, flows into me, and still my arms hold on to the steady motion. I hum, sing, chant centuries-old charms Gram never taught me but that I somehow know.

The energy pours into me, through me, fills me up, and then, when I'm sure I've mended it all, I reach down, deep, deep down into my most inner self and push it—everything good—back into Kye.

Fire spreads in my blood, hot like lava, pressing weight on my lungs, and oxygen feels precious but so hard to catch. I try to cough it up, to become an erupting volcano and expel the horrible pressure building inside me, but it keeps building, and my body feels hotter and hotter. The pendant spins like a top, hovering over Kye, glowing like a light bulb. My chest feels tight, I can't breathe, and then I'm falling down a tunnel. Sinking. Falling. Sinking.

"Abby!" Eric sounds alarmed, but so far away.

The room is in motion. Kye reaches up to touch my face, his cobalt eyes stare into mine, through mine. "No, Abby, stop." His wide eyes reflect his panic, but his voice is stronger now. "Don't do this. Stop it. I don't want you to do this."

My eyes are heavy, so very heavy, but I fight them open. "It's already done."

His hand falls away and his eyes close again.

I keep going, keep working until the energy around me swirls and melds together and I can no longer feel Eric's touch on my shoulder, until my toes go numb and my lungs can't catch air. And then everything goes black.

It's over.

FORTY-TWO

Choices

Bright light shines through my closed eyelids and the air sighs with music. I'm floating, surrounded by luxurious fabric that feels like feathers on my skin. There is no trace of hunger or the nausea and ache I expect, but something is familiar. A soft scent I can't quite place. Baby powder, ocean breeze, fresh-baked bread, fruit on the vine, rain, all mixed together to make a unique and wonderful perfume.

I'm warm, relaxed, content, until I reach for Kye, expecting him to be lying beside me in this heaven, but my hands clutch empty space.

"Open your eyes, Abigail." The words glide over me, the sound of angels singing, of rain softly falling, of waves crashing on the shore of a perfect, untouched beach. It floats over my skin, into my ears, the voice of a mother to her child.

So I obey.

My bed is circular and surrounded by a flowing, gauzy substance. Three women hover near my feet. The one on my left smiles. A mane of blonde hair cascades past her waist, and without reason, I know her as Macha, goddess of war. To my right is Badb, goddess of death, with her rippling waves of midnight hair and shrewd, unblinking eyes.

Between them, with fiery ringlets of red hair curling around her body and eyes the same green as the emeralds in the Pendant of

Sadira, is Morrigan, the supreme fertility goddess. The oracle. The head goddess of the Morrigana.

These three great queens are the heart of war and rebirth, regeneration. Their presence is all at once overwhelming and familiar, as if I've met them before, known them as friends or mother figures in another existence.

I push myself up and realize I'm no longer wearing the silver dress from New York, but a soft white one that drapes around me, flowing down my legs to my toes. Warm calm spreads from the bottom of my heels into the rest of my body, blurring my memory until everything feels fuzzy, faded. "Am I dead?"

Badb answers in a throaty, seductive voice. "Do you wish to be dead?"

Confused, I tip my head to the side. "I don't know. Is this what dead is like? Am I in heaven?"

Macha's laugh sounds like tinkling bells. "Oh no, Abigail. This is the crystal castle. You'll remain here until your true destiny is decided."

I rub my hands over the silk bedding, feeling it glide between my fingers and tickle my palms. "Decided?"

"Your body has taken in a great deal of broken energy, but your soul is strong and fighting, your life purpose incomplete," Morrigan says, clasping hands with her sisters. "What do you desire, Abigail?"

I slip to the edge of the bed, curling my legs under me. "What are my choices?"

Morrigan spreads her right arm wide. "You may choose to continue your human life. There will be anguish and sorrow in your future, broken hearts and death. Wars will rage, battles will be won and lost. Some humans find joy and then they create more life, more humans who will suffer for their own happiness." Her left arm spreads now. "You may choose a life of paradise in the world of eternal youth and beauty, located on the Phantom Island of the legendary Tir na nog. In this place there is no heartache, no war, no death. Only joy. You will need no one, and be needed by no one. You will be free from the burdens that bind you in the mortal world. But you will go there alone. There is no returning from Tir na nog, where unions between souls do not exist. The man you loved will be erased from your mind, replaced by the pleasure of paradise. You will know nothing but singular contentment."

For the first time in my life, my heart feels free, light.

Empty.

Why am I here? My mind is full of clouds, my memories fuzzy, broken. It takes a great deal of effort, but a face shimmers in my mind. Eyes blue as sapphires that seem as deep and endless as the sea, a dimple bending his left cheek, a lock of wavy blond hair falling across a tanned forehead. A familiar voice. *I love you too ... I'll find you again ... I'll never stop looking. Never.*

Kye.

"Did I save him? Did I Heal him?"

The women nod in sync. Morrigan answers. "He lives."

The voice burns like sunshine in my memory, bringing back flashes of other people, other places, other things I know I should be doing. A deep ache of longing settles in my chest. *I don't want to forget.* "I promised I'd come back."

Morrigan's hands flutter across my forehead. "Your body has endured much. Should you return, you'll experience excruciating pain."

My fingers run curiously along my arms, touch my skin, pull hairs, pinch. There is no pain, only a pleasant sensation of pressure. "But ..." *The boy.* Already, I've forgotten his name again. A sense of panic wells up and squeezes my throat, though I'm not sure why it's so important that I remember this one detail. "Why? Why can't I remember?"

Macha pats the sheets near my foot in a maternal gesture. "The boy lives. This pain will be yours and yours alone."

Badb frowns.

Morrigan reaches inside her gown and produces a silver bough with white flowers blooming up the length of the branches. She plucks one and offers it to me. "There is a third choice. By eating this, you may return home for a time."

The bloom brings to mind another face, a gray-haired man. Relieved to have a face in my mind again, I hesitate and don't accept the offered gift. "The bloom of eternal life."

The women nod again. Their singularity is getting annoying. "What happens if I eat it?"

"You'll return home for a while," Morrigan says again. "And when your purpose has been served, you'll be taken across the crystal bridge."

The memory of the man fades as well, and my remaining contentment along with it. My mind continues reaching, but is unable to grasp anything solid. "What about the people I love? The ... others." The blue-eyed boy, the woman who held me when I cried, the friend with the hypnotizing voice. *Why can't I remember their names? Their faces?*

"They are still mortal, and as such, will someday die while you'll continue living for many years. It is the best of both worlds."

I have no pain, nothing binding me to earth. Nothing but a pair of deep blue eyes and the words *I'll find you again.*

Then I manage to grasp an agonizing memory of deep, unforgiving ache. "If I eat this blossom, will I feel pain?"

Macha shakes her head.

Another memory. A hand holding mine, keeping me grounded, arms pulling me close. "Then how will I know joy?"

No answer.

More memories fight through the fog, leaving me confused, frowning. A dark-haired boy who betrayed but then saved me. A woman tenderly combing my hair when I was little, trying so hard to understand me, to help me. The older woman, the Healer, what she wanted for me, what she always told me I would someday become. My own desires for future possibilities. Blue eyes. The boy in my dreams. The boy who always finds me.

"If I go, he won't be able to find me."

A cloud of confusion darkens Macha's face. "Immortality is a great honor offered to few chosen souls."

"But I have to be mortal so he can find me again. So I can find him," I murmur, shaking my head. "I need to find him."

"I will never understand the attachments of humans." Morrigan presses the flower hard in my palm. When she removes her hand, the bud has morphed into a large pink diamond. "The tasks ahead will be more difficult than the ones you've yet survived. You will call on us again. Swing this diamond over your palm in a clockwise circle and sing the calling tones. They are the same ones you used to call the broken energy out of your beloved and save his life, and which summoned us to your aid. Be warned; with the next summons, your choices will not be the same."

My fingers close around the precious stone. *I'm going home. I'm going back to him.*

"Beware that charm, young one," Badb says. "The Morrigana always requires payment. A summons will cost you."

I hope I never have to find out what that cost is.

"Fate has decided." With soft hands on my arms, Macha urges me to lie back. "Close your eyes, and prepare for pain. "

Morrigan hums. Soon the other two join her, and then I'm spinning. Spinning and spinning and spinning and spinning until I land. *Thud.* Smack into hell.

FORTY-THREE

Strong. Determined

A freight train is parked on my chest. I try to thrash about, but my limbs are too heavy. Every inch of me aches. My skin, organs, and muscles throb with the slightest touch. Something rolls under my back, lifting me from a fiery hot surface and submerging me into icy, frigid water. I steal a mouthful of air, but it refuses to travel down my throat and I choke on it. When I finally find enough breath to scream, needles dig into my arms, thousands of them, until the pain becomes too much and I slither into oblivion.

A voice reaches me down a tunnel far, far away. Rivers of cold hold my heavy eyes closed. Something touches my skin and my fuzzy brain struggles to figure out what's happening. My fingers twitch, trapped. A hand. Someone's holding my hand.

The voice says my name and I force an eye open. A blurry face looms above. Valdemar. His words are caught in the tunnel and I can't understand them, but as my eyes focus, my ears clear a little. He's chanting, quick and sharp, in a language I don't recognize. Someone lifts me, and every step, every tiny movement is torture. "It hurts," I moan, thankfully falling back into the dark.

The first thing I see upon opening my eyes is Kye's face on the pillow, next to mine. His smooth skin is perfect, unscarred, untouched. His eyes are closed, but I know their color well.

I don't hurt so much anymore, but my chest feels tight. Kye's arm is draped across my stomach, holding me to his side. A soft light flickers in the room, but the only sound is his steady breathing. He jerks and his arm flexes, tightens. He's sleeping.

"Kye," I croak. "Can't breathe." His eyes pop open and his brows draw together. Then his expression softens into that familiar half smile. He loosens his grip but doesn't let go.

"Hey, you," he murmurs. "How are you feeling? Are you warm enough?"

"Hot." My voice is rough from disuse. "Heaven's warmer than I expected, but I'll take it as long as they let you stay with me."

Kye brushes tangled hair away from my eyes. "I have to go home at some point. But lucky you, you're already here."

"Home?"

"Yes. Your mom's here. And Erda. You can go back to school. Live your life now."

"I can't go home," I say, teasing. "I'm dead."

"That's not funny." He grimaces, shaking his head. "You really had us worried."

I struggle out of his arms and sit up, feeling a deep ache I can't pinpoint. I pretty much hurt everywhere. Soft, white light filters through the curtains and four or five stubby candles burn on my dresser, reflecting off handfuls of colorful crystals placed around my room. Kye has cleaned himself up since I last saw him. There is no trace of blood or dirt on his skin or clothes and his breath smells like mint toothpaste.

My mouth, on the other hand, tastes like I ate dirt, and my head throbs like I've been buried in it. When I look at myself, I half expect to be filthy. Instead, I realize someone has changed me into flannel pajamas. My sleeve is pushed up to my elbow to reveal fading purple bruises dotting my pale skin.

"You don't want to see the rest," Kye says, pulling my sleeve down. "Your mother about fainted the first time she changed your clothes."

"How long have I been asleep?"

He props his head on his arms. "Way too long."

I lift an eyebrow, waiting for him to elaborate.

"Nine days."

"Nine days?" I squeak, shocked.

"We've been really glad you weren't in an actual coma." His words come out in a rush. "You mumbled a little, moaned, and drank through a straw when we really pushed it down your throat. You even drank some herbal stuff Val forced on you."

"No way. No way, Kye. Do not tell me I now have two weeks of missed school to make up."

"Technically, just over one. And I can't believe you would worry about school at a time like this." He sits up, shaking his head again, irritated. "You risked your life to save mine, fought against the Dark Prince, and resealed the tomb to save the rest of the world from destruction. There are shadow demons on the loose, and you're worried about homework? You almost died, Abby!" He drops his head into his hands, threading his fingers through his hair. "Why did you do that? Huh? Why?"

"Which part?"

"Why did you sacrifice yourself to save me?"

I let out a long breath. "Clearly I didn't, since I'm still alive."

"But you tried, and I want to know why. Your heart stopped. Val said your heart stopped for about three minutes. I almost lost you. You almost died because of me." He sits up and pulls me to him, his expression fierce. "Don't you know your death would have killed me too?"

I run my fingers through my matted hair until they're completely tangled and I have to forcefully rip them out.

"I want an answer," he demands. "Why?"

"Because I love you!" I shout. "And I couldn't just stand there and watch you die. I had to do something."

Gently, he scoots me into his lap and wraps his arms around me, resting his cheek on my head. "Say it again," he murmurs.

I breathe into his neck. "I've said it before."

"Say it anyway." He squeezes harder, though still not tight.

"I love you." I wrap my arms around his waist and lay my head on his shoulder. "Stay here with me. Please, stay here with me and don't go away."

"You want to stay with me while I drag you all over the world? Sleeping on benches in malls and getting attacked on the street? Having to catch a plane by yourself in the middle of the night, not knowing what happened to me? Running through a dark cave barefoot in a silk dress? Facing impossible odds to correct something that went wrong in a life you don't even remember?"

"Yes." I pull him into my arms, blinking my misty eyes.

"How? How can you want this?"

"How can I not?" I press my hands to his cheeks. "There's no going back to my old life now. I'll never be the same after everything that's happened. After loving you. I do remember a little bit of my life as Raina, of her love for Theron all those years ago. It's part of me forever. I'll never stop loving you, so how can I not want to be with you for as long as I can?"

Kye blinks rapidly, closes his eyes, and draws a deep breath. "They'll never leave us alone. I don't know how to protect you except to leave and let Raina fade back into Abby. That's what would happen, you know. You don't feel Raina and I don't feel Theron as much when we're apart. So, if I left, maybe—maybe you would have a chance at a partially normal life."

My heart cracks open a little and I drop my hands away from his face. I need to know. "Do you love me?"

"I do." His voice sounds tortured. "So much it hurts. I don't know how to protect you, but how can I possibly leave you? It'll kill me."

I sigh, relieved. "So, what do we do now?"

He pauses, thinks about it, and then points at a stack of books on the floor. "Homework."

I giggle at his mood swings, because I love him.

So.

Much.

He rubs my shoulders again, and my skin heats at the touch. I wrap my arms around his neck and lean in, prepared to put off homework for a little while longer.

The door bangs open and a muffled giggle is drowned out by a bark. Erda bounds into the room, jumps up to put her front paws on my thighs. I yelp. "Off, Erda. Get down. You know better than to jump on people."

Her long, pink tongue smears slobber on my chin in answer and I melt. "I love you too."

"You're awake." Jen clears her throat, standing in the doorway. "We thought we heard voices in here."

"Actually, we thought Kye's cookies had finally crumbled and he was having a conversation with himself." Rose pushes past Jen. "We came to see if it's time to send him to the crazy farm."

Kye makes a face, then picks up my pillow and lobs it at her head. "Very funny."

"Well, you have been acting rather nuts." Rose tosses the pillow on my bed, then shoves Kye away and hugs me tight. "I've been worried to puking over you, you know."

I squeeze her back, feeling weak. "I know. I'm sorry."

Jen joins our hug. "Me too," she says. "I burned a hole in your mom's shower curtain when Val told us there was nothing more he could do. I went in there to throw up and started the thing on fire instead."

The mental picture makes me giggle. "Seriously?"

She nods, blushing.

Another voice, quieter, more hesitant, comes from the hallway. "You're awake."

Kye scowls at Eric. "All right, she's awake and you've seen her. Now go home."

"Ahem." My mom pats Eric's shoulder, shooting Kye a stern look. "Actually, that's my call, Kye." A softer, more sympathetic look goes to Eric. "Stay as long as Abby likes." Her gaze veers back to Kye. "No fighting, you two."

Eric looks smug and Kye's scowl deepens.

Mom takes me in her arms. "Oh, sweetheart. I'm glad you're okay. I've never been so worried in my life." She draws away, a wrinkle forming on her forehead. "Don't ever do that to me again."

I lean my head on her shoulder, feeling safe, loved. "I'm sorry, Mom. I didn't mean to worry you. Everything happened so fast."

"I know," she says, frowning. "I've heard the story—several times." I glare at Kye.

He makes a face. "Hey, don't look at me. I wasn't the chatty one."

Suddenly, no one will look me in the eye except Eric. I'm all set to yell at him—because he's there and I'm still mad at him—when the door slams downstairs and someone yells, "Marian? Kye? I brought pizza. Where is everyone?" Heavy footfalls clamber up the stairs. "Marian?"

"Landon, we're in here." Mom flushes and her hands flutter up to pat her hair. Kye grins.

Apparently, I've missed a lot while I was sleeping.

A ball of light whizzes to the bed and stops abruptly near the empty pillow. Murtagh whips around, hands on hips, looking confused. "*Cailín* girl? Bed empty. Where *mo chara?*"

I pull out of my mother's arms. "I'm here, Murtagh. Right here."

He seems relieved, and flits closer to hover near my face. "*Cailín* better now?"

I offer my hand for him to land on. "Yes, I feel a lot better, thanks. What have you been up to?"

Murtagh explains his story with gusto, using his arms and legs and blinking light. Too bad none of us understands a word of his language.

Kye murmurs in my ear. "Valdemar says Murtagh showed up after you and Eric disappeared through the portal. You took the hard way in. That little guy had information about a sacred well. A thimble full of water from the well turned the boiling acid-mud into a calm, glass surface and opened the portal like a door. After Murtagh showed up with the water, he led the others into the tunnels where they found all three of us—you, me, and Eric—unconscious in the cavern." I notice he says nothing about Juri and decide not to ask right now.

"We were all unconscious? What happened to Eric?"

"We figured out that while you funneled your energy into me, Eric was doing the same thing to you." Kye sighs, reluctantly adding, "He probably saved your life."

Murtagh finishes his story and poses dramatically with one fist on his hip, waving the other in the air triumphantly. "Murtagh, hero. Find sacred place, fight battle, save queen. Queen healthy now. Good day."

Everyone laughs. Akers has his arm around my mother and I smile at them, because I like feeling the brush of romance in the air—and not just my own. The eight of us—counting Murtagh and Erda—filter downstairs to the kitchen and spend the evening catching up on what I've missed at school and during spring break.

As night falls, Jen and Rose leave for home. Akers eventually mumbles something about an early morning class and goes too. Mom kisses my head, reminds Kye he has school tomorrow, and then closes herself in her bedroom looking twitterpated. Erda dozes on the floor in front of the fireplace, with Murtagh curled up and snoring on her fluffy back.

Kye and I sprawl on the sofa watching Cake Boss. He could stay all night. I doubt my mom would notice before breakfast. I know eventually he'll have to go do whatever he does when the elementals call on him. It's part of why I love him. Plus, he doesn't actually live here.

"When do you leave?" I ask.

His head is tipped against a cushion, eyes closed, but he forces one open. "Huh?"

"I know you can't stay forever. You have an obligation to the elementals. Especially the faeries. I won't keep you from it, I just need to prepare in advance, that's all."

Both eyes are open now. He lifts his head. "I told you before, Abby. I don't know how to protect you, but I'm not going anywhere for now."

I blink. His smile blooms at my disbelieving expression. "Like it or not, princess, you're stuck with me for a while."

"Wait," I say, confused. "You're staying here? With me?"

"Looks like it." He picks up my hand and plays with my ring. "We're stronger together. Having me leave for a while, then come back and leave again ... well, I don't know how that'll affect Raina and Theron. Val and I discussed it, and we both feel like it's too much of a risk. So, like I said, I'm here for the duration."

My heart races. This is not at all what I expected. It makes me happy. So happy. I throw my arms around him. "What about the curse?"

He bites his lip. "Val has another theory about that. It isn't a sure thing, but he thinks we should test it. When you took my life energy into yourself, you connected us with a sacrificial bond that could possibly be stronger than the curse."

"What does that mean?"

"It means we're connected, maybe even responsible for each other. No way to know for sure until we test it out."

I brush a lock of hair off his forehead. "Huh." A thought has me pulling away, worried. "How does my mom feel about you moving in?"

Erda growls in her sleep when Kye bursts out laughing. "Abby, I love you, but I'm not moving into your house. None of my many parents would be happy with that scenario."

I blush, looking down at my knees, wondering what he thinks I was asking.

Kye tips my chin up with his finger. "And however liberal you think your mother is, she already had 'the chat' with me."

"The chat?"

"The one in which she grilled me on my behavior during our trip and in which I assured her about my manners and how I treated you like a lady. Also, she happened to be present when future plans were being discussed. My moving into this house is clearly not an option for her either."

I roll my stiff neck, stretch, and yawn. "I'm relieved she voiced an opinion. Though, I still wonder if she's more worried about what the neighbors think than what's really happening."

"Give her some credit, Abby." When he stretches, the long, lean muscles in his chest ripple under his T-shirt. "Anyway, I'll still be spending lots of time here, parents or not."

"I'm good with that."

He stands, helps me up, and twines his hands lightly around the small of my back. "Guess I'm going to be a regular at school again." He pulls me close and kisses me. A long, drawn out kiss that speaks of ... well, goodbye.

"Abby." He sighs my name—just my name—then leans his forehead on mine.

"You have to go, don't you?"

He nods, wrinkling his nose. "For tonight. I'll crash at Akers's house until Val can find us a place closer to town." He touches the tip of my nose with his finger. "You, Princess Abby, should get to bed. You have a big day back at school tomorrow."

He zips his coat, touches his fingers to his lips, and whispers, "Night."

As he drives away, I think back to the day we met and realize it was a turning point for me. Possibly the biggest one I'll ever experience.

Longing for Gram rises in my chest, but suddenly I understand why she had to go when she did. She was ready to move on to another life, one where she could find my grandfather, her one and only true love. I can't fault her for that. She knew I had to stay and fulfill my destiny—both Abby's and Raina's. And even though I wish she had been more forthcoming, I don't fault her for that either.

Guilt makes my stomach flutter. I should have read her letter to me that very first day. My bare feet slap on the wood floor on the way to my room, where I crouch in front of the bottom drawer, groaning with the pain caused by every movement, and remove the unopened letter.

My name is scrolled across the front in Gram's feminine handwriting as I turn it over and finally break the seal.

My dearest Abigail,

Since you're reading this letter, my time in this life has come to an end. There are so many things I've tried to teach you, but Healing is an art you'll have to learn on your own. And you will. When someone important to you is in jeopardy, you'll find your hidden memories. Memory becomes knowledge, and once you know, you'll never forget.

The world is vast, and the things you've experienced such a small portion of the whole. I could try to explain the existence of other worlds, other creatures, but there are things you won't understand until you see and experience them for yourself.

I'd give my life to wrap you in a protective bubble and keep you from your future. Fate has plenty in store for you, I'm afraid.

Your soul is so much older than your body. Even though many layers have been piled upon her in the past several hundred years, I believe you were once a young maiden who fell in love with a prince and became his bride.

The two of you died, each attempting to save the other from an evil curse, pronounced on you by the Dark Prince Tynan of the Otherworld Nairn. The curse has held strong for all the centuries since the maiden Raina sealed Tynan and his demon army inside a poisonous tomb, using the power of her wedding ring, the very ring I'm leaving to you. It must be protected at all costs—even your life. To this day, Gifted scholars dedicate themselves to finding a way to break the curse that keeps the lovers apart. Until then, we are limited in our powers and must rely on the Dragons to keep peace and order among our kind.

By staying together, Prince Theron and Raina bring illness and death on each other. Their love is strong, and when one passes on, the other follows quickly behind. Because of this, Theron and Raina never live long in any existence after they find each other. It makes sense that paradise can't last forever, but it's a bittersweet crust to bite. Especially to Theron's people, who wait to see his throne restored.

In this life, the blood bonds remain strong. You are descended from the child Raina bore before she died. Theron's child. The only remaining royal flesh and blood. I believe it will be you, my darling, who will lead the Gifted into peace and who will destroy the immortal Elen.

You're young, Abby, and Raina's soul is stronger than it's ever been. I see it in your face every time you open your eyes. Every time I hear your voice, I feel the jolt of recognition I first experienced on the day you were born. This time the curse will be broken. You have the power, strength, and knowledge to see this through and finish it.

When you find Theron, cling to him. Love him with everything you have—the same way you always did. Only together will you break the spell that has held our people bound for so many years.

I believe in you.

All my love until we meet again,
Your Gram.

A giggle bubbles in my throat as I fall back on my bed. Gram knew. The day I was born, she knew who I was. Who I am. And while she may have pushed me to learn, she never tried to force me to see what she must have known I couldn't understand.

Not then.

Reading her words now gives me strength and confidence. Things I'm going to need. I feel her spirit hovering near, holding me close. Giving me strength.

Kye's mention of loose shadow demons hasn't escaped me. We have lots to do, curses to break, secrets to protect. And learning. About Healing, about Sight, about the Witch Light I've never heard of before now. Not to mention the amount of time it's going to take for me to make up all my missed schoolwork.

Ugh.

The full moon glows like a lemon outside my window and the wind sings in the trees, whistling Gram's happy tones. My life has never been better. Right now, I'm going to live moment by moment and take the rest as it comes.

Because no matter what Val told Kye, deep down I know.

The battle isn't over. Not by a long shot.

Read on for a sneak peek at Birthright, the captivating sequel to Descendant

BIRTHRIGHT

ONE

Sick

My new cell phone buzzes as I scramble out of bed with one of two destinations in mind. This time, I manage to make it to the bathroom to pay homage to the porcelain throne. I swear, I spend more time doubled over wishing I could throw up than I spend upright—or even lying flat, for that matter. And there's no telling what tomorrow will bring.

Except more of the same sick symptoms. Val assures me that there will continue to be lots more of this.

Joy.

The phone buzzes again, Kye's ringtone growing progressively louder until it stops altogether. He'll call back, so I stay put, afraid that if I stand too fast, I'll pass out again like last week. My days have become an endless cycle of horrendous pain, passing out, and attempting to finish high school before I die.

Some days dying doesn't sound like the worst option. But I would like to graduate first. Feel like I accomplished something this time around.

When my phone buzzes a third time in as many minutes, I have to answer and save Kye a trip. I need to see him like I need to breathe, but I have to trick my body into accepting fluids. Otherwise, my mom has threatened to take me to the hospital for an IV—something we all want to avoid. So I get up slowly, rinse my mouth and wipe my face, determined to make it back before Kye calls again.

The wall is my anchor as I stumble to my room and collapse in a heap on the bed. Healing crystals dangle from each post, and pieces of other natural stones mingle among the potted herbs lining my room. Landon even drilled wires into the ceiling so Mom could hang Gram's most powerful gems. But none of it is enough.

I pull the comforter over me, shivering. Winter has passed, and we're experiencing the balmiest spring in recent Jackson history, but I'm always cold. And sick. And exhausted. Thoughts of giving up hover in the back of my mind until the phone rings again. This time, I pick it up, managing a weak smile when Kye's voice tickles my ear. "Please tell me something has changed," he pleads, a desperate edge to his voice. "That you were downstairs noshing on potato chips rather than ... you know."

"Sour cream and onion," I manage, shoving aside thoughts of any and all food, and reaching out to bring the garbage can closer, just in case. Please.

"Tell me you're getting better," he continues, his voice softening. "Make me believe this is something that will pass, something we can overcome. Convince me we're not dying."

"Actually, I was outside gardening," I lie. I know he knows better, but it's nice to pretend. "My herbs are thriving, and I'm going to plant tomatoes in a few weeks. And you wouldn't believe what Murtagh's done with the flower beds. He's a gardening genius."

"Ah," he says. "I was wondering where your mother found the juicy carrots that were in the soup she sent over yesterday. I've only seen the little stubby ones at the grocery store."

"Oh, yes. Most of the ingredients were home grown. No one does vegetable noodle soup like Marian." I lean against the wall of pillows, tucking the comforter up to my chin.

"Now tell me you ate some of that soup," he says. "Convince me that there's no way you're going to end up in the hospital this week."

Stifling a yawn, I stare out the window at the sun-lit mountains. "I finished the whole pot. Marian was angry because I didn't leave any for her and Gabe."

"That's my girl," he says, sounding satisfied, if unconvinced. I haven't been able to eat more than a few bites of anything for over a week. But the rest is true. My mom did make soup, and Murtagh really has been hard at work caring for my plants.

"So, about school tomorrow ..." Kye starts.

"I know we're going to pay for it. Believe me, I'm so weak I can barely stand, and it's been three days since you kissed me in that alcove. But I can't breathe. Do you understand? Missing you is more painful than seeing you, so please don't cancel on me. Please."

"Relax, babe. I'll be there. Just making sure you've got Gabe covered."

Gabe = part Dragon, part bodyguard, part babysitter, and total tattletale. He's been assigned to guard me. All the freaking time. But he does genuinely worry, which is something I use to my advantage, frequently. "I'm thinking of developing a sudden, inexplicable need for a hamburger between sixth and seventh period. A craving he couldn't possibly deny."

"Good one."

"I know. Especially since it's probably going straight in the garbage can so I don't have to smell it."

"Are you sure he'll go, rather than sending someone else?"

"I'll convince him I don't know how long my craving will last, and that I need it right away. It'll only buy us fifteen minutes or so, but ..."

Kye finishes my thought for me. "It's fifteen minutes more than we're supposed to have together."

"I'll take whatever I can get," I tell him.

His answering sigh is shaky. "I feel like there's an enormous hole in my chest when we're apart like this."

"Me too," I answer, reminding myself I should be glad for the small fragments of time we've learned how to steal. Eventually, there will be no more secret meetings behind the curtains in the auditorium, or blissful seconds in the janitor's closet during lunch. Eventually, someone will see Kye sneaking into my room to hold me in the middle of the night after a particularly hard week, and they'll send one of us away. At some point, parting will become permanent for us, and we'll have to learn how to accept it. Somehow. Unfortunately, I'm afraid that point is coming very, very soon.

"Back off, Gabe." I remove the pizza he just plopped on my tray and toss it on his, shuddering. "If you're so excited about carbs and processed meat, then you take this."

"Abby, you have to start eating better." Gabe follows behind, filling his tray with everything I refuse to put on mine. "You're withering away."

I add a side of vinaigrette next to my salad. "I can't help it. You know I can't. Eating fatty foods only makes it worse."

"Maybe if you—"

"Stop." My tray clatters on the table, flatware clinking against my unopened pop can. "Just stop trying to fix me, all right? There's nothing you can do. There's nothing anyone can do." The all-too-familiar burn of tears throbs behind my eyes. "I'm dying, Kye's dying, and Tynan wins. Again."

Gabe eases me onto the bench, murmuring words meant to comfort. He knows how weak I am—all the Dragons do. It's their job to know, just like it's their job to do everything in their power to protect me, to keep me alive as long as possible while we search for a way to break the stupid curse. But all that effort—it's not for me. It's for them. They think I'm here to save them.

They don't seem to understand that I don't even have the power to save myself.

"We're not going to let him win." Gabe leans close, speaking low so no one else will hear. "The royal blood has finally been restored after all this time. Do you really think we'll let our queen go without a hell of a fight?"

Arguing is pointless, so I rest my forehead on the table, wondering if anyone ever listens to me. "I just want Kye—alive. Living and breathing and by my side. And I don't care about the rest. I don't want to be your stupid queen."

Gabe's hand rubs circles on the small of my back. "You'll have to take that up with Zane and Val. Again."

"They don't care."

Another hand rests on my shoulder, and the energy around me shifts with a warm, welcoming light. I don't have to look up to know Rose and Jen are here.

"We'll figure it out, Abby," Rose murmurs. "You'll both be fine."

Jen remains silent, so I glance up. Why does she feel so distant? Maybe she doesn't know what to say. How do you comfort a friend you know is dying? My stomach burns and gurgles with acid, doubling me over with a moan. "Has anyone seen Akers today?"

Our beloved Dragon-turned-teacher allows us to call him Landon, except at school. It's a respect thing, and I totally get it. But under the circumstances, Mr. Akers feels too formal, so we've taken to referring to him as Akers.

"His car's in the parking lot," Rose says.

Unable to move, I hold a shaking hand to my head. "I need him."

"Eat something first." Gabe sounds exasperated. "You know he won't help you unless you try to eat."

"I can't!" I snap. "You can bring the salad with us, but I'm not going to be able to eat until my chakras are realigned."

Gabe leans close as if he means to support me, so I shove him away and push to my feet on my own. My first step is wobbly, so I accept Rose's steadying arm. "I hate this."

"Me too." She asks Jen to guard her food while she walks with me.

"What am I going to do?"

"I hate to say this—because just thinking about it hurts—but it might be time for you to leave." She pauses to clear her throat. "I love you, and I'm going to miss you something fierce, but I can't—I won't—watch you die. Not when it can be prevented."

The lump in my throat keeps me from answering as we round the corner and enter the open doorway that leads us onstage.

"Akers?" Gabe calls. "Abby needs you."

I head for the office, though the window is dark. "Check the prop room," I tell Gabe. "He's probably cataloguing or building a set piece or something." I flip on the office light. As always, the desk is clear of any clutter. There's a locked drawer on the right, where Akers keeps his laptop, phone, and printer. I've watched him meticulously store everything in a very precise manner a number of times. Something about balanced Chi. Or maybe it's for my benefit, because I need somewhere to lie while he gives me the energy treatments that keep me going on days like today.

While I spread out on the massive oak desk, Rose retrieves a block of smoky quartz from a shelf in the corner and places it between my knees. "Where are the rest?"

"I have them." I hand her nuggets of amber and tigers eye from my jacket pocket, and then quartz and aquamarine from the chain around my neck. She situates them along my torso, on my abdomen, ribs, and throat. As footsteps clip-clop across the stage, she retrieves amethyst from a glass display case and balances it on my forehead.

"Looks like Rose has things under control," Akers says, his piercing blue eyes landing on me. "I'm starting to feel unneeded."

Rose clears her throat. "I may be learning where to put the crystals, but I'm no Healer. Besides, we're still missing the heart stone."

"I'm not a Healer either. I just do what Val tells me." Akers signals for Gabe to close the blinds and lifts a long chain from under his shirt, drawing it over his head. "You know the drill, kids." While others turn to face the window, I close my eyes and wait for the swish and click that means Akers has closed the hidden security safe. Then the warm pendant falls into my open hand.

Eyes still closed, I hold it suspended over my heart, willing my weakening Healing powers to draw power from the emeralds. Akers, Rose, and Gabe join hands, closing their eyes and channeling their positive energy at me. Val has explained that this is the only way for a Healer to actually treat herself. At first it was just Akers and me in this little room, but we recently discovered that having Gabe and Rose present helps me to spin the crystals faster, stronger, making the stones more potent as my friends' combined energy fills the cracks in mine and my chakras realign.

After a minute, our energy holds the pendant aloft, and a number of the smaller crystals lift into the air as well. The stones revolve together, synchronized in a clockwise formation, faster and faster as I feel a jolt. Lights flicker, dance, and warmth from my Healing stones surrounds me like a tropical breeze.

"Abby." Rose's voice breaks my concentration, and the crystals drift to rest on my body. I take a deep breath and open my eyes.

Gabe smiles down at me. "Feel better?"

I nod, accepting his hand so he can help me into a sitting position. As I hang my head, waiting for it to clear, Akers doubles over, clutching his middle while Rose helps him to his chair.

"Sorry, Landon!"

A bead of sweat rolls off his forehead and drips onto the floor. The hue of his skin looks the slightest shade of green. "It's fine, Abby. Part of my job. Can't imagine what it's like dealing with this all day, every day."

"I wouldn't wish it on anyone, which is why I hate sharing it with you just so I can survive the day. It's not very fair."

Rose frowns, for once in her life seeming to be at a loss for words.

Landon mops his forehead with a discarded T-shirt. "As you have so vehemently pointed out in recent weeks, none of our circumstances are fair, least of all yours."

A guilty flush warms my cheeks when I think of the clandestine meeting I'm planning with Kye and how many people will pay for our fifteen minutes of happiness. Uncomfortable with the thought, I slide off the desk, muttering, "I just wish I knew what to do."

Always solicitous, Gabe hovers near. "You okay?"

I nod, kneeling in front of Akers. If he's going to be sick because of me, the least I can do is hold the trash can for him. But he shoves it away and sits up. "I'm fine," he says. "I'll be fine. My relief will come ten times more quickly than yours. I only need a few minutes."

Rose squeezes my arm when I turn to her and say, "We can't keep this up. I have to do something."

Our eyes connect, hers pleading for me to go—even as she begs me to stay.

I know she's right. I don't know how or where, but the when is now—maybe this week. Because if I don't do something soon—leave this place that finally feels like home, and these people I love like family—it will be too late.

And Kye and I might not be the only ones who die.

Nichole Giles was born in Nevada and has lived in a number of cities in and around the Midwest. Her early career plans included becoming an actress or a rock star, but she decided instead to have a family and then become a writer. Writing is her passion, but she also loves to spend time with her husband and four children, travel to tropical and exotic destinations, drive in the rain with the convertible top down, and play music at full volume so she can sing along.

Acknowledgements

If publishing a book is a journey, mine has been a thousand miles long, with people cheering for my every step.

Those steps begin and end with my family. Biggest, most important thanks to Gary, who held me up and loved me through hundreds of rejections, who let me be who I am, and who worked extra hours to pay for all my most favorite writing conferences. To Brayden for brainstorming genius, endless nights spent helping me build worlds and plots, and then for painting them, and Brittany, Madison, and McKay for all the do-it-yourself dinners, missed games, messy house, clothes washed but not dried, and for always patiently waiting for me to "just finish this page." You five are my world and I love you bigger than the universe.

I have progressed by miles since I joined forces with the spectacular people at Authors Incognito, and then miles more, thanks to my Super Edits group: Tristi Pinkston, Keith Fisher, Heather Justesen, and Kimberly Job, who have read and red-lined thousands of words for me. My Novel Thoughts group: Cindy and Russ Beck, Connie Hall, and Rachelle Christensen used colors other than red, but the results were the same, and I would not be where I am without each of you.

Special thanks to Elana Johnson for being my other half at events, for countless hours of conversations, and for rescuing me from the ledge every time I find one. To James Dashner for challenging me to finish a full draft when I was a wide-eyed beginner, J. Scott Savage for inspiring me to keep going when I'd had hundreds of rejections, and Darvell Hunt for telling me it would be my year. Also to TJR who told me I should try in the first place. You were all right.

Lots of people write books, but very few manage to find a publisher to help breathe life into them. Michelle Davidson Argyle pointed me toward mine and left me forever in her debt. Hugs to you and to Rhett and Emmaline Hoffmeister for open minds, creative hearts, and for giving me choices I never knew I could have. Thanks to the Rhemalda crew for helping me pull this off, and also to my lovely agent, Brittany Howard, for believing in me and championing my work. I am so blessed to have you all in my support car.

Karen Hoover, L.T. Elliott, Carolyn Vawdrey, Jenn Johansson, Debbie Davis, Windy Aphayrath, Sheralyn Pratt, Ali Cross, and Christine Bryant have made incredible cheerleaders as well as friends. I'm lucky to have you on the road with me.

Positive energy and love to Tova Heaton, at www.thewayofthewitch.com, for running a workshop that became the inspiration behind Abby's healing ability, and who is my number one source of information on holistic healing. Also for life-long friendship and hundreds of lunches filled with endless possibilities.

Loves and kisses to my FABs, Lori Smith, Raylene Long, Jennifer Brown and Tiffany Wood-McCarthy, for giving me courage when I didn't know where to borrow it, for knowing the real me and loving me anyway, for Mexico and Midway and any future destinations, and who are the best, best, best friends a girl could have. Most people are lucky if they find one. I have four.

Thanks to my brothers and sisters, who are always there when it matters most, and who will shove me from behind when I start to lose momentum. To my parents, Joe and Pam Petersen and Steve and Deanne Hechtle, for teaching me that families are as much about love as about blood, and for raising me to believe in our power of choice. Thanks to my grandparents, Ernie and Mona Ketchum and Mel and Jeneal Petersen, who was the inspiration behind Gram. Special thanks to Kay and Carol Giles, for accepting, teaching, and loving me as their own. And to my extended family, just for being awesome.

The steps have been long and the road treacherous. I wouldn't be where I am without the influence of countless other important people. If you are one of those I was unable to name, I remember, I love you, and I thank you for being part of my journey. This, my friends, is only the beginning.